PENGUIN TWENTIETH-CENTURY CLASSICS

WRITINGS ON IRISH FOLKLORE, LEGEND AND MYTH

William Butler Yeats was born in Dublin in 1865 into an artistic family and spent his childhood in Sligo, Dublin and London. In Dublin he enrolled at the Metropolitan School of Art in 1884. The next year he became a founder-member of the Dublin Hermetic Society; in time this led him to the Esoteric Section of the Theosophical Society and the Hermetic Order of the Golden Dawn (1890). He developed a life-long interest in magic, the occult and the supernatural, which influenced much of his thinking and writing, and which achieved its most complete expression in the expository speculations of *A Vision* (1925; revised version 1937). His early poetry was influenced by Victorian models, which he largely came to reject in the search for a personal utterance and for a voice which was distinctively Irish.

Yeats's home was most often in London, though he visited Ireland frequently. For a while he was close to the politics of Irish nationalism, not least because of his long infatuation with the revolutionary Maud Gonne, to whom he unsuccessfully proposed on many occasions. From an early stage, he devoted his energies much less to direct political action than to the cause of an imaginative nationalism which involved him in the collection of folklore (notably in *The Celtic Twilight*, 1893), in the creation and management of a national theatre for which he wrote a body of plays (five of which presented the epic hero Cuchulain), and in the critical reinterpretation and advancement of the Irish literary tradition. Like his plays, Yeats's poetry constantly redefined itself; it is particularly remarkable for its expansive development after *Responsibilities* (1914) and for the imaginative rigour of its frequent revisions.

In 1915 Yeats refused a knighthood from the British government; in 1922 he became a Senator of the newly founded Irish Free State, and finally settled in Dublin with Georgie Hyde-Lees, whom he had

married in 1917 and whose automatic writing became the basis of *A Vision*. In 1917 he also purchased a Norman stone tower in Ballylee Co. and this provided the symbolic focus for *The Tower* (1928) which is, arguably, his richest collection of poetry. Yeats left a vivid record of his life and of his friends and acquaintances in the volumes which were collected as *Autobiographies*, also published by Penguin, and in the franker *Memoirs* (not published until 1972). He died at Roquebrune, France, in January 1939.

Robert Welch is Professor of English at the University of Ulster, Coleraine. He has published *Irish Poetry from Moore to Yeats* (1980), *A History of Verse Translation from the Irish* (1988) and *Changing States: Transformations in Modern Irish Literature* (1993). He is editor of *The Oxford Companion to Irish Literature* and was chairman of the International Association for the Study of Anglo-Irish Literature from 1988 to 1991. He has edited a number of volumes of essays, and a book of his poems, *Muskerry*, appeared in 1991. He is married with four children and lives in Portstewart.

Timothy Webb is General Editor for the works of W. B. Yeats in Penguin Twentieth-Century Classics.

W. B. YEATS

WRITINGS ON IRISH FOLKLORE, LEGEND AND MYTH

EDITED WITH AN INTRODUCTION AND NOTES BY ROBERT WELCH

PENGUIN BOOKS

PENGUIN BOOKS

Published by the Penguin Group
Penguin Books Ltd, 27 Wrights Lane, London W8 5TZ, England
Penguin Books USA Inc., 375 Hudson Street, New York, New York 10014, USA
Penguin Books Australia Ltd, Ringwood, Victoria, Australia
Penguin Books Canada Ltd, 10 Alcorn Avenue, Toronto, Ontario, Canada M4V 3B2
Penguin Books (NZ) Ltd, 182–190 Wairau Road, Auckland 10, New Zealand

Penguin Books Ltd, Registered Offices: Harmondsworth, Middlesex, England

This edition first published in Penguin Books 1993
1 3 5 7 9 10 8 6 4 2

Typeset by Datix International Limited, Bungay, Suffolk
Set in 10/12 pt Monophoto Sabon
Printed in England by Clays Ltd, St Ives plc

CONTENTS

ACKNOWLEDGEMENTS

I would like to thank the British Academy for a personal research grant, which allowed me to undertake research at the British Library; the Research Subcommittee of the Faculty of Humanities, University of Ulster, under its chairman, Dr John Gillespie, for its assistance; Professor Peter Roebuck; Professor A. N. Jeffares; Dr John Kelly; Dr John Pitcher; Professor Timothy Webb, for guidance and encouragement; Dr Bruce Stewart; Dr Lis Lillie; Mr Philip Tilling; Mr Brian Baggett; Dr Rory McTurk; Dr Daithí Ó hÓgáin; Mr Alan Peacock; Van Morrison, for his kind permission to reproduce a verse from *Beautiful Vision*; Donna Poppy at Penguin; Mrs Elizabeth Holmes; and Mrs Mary McCaughan.

A TEXTUAL AND EDITORIAL NOTE

Content

This volume consists of all of Yeats's discursive published writings on Irish folklore, legend and myth, where these topics constitute the main subject of the essay, introduction or sketch. It excludes poetry, drama and prose fiction based on this material, and incidental discussion of it in occult works such as *A Vision* or in the autobiographical writings. The great bulk of the work presented here was written between 1887 and 1904, the years during which he familiarized himself with Irish tradition, particularly in its folk and legendary aspects. These writings reveal the development of a critical, analytical, and interpretative approach to Irish tradition during this period in particular, but extending beyond it to 1933, when he considered again the scope and quality of life on the islands off the west coast of Ireland. At the outset, as in the discussion and classification of fairies in the late 1880s, there is analysis and youthful fascination, which develops, throughout the 1890s, into a world view of considerable psychological and philosophical depth; until, in the 1900s, this material, and the spiritual, intellectual and cultural interests it generated, became part of the quality of awareness deployed in all his writings.

Order

A pattern of developing complexity is evident in the writings gathered here, for which reason it was decided to present them chronologically, in the order of publication. This decision might seem to involve a major disadvantage: *The Celtic Twilight* in its two overlapping versions (1893 and 1902) is not presented as a unified text; rather the constituent elements out of which it was originally assembled (on two occasions) are given as they were first printed in newspapers and magazines, thus allowing the reader a clear sense of Yeats's persistent intellectual toil on his material and his increasing mastery of it. The contents of both editions of *The Celtic Twilight* are given in an appendix. This chronological guideline is breached in a few instances: the note on 'The Valley of the Black Pig' is given in its fullest, not its earliest, form; and in a number of other cases a later version develops an incidental sketch into a free-standing piece, and where this occurs the latter is preferred.

Texts

The texts given are normally the texts of first printings. Sometimes Yeats reused a part of an essay or review in a later publication. Wherever this occurs, the text followed is nearly always that of the fuller version. Details of such editorial decisions are given in the notes to relevant items. Very few of Yeats's idiosyncratic spellings have been altered; however, his spellings of the proper names Cuchulain, Fionn mac Cumhail, Tír na nÓg, Tuatha Dé Danann, and of lepracaun, have been standardized throughout to avoid irritation, and obvious printers' errors have been corrected.

Notes

Each item has a headnote that provides relevant biographical and bibliographical information. These headnotes are followed by annotations numbered separately for each item.

Glossary

After the notes a glossary of anglicized Irish words, names and phrases is given. This includes Yeats's explanation of the term or terms; any necessary correction of this explanation; and a transliteration of the term or terms into standard modern Irish. This procedure has the advantage of giving the reader a brief, consolidated dictionary of Irish terms, many of which are used frequently throughout the writings gathered here. The alternative would have been to gloss them in the notes, but the information would then have been too widely dispersed and too difficult of access. Yeats's anglicized spelling of Irish words is not consistent, so the practice adopted has been to retain the orthography as it first occurs, chronologically, except for the very common words listed in 'Texts' above. In those cases where the pronunciation is not self-evident from the spelling a phonetic transcription is given.

ABBREVIATIONS

A	W. B. Yeats, *Autobiographies* (London, 1955, 1970 reprint)
CL, I	John Kelly and Eric Domville (eds.), *The Collected Letters of W. B. Yeats. Vol. I, 1865–1895* (Oxford, 1986)
CM	Proinsias Mac Cana, *Celtic Mythology* (Middlesex, 1970)
CP	W. B. Yeats, *Collected Poems* (London, 1958 reprint)
CT, 1893	W. B. Yeats, *The Celtic Twilight, Men and Women, Ghosts and Fairies* (London, 1893)
CT, 1902	W. B. Yeats, *The Celtic Twilight* (London, 1902)
FFTIP	W. B. Yeats (ed.), *Fairy and Folk Tales of the Irish Peasantry* (London, New York, Toronto, 1888)
NCJ	A. Norman Jeffares, *A New Commentary on the Poems of W. B. Yeats* (London, 1984)
UP, I & II	John P. Frayne (ed.), *Uncollected Prose by W. B. Yeats. Vol. I: First Reviews and Articles 1886–1896* (London, 1970); John P. Frayne and Colton Johnson (eds.), *Uncollected Prose by W. B. Yeats. Vol. II: Later Reviews, Articles and Other Miscellaneous Prose 1897–1939* (London, 1975)
WBYIF	Mary Helen Thuente, *W. B. Yeats and Irish Folklore* (Totowa, NJ, 1980)

INTRODUCTION

> ... I have all-ways considered my self a voice of what I beleive to be a greater renaisance – the revolt of the soul against the intellect – now begining in the world.
>
> W. B. Yeats, letter to John O'Leary, July 1892

> I accept ... I accept ... totally without
> reservation my race that no ablution
> of hyssop mixed with lilies could purify
> my race pitted with blemishes
> my race a ripe grape for drunken feet.
>
> Aimé Césaire, *Cahier d'un retour*[1]

I

The Co. Sligo of Yeats's childhood was a place full of legend, fairy lore, mythological or quasi-mythological tales. As a nursery for a mind that was to revolt against nineteenth-century materialism and scientific method, it could not have been more appropriate. During his earliest years his family stayed in Sligo for long periods of time, and from the age of seven to nine he lived there for two years entirely with his brother and sisters.

In his boyhood Yeats, like many others of his class throughout Ireland, spent a great deal of time wandering about the countryside – the names are well known, Rosses Point, Ballisodare, Ben Bulben, Knocknarea – talking to the country people, listening to their stories. Douglas Hyde was finding out about the Irish language in Co. Roscommon, in a similar way; in Co. Donegal Joyce Cary, on his summer holidays near Quigley's Point, was listening to fierce tales of agrarian outrage; and Edith Somerville in Cork was taking in the linguistic energy and inventiveness of Castletownshend. For a variety of reasons, including political ones, the Anglo-Irish were intrigued by the supernatural, fairies and the afterlife. Up to a point this interest sprang from a curiosity about the imaginative life of a subject class growing less disadvantaged with increasing modernization; but tales of ghosts, hauntings and fairies provided the Anglo-Irish with an imagery that reflected their own sense of insecurity and baffled unease. Yeats's relations, the Middletons and the Pollexfens, were interested in fairy lore, ghosts and the occult. 'Regina, Regina Pigmeorum, Veni' in *The Celtic Twilight* (p. 117) tells of an experiment Yeats conducted in 1892 with his uncle George Pollexfen and his cousin Lucy Middleton (known in Sligo as a witch) when they (successfully) summoned the local fairy queen.

Sligo seems to have been a locale unusually rich in fairy lore and tales of hauntings, ghosts and eerie happenings. Mary Helen Thuente points out that the folklorist W. Y. Evans-Wentz found the area around Ben Bulben 'full of fairy lore' in 1911; he compared notes with Hyde, who informed him that Roscommon, Hyde's own native county, had much less in the way of supernatural tradition.[2]

Yeats began to accumulate stories of this kind from very early on. He maintained this interest when the family moved to Howth in 1881, and the article 'Village Ghosts' is based on lore collected there when he was sixteen. At this time, too, Yeats was interested in natural history and the classification of species of plants and animals: the two aspects of his mind merge, strangely, in the classification of fairies he developed in his anthology *Fairy and Folk Tales of the Irish Peasantry* (1888).

It may be said that Yeats became a folklorist and a student of legend, myth and magic because of his exposure to this material while at an impressionable age. He shared the interest of his class in this material; and, in addition, these tales of the supernatural were imaginative nourishment to a mind conscious of a need to break with the agnosticism and scientific scepticism of his father, John B. Yeats. His memory for anything that moved his creative instinct was always good; and the recollections of boyhood, supplemented by research and further actual fieldwork, produced the material gathered in *The Celtic Twilight* (1893 and 1902). This volume contained, he said, 'all real stories heard among the people or real incidents with but a little disguise in names and places'.[3]

But before *The Celtic Twilight* there were the anthologies: *Fairy and Folk Tales of the Irish Peasantry* and *Irish Fairy Tales* (1892). It has been shown that these collections grew out of the most careful and painstaking research on Yeats's part into everything published in the field of Irish folklore.[4] By the time he had prepared his texts and written his commentary and analysis, he had mastered the material and decided on its imaginative value. His researches on folklore did not cease there. They expanded and further deepened his study of Irish myth and legend, which he was making for his poems; and they integrated his desire to promote his country imaginatively with his occult learning. 'All his twenties crammed with toil', he wrote in 'What Then?' (1937),[5] and a not inconsiderable part of this toil was involved in attempting to order *anarchic* and difficult material (see p. 53). Behind all this labour lay an ambition to serve his country by uniting an imaginative movement in literature with all aspects of native tradition: folklore, myth, legend, religion, custom and thought. And intertwined with this ambition was another strand in the fabric of his thinking: the 'revolt of the soul' against the materialist intellect, which he saw dominating life and repressing imaginative thought in the modern world.

When he stayed with Lady Gregory in Coole in 1897, he recommenced fieldwork on folk legend and belief, this time in Galway, in a collaboration that was to last many years and that led to a series of essays by Yeats (see headnote to item 37) and to Lady Gregory's *Visions and Beliefs in the West of Ireland* (1920). Fieldwork on folklore and folk belief fed into his work on myth and legend; and this body of knowledge, along with his occult learning, was a network of relationships, a field of significances, he could deploy in his ambition to write for his country a literature that would be urgent, risky, troublesome and, at the same time, totally in line with tradition.

II

Yeats, though often disillusioned with Ireland, never ceased to write about it. He studied its folklore, history and literature with an energy that sprang from a volume of need going much deeper than anything patriotic sentiment, antiquarianism or political commitment could supply. Yeats never ceased to be convinced that there was, at the back of Irish experience, a 'mathematics'[6] of being, a law of energy, that moved into action at certain moments of clarity and heroic density: when Pearse strode in the Post Office, Cuchulain 'stalked' by his side. In his advice to Irish poets, an order rings out, enjoining them to legitimate their present imagining with the strength and order of the past:

Cast your mind on other days
That we in coming days may be
Still the indomitable Irishry.[7]

By September 1938, when he wrote these lines, Yeats had acquired much confidence and daring, but back in the 1880s and 1890s we see him attempting to claim a space for Ireland and for himself. He wanted to create an image of Ireland that would be different from the idealized picture promulgated by Young Ireland, or the democratic modern state envisaged by Gladstone and Parnell.

He wished, too, to advance a notion of 'Irishness' that would resist the stereotype of the fine but unbridled Celtic temperament invented by Matthew Arnold. Whenever the 'Celtic Twilight' is mentioned, Arnold, whether consciously or not, is being invoked. It was he, in lectures delivered as Professor of Poetry at Oxford in 1866, who developed the notion of the sane and solid Saxon as against the wild and imaginative Celt. The 'despotism of fact' was something the Celt reacted against, with his capacity for dreaming, his sensitivity, his hatred of empiricism. Arnold's racial stereotypes were well intentioned, because he did envisage an imperial culture in which Celtic emotionalism (something present in the substrata of Saxon psychology but normally repressed) would, once liberated, mitigate the harsh and stolid practicality of the empire-builder. But this compliment, Yeats saw, was double-edged. To imagine the Celt as soft consigned him to an inferior role; whereas to imagine the Saxon as harsh offered the Celt a justification for dislike as well as providing the Saxon with the opportunity for masochistic self-laceration; thereby creating a psychological tangle crucial to the nuanced shiftings of guilt, the blaming of self rapidly becoming the blaming of the other, characteristic of colonial psychology.[8] In this world of murky self-doubt and blurred accusation the notion of a 'Celtic Twilight', where differences would merge in a unity involving the surrender of social and political reality, was attractive. It was an aesthetic sensuality parallel to the more obvious and perhaps therefore more wholesome submissions imagined in Aubrey Beardsley's *Under the Hill* or Arthur Symons's *London Nights*; but whatever the attractions of this kind of Celtic Twilight (or 'cultic twalette' as Joyce termed it[9]) for Fiona Macleod (the pen-name for the Celtic enthusiast William Sharp, from Scotland) and George Russell (AE), it had little or no effect on Yeats. He never bought this illusion.

Yeats addressed the matter directly in 1898 in his crucial essay on 'The Celtic Element in Literature', which clearly states his attitude to Arnold. He was misread and misinterpreted, particularly by hard-nosed and emphatically bullish Irish nationalists like D. P. Moran (see headnote, item 51), who found it convenient to bracket Yeats with the purveyors of Celtic Twilight effeminacy and label him as a 'fraud'.[10] In September 1900 Yeats contributed a letter on Irish language and literature to the *Leader*, a nationalist weekly edited by Moran, in which he points out that what he has had to say about Arnold was specifically intended as a challenge to the shallow cultural stereotypes of the period: 'I have avoided "Celtic note" and "Celtic renaissance" partly because both are vague and one is grandiloquent, and partly because the journalist has laid his ugly hands upon them' (p. 279). The essay of 1898 takes on Arnold (and Ernest Renan, from whom Arnold drew a great deal) by completely transforming their intellectual strategy. Arnold (and Renan) must be considered 'a little'; if we do not, Yeats writes, 'we may go mad some day, and the enemy . . . root up our rose garden and plant a cabbage garden instead' (p. 190). Yeats's method is not so much to contradict Arnold as to write against him, to formulate a language different from the stereotyped categories Arnold has stated, whilst also giving him his due. Arnold had praised the 'Celtic note', suggesting that English literature derives its 'natural magic' from a Celtic source. Yeats refuses the compliment, and opens the field of discourse to a vastly wider perspective:

> I will put this differently and say that literature dwindles to a mere chronicle of circumstance, or passionless phantasies, and passionless meditations, unless it is constantly flooded with the passions and beliefs of ancient times, and that of all the fountains of the passions and beliefs of ancient times in Europe, the Slavonic, the Finnish, the Scandinavian, and the Celtic, the Celtic alone has been for centuries close to the main river of European literature (p. 198).

Far from being eccentric, Celtic tradition matters because it is central to European literature, since it proves to be entirely at one with ancient knowledge. Not an attack on Arnold (Yeats is too intelligent not to realize that such crude methods collaborate with power and are ultimately self-destructive), this view of tradition transforms the polarity of the Celt/Saxon opposition with its universalizing scope and in its open acceptance of its own ground, its 'rose-garden'. Later in the same paragraph Yeats expands the range of reference to unite the Irish tradition of pilgrimage to Lough Derg with the framework of the *Divine Comedy*. The method is not argument; it is the open acknowledgement of a difference, which is then said to be deeply integrative, profoundly unifying, because it leads into the 'main river' of European tradition.

Yeats's writing against Arnold is hieratic, charged with characteristic Yeatsian rhetoric ('passion', 'ancient', 'fountain', 'river'), powerfully invoking a certain quality of knowledge, potentially there in Celtic/Irish tradition and waiting to be released. This knowledge is not the information produced by 'the clatter of printing presses' or purveyed by 'the lecturers with their black coats and tumblers of water' (p. 77), but a knowledge residing at the core of reality itself, with which the supernatural worlds of folklore, legend and myth are intimately connected. This sort of knowledge is not empirical but imaginative knowledge, a fully human quality of awareness, as William Blake conceived it; or 'liberating' as Edward W. Said employs the term.[11]

Image, symbol and folktale; saga and legend; certain strong and passionate natures embody this knowledge when it becomes power. This is not, as Yeats conceived it, a rhetoric to upset the balance of political or social power but an enabling set of ideas charged with imaginative wonder. In the same essay he describes the process of this wisdom, in a passage arising from his delight in the love songs of Connacht, as collected by Douglas Hyde in 1893, and his researches into the Ossianic poems and stories of Fionn and Oisín. This passage, worth setting beside the troubled and confident insights of the late 'A General Introduction for my Work' (1937), represents a more optimistic, perhaps even more liberating, statement of his aesthetic convictions:

> The lover in the Irish folk song bids his beloved come with him into the woods, and see the salmon leap in the rivers, and hear the cuckoo sing, because death will never find them in the heart of the woods. Oisin, new come from his three hundred years of faeryland, and of the love that is in faeryland, bids St Patrick cease his prayers a while and listen to the blackbird, because it is the blackbird of Darrycarn that Fionn brought from Norway, three hundred years before, and set its nest upon the oak tree with his own hands. Surely if one goes far enough into the woods, there one will find all that one is seeking? (p. 194)

The intensity and depth of imaginative response to Irish tradition is remarkable here – no less than the originality and courage of the ambition. Death will never find the lover in the heart of the woods: an absurd statement, on the face of it, and easily cast aside as mystagogic burbling; but we should remember that Yeats was committed to an imaginative process of thought that aims to give actuality to forms that are beyond the categories of space, time and personality: 'it may be the arts are founded on the life beyond the world, and that they must cry in the ears of our penury until the world has been consumed and become a vision' (p. 197).

In 'Sailing to Byzantium' the sages standing in God's 'holy fire' ('As in the gold mosaic of a wall') are implored to be the singing masters of Yeats's soul. He beseeches them to come from this 'beyond' where they vibrate in fire, to whirl towards him and:

> Consume my heart away; sick with desire
> And fastened to a dying animal
> It knows not what it is; and gather me
> Into the artifice of eternity.[12]

Though what the Yeats of 'Sailing to Byzantium' imagines (all fire, intensity, joy fuelled by bitterness) is quite different to that envisaged by the Yeats of 1898, formally the process is exactly the same in the prose and in the verse. The object of the search (energetically invoked in 1927; calmly envisioned in trance-like prose in 1898) is beyond; because it is independent of human categories it has its own identity. Seeking this knowledge is empowering; to Yeats's understanding the learning and mental discipline of the traditional Irish storyteller embodied procedures for gaining such knowledge.

In the preface to Lady Gregory's *Cuchulain of Muirthemne* (1902), Yeats attempts to describe his idea of what the old Irish storyteller was like: his technique, attitude, imaginative approach. Not surprisingly, perhaps, the storyteller turns out to be a very Yeatsian type; even though Yeats is here thinking of the *filidh*, or chief poets of early Christian Ireland, those who would have recited the tales of Cuchulain before the earliest versions were written down, perhaps in the seventh or eighth centuries. Yeats is trying to imagine a favourite, indeed emblematic, figure of his: the poet–seer still in touch with Druidic methods and practices. The Irish poets had, he says, 'a supernatural sanction, for a chief poet had to understand not only innumerable kinds of poetry, but how to keep himself for nine days in a trance' (p. 330). This, from the accounts available, in such sources as the *Memoirs of the Marquis of Clanricarde*,[13] seems to be quite accurate. The mind of the poet–seer 'constantly escaped out of daily circumstance, as a bough that has been held down by a weak hand suddenly straightens itself out'. This cast of mind constantly seeks the 'beyond', and goes to Tír na nÓg or Tír Tairngire (The Land of Youth, The Land of Promise), places as near to the ancient poet reciting the heroic life of Cuchulain as to the country people of 'today'. And the tales recited out of the depth induced by trance, the imaginative forms thus created, in mythic narrative or folktale, have *their own life*, are moved by contact with this otherworld, and so move us. These stories are impersonal, indifferent to us, ghostly: 'the Irish stories make one understand why the Greeks called myths the activities of the dæmons' (p. 332). Trance, in which the images of common day recede, enables the otherworld to draw near. Dead and living communicate in the new, different life inhering in this imaginative creation. Irish folk tradition preserves this method, these powers.

In the same year in which he wrote his preface to *Cuchulain of Muirthemne*, he produced a second edition of *The Celtic Twilight*, first published in 1893. His thinking on the relationship between the kind of imaginative knowledge he sought and folk tradition evolved steadily from 1887 through the 1890s. The response to Arnold, which he forcefully clarified in the essay on Celtic literature, cleared much ground, so that by the early 1900s he could confidently bring himself to speak of techniques of awareness and trance that allow the creative imagination access to levels of meaning central to being but inherent in Irish folk tradition. In the 1902 edition of *The Celtic Twilight* he added a piece on trance, imaginative receptivity, the interanimation of the living and the dead, capabilities and practices that he found amongst the Irish country people:

> Even to-day our country people speak with the dead and with some who perhaps have never died as we understand death; and even our educated people pass without great difficulty into the condition of quiet that is the condition of vision. We can make our minds so like still water that beings gather about us that they may see, it may be, their own images, and so live for a moment with a clearer, perhaps even with a fiercer, life because of our quiet (p. 298).

'For wisdom is the property of the dead',[14] he wrote in the poem 'Blood and the Moon' in 1927 (first published 1928), but this thinking derives from his supernatural meditations, his trance practices, and his fieldwork on folklore in the 1890s. Fairy lore; folk beliefs and practices; Irish mythology and legend as preserved in the cycles of tales that have come down in manuscript versions – all these radiated from a core of faith and belief that was still capable of awakening in the Irish mind. This was possible because the Celt remained conscious of the depth and volume of the mainstream of European tradition. So, instead of being the subject of Arnold's condescension and glad of the notice he was thereby afforded, Yeats's Celt is a European in the same tradition as Homer. Moreover, this is the tradition of Porphyry, Dante, Blake; and so he can be self-assertive with the confidence of an esoteric power and wisdom.

Lady Wilde ('Speranza'), Oscar's mother, was a collector of, and commentator on, folk practice and belief. More than any previous student of Irish folklore, she impressed Yeats with her view that this material preserved the spiritual outlook of the ancient Irish.[15] The study of magic (which, in a letter to John O'Leary in July 1892, he described as 'next to my poetry the most important pursuit of my life'[16]); his researches into the written sources for folklore, legend and myth; and his experiments in symbol, vision and trance – all these formed part of his quest for a language adequate to his urgent sense that Ireland was waiting to receive expression through his art.

III

The vision that Yeats developed was one that sought to unify folk belief; legend; the passionate 'thrusts of power' he found in love song; the quality of metaphysical awareness he attributed to Irish country-people; and the 'wasteful virtues' of an Anglo-Irish aristocracy, who, he said, played their part before the 'exacting tribunal' (p. 361) of the collective he termed 'the people'.[17] He praised the Irish writer William Carleton as a faithful transcriber, particularly in his stories rather than his novels, of the vitality and colour of the life out of which he had come. But Carleton, like other nineteenth-century predecessors – Gerald Griffin, James Clarence Mangan, William Allingham – failed because he and they did not create a world; they, in Yeats's view, were like flies struggling in the marmalade of history,[18] encumbered, tormented, drowning either in sweetness or bitterness. The art he wanted would take on the disgrace of the Irish, their lack of pride, their arrogance, their (to use a phrase of Seamus Heaney's) 'wet centre',[19] and transform the situation by awakening a creative spirit inherent in Irish tradition, a spirit not eccentric but consistent with ancient wisdom.

The Order of the Golden Dawn, which he joined in 1890, helped to reactivate Celtic mysteries; his twilight was not a *fin de siècle* decline but an anticipation of transformations, a dawn to the new day.

It is difficult now to assess the energy of Yeats's commitment when he set to work classifying folklore and fairy belief, studying translations of Gaelic legends and myths, researching his nineteenth-century predecessors in Anglo-Irish literature. In the 1890s and in the first decade of this century there cannot have been many with such an extensive and interrogative understanding of so many phases of Irish tradition as he, and this in spite of the fact that he knew no Irish and failed to learn it. His needs were creative, not scholarly; he wanted to hammer his thoughts into unity, thoughts based upon fieldwork, study, experiment, the practice of the craft of poetic knowledge, in order to create a living thing, an art work or artifice that would have its own life, and therefore be an activity of the Irish spirit. In *The Spirit of the Nation* of Young Ireland, a collection of verses republished many times in the nineteenth century, this 'spirit' was envisaged as political enthusiasm for self-government; Yeats's spirit was the animation of a body of knowledge, hitherto neglected, Irish knowledge, based upon Irish life, empowered by an attitude of acceptance and temperate self-recognition. Joyce sought to create a humane conscience for his race; Yeats, romantically, summoned the 'shaping spirit of imagination'.[20] It is hard for us to see past Yeats into the nineteenth century, so integrative was his view of Irish tradition, but, when we do, we find (to put it bluntly) a literary culture on its knees, with no properly expressive set of representations of itself, the Irish language going, in many places gone, no readership, the Anglo-Irish aristocracy and middle class increasingly marginalized, and an emergent but poorly educated peasant or lower middle-class Catholic readership. We see a great deal of effort, little focused energy.

This essay began with an extract from Aimé Césaire's *Cahier d'un retour*. We may now quote another extract:

> man still must overcome all the interdictions wedged in the recesses of his fervour and no race has a monopoly on beauty, on security, on intelligence, on strength.[21]

Yeats made a strong attempt to overcome the 'interdictions wedged in the recesses of his fervour', all the doubts and prohibitions that hedged around the matter of Ireland at the end of the nineteenth century and the first decades of this. These 'interdictions' were not just the scientific rationalism of his time, but his *own* self-doubt about the wisdom of being associated with lunatics like MacGregor Mathers, the zany occultist, or vague optimists like his friend AE. But he stuck it out and stayed with his method, which was to unify the 'wild anarchy' (p. 53) of legend, myth, folklore, into an imaginative body of knowledge, a tissue (text) to set against the authoritative texts of English.[22] While always aware of how much he owed to English (Shakespeare, Chaucer, Donne, Blake, Landor, to name but a few of his master-spirits), he also wanted to bring into play a counter-text or set of counter-texts expressive of his own Irishness and of Ireland itself, arguing all the time that such elements were not merely nationalist but that they connected to the mother-lode, from which all master-spirits drew.

IV

In the magisterial late essay 'A General Introduction for my Work' Yeats wrote of the time, two or three generations ahead (the year 2000), when Europe may find something attractive in the idea of a 'Druidic' background to its (Christian) civilization. This is his 'faith',[23] he asserts. The conviction informing all his study of Irish material – whether saga, myth, legend or folklore – is that this knowledge is ancient European knowledge, and that Dante, Shakespeare and Blake drew upon it. This background is composed of many elements, and it may be useful to separate a few of these from the complex weave.

Throughout his folk researches and the redactions of the fieldwork he did in Sligo, Aran or Galway (with Lady Gregory), the theme of the interanimation of the living and the dead continually recurs. In 1898 he wrote:

> last year I met a man on the big island of Aran who heard fighting when two of his children died. I did not write his story down at the time, and so cannot give his very words. One night he heard a

> sound of fighting in the room. He lit the light, but everything became silent at once and he could see nothing. He put out the light and the room was full of the sound of fighting as before. In the morning he saw blood in a box he had to keep fish in, and his child was very ill. I do not remember if his child died that day, but it died soon. He heard fighting another night, and he tried to throw the quilt on the people who were fighting, but he could not find anybody. In the morning he found blood scattered about and his second child dead. A man he knew was in love with a girl who lived near and used to sleep with her at night, and he was going home that morning and saw a troop of them, and the child in the middle of them. Once, while he was telling this story, he thought I was not believing him, and he got greatly excited and stood up and said he was an old man and might die before he got to his house and he would not tell me a lie, before God he would not tell me a lie (pp. 168–9).

He goes on to say that the second child is seen by a third party with the *slua sí*, the fairy host, who have taken it away, leaving behind the sign of blood. Yeats's folklore is full of these tales of changelings, and the theme impregnates the poetry from 'The Stolen Child' to 'Sailing to Byzantium', where he implores the otherworld to take him into its living artifice. The theme is plain enough, but what does it connect to, what is its place in Yeats's unity?

Yeats held that poetic knowledge came from 'out there', from 'beyond', from what, to the normal sane way of beholding, is 'dead'. There is a radical kind of strategy at work here: what to you (the modern world, Britain, materialism) is dead, to us is alive and full of strange complexity. Where your opinionatedness cannot allow you to go, we ('Irish'[24]) can find a core of energy, a living mathematics. As is often the case there is a method behind the assertion. You think we have no tradition, no power, no knowledge: but the material, unified by imagination, reveals a capacity for vision and wonder. Life is not as the opinionated, the industrialists, and the citizenry think it is; in the world of Irish country belief, in Irish legend and myth, life is continually animated by death.

The people in Yeats's folklore (and in Irish folklore in general) live in a world that is precariously balanced between opposing forces. Such opposition is the dynamic of reality:

> cold and barrenness with us are warmth and abundance in some inner world; while what the Aran people call 'the battle of the friends' believed to be fought between the friends and enemies of the living among the 'others', to decide whether a sick person is to live or die, and the battle believed to be fought by the 'others' at harvest time, to decide, as I think, whether the harvest is to stay among men, or wither from among men and belong to the 'others' and the dead, show, I think, that the gain of the one country is the other country's loss (pp. 325–6).

This passage is badly written, but it is clumsy and inelegant because of the intellectual and indeed stylistic tension that often shows itself in Yeats when he approaches the central knots in the fabric of his vision. It is a measure of his artistic achievement that such hesitancy and awkwardness are transformed into the profound and spine-tingling uncertainty and awesome openness in the poetic method of 'Byzantium' (written in 1930), the second stanza of which explores the idea of interaction between living and dead:

> Before me floats an image, man or shade,
> Shade more than man, more image than a shade;
> For Hades' bobbin bound in mummy-cloth
> May unwind the winding path;
> A mouth that has no moisture and no breath
> Breathless mouths may summon;
> I hail the superhuman;
> I call it death-in-life and life-in-death.[25]

The complex narrative of the play *The Only Jealousy of Emer* (1919) also interrogates and develops upon this master-theme.

The otherworld is not distant; it is as near as the air one breathes. Order, attentiveness, discipline and courtesy are essential to life because the 'others' may use anarchy of emotion or behaviour to usurp the conscious mind and the will. It must be stressed that Yeats's fairies, the *sí* ('others'), belong to Gaelic tradition, in which the otherworld has its own separate life, with hierarchies, locations, histories and war-like beings. A complex and densely populated world, it is a commonwealth, as the Scot Robert Kirk described it, but one which, given spiritual blindness, insensitivity or thoughtless behaviour, can overwhelm this world. Ceremony, custom, the mask, as Yeats developed the idea, are means of governing the potential lawlessness of the unconscious otherworld. For example, to admire a beautiful woman without wishing her well in the form of blessing can open up a channel between her and the fairies by means of which they can take her away (p. 315). Violent emotion of any kind can do great damage; it can be 'a rope to drag us out of the world' (p. 164). Or, as he put it earlier in various ways: 'every emotion, which is not governed by our will . . . is the emotion of spirits who are always ready to bring us under their power' (p. 264); 'mystics believe that sicknesses and the elements do the will of spiritual powers' (p. 161).

Yeats's idea of the otherworld, which he takes from Gaelic tradition, becomes, in his mental arena, a kind of uncertainty principle. Things are not what they seem to be. We live in a world, apparently solid, but actually, to the eyes of an understanding schooled in ancient wisdom, 'flowing' and 'phenomenal', two words he used in 'A General Introduction for my Work'.[26] This phenomenal, flowing view of the world was, he also asserted, 'concrete', because it was rooted in actual things seen by the eye of imagination, not obstructed by the tired categories of the materialist mind, and thereby rendered static, solidified.

Yeats's aim was to create a vital Irish imagination based on ancient knowledge, ancient wisdom. He researched and studied all material on Irish folklore, legend and myth available to him at the time, with energy, thoroughness and commitment. The insights and knowledge this material embodied were Irish, but it also, to his view, connected him to the main line of European tradition. To follow this line of inquiry meant a profound refusal of the Arnold view of Celticism, and of the contemporary Irish middle class's view of itself. He set about unifying a 'wild anarchy' of legends, as he saw it, to create an Ireland of the imagination: eloquent, searching and modern; questioning, open and traditional.

Some contemporary critics have pointed to Yeats's imagined Ireland, with all its spookcraft, and derided it (something he was good at himself); or, more persuasively, they have argued that his search for 'authentic Irishness' and 'ancient' tradition is a phase of the post-colonial experience when the native or the native's spokesman asserts the continuity of the racial substrate of the colony in mystical terms. But this intellectual formulation does not take account of the fact that Yeats's commentary upon, and use of, folklore, legend and myth moves us profoundly by releasing a freedom of imagining, and by inviting us to participate in this freedom:

One man, one man alone
In that outlandish gear,
One solitary man
Of all that rambled there
Had turned his stately head.
'That is a long way off,
And time runs on,' he said,
'And the night grows rough.'

'I am of Ireland,
And the Holy Land of Ireland,
And time runs on,' cried she.
'Come out of charity
And dance with me in Ireland.'[27]

The famous songwriter and neglected poet, Van Morrison, puts the same case in a different tonality:

There's a dream where the contents are visible
Where the poetic champions compose.
Will you breathe not a word of this secrecy and
Will you still be my special rose?[28]

Samhain 1992

Notes

In the introduction page references are given in brackets to the texts in this volume.

1. W. B. Yeats quotation from *CL, I*, p. 303.

Aimé Césaire quotation from Edward W. Said, *Yeats and Decolonization*, Field Day Pamphlet 15 (1989), p. 16. See Robert O'Driscoll, 'Continuity in Loss: The Irish and Anglo-Irish Traditions' in Birgit Bramsbäck and Martin Croghan (eds.), *Anglo-Irish and Irish Literature: Aspects of Language and Culture*, Vol. I (1988), pp. 143–58.

2. *WBYIF*, p. 129.
3. *WBYIF*, p. 128.
4. *WBYIF*, *passim*.
5. *CP*, p. 347.
6. *CP*, p. 375.
7. *CP*, p. 400.
8. See David Cairns and Shaun Richards, '"Woman" in the Discourse of Celticism', in Birgit Bramsbäck and Martin Croghan (eds.), *Anglo-Irish and Irish Literature: Aspects of Language and Culture*, Vol. II (1988), pp. 31–3, for a discussion of the 'effeminate' discourse of Celticism. Cairns and Richards also point out that Ernest Renan anticipates Arnold, and that he describes the Celts as an 'essentially feminine race'.
9. James Joyce, *Finnegans Wake* (1939), p. 344.
10. *UP, II*, p. 237.
11. Said writes of 'the power of Yeats's accomplishment in restoring a suppressed history, and rejoining the nation to it', a form of imaginative decolonization moving in the direction of liberation. Edward W. Said, *Yeats and Decolonization*, p. 20.
12. *CP*, p. 217.
13. Osborn Bergin, 'Bardic Poetry', preface to his *Irish Bardic Poetry* (1970), pp. 5–8.
14. *CP*, p. 269.
15. *WBYIF*, p. 269.
16. *CL, I*, p. 313.
17. *CP*, p. 276.
18. A phrase from 'Ego Dominus Tuus', *CP*, p. 181.
19. Seamus Heaney, 'Bogland', *Door into the Dark* (1972), p. 56.
20. Samuel Taylor Coleridge, 'Dejection: An Ode', *The Poems of Samuel Taylor Coleridge* ([n.d.]), p. 243.
21. Edward W. Said, *Yeats and Decolonization*, p. 17.
22. Roland Barthes in 'The Theory of the Text', included in Robert Young (ed.), *Untying the Text* (1981), p. 39, writes of the etymology of 'text': 'it is a tissue, something woven'.
23. *Essays and Introductions* (1961), p. 518.

24. *CP*, p. 376.
25. *CP*, p. 280.
26. *Essays and Introductions*, p. 518.
27. *CP*, p. 304.
28. 'Queen of the Slipstream' in *Poetic Champions Compose* (Caledonia Productions Ltd, Phonogram, 1987).

I

INTRODUCTION TO *FAIRY AND FOLK TALES OF THE IRISH PEASANTRY*

(1888)

Dr Corbett,[1] Bishop of Oxford and Norwich, lamented long ago the departure of the English fairies. 'In Queen Mary's time' he wrote –

When Tom came home from labour,
  Or Cis to milking rose,
Then merrily, merrily went their tabor,
  And merrily went their toes.

But now, in the times of James, they had all gone, for 'they were of the old profession', and 'their songs were Ave Maries'. In Ireland they are still extant, giving gifts to the kindly, and plaguing the surly. 'Have you ever seen a fairy or such like?' I asked an old man in County Sligo. 'Amn't I annoyed with them,' was the answer. 'Do the fishermen along here know anything of the mermaids?' I asked a woman of a village in County Dublin. 'Indeed, they don't like to see them at all,' she answered, 'for they always bring bad weather.' 'Here is a man who believes in ghosts,' said a foreign sea-captain, pointing to a pilot of my acquaintance. 'In every house over there,' said the pilot, pointing to his native village of Rosses, 'there are several.' Certainly that now old and much respected dogmatist, the Spirit of the Age,[2] has in no manner made his voice heard down there. In a little while, for he has gotten a consumptive appearance of late, he will be covered over decently in his grave, and another will grow, old and much respected, in his place, and never be heard of down there, and after him another and another and another. Indeed, it is a question whether any of these personages will ever be heard of outside the newspaper offices and lecture-rooms and drawing-rooms and eel-pie houses of the cities, or if the Spirit of the Age is at any time more than a froth. At any rate, whole troops of their like will not change the Celt much. Giraldus Cambrensis[3] found the people of the western islands a trifle paganish. 'How many gods are there?' asked a priest, a little while ago, of a man from the Island of Innistor.[4] 'There is one on Innistor; but this seems a big place,' said the man, and the priest held up his hands in horror, as Giraldus had, just seven centuries before. Remember, I am not blaming the man; it is very much better to believe in a number of gods than in none at all, or to think there is only one, but that he is a little sentimental and impracticable, and not constructed for the nineteenth century. The Celt, and his cromlechs,[5] and his pillar-stones, these will not change much – indeed, it is doubtful if anybody at all changes at any time. In spite of hosts of deniers, and asserters, and wise-men, and professors, the majority still are averse to sitting down to dine thirteen at table, or being helped to salt, or walking under a ladder, or seeing a single magpie flirting his chequered tail. There are, of course, children of light who have set their faces against all this, though even a newspaper man, if you entice him into a cemetery at midnight, will believe in phantoms, for every one is a visionary, if you scratch him deep enough. But the Celt is a visionary without scratching.

Yet, be it noticed, if you are a stranger, you will not readily get ghost and fairy legends, even in a western village. You must go adroitly to work, and make friends with the children, and the old men, with those who have not felt the pressure of mere daylight existence, and those with whom it is growing less, and will have altogether taken itself off one of these days. The old women are most learned, but will not so readily be got to talk, for the fairies are very secretive, and much resent being talked of; and are there not many stories of old women who were nearly pinched into their graves or numbed with fairy blasts?

At sea, when the nets are out and the pipes are lit, then will some ancient hoarder of tales become loquacious, telling his histories to the tune of the creaking of the boats. Holy-eve night,[6] too, is a great time, and in old days many tales were to be heard at wakes. But the priests have set their faces against wakes.

In the *Parochial Survey of Ireland*[7] it is recorded how the story-tellers used to gather together of an evening, and if any had a different version from the others, they would all recite theirs and vote, and the man who had varied would have to abide by their verdict. In this way stories have been handed down with such accuracy, that the long tale of Deirdre was, in the earlier decades of this century, told almost word for word, as in the very ancient manuscripts in the Royal Dublin Society.[8] In one case only it varied, and then the manuscript was obviously wrong – a passage had been forgotten by the copyist. But this accuracy is rather in the folk and bardic tales than in the fairy legends, for these vary widely, being usually adapted to some neighbouring village or local fairy-seeing celebrity. Each county has usually some family, or personage, supposed to have been favoured or plagued, especially by the phantoms, as the Hackets of Castle Hacket, Galway, who had for their ancestor a fairy, or John-o'-Daly of Lisadell, Sligo, who wrote 'Eileen Aroon', the song the Scotch have stolen and called 'Robin Adair', and which Handel* would sooner have written than all his oratorios, and the 'O'Donahue of Kerry'.[9] Round these men stories tended to group themselves, sometimes deserting more ancient heroes for the purpose. Round poets have they gathered especially, for poetry in Ireland has always been mysteriously connected with magic.

These folk-tales are full of simplicity and musical occurrences, for they are the literature of a class for whom every incident in the old rut of birth, love, pain, and death has cropped up unchanged for centuries: who have steeped everything in the heart: to whom everything is a symbol. They have the spade over which man has leant from the beginning. The people of the cities have the machine, which is prose and a *parvenu*. They have few events. They can turn over the incidents of a long life as they sit by the fire. With us nothing has time to gather meaning, and too many things are occurring for even a big heart to hold. It is said the most eloquent people in the world are the Arabs, who have only the bare earth of the desert and a sky swept bare by the sun.

* He lived some time in Dublin, and heard it then.

'Wisdom has alighted upon three things,' goes their proverb; 'the hand of the Chinese, the brain of the Frank, and the tongue of the Arab.'[10] This, I take it, is the meaning of that simplicity sought for so much in these days by all the poets, and not to be had at any price.

The most notable and typical story-teller of my acquaintance is one Paddy Flynn, a little, bright-eyed, old man, living in a leaky one-roomed cottage of the village of B—,[11] 'The most gentle – *i.e.*, fairy – place[12] in the whole of the County Sligo,' he says, though others claim that honour for Drumahair or for Drumcliff. A very pious old man, too! You may have some time to inspect his strange figure and ragged hair, if he happen to be in a devout humour, before he comes to the doings of the gentry.[13] A strange devotion![14] . . .

Not that the sceptic[15] is entirely afar even from these western villages. I found him one morning as he bound his corn in a merest pocket-handkerchief of a field. Very different from Paddy Flynn – Scepticism in every wrinkle of his face, and a travelled man, too! – a foot-long Mohawk Indian tattooed on one of his arms to evidence the matter. 'They who travel,' says a neighbouring priest, shaking his head over him, and quoting Thomas à Kempis, 'seldom come home holy.' I had mentioned ghosts to this Sceptic. 'Ghosts,' said he; 'there are no such things at all, at all, but the gentry, they stand to reason; for the devil, when he fell out of heaven, took the weak-minded ones with him, and they were put into the waste places. And that's what the gentry are. But they are getting scarce now, because their time's over, ye see, and they're going back. But ghosts, no! And I'll tell ye something more I don't believe in – the fire of hell'; then, in a low voice, 'that's only invented to give the priests and the parsons something to do.' Thereupon this man, so full of enlightenment, returned to his corn-binding.

The various collectors of Irish folk-lore have, from our point of view, one great merit, and from the point of view of others, one great fault. They have made their work literature rather than science, and told us of the Irish peasantry rather than of the primitive religion of mankind, or whatever else the folk-lorists are on the gad after. To be considered scientists they should have tabulated all their tales in forms like grocers' bills – item the fairy king, item the queen. Instead of this they have caught the very voice of the people, the very pulse of life, each giving what was most noticed in his day. Croker[16] and Lover,[17] full of the ideas of harum-scarum Irish gentility, saw everything humorised. The impulse of the Irish literature of their time came from a class that did not – mainly for political reasons – take the populace seriously, and imagined the country as a humorist's Arcadia; its passion, its gloom, its tragedy, they knew nothing of. What they did was not wholly false; they merely magnified an irresponsible type, found oftenest among boatmen, carmen, and gentlemen's servants, into the type of a whole nation, and created the stage Irishman. The writers of 'Forty-eight, and the famine[18] combined, burst their bubble. Their work had the dash as well as the shallowness of an ascendant and idle class, and in Croker is touched everywhere with beauty – a gentle Arcadian beauty. Carleton,[19] a peasant born, has in many of his stories, more especially in his ghost stories, a much more serious way with him, for all his humour. Kennedy,[20] an old bookseller in Dublin, who seems to have had a something of genuine belief in the fairies, came next in time. He has far less literary faculty, but is wonderfully accurate, giving often the very words the stories were told in. But the best book since Croker is Lady Wilde's[21] *Ancient Legends*. The humour has all given way to pathos and tenderness. We have here the innermost heart of the Celt in the moments he has grown to love through years of persecution, when, cushioning himself about with dreams, and hearing fairy-songs in the twilight, he ponders on the soul and on the dead. Here is the Celt, only it is the Celt dreaming.

Besides these are two writers of importance, who have published, so far, nothing in book shape – Miss Letitia Maclintock[22] and Mr Douglas Hyde.[23] Miss Maclintock writes accurately and beautifully the half Scotch dialect of Ulster; and Mr Douglas Hyde is now preparing a volume of folk tales in Gaelic, having taken them down, for the most part, word for word among the Gaelic speakers of Roscommon and Galway. He is, perhaps, most to be trusted of all. He knows the people thoroughly. Others see a phase of Irish life; he understands all its elements. His work is neither humorous nor mournful; it is simply life. I hope he may put some of his gatherings into ballads, for he is the last of our ballad-writers of the school of Walsh and Callanan[24] – men whose work seems fragrant with turf smoke. And this brings to mind the chap books.[25] They are to be found brown with turf smoke on cottage shelves, and are, or were, sold on every hand by the pedlars, but cannot be found in any library of this city of the Sassanach.[26] *The Royal Fairy Tales*, *The Hibernian Tales* and *The Legends of the Fairies* are the fairy literature of the people.

Several specimens of our fairy poetry are given. It is more like the fairy poetry of Scotland than of England. The personages of English fairy literature are merely, in most cases, mortals beautifully masquerading. Nobody ever believed in such fairies. They are romantic bubbles from Provence. Nobody ever laid new milk on their doorstep for them.

As to my own part in this book, I have tried to make it representative, as far as so few pages would allow, of every kind of Irish folk-faith. The reader will perhaps wonder that in all my notes I have not rationalised a single hobgoblin. I seek for shelter to the words of Socrates.[27]

Phædrus. I should like to know, Socrates, whether the place is not somewhere here at which Boreas is said to have carried off Orithyia from the banks of the Ilissus?

Socrates. That is the tradition.

Phædrus. And is this the exact spot? The little stream is delightfully clear and bright; I can fancy that there might be maidens playing near.

Socrates. I believe the spot is not exactly here, but about a quarter-of-a-mile lower down, where you cross to the temple of Artemis, and I think that there is some sort of an altar of Boreas at the place.

Phædrus. I do not recollect; but I beseech you to tell me, Socrates, do you believe this tale?

Socrates. The wise are doubtful, and I should not be singular if, like them, I also doubted. I might have a rational explanation that Orithyia was playing with Pharmacia, when a northern gust carried her over the neighbouring rocks; and this being the manner of her death, she was said to have been carried away by Boreas. There is a discrepancy, however, about the locality. According to another version of the story, she was taken from the Areopagus, and not from this place. Now I quite acknowledge that these allegories are very nice, but he is not to be envied who has to invent them; much labour and ingenuity will be required of him; and when he has once begun, he must go on and rehabilitate centaurs and chimeras dire. Gorgons and winged steeds flow in apace, and numberless other inconceivable and portentous monsters. And if he is sceptical about them, and would fain reduce them one after another to the rules of probability, this sort of crude philosophy will take up all his time. Now, I have certainly not time for such inquiries. Shall I tell you why? I must first know myself, as the Delphian inscription says; to be curious about that which is not my business, while I am still in ignorance of my own self, would be ridiculous. And, therefore, I say farewell to all this; the common opinion is enough for me. For, as I was saying, I want to know not about this, but about myself. Am I, indeed, a wonder more complicated and swollen with passion than the serpent Typho, or a creature of gentler and simpler sort, to whom nature has given a diviner and lowlier destiny?

2

'THE IRISH FAIRIES'

from *Fairy and Folk Tales of the Irish Peasantry* (1888)

The Trooping Fairies

The Irish word for fairy is *sheehogue* [*sidheóg*], a diminutive of 'shee' in *banshee*. Fairies are *deenee shee* [*daoine sidhe*] (fairy people).

Who are they? 'Fallen angels who were not good enough to be saved, nor bad enough to be lost,' say the peasantry. 'The gods of the earth,' says the *Book of Armagh*.[1] 'The gods of pagan Ireland,' say the Irish antiquarians, 'the Tuatha Dé Danann,[2] who, when no longer worshipped and fed with offerings, dwindled away in the popular imagination, and now are only a few spans high.'

And they will tell you, in proof, that the names of fairy chiefs are the names of old Danann heroes, and the places where they especially gather together, Danann burying-places, and that the Tuatha Dé Danann used also to be called the *slooa-shee* [*sluagh sidhe*] (the fairy host), or *Marcra shee* (the fairy cavalcade).

On the other hand, there is much evidence to prove them fallen angels. Witness the nature of the creatures, their caprice, their way of being good to the good and evil to the evil, having every charm but conscience – consistency. Beings so quickly offended that you must not speak much about them at all, and never call them anything but the 'gentry', or else *daoine maithe*, which in English means good people, yet so easily pleased, they will do their best to keep misfortune away from you, if you leave a little milk for them on the window-sill over night. On the whole, the popular belief tells us most about them, telling us how they fell, and yet were not lost, because their evil was wholly without malice.

Are they 'the gods of the earth'? Perhaps! Many poets, and all mystic and occult writers, in all ages and countries, have declared that behind the visible are chains on chains of conscious beings, who are not of heaven but of the earth, who have no inherent form but change according to their whim, or the mind that sees them. You cannot lift your hand without influencing and being influenced by hoards. The visible world is merely their skin. In dreams we go amongst them, and play with them, and combat with them. They are, perhaps, human souls in the crucible – these creatures of whim.

Do not think the fairies are always little. Everything is capricious about them, even their size. They seem to take what size or shape pleases them. Their chief occupations are feasting, fighting, and making love, and playing the most beautiful music. They have only one industrious person amongst them, the *lepracaun* – the shoemaker. Perhaps they wear their shoes out with dancing. Near the village of Ballisodare is a little woman who lived amongst them seven years. When she came home she had no toes – she had danced them off.

They have three great festivals in the year – May Eve, Midsummer Eve, November Eve. On May Eve, every seventh year, they fight all round, but mostly on the 'Plain-a-Bawn' (wherever that is), for the harvest, for the best ears of grain belong to them.[3] An old man told me he saw them fight once; they tore the thatch off a house in the midst of it all. Had anyone else been near they would merely have seen a great wind whirling everything into the air as it passed. When the wind makes the straws and leaves whirl as it passes, that is the fairies, and the peasantry take off their hats and say, 'God bless them.'

On Midsummer Eve, when the bonfires are lighted on every hill in honour of St John, the fairies are at their gayest, and sometime steal away beautiful mortals to be their brides.

On November Eve they are at their gloomiest, for, according to the old Gaelic reckoning, this is the first night of winter. This night they dance with the ghosts, and the *pooka* is abroad, and witches make their spells, and girls set a table with food in the name of the devil, that the fetch[4] of their future lover may come through the window and eat of the food. After November Eve the blackberries are no longer wholesome, for the *pooka* has spoiled them.

When they are angry they paralyse men and cattle with their fairy darts.

When they are gay they sing. Many a poor girl has heard them, and pined away and died, for love of that singing. Plenty of the old beautiful tunes of Ireland are only their music, caught up by eavesdroppers. No wise peasant would hum 'The Pretty Girl Milking the Cow' near a fairy rath,[5] for they are jealous, and do not like to hear their songs on clumsy mortal lips. Carolan,[6] the last of the Irish bards, slept on a rath, and ever after the fairy tunes ran in his head, and made him the great man he was.

Do they die? Blake saw a fairy's funeral;[7] but in Ireland we say they are immortal.

CHANGELINGS

Sometimes the fairies fancy mortals, and carry them away into their own country, leaving instead some sickly fairy child, or a log of wood so bewitched that it seems to be a mortal pining away, and dying, and being buried. Most commonly they steal children.[8] If you 'over look a child', that is look on it with envy, the fairies have it in their power. Many things can be done to find out in a child a changeling, but there is one infallible thing – lay it on the fire with this formula, 'Burn, burn, burn – if of the devil, burn; but if of God and the saints, be safe from harm' (given by Lady Wilde). Then if it be a changeling it will rush up the chimney with a cry, for, according to Giraldus Cambrensis, 'fire is the greatest of enemies to every sort of phantom, in so much that those who have seen apparitions fall into a swoon as soon as they are sensible of the brightness of fire'.[9]

Sometimes the creature is got rid of in a more gentle way. It is on record that once when a mother was leaning over a wizened changeling the latch lifted and a fairy came in, carrying home again the wholesome stolen baby. 'It was the others,' she said, 'who stole it.' As for her, she wanted her own child.

These who are carried away are happy, according to some accounts, having plenty of good living and music and mirth.

Others say, however, that they are continually longing for their earthly friends. Lady Wilde gives a gloomy tradition that there are two kinds of fairies – one kind merry and gentle, the other evil, and sacrificing every year a life to Satan, for which purpose they steal mortals. No other Irish writer gives this tradition – if such fairies there be, they must be among the solitary spirits – *pookas*, *Fir Darrigs*, and the like.

THE MERROW

The *Merrow*, or if you write it in the Irish, *Moruadh* or *Murrúghach*, from *muir*, sea, and *oigh*, a maid, is not uncommon, they say, on the wilder coasts. The fishermen do not like to see them, for it always means coming gales. The male *Merrows* (if you can use such a phrase – I have never heard the masculine of *Merrow*) have green teeth, green hair, pig's eyes, and red noses; but their women are beautiful, for all their fish tails and the little duck-like scale between their fingers. Sometimes they prefer, small blame to them, good-looking fishermen to their sea lovers. Near Bantry, in the last century, there is said to have been a woman covered all over with scales like a fish, who was descended from such a marriage. Sometimes they come out of the sea, and wander about the shore in the shape of little hornless cows. They have, when in their own shape, a red cap, called a *cohullen druith*, usually covered with feathers. If this is stolen, they cannot again go down under the waves.

Red is the colour of magic in every country, and has been so from the very earliest times. The caps of fairies and magicians are well-nigh always red.

The Solitary Fairies

LEPRACAUN, CLURICAUN AND FAR DARRIG

'The name *Lepracaun*,' Mr Douglas Hyde writes to me, 'is from the Irish *leith brog* – *i.e.*, the One-shoemaker, since he is generally seen working at a single shoe. It is spelt in Irish *leith bhrogan*, or *leith phrogan*, and is in some places pronounced Luchryman, as O'Kearney[10] writes it in that very rare book, the *Feis Tigh Chonain*.'[11]

The *Lepracaun*, *Cluricaun*, and *Far Darrig*. Are these one spirit in different moods and shapes? Hardly two Irish writers are agreed. In many things these three fairies, if three, resemble each other. They are withered, old, and solitary, in every way unlike the sociable spirits of the first sections. They dress with all unfairy homeliness, and are, indeed, most sluttish, slouching, jeering, mischievous phantoms. They are the great practical jokers among the good people.

The *Lepracaun* makes shoes continually, and has grown very rich. Many treasure-crocks, buried of old in war-time, has he now for his own. In the early part of this century, according to Croker, in a newspaper office in Tipperary, they used to show a little shoe forgotten by a Lepracaun.

The *Cluricaun* (*Clobhair-ceann*, in O'Kearney) makes himself drunk in gentlemen's cellars. Some suppose he is merely the Lepracaun on a spree. He is almost unknown in Connacht and the north.

The *Far Darrig* (*fear dearg*), which means the Red Man, for he wears a red cap and coat, busies himself with practical joking, especially with gruesome joking. This he does, and nothing else.

The *Fear-Gorta* (Man of Hunger) is an emaciated phantom that goes through the land in famine time, begging an alms and bringing good luck to the giver.

There are other solitary fairies, such as the House-spirit and the *Water-sheerie*, own brother to the English Jack-o'-Lantern; the *Pooka* and the *Banshee* – concerning these presently; the *Dallahan*, or headless phantom – one used to stand in a Sligo street on dark nights till lately; the Black Dog, a form, perhaps, of the *Pooka*. The ships at the Sligo quays are haunted sometimes by this spirit, who announces his presence by a sound like the flinging of all 'the tin porringers in the world' down into the hold. He even follows them to sea.

The *Leanhaun Shee* (fairy mistress) seeks the love of mortals. If they refuse, she must be their slave; if they consent, they are hers, and can only escape by finding another to take their place. The fairy lives on their life, and they waste away. Death is no escape from her. She is the Gaelic muse, for she gives inspiration to those she persecutes. The Gaelic poets die young, for she is restless, and will not let them remain long on earth – this malignant phantom.

Besides these are divers monsters – the *Augh-iska*, the Water-horse, the *Payshtha* (*piast = bestia*), the Lake-dragon, and such like; but whether these be animals, fairies or spirits, I know not.

Ghosts

Ghosts, or as they are called in Irish *Thevshi* or *Tash* (*taidhbhse, tais*) live in a state intermediary between this life and the next. They are held there by some earthly longing or affection, or some duty unfulfilled, or anger against the living. 'I will haunt you,' is a common threat; and one hears such phrases as, 'She will haunt him, if she has any good in her.' If one is sorrowing greatly after a dead friend, a neighbour will say, 'Be quiet now, you are keeping him from his rest'; or, in the Western Isles, according to Lady Wilde, they will tell you, 'You are waking the dog that watches to devour the souls of the dead.' Those who die suddenly, more commonly than others, are believed to become haunting Ghosts. They go about moving the furniture, and in every way trying to attract attention.

When the soul has left the body, it is drawn away, sometimes, by the fairies. I have a story of a peasant who once saw, sitting in a fairy rath, all who had died for years in his village. Such souls are considered lost. If a soul eludes the fairies, it may be snapped up by the evil spirits. The weak souls of young children are in especial danger. When a very young child dies, the western peasantry sprinkle the threshold with the blood of a chicken, that the spirits may be drawn away to the blood. A Ghost is compelled to obey the commands of the living. 'The stable-boy up at Mrs G—'s there,' said an old countryman, 'met the master going round the yards after he had been two days dead, and told him to be away with him to the lighthouse, and haunt that; and there he is far out to sea still, sir. Mrs G— was quite wild about it, and dismissed the boy.' A very desolate lighthouse poor devil of a Ghost! Lady Wilde considers it is only the spirits who are too bad for heaven, and too good for hell, who are thus plagued. They are compelled to obey someone they have wronged.

The souls of the dead sometimes take the shapes of animals. There is a garden at Sligo where the gardener sees a previous owner in the shape of a rabbit. They will sometimes take the forms of insects, especially of butterflies. If you see one fluttering near a corpse, that is the soul, and is a sign of its having entered upon immortal happiness. The author of the *Parochial Survey of Ireland*, 1814, heard a woman say to a child who was chasing a butterfly, 'How do you know it is not the soul of your grandfather.' On November eve[12] the dead are abroad, and dance with the fairies.

As in Scotland, the fetch is commonly believed in. If you see the double, or fetch, of a friend in the morning, no ill follows; if at night, he is about to die.

Witches, Fairy Doctors

Witches and fairy doctors receive their power from opposite dynasties; the witch from evil spirits and her own malignant will; the fairy doctor from the fairies, and a something – a temperament – that is born with him or her. The first is always feared and hated. The second is gone to for advice, and is never worse than mischievous. The most celebrated fairy doctors are sometimes people the fairies loved and carried away, and kept with them for seven years; not that those the fairies love are always carried off – they may merely grow silent and strange, and take to lonely wanderings in the 'gentle' places. Such will, in after-times, be great poets or musicians, or fairy doctors; they must not be confused with those who have a *Leanhaun shee* [*leannán sídhe*], for the *Leanhaun shee* lives upon the vitals of its chosen, and they waste and die. She is of the dreadful solitary fairies. To her have belonged the greatest of the Irish poets, from Oisin[13] down to the last century.

Those we speak of have for their friends the trooping fairies – the gay and sociable populace of raths and caves. Great is their knowledge of herbs and spices. These doctors, when the butter will not come on the milk, or the milk will not come from the cow, will be sent for to find out if the cause be in the course of common nature or if there has been witchcraft. Perhaps some old hag in the shape of a hare has been milking the cattle. Perhaps some user of 'the dead hand' has drawn away the butter to her own churn. Whatever it be, there is the counter-charm. They will give advice, too, in cases of suspected changelings, and prescribe for the 'fairy blast'[14] (when the fairy strikes any one a tumour rises, or they become paralysed. This is called a 'fairy blast' or a 'fairy stroke'). The fairies are, of course, visible to them, and many a new-built house have they bid the owner pull down because it lay on the fairies' road. Lady Wilde thus describes one who lived in Innis Sark: – 'He never touched beer, spirits, or meat in all his life, but has lived entirely on bread, fruit, and vegetables. A man who knew him thus describes him – "Winter and summer his dress is the same – merely a flannel shirt and coat. He will pay his share at a feast, but neither eats nor drinks of the food and drink set before him. He speaks no English, and never could be made to learn the English tongue, though he says it might be used with great effect to curse one's enemy. He holds a burial-ground sacred, and would not carry away so much as a leaf of ivy from a grave. And he maintains that the people are right to keep to their ancient usages, such as never to dig a grave on a Monday, and to carry the coffin three times round the grave, following the course of the sun, for then the dead rest in peace. Like the people also, he holds suicides as accursed; for they believe that all its dead turn over on their faces if a suicide is laid amongst them.

'"Though well off, he never, even in his youth, thought of taking a wife; nor was he ever known to love a woman. He stands quite apart from life, and by this means holds his power over the mysteries. No money will tempt him to impart his knowledge to another, for if he did he would be struck dead – so he believes. He would not touch a hazel stick, but carries an ash wand, which he holds in his hand when he prays, laid across his knees; and the whole of his life is devoted to works of grace and charity, and though now an old man, he has never had a day's sickness. No one has ever seen him in a rage, nor heard an angry word from his lips but once, and then being under great irritation, he recited the Lord's Prayer backwards as an imprecation on his enemy. Before his death he will reveal the mystery of his power, but not till the hand of death is on him for certain." When he does reveal it, we may be sure it will be to one person only – his successor.' There are several such doctors in County Sligo, really well up in herbal medicine by all accounts, and my friends find them in their own counties. All these things go on merrily. The spirit of the age laughs in vain, and is itself only a ripple to pass, or already passing, away.

The spells of the witch are altogether different; they smell of the grave. One of the most powerful is the charm of the dead hand. With a hand cut from a corpse they, muttering words of power, will stir a well and skim from its surface a neighbour's butter.

A candle held between the fingers of the dead hand can never be blown out. This is useful to robbers, but they appeal for the suffrage of the lovers likewise, for they can make love-potions by drying and grinding into powder the liver of a black cat. Mixed with tea, and poured from a black teapot, it is infallible. There are many stories of its success in quite recent years, but, unhappily, the spell must be continually renewed, or all the love may turn into hate. But the central notion of witchcraft everywhere is the power to change into some fictitious form, usually in Ireland a hare or a cat. Long ago a wolf was the favourite. Before Giraldus Cambrensis came to Ireland, a monk wandering in a forest at night came upon two wolves, one of whom was dying. The other entreated him to give the dying wolf the last sacrament. He said the mass, and paused when he came to the viaticum. The other, on seeing this, tore the skin from the breast of the dying wolf, laying bare the form of an old woman. Thereon the monk gave the sacrament. Years afterwards he confessed the matter, and when Giraldus visited the country, was being tried by the synod of the bishops. To give the sacrament to an animal was a great sin. Was it a human being or an animal? On the advice of Giraldus they sent the monk, with papers describing the matter, to the Pope for his decision. The result is not stated.[15]

Giraldus himself was of opinion that the wolf-form was an illusion, for, as he argued, only God can change the form. His opinion coincides with tradition, Irish and otherwise.

It is the notion of many who have written about these things that magic is mainly the making of such illusions. Patrick Kennedy tells a story of a girl who, having in her hand a sod of grass containing, unknown to herself, a four-leaved shamrock, watched a conjurer at a fair. Now, the four-leaved shamrock guards its owner from all *pishogues* (spells), and when the others were staring at a cock carrying along the roof of a shed a huge beam in its bill, she asked them what they found to wonder at in a cock with a straw. The conjurer begged from her the sod of grass, to give to his horse, he said. Immediately she cried out in terror that the beam would fall and kill somebody.

This, then, is to be remembered – the form of an enchanted thing is a fiction and a caprice.

Tír na nÓg

There is a country called Tír na nÓg, which means the Country of the Young, for age and death have not found it; neither tears nor loud laughter have gone near it. The shadiest boskage covers it perpetually. One man has gone there and returned. The bard, Oisin, who wandered away on a white horse, moving on the surface of the foam with his fairy Niamh, lived there three hundred years, and then returned looking for his comrades. The moment his foot touched the earth his three hundred years fell on him, and he was bowed double, and his beard swept the ground. He described his sojourn in the Land of Youth to Patrick before he died. Since then many have seen it in many places; some in the depths of lakes, and have heard rising therefrom a vague sound of bells; more have seen it far off on the horizon, as they peered out from the western cliffs. Not three years ago a fisherman imagined that he saw it. It never appears unless to announce some national trouble.

There are many kindred beliefs. A Dutch pilot, settled in Dublin, told M. De La Boullage Le Cong,[16] who travelled in Ireland in 1614, that round the poles were many islands; some hard to be approached because of the witches who inhabit them and destroy by storms those who seek to land. He had once, off the coast of Greenland, in sixty-one degrees of latitude, seen and approached such an island only to see it vanish. Sailing in an opposite direction, they met with the same island, and sailing near, were almost destroyed by a furious tempest.

According to many stories, Tír na nÓg is the favourite dwelling of the fairies. Some say it is triple – the island of the living, the island of victories, and an underwater land.[17]

Saints, Priests

Everywhere in Ireland are the holy wells. People as they pray by them make little piles of stones, that will be counted at the last day and the prayers reckoned up. Sometimes they tell stories. They deal with the old times, whereof King Alfred of Northumberland[18] wrote –

I found in Innisfail the fair,
In Ireland, while in exile there,
Women of worth, both grave and gay men,
Many clericks and many laymen.

Gold and silver I found, and money,
Plenty of wheat, and plenty of honey,
I found God's people rich in pity,
Found many a feast, and many a city.

There are no martyrs in the stories. That ancient chronicler Giraldus taunted the Archbishop of Cashel because no one in Ireland had received the crown of martyrdom. 'Our people may be barbarous,' the prelate answered, 'but they have never lifted their hands against God's saints; but now that a people have come amongst us who know how to make them (it was just after the English invasion), we shall have martyrs plentifully.'

The bodies of saints are fastidious things. At a place called Four-mile-Water, in Wexford, there is an old graveyard full of saints. Once it was on the other side of the river, but they buried a rogue there, and the whole graveyard moved across in the night, leaving the rogue-corpse in solitude. It would have been easier to move merely the rogue-corpse, but they were saints, and had to do things in style.

3

'IRISH FAIRIES, GHOSTS, WITCHES'

from *Lucifer* (1889)

It has occurred to me that it would be interesting if some spiritualist or occultist would try to explain the various curious and intricate spiritualistic beliefs of peasants. When reading Irish folk-lore, or listening to Irish peasants telling their tales of magic and fairyism and witchcraft, more and more is one convinced that some clue there must be. Even if it is all dreaming, why have they dreamed this particular dream? Clearly the occultist should have his say as well as the folk-lorist. The history of a belief is not enough, one would gladly hear about its cause.

Here and there an occult clue is visible plainly. Some of the beliefs about ghosts are theosophical; the Irish ghost or *thivish*, for instance, is merely an earth-bound shell, fading and whimpering in the places it loved. And many writers, from Paracelsus to d'Assier,[1] have shed a somewhat smoky light on witches and their works, and Irish witches do not differ much from their tribe elsewhere, except in being rather more harmless. Perhaps never being burnt or persecuted has lessened the bitterness of their war against mankind, for in Ireland they have had on the whole, a very peaceable and quiet time, disappearing altogether from public life since the 'loyal minority' pilloried and imprisoned three and knocked out the eye of one with a cabbage stump, in 1711, in the town of Carrickfergus.[2] For many a long year now have they contented themselves with going out in the grey of the morning, in the shape of hares, and sucking dry their neighbour's cows, or muttering spells while they skimmed with the severed hand of a corpse the surface of a well gathering thereon a neighbour's butter.

It is when we come to the fairies and 'fairy doctors', we feel most the want of some clue – some light, no matter how smoky. These 'fairy doctors', are they mediums or clairvoyants? Why do they fear the hazel tree, or hold an ash tree in their hands when they pray? Why do they say that if you knock once at their doors they will not open, for you may be a spirit, but if you knock three times they will open. What are these figures, now little, now great, now kindly, now fierce, now ugly, now beautiful, who are said to surround them – these fairies, whom they never confuse with spirits, but describe as fighting with the spirits though generally having the worst of it, for their enemies are more God-fearing? Can any spiritualist or occultist tell us of these things? Hoping they can, I set down here this classification of Irish fairyism and demonology. The mediaeval divisions of sylphs, gnomes, undines and salamanders will not be found to help us. This is a different dynasty.

Fairy Doctors

Unlike the witch, who deals with ghosts and spirits, the fairy doctor is never malignant; at worst, he is mischievous like his masters and servants the fairies. Croker, in the *Confessions of Tom Bourke*, said by Keightly,[3] of the *Fairy Mythology*, to be the most valuable chapter in all his writings, describes the sayings and doings of such a man. Each family has its particular adherent among the 'good people', as the fairies are called, and sometimes when a man died the factions of his father and mother would fight as to the grave-yard he was to be buried in, the relations delaying the funeral until Tom Bourke told them one party or other had won. If they buried in the wrong grave-yard all kinds of ill luck would follow, for fairies know how to kill cattle with their fairy darts, and do all kinds of mischief.

The fairy doctor is great with herbs and spells. He can make the fairies give up people they have carried off, and is in every way the opposite of the witch.

The Sociable Fairies

These are the Sheogues (Ir. *Sidheog*, 'a little fairy'), and are usually of small size when first seen, though seeming of common human height when you are once glamoured. It sometimes appears as if they could take any shape according to their whim. Commonly, they go about in troops, and are kind to the kindly and mischievous to the evil and ill-tempered, being like beautiful children, having every charm but that of conscience – consistency.

Their divisions are sheogue, a land fairy, and merrow, Ir. *moruadh*, or 'sea maid' (the masculine is unknown), a water fairy. The merrow is said not to be uncommon. I asked a peasant woman once whether the fishermen of her village ever saw one. 'Indeed, they don't like to see them at all,' she answered, 'for they always bring bad weather.'

All over Ireland are little fields circled by ditches, and supposed to be ancient fortifications and sheep folds. These are the raths or forts. Here, marrying and giving in marriage, live the land fairies. Many a mortal have they enticed down into their dim world. Many more have listened to their fairy music, till all human cares and joys drifted from their hearts, and they became great fairy doctors, or great musicians, or poets like Carolan,[4] who gathered his tunes while sleeping on a fairy rath; or else they died in a year and a day, to live ever after among the fairies.

These sociable fairies are in the main good, but one most malicious habit have they – a habit worthy of a witch. They steal children, and leave a withered fairy a thousand, or may be two thousand years old, for the matter of that, instead. Two or three years ago a man wrote to one of the Irish papers, telling of a case in his own village, and how the parish priest made the fairies deliver up again the stolen child.

The sociable fairies are very quarrelsome.

Lady Wilde tells about one battle in which, no stones being at hand, they stole butter and flung it at each other. A quantity stuck in the branches of an alder-tree. A man in the neighbourhood mended the handle of the dash of his churn with a branch of this tree. As soon as he began churning, the butter, until now hanging invisible in the alder branches, flowed into his churn. The same happened every churning-day, until he told the matter to a fairy doctor, which telling broke the spell, for all these things have to be kept secret.

Kennedy[5] describes a battle heard by a peasant of his acquaintance. The sheogues were in the air over a river. He heard shots and light bodies falling into the water, and a faint sound of shouting, but could see nothing. Old Patrick Kennedy, who records this, was a second-hand bookseller in Dublin, and claimed in one of his works to know spells for making the fairies visible, but would not tell them for fear they might set dangerous forces in action – forces that might destroy the user of the spell. These battles are often described by Irish fairy seers. Sometimes the sociable sheogues, dressed in green coats, fight with the solitary red-coated fairies.

The Solitary Fairies

The best known of these is the Lepracaun (Ir. *Leith bhrogan*, *i.e.*, the 'one shoe maker'). He is seen sitting under a hedge mending a shoe, and one who catches him and keeps his eyes on him can make him deliver up his crocks of gold, for he is a rich miser; but if he takes his eyes off him, the creature vanishes like smoke. He is said to be the child of a spirit and a debased fairy, and, according to McAnally,[6] wears a red coat with seven rows of buttons, seven buttons in each row, and a cocked hat, on the point of which he sometimes spins like a top.

Some writers have supposed the Cluricaun to be another name of the same fairy, given him when he has laid aside his shoe-making at night and goes on the spree. The Cluricaun's one occupation is robbing wine-cellars.

The Gonconer or Gancanagh (Ir. *Gean-canagh*, *i.e.*, 'Love talker')[7] is a little creature of the Lepracaun type, unlike him, however, in being an idler. He always appears with a pipe in his mouth in lonely valleys, where he makes love to shepherdesses and milkmaids.

The Far Darrig (Ir. *Fear-Dearg*, *i.e.*, red man) plays practical jokes continually. A favourite trick is to make some poor mortal tramp over hedges and ditches, carrying a corpse on his back, or to make him turn it on a spit. Of all these solitary, and mainly evil, fairies there is no more lubberly wretch than this same Far Darrig. Like the next phantom, he presides over evil dreams.

The Pooka seems to be of the family of the nightmare. He has most likely never appeared in human form, the one or two recorded instances being probably mistakes, he being mixed up with the Far Darrig. His shape is that of a horse, a bull, goat, eagle, ass and perhaps of a black dog, though this last may be a separate spirit. The Pooka's delight is to get a rider, whom he rushes with through ditches and rivers and over mountains, and shakes off in the grey of the morning. Especially does he love to plague a drunkard – a drunkard's sleep is his kingdom.

The Dullahan is another gruesome phantom. He has no head, or carries it under his arm. Often he is seen driving a black coach, called the coach-a-bower (Ir. *Coise-bodhar*),[8] drawn by headless horses. It will rumble to your door, and if you open to it, a basin of blood is thrown in your face. To the houses where it pauses it is an omen of death. Such a coach, not very long ago, went through Sligo in the grey of the morning (the spirit hour). A seaman saw it, with many shudderings. In some villages its rumbling is heard many times in the year.

The Leanhaun Shee (fairy mistress) seeks the love of men. If they refuse, she is their slave; if they consent, they are hers, and can only escape by finding one to take their place. Her lovers waste away, for she lives on their life. Most of the Gaelic poets, down to quite recent times, have had a Leanhaun Shee, for she gives inspiration to her slaves. She is the Gaelic muse, this malignant fairy. Her lovers, the Gaelic poets, died young. She grew restless, and carried them away to other worlds, for death does not destroy her power.

Besides these, we have other solitary fairies, such as the House Spirit and Water Sheerie, a kind of Will-o'-the-Wisp, and various animal spirits, such as the Aughiska, the water-horse, and the Paystha (*Piast bestea*), the lake dragon, a guardian of hidden treasure, and two fairies, the Far-gorta and the Banshee, who are technically solitary fairies, though quite unlike their fellows in disposition.

The Far-gorta (man of hunger) is an emaciated fairy that goes through the land in famine time, begging, and bringing good luck to the giver of alms.

The Banshee (*Bean-sidhe*) seems to be one of the sociable fairies grown solitary through the sorrow or the triumph of the moment; her name merely means woman-fairy, answering to the less common word Farshee, man fairy. She wails, as most people know, over the death of some member of an old Irish family. Sometimes she is an enemy of the house, and wails with triumph; sometimes a friend, and wails with sorrow. When more than one Banshee comes to cry, the man or woman who is dying must have been very holy or very brave. Occasionally she is undoubtedly believed to be one of the sociable fairies. Cleena, once an ancient Irish goddess, is now a Munster sheogue.

O'Donovan,[9] one of the very greatest of the Irish antiquarians, wrote in 1849 to a friend, who quoted his words in the *Dublin University Magazine*: 'When my grandfather died in Leinster, in 1798, Cleena came all the way from Tonn Cleena, at Glandore, to lament him; but she has not been heard ever since lamenting any of our race, though I believe she still weeps in the mountains of Drimoleague in her own country, where so many of the race of Eoghan More[10] are dying of starvation.'

The Banshee who cries with triumph is often believed to be no fairy, but the ghost of one wronged by an ancestor of the dying. Besides these are various fairies who fall into none of the regular groups, such as 'Dark Joan of the Boyne'. This fairy visits houses in the form of a hen with a lot of chickens, or a pig with a litter of banyans.[11] Several now living say they have fought with this fairy pig. This taking the appearance of several animals at one time is curious, and brings to mind how completely a matter of whim, or symbolism the form of an enchanted being must be thought. Indeed, the shape of Irish fairies seems to change with their moods – symbolizing or following the feelings of the moment.

When we look for the source of this spirit rabble, we get many different answers. The peasants say they are fallen angels who were too good to be lost, too bad to be saved, and have to work out their time in barren places of the earth. An old Irish authority – the *Book of Armagh* – calls them gods of the earth, and quite beyond any kind of doubt many of them were long ago gods in Ireland.

Once upon a time the Celtic nations worshipped gods of the light, called in Ireland Tuatha Dé Danann and corresponding to Jupiter and his fellows, and gods of the great darkness corresponding to the Saturnian Titans.[12] Among the sociable fairies are many of the light gods; perhaps, some day, we may learn to look for the dark gods among the solitary fairies. The Pooka we can trace, a mysterious deity of decay, to earliest times. Certainly, he is no bright Tuatha Dé Danann. Around him hangs the dark vapour of Domnian[13] Titanism.

4

'SCOTS AND IRISH FAIRIES'

from the *Scots Observer* (1889)

Most men know the prophecy of Thomas of Ercildoune:[1] 'The time is coming when all the wisdom of the world shall centre in the grey goose quill.' So much of prophecy has been fulfilled. Tradition seems half gone. Thomas of Ercildoune and his like go with it. The newspaper editors and other men of the quill, this long while have been elbowing fairy and fairy seer from hearth and board. Maybe yet the creatures have more vitality than they think. Two lady friends of the present writer's believe firmly that the West of Ireland goblins tried to carry them off some odd years since. They were glamoured,[2] and wandered up and down in their own field for an hour, everything having grown strange to them. Suddenly the fairies changed their minds. The ladies looked round, everything was familiar again. A man was working a few yards away. They had been glamoured an hour. One carried in her hand her brother's silver-mounted walking-stick. The silver was gone. 'They stole it instead of you, for you have good friends among the gentry (fairies),' said a 'knowledgeable woman', in the neighbourhood. One of these ladies, when a young girl, used to kneel down over the *bucalauns* or ragweed, and sing, thinking that the fairies heard her underground, and were pleased. For *bucalauns* are fairy plants. At night the green-coated troop come out of their green hills and change the *bucalauns* into horses, and ride furiously all night long.

Not only in Ireland is fairy belief still extant. It was only the other day I heard of a Scottish farmer who believed that the lake in front of his house was haunted by a water-horse. He was afraid of it, and dragged the lake with nets, and then tried to pump it empty. It would have been a bad thing for the water-horse had he found him. An Irish peasant would have long since come to terms with the creature. For in Ireland there is something of timid affection between men and spirits. They only ill-treat each other in reason. Each admits the other side to have feelings. There are points beyond which neither will go. No Irish peasant would treat a captured fairy as the man in Campbell did.[3] He caught a kelpie,[4] and tied her behind him on his horse. She was fierce, but he kept her quiet by driving an awl and a needle into her. They came to a river, and she grew very restless, fearing to cross the water. Again he drove the awl and needle into her. She cried out, 'Pierce me with the awl, but keep that slender, hair-like slave (the needle) out of me.' They came to an inn. He turned the light of a lantern on her; immediately she dropped down like a falling star, and changed into a lump of jelly. She was dead. Nor would they treat the fairies as one is treated in an old Gaelic poem. A fairy loved a little child who used to cut turf at the side of a fairy hill. Every day the fairy put out his hand from the hill with an enchanted knife. The child used to cut the turf with the knife. It did not take long, the knife being charmed. Her brothers wondered why she was done so quickly. At last they resolved to watch, and find out who helped her. They saw the small hand come out of the earth, and the little child take from it the knife. When the turf was all cut, they saw her make three taps on the ground with the handle. The small hand came out of the hill. Snatching the knife from the child, they cut the hand off with a blow. The fairy was never again seen. He drew his bleeding arm into the earth, thinking, as it is recorded, he had lost his hand through the treachery of the child.

In Scotland you are too theological, too gloomy. You have made even the Devil religious. 'Where do you live, good-wyf, and how is the minister?' he said to the witch when he met her on the high-road, as it came out in the trial.[5] You have burnt all the witches. In Ireland we have left them alone. To be sure, the 'loyal minority' knocked out the eye of one with a cabbage-stump on the 31st of March, 1711, in the town of Carrickfergus.[6] But then the 'loyal minority' is half-Scottish. You have discovered the fairies to be pagan and wicked. You would like to have them all up before the magistrate. In Ireland warlike mortals have gone amongst them, and helped them in their battles, and they in turn have taught men great skill with herbs, and permitted some few to hear their tunes. Carolan slept upon a fairy rath.[7] Ever after their tunes ran in his head, and made him the great musician he was. In Scotland you have denounced them from the pulpit. In Ireland they have been permitted by the priests to consult them on the state of their souls. Unhappily the priests have decided that they have no souls, that they will dry up like so much bright vapour at the last day; but more in sadness than in anger have they said it. The Catholic religion likes to keep on good terms with its neighbours.

These two different ways of looking at things uncanny have influenced in each country the whole world of sprites and goblins. For their gay and graceful doings you must go to Ireland; for their deeds of terror to Scotland. Our Irish fairy terrors have about them something of make-believe. When a peasant strays into an enchanted hovel, and is made to turn a corpse all night on a spit before the fire, we do not feel anxious; we know he will wake in the midst of a green field, the dew on his old coat. In Scotland it is altogether different. You have soured the naturally excellent disposition of ghosts and goblins. The piper McCrimmon, of the Hebrides, shouldered his pipes, and marched into a sea cavern, playing loudly, and followed by his dog. For a long time the people could hear the pipes. He must have gone nearly a mile, when they heard the sound of a struggle. Then the piping ceased suddenly. Some time went by, when his dog came out of the cavern completely flayed, too weak even to howl. Nothing else ever came out of the cavern. Then there is the tale of the man who dived into a lake where treasure was thought to be. He saw a great coffer of iron. Close to the coffer lay a monster, who warned him to return whence he came. He rose to the surface; but the bystanders, when they heard he had seen the treasure, persuaded him to dive again. He dived. In a little while his heart and liver floated up, reddening the water. No man ever saw the rest of his body.

These water-goblins and water-monsters are prominent in Scottish folk-lore. We have them too, but take them much less dreadfully. Our tales turn all their doings to favour and to prettiness, or hopelessly humorise the creatures. A hole in the Sligo River is haunted by one of these monsters. He is ardently believed in by many, but that does not prevent the peasantry playing with the subject, and surrounding it with conscious phantasies. When I was a small boy I fished one day for congers in the monster-hole. Returning home, a great eel on my shoulder, his head flapping down in front, his tail sweeping the ground behind, I met a fisherman of my acquaintance. I began a tale of an immense conger, three times larger than the one I carried, that had broken my line and escaped. 'That was him,' said the fisherman. 'Did you ever hear how he made my brother emigrate? My brother was a diver, you know, and grubbed stones for the Harbour Board. One day the beast comes up to him, and says, "What are you after?" "Stones, sur," says he. "Don't you think you had better be going?" "Yes, sur," says he. And that's why my brother emigrated. The people said it was because he got poor, but that's not true.'

You – you will make no terms with the spirits of fire and earth and air and water. You have made the Darkness your enemy. We – we exchange civilities with the world beyond.

5

'IRISH WONDERS'

from the *Scots Observer* (1889)

In the matter of folk-tales, the scientific-minded wish for the very words they are told in. Others would allow some equivalent for the lost gesture, local allusions, and quaint manners of the story-tellers – some concentrating on humour and dialect. They consider that a folk-tale told by Carleton[1] gives a truer impression of what it sounds like when some old voice is reciting in the turf smoke, than any word-for-word version. Carleton has never added anything untrue, anything incongruous: no other man ever knew the Irish peasantry as he did; none other ever touched Irish folk-lore with like genius. But because genius is justified of all her children, that does not prove Mr McAnally right in leaving the accurate, reverent way, to dress up his fine tales in a poor slatternly patchwork of inaccurate dialect and sham picturesqueness. Had he told them word for word, or even in common literary English, he might have produced a book that students would turn to for years to come. Instead, he has made his whole work smack of the tourist's car. The dialects of north and south, and east and west, are all rolled into one ridiculous mixture. Why, the village children in Ireland laugh at the speech of the next county, almost at that of the next village. Mr McAnally is an Irish-American. In his feelings for the old country there is a touch of genuine poetry. But the Ireland he loves is not the real Ireland: it is the false Ireland of sentiment. He strains to make everything humorous, according to the old convention, pretty according to the old prepossession. From his desperate search for the pretty and humorous, he has brought home some strange baggage. He fathers, or rather mothers, the following on a 'knowledgeable woman' of Colooney, Sligo. The matter discussed is a fairy ball, seen by her grandmother's aunt: 'It was the 'cutest sight alive. There was a place for thim to shtand on, an' a wondherful big fiddle av the size ye cud slape in it, that was played be a monsthrous frog, an' two little fiddles that two kittens fiddled on, an' two big drums baten be cats, an' two trumpets, played be fat pigs. All round the fairies were dancin' like angels, the fire-flies givin' thim light to see by, an' the moon-bames shinin' on the lake, for it was be the shore it was; an' if ye don't belave it, the glen's still there, that they call the Fairy Glen to this blessed day.'

The writer of this article, though he has not gathered folk-tales in Colooney, has done so within two miles of it, as well as reading most, if not all, recorded Irish fairy tales, but never has he heard anything like this. Even if the fire-fly were forgiven, this would remain the worst-invented piece of folk-lore on record. These fiddling and trumpeting beasts are quite alien to Celtic myth; for Celtic fairies are much like common men and women. Often the fairy-seer meets with them on some lonely road, and joins in their dance, and listens to their music; and does not know what people they are till the whole company melts away into shadow and night. On those occasions when it pleases them to take on diminutive size, and so be known at once, they are still, in well-nigh all their works and ways, like human beings. This fiddling fancy may be German; good Celtic it cannot be. The whole surroundings of the *deenee shee* (fairy people) are simple and matter-of-fact. The peasant credits them with what he himself admires. 'They have,' said one old peasant to the writer, 'the most beautiful parlours and drawing-rooms.' By saying it was the poor 'knowledgeable woman's' grandmother's aunt that saw the fiddling, Mr McAnally means, we suppose, to suggest the old calumny that nobody but somebody's distant relation ever saw a spirit. There is probably not a village in Ireland where a fairy-seer or two may not be found. As to the last sentence of Mr McAnally's amusing nine lines, there is, of course, not a peasant in Ireland who would use such an argument.

It is sincerely to be regretted that Mr McAnally has not the convincing art: one often really wishes to believe him, as in the lepracaun chapter – the most full of detail of anything ever written about that goblin shoemaker. It sounds for the most part like honest folk-lore; but then that fire-fly! There is one tale in the chapter too good, however, to have been changed in any essential. There was a child who was stolen at birth by the fairies of Lough Erne. When she began to grow up, they gave her a dance every night down under the lake. The queen meant to find her a good husband among the fairies, but she fell in love with an old lepracaun. Thereupon the queen, 'to circumvent her', gave her leave to walk on the shore of the lake, where she met Darby O'Hoolighan, and loved him. They married, and the queen gave them cattle and household things, but told her to tell her husband she would return to the fairies if he struck her three blows. For seventeen years they lived happily, and had two big sons. At last, one day they were going to a wedding, and she was very slow. Darby struck her on the shoulder with his hand, and she began to cry, and said it was the first of the three blows. A year later he was teaching his boy to use a shillaly, and she got behind and was struck. That was the second blow. 'Divil take the stick,' he cried, and flung it against the wall. The stick bounced back and struck her, and made the third blow. She kissed her sons, and went and called the cows in the fields, and they quit grazing and followed her; and the oxen in the stalls heard her, and stopped eating and followed. She spoke to the calf they had killed that morning, and it came down from where it was hanging in the yard and followed her. The lamb that was killed the day before, and the pigs that were salted and hung up to dry, went after her in a string. Next she called the things in the house. The chairs and tables, and the chest of drawers, and the boxes, and the pots and pans and gridirons, and buckets, and noggins, all put out legs 'like bastes', and walked after her; and the house was left bare and empty. They came to the edge of the lake, and all went under, down again to fairy-land. After this she used sometimes to come close to the shore to see her two sons. One day there was seen 'a little atomy of a man along wid her, that was a lepracaun'; therefore it got about that the real reason she left her husband was to get back to the old lepracaun she was in love with before she married Darby.

Mr McAnally's stories are nearly all good in themselves. His sentences, too, have often an Irish turn in them, though the pronunciation is written anyhow. It is mainly his isolated assertions that trouble. He says the most momentous things in the most jaunty, careless way. He tells us, for instance, that, of the spirits of the bad, 'some are chained at the bottom of the lakes, others buried under ground, others confined in mountain gorges; some hang on the sides of precipices, others are transfixed on the tree-tops, while others haunt the houses of their ancestors: all waiting till the penance has been endured, and the hour of release arrives'. There is a fine gloomy suggestion about the ghosts swinging on the tree-tops which we feel sure that Mr McAnally has honestly reported. But why is there not some authority reverently given for so strange a thing? In what part of Ireland was it said, this saying recalling *Mahabharata*[2] and *Divine Comedy*? We believe it to be honest folk-lore and defy that shining insect circling and flickering before us, anxious to remind us of another name for the God of Flies.[3]

6

'VILLAGE GHOSTS'

from the *Scots Observer* (1889)

In the great cities we see so little of the world, we drift into our minority. In the little towns and villages there are no minorities; people are not numerous enough. You must see the world there, perforce. Every man is himself a class; every hour carries its new challenge. When you pass the inn at the end of the village you leave your favourite whimsy behind you; for you will meet no one who can share it. We listen to eloquent speaking, go to discussions, read books and write them, settle all the affairs of the universe. The dumb village multitudes pass on unchanging; the feel of the spade in the hand is no different for all our talk: good seasons and bad follow each other as of old. The dumb multitudes are no more concerned with us than is the old horse peering through the rusty gate of the village pound. The ancient map-makers wrote across unexplored regions, 'Here are the lions.' Across the villages of fishermen and turners of the earth so different are these from us, we can write but one line that is certain, 'Here are ghosts.'

My ghosts inhabit the village of H—,[1] in Leinster, Ireland. History has in no manner been burdened by this ancient village, with its crooked lanes, its old abbey churchyard full of long grass, its green background of small fir trees, and its quay, where lie a few tarry fishing luggers. In the annals of entomology it is well known. For a small bay lies westward a little, where he who watches night after night may see a certain rare moth fluttering along the edge of the tide, just at the end of twilight or the beginning of dawn. A hundred years ago it was carried here from Italy by smugglers in a cargo of silks and laces. If the moth-hunter would throw down his net, and go hunting for short tales or tales of the fairies and such like children of Lilith,[2] he would have need for far less patience. To approach the village at night a timid man requires great strategy. A man was once heard complaining, 'By the cross of Jesus! how shall I go? If I pass by the hill of Dunboy old Captain B— may look out on me. If I go round by the water, and up by the steps, there is the headless one and another on the quays, and a new one under the old churchyard wall. If I go right round the other way, Mrs Stewart is appearing at Hillside Gate, and the devil himself is in the Hospital Lane.'

I never heard which spirit he braved, but feel sure it was not the one in the Hospital Lane. In cholera times a shed had been there set up to receive patients. When the need had gone by, it was pulled down, but ever since the ground where it stood has broken out in ghosts and demons and fairies. There is a farmer at H—, Paddy Brian by name – a man of great strength, and a teetotaller. His wife and sister-in-law, musing on his great strength, often wonder what he would do if he drank. One night, when passing through the Hospital Lane, he saw what he supposed at first to be a tame rabbit; after a little he found that it was a white cat. When he came near, the creature slowly began to swell larger and larger, and as it grew he felt his own strength ebbing away, as though it were sucked out of him. He turned and ran.

By the Hospital Lane goes the 'Fairies' Path'. Every evening they travel from the hill to the sea, from the sea to the hill. At the sea end of their path stands a cottage. One night, Mrs Arbunathy, who lived there, left her door open, as she was expecting her son. Her husband was asleep by the fire; a tall man came in and sat beside him. After he had been sitting there for a while, the woman said, 'In the name of God, who are you?' He got up and went out, saying, 'Never leave the door open at this hour, or evil may come to you.' She woke her husband, and told him. 'One of the good people has been with us,' said he.

Probably the man braved Mrs Stewart at Hillside Gate. When she lived she was the wife of the Protestant clergyman. 'Her ghost was never known to harm any one,' say the village people; 'it is only doing a penance upon the earth.' Not far from Hillside Gate, where she haunted, appeared for a short time a much more remarkable spirit. Its haunt was the bogeen, a green lane leading from the western end of the village. I quote its history at length: a typical village tragedy. In a cottage at the village end of the bogeen lived a house-painter, Jim Montgomery, and his wife. They had several children. He was a little dandy, and came of a higher class than his neighbours. His wife was a very big woman. Her husband, who had been expelled from the village choir for drink, gave her a beating one day. Her sister heard of it, and came and took down one of the window shutters – Montgomery was neat about everything, and had shutters on the outside of every window – and beat him with it, being big and strong like her sister. He threatened to prosecute her; she answered that she would break every bone in his body if he did. She never spoke to her sister again, because she had allowed herself to be beaten by so small a man. Jim Montgomery grew worse and worse: his wife soon began to have not enough to eat. She told no one, for she was very proud. Often, too, she would have no fire on a cold night. If any neighbours came in she would say she had let the fire out because she was just going to bed. The people about often heard her husband beating her, but she never told any one. She got very thin. At last one Saturday there was no food in the house for herself and the children. She could bear it no longer, and went to the priest and asked him for some money. He gave her thirty shillings. Her husband met her, and took the money, and beat her. On the following Monday she got very ill and sent for a Mrs Kelly. Mrs Kelly, as soon as she saw her, said, 'My woman, you are dying,' and sent for the priest and the doctor. She died in an hour. After her death, as Montgomery neglected the children, the landlord had them taken to the workhouse. A few nights after they had gone, Mrs Kelly was going home through the bogeen, when the ghost of Mrs Montgomery appeared and followed her. It did not leave her until she reached her own house. She told the priest, Father S—, a noted antiquarian, and could not get him to believe her. A few nights afterwards Mrs Kelly again met the spirit in the same place. She was in too great terror to go the whole way, but stopped at a neighbour's cottage midway, and asked them to let her in. They answered they were going to bed. She cried out, 'In the name of God let me in, or I will break open the door.' They opened, and so she escaped from the ghost. Next day she told the priest again. This time he believed, and said the spirit would follow her until she spoke to it. The third time she met the spirit in the bogeen as before. She asked what kept it from its rest. The spirit said that its children must be taken from the workhouse, for none of its relations were ever there before, and that three masses were to be said for the repose of its soul. 'If my husband does not believe you,' she said, 'show him that,' and touched Mrs Kelly's wrist with three fingers. The places where they touched swelled up and blackened. She then vanished. For a time Montgomery would not believe that his wife had appeared: 'she would not show herself to Mrs Kelly,' he said – 'she with respectable people to appear to.' He was convinced by the three marks, and the children were taken from the workhouse. The priest said the masses, and the soul must have been at rest, for the shade has not since appeared. Some time afterwards Jim Montgomery died in the workhouse, having come to great poverty through drink.

I know some who believe they have seen the headless ghost upon the quay, and one who, when he passes the old cemetery wall at night, sees a woman with white borders to her cap[3] creep out and follow him. The apparition only leaves him at his own door. The villagers imagine she must follow him to avenge some wrong. 'I will haunt you when I die' is a favourite threat. His wife was once half-scared to death by what she considers a demon in the shape of a dog. These are a few of the open-air spirits; the more domestic of their tribe gather within doors, plentiful as swallows under southern eaves.

One night a Mrs Nolan was watching by her dying child in Fluddey's Lane. Suddenly there was a sound of knocking heard at the door. She did not open, fearing it was some unhuman thing that knocked. The knocking ceased. After a little the front-door and then the back-door were burst open, and closed again. Her husband went to see what was wrong. He found both doors bolted. The child died. The doors were again opened and closed as before. Then Mrs Nolan remembered that she had forgotten to leave window or door open, as the custom is, for the departure of the soul. These strange openings and closings and knockings were warnings and reminders from the spirits who attend the dying.

The house ghost is usually a harmless and well-meaning creature. It is put up with as long as possible. It brings good luck to those who live with it. The writer remembers two children who slept with their mother and sisters and brothers in one small room. In the room was also a ghost. They sold herrings in the Dublin streets, and did not mind the ghost much, because they knew they would always sell their fish easily while they slept in the 'ha'nted' room.

The writer has some acquaintance among the ghost-seers of western villages. The Connacht tales are very different from those of Leinster. These H— spirits have a gloomy matter-of-fact way with them. They come to announce a death, to fulfil some obligation, to revenge a wrong, to pay their bills even – as did a fisherman's daughter the other day – and then hasten to their rest. All things they do decently and in order. It is demons, and not ghosts, that transform themselves into white cats or black dogs. The people who tell the tales are poor, serious-minded fishing people, who find in the doings of the ghosts the fascination of fear. In the western tales is a whimsical grace, a curious extravagance. The people who recount them live in the most wild and beautiful scenery, under a sky ever loaded and fantastic with flying clouds. They are farmers and labourers, who do a little fishing now and then. They do not fear the spirits too much to feel an artistic and humorous pleasure in their doings. The ghosts themselves share in their quaint hilarity. In one western town, on whose deserted wharf the grass grows, these spirits have so much vigour that, when a misbeliever ventured to sleep in a haunted house, I have been told they flung him through the window, and his bed after him. In the surrounding villages the creatures use the most strange disguises. A dead old gentleman robs the cabbages of his own garden in the shape of a large rabbit. A wicked sea-captain stayed for years inside the plaster of a cottage wall, in the shape of a snipe, making the most horrible noises. He was only dislodged when the wall was broken down; then out of the solid plaster the snipe rushed away whistling.

7

'KIDNAPPERS'

from the *Scots Observer* (1889)

A little north of the town of Sligo, on the southern side of Ben Bulben, some hundreds of feet above the plain, is a small white square in the limestone. No mortal has ever touched it with his hand; no sheep or goat has ever browsed grass beside it. There is no more inaccessible place on the planet, and few more encircled by awe to the deep considering. It is the door of fairy-land. In the middle night it swings open, and the unearthly troop rush out. All night the gay rabble sweeps to and fro across the land, invisible to all, unless perhaps where, in some more than commonly 'gentle' place – Drumcliff or Drum-a-hair – the night-capped heads of fairy-doctors may be thrust from their doors to see what mischief the 'gentry' are doing. To their trained eyes and ears the fields are covered by red-hatted riders, and the air full of shrill voices – a sound like whistling, as an ancient Scottish seer has recorded, and wholly different from the talk of the angels, who 'speak much in the throat, like the Irish', as Lilly,[1] the astrologer, has wisely said. If there be a new-born baby or new-wed bride in the neighbourhood, the night-capped 'doctors' will peer with more than common care, for the unearthly troop do not always return empty-handed. Sometimes a new-wed bride or a new-born baby goes with them into their mountains; the door swings-to behind, and the new-born or the new-wed moves henceforth in the bloodless land of Fairy; happy enough, but doomed to melt out at the last judgment like bright vapour, for the soul cannot live without sorrow. Through this door of white stone, and the other doors of that land where *geabheadh tu an sonas aer pighin* ('you can buy joy for a penny'), have gone kings, queens, and princes, but so greatly has the power of Fairy dwindled, that there are none but peasants in these sad chronicles of mine.

Somewhere about the beginning of this century appeared at the western corner of Market Street, Sligo, where the butcher's shop now is, not a palace, as in Keats's *Lamia*,[2] but an apothecary's shop, ruled over by a certain unaccountable Dr Opendon. Whence he came from, none ever knew. There also was in Sligo, in those days, a woman, Ormsby by name, whose husband had fallen mysteriously sick. The doctors could make nothing of him. Nothing seemed wrong with him, yet weaker and weaker he grew. Away went the wife to Dr Opendon. She was shown into the shop parlour. A black cat was sitting straight up before the fire. She had just time to see that the sideboard was covered with fruit, and to say to herself, 'Fruit must be wholesome when the doctor has so much,' before Dr Opendon came in. He was dressed all in black, the same as the cat, and his wife walked behind him dressed in black likewise. She gave him a guinea, and got a little bottle in return. Her husband recovered that time. Meanwhile the black doctor cured many people; but one day a rich patient died, and cat, wife, and doctor all vanished the night after. In a year the man Ormsby fell sick once more. Now he was a good-looking man, and his wife felt sure the 'gentry' were coveting him. She went and called on the 'fairy-doctor' at Cairnsfoot. As soon as he had heard her tale, he went behind the back door and began muttering, muttering, muttering – making spells. Her husband got well this time also. But after a while he sickened again, the fatal third time, and away went she once more to Cairnsfoot, and out went the fairy-doctor behind his back door and begun muttering, but soon he came in and told her it was no use – her husband would die; and sure enough the man died, and ever after when she spoke of him Mrs Ormsby shook her head saying she knew well where he was, and it wasn't in heaven or hell or purgatory either. She probably believed that a log of wood was left behind in his place, but so bewitched that it seemed the dead body of her husband. She is dead now herself, but many still living remember her. She was, I believe, for a time a servant or else a kind of pensioner of some relations of my own.

Sometimes those who are carried off are allowed after many years – seven usually – a final glimpse of their friends. Many years ago a woman vanished suddenly from a Sligo garden where she was walking with her husband. When her son, who was then a baby, had grown up he received word in some way, not handed down, that his mother was glamoured by fairies and imprisoned for the time in a house in Glasgow and longed to see him. Glasgow in those days of sailing-ships seemed to the peasant mind almost over the verge of the known world, yet he, being a dutiful son, started away. For a long time he walked the streets of Glasgow; at last down in a cellar he saw his mother working. She was happy, she said, and had the best of good eating, and would he not eat, and therewith laid all kinds of food on the table; but he, knowing well that she was trying to cast on him the glamour by giving him fairy food, that she might keep him with her, refused and came home to his people in Sligo.

Some five miles southward of Sligo is a gloomy and tree-bordered pond, a great gathering-place of water-fowl, called, because of its form, the Heart Lake. It is haunted by stranger things than heron, snipe, or wild duck. Out of this lake, as from the white square stone in Ben Bulben, issues an unearthly troop. Once men began to drain it; suddenly one of them raised a cry that he saw his house in flames. They turned round, and every man there saw his own cottage burning. They hurried home to find it was but fairy glamour. To this hour on the border of the lake is shown a half-dug trench – the signet of their impiety. A little way from this lake I heard a beautiful and mournful history of fairy kidnapping. I heard it from a little old woman in a white cap, who sings to herself in Gaelic, and moves from one foot to the other as though she remembered the dancing of her youth.

A young man going at nightfall to the house of his just-married bride, met in the way a jolly company, and with them his bride. They were fairies, and had stolen her as a wife for the chief of their band. To him they seemed only a company of merry mortals. His bride, when she saw her old love, bade him welcome, but was most fearful lest he should eat the fairy food, and so be glamoured out of the earth into that bloodless, dim nation, wherefore she set him down to play cards with three of the cavalcade, and he played on, realising nothing until he saw the chief of the band carrying his bride away in his arms. Immediately he started up, and knew that they were fairies; for slowly all that jolly company melted into shadow and night. He hurried to the house of his beloved. As he drew near came to him the cry of the keeners. She had died some time before he came. Some noteless Gaelic poet had made this into a forgotten ballad, some odd verses of which my white-capped friend remembered and sang for me.[3]

Sometimes one hears of stolen people acting as good genii to the living, as in this tale, heard also close by the haunted pond, of John Kirwan of Castle Hacket. The Kirwans[4] are a family most rumoured of in peasant lore, and believed to be the descendants of a man and a spirit. They have ever been famous for beauty, and I have read that the mother of the present Lord Cloncurry was of their tribe.

John Kirwan was a great horse-racing man, and once landed in Liverpool with a fine horse, going racing somewhere in middle England. That evening, as he walked by the docks, a slip of a boy came up and asked where he was stabling his horse. In such and such a place, he answered. 'Don't put him there,' said the slip of a boy; 'that stable will be burnt to-night.' He took his horse elsewhere, and sure enough the stable was burnt down. Next day the boy came and asked as reward to ride as his jockey in the coming race, and then was gone. The race-time came round. At the last moment the boy ran forward and mounted, saying, 'If I strike him with the whip in my left hand I will lose, but if in my right hand bet all you are worth.' For, said Paddy Flynn,[5] a noted fairy seer, who told me the tale, 'the left arm is good for nothing. I might go on making the sign of the cross with it, and all that, come Christmas, and a Banshee, or such like, would no more mind than if it was that broom'. Well, the slip of a boy struck the horse with his right hand, and John Kirwan cleared the field out. When the race was over, 'What can I do for you now?' said he. 'Nothing but this,' said the boy: 'My mother has a cottage on your land – they stole me from the cradle. Be good to her, John Kirwan, and wherever your horses go I will watch that no ill follows them; but you will never see me more.' With that he made himself air, and vanished.

Sometimes animals are carried off – apparently drowned animals more than others. In Claremorris, Mayo, Paddy Flynn told me, lived a poor widow with one cow and its calf. The cow fell into the river, and was washed away. There was a man thereabouts who went to a red-haired woman – for such are supposed to be wise in these things – and she told him to take the calf down to the edge of the river, and hide himself and watch. He did as she had told him, and as evening came on the calf began to low, and after a while the cow came along the edge of the river and commenced suckling it. Then, as he had been told, he caught the cow's tail. Away they went at a great pace, across hedges and ditches, till they came to a royalty (a name for the little circular ditches, commonly called raths or forts, with which Ireland is covered since pagan times). Therein he saw walking or sitting all the people who had died out of his village in his time. A woman was sitting on the edge with a child on her knees, and she called out to him to mind what the red-haired woman had told him, and he remembered she had said bleed the cow. So he stuck his knife into the cow and drew blood. That broke the spell, and he was able to turn her homeward. 'Do not forget the spancel,'[6] said the woman with the child on her knees; 'take the inside one.' There were three spancels on a bush; he took one, and the cow was driven safely home to the widow.

There is hardly a valley or mountain-side where folk cannot tell you of someone pillaged from amongst them. Two or three miles from the Heart Lake lives an old woman who was stolen away in her youth. After seven years she was brought home again for some reason or other, but she had no toes left. She had danced them off. Many near the white stone door in Ben Bulben have been stolen away.

It is far easier to be sensible in cities than in many country places I could tell you of. When one walks on those grey roads at evening by the scented elder bushes of the white cottages, watching the faint mountains gathering the clouds upon their heads, one all too readily seems to discover, beyond the thin cobweb veil of the senses, those creatures, the goblins, hurrying from the white square stone door to the north, or from the Heart Lake in the south.

8

'COLUMKILLE AND ROSSES'

from the *Scots Observer* (1889)

High upon the hill-top
The old king sits;
He's now so old and grey,
He's nigh lost his wits.
With a bridge of white mist
Columkille he crosses,
On his stately journeys
From Sleive-league to Rosses.[1]

As befits so delicate and precise a writer, Mr Allingham has not used any loose poetic licence in the matter of fairy localities. 'Columkille' and Rosses were, are, and ever shall be, please Heaven! places of unearthly resort. I have lived near by them and in them, time after time, and, with the sweet child-verses ringing in my ears, have gathered any crumbs of fairy lore I could find therein, looking for some trace of the old king on his journey. Columkille is a fancy name of Mr Allingham's own spinning for wide, green Drumcliff valley, lying at the foot of Ben Bulben, the mountain in whose side the square white door, described here a while since,[2] swings open at nightfall to loose the fairy riders on the world. The great St Columba himself was 'at the bigging'[3] of all the old ruins in the valley, and climbed the mountains more than once to get near heaven with his prayers. Rosses is a little sea-dividing, sandy plain, covered with short grass, like a green table-cloth, and lying in the foam midway between the round cairn-headed Knocknarea and 'Ben Bulben, famous for hawks':

But for Ben Bulben and Knocknarea
Many a poor sailor 'd be cast away,

as the rhyme goes.

At the northern corner of Rosses is a little promontory of sand and rocks and grass: a mournful haunted place. Here, probably, the old king's journey ended. No wise peasant would fall asleep under its low cliff, for he who sleeps here may wake 'silly', the 'good people' having carried off his soul. There is no more ready short cut to the dim kingdom than this plovery headland, for, covered and smothered now from sight by mounds of sand, a long cave goes thither 'full of gold and silver and the most beautiful parlours and drawing-rooms'. Once, before the sand covered it, a dog strayed in, and was heard yelping vainly deep underground in a fort far inland. These forts or raths, low circular ditches made before history began, cover all Rosses and all Columkille. The one where the dog yelped has, like most others, an underground beehive chamber in the midst. Once when I was poking about there, an unusually intelligent and 'reading' peasant who had come with me, and waited outside, knelt down by the opening, and whispered in a timid voice, 'Are you all right sir?' I had been some little while underground, and he feared I had been carried off like the dog.

No wonder he was afraid, for the fort has long been circled by ill-boding rumours. It is on the ridge of a small hill, on whose northern slope lie a few stray cottages. One night a farmer's young son came from one of them and saw the fort all flaming, and ran towards it, but the 'glamour' fell on him, and he sprang on to a fence, cross-legged, and commenced beating it with a stick, for he imagined the fence was a horse and that all night long he went on the most wonderful ride through the country. In the morning he was still beating his fence and they carried him home, where he remained a simpleton for three days before he came to himself again. A little later a farmer tried to level the fort. His cows and horses died, and all manner of trouble overtook him, and finally he himself was led home, and left useless with 'his head on his knees by the fire to the day of his death'.

A few hundred yards southwards of the northern angle of Rosses is another angle having also its cave, though this one is not covered with sand. About twenty years ago a brig was wrecked near by, and three or four fishermen were put to watch the deserted hulk through the darkness. At midnight they saw sitting on a stone at the cave's mouth two red-capped fiddlers fiddling with all their might. The men fled. A great crowd of villagers rushed down to the cave to see the strange musicians, but the creatures had gone.

To the wise peasant the green hills and woods round him are full of never-fading mystery. When the aged countrywoman stands at her door in the evening, and, in her own words, 'looks at the mountains and thinks of the goodness of God', God is all the nearer, because the pagan powers are not far: because northward in Ben Bulben, famous for hawks, the white square door swings open at sundown, and those wild unchristian riders rush forth upon the fields, while southward the White Lady still wanders under the broad cloud night-cap of Knocknarea. How may she doubt these things, even though the priest shakes his head at her? Did not a herd boy, no long while since, see the White Lady? She passed so close that the skirt of her dress touched him. 'He fell down, and was dead three days.' But this is merely the small gossip of fairydom – the little stitches that join this world and the other.

One night as I sat eating Mrs Hart's[4] soda-bread her husband told me a longish story, much the best of all I heard in Rosses. Those creatures, the 'good people', love to repeat themselves, and many a poor man from Fionn mac Cumhail[5] to our own days has happened on some such adventure.

'In the times when we used to travel by canal,' said my entertainer, 'I was coming down from Dublin. When we came to Mullingar the canal ended, and I began to walk, and stiff and fatigued I was after the slowness. I had some friends with me, and now and then we walked, now and then we rode in a cart. So on till, we being walking, over a wall in a field we saw some girls milking a cow, and stopped to joke with them. After a while we asked them for a drink of milk. "We have nothing to put it in here," they said, "but come to the house with us." We went home with them, and sat round the fire talking. After a while the others went, and left me, loth to stir from the good fire. I asked the girls for something to eat. There was a pot on the fire, and they took the meat out and put it on a plate, and told me to eat only the meat that came off the head. When I had eaten, the girls went out, and I did not see them again. It grew darker and darker, and there I still sat, loth as ever to leave the good fire, and after a while two men came in, carrying between them a corpse. When I saw them coming I hid behind the door. Says one to the other, putting the corpse on the spit, "Who'll turn the spit?" Says the other, "Michael Hart, come out of that and turn the meat." I came out all a tremble, and began turning the spit. "Michael Hart," says the one who spoke first, "if you let it brown we'll have to put you on the spit instead"; and on that they went out. I sat there trembling and turning the corpse till towards midnight. The men came again, and the one said it was burnt, and the other said it was done right. But having fallen out over it, they both said they would do me no harm that time; and, sitting by the fire, one of them cried out: "Michael Hart, can you tell me a story?" "Divil a one," said I. On which he caught me by the shoulder, and put me out like a shot. It was a wild blowing night. Never in all my born days did I see such a night – the darkest night that ever came out of the heavens. I did not know where I was for the life of me. So when one of the men came after me and touched me on the shoulder, with a "Michael Hart, can you tell a story now?" "I can," says I. In he brought me; and, putting me by the fire, says: "Begin." "I have no story but the one," says I, "that I was sitting here, and you two men brought in a corpse and put it on the spit, and set me turning it." "That will do," says he; "ye may go in there and lie down on the bed." And I went, nothing loth; and in the morning where was I but in the middle of a green field?'

The true version of this wild folk-tale has never been printed before.

'Columkille' is a great place for omens. Before a prosperous fishing season a herring-barrel appears in the midst of a storm-cloud; and at a place called Columkille's Strand – a place of marsh and mire – on a moonlight night an ancient boat, with St Columba himself, comes floating in from sea: a portent of a brave harvesting. They have their dread portents, too. Some four or five seasons since a fisherman saw, far on the horizon, renowned Hy

Brazel,[6] where he who touches shall find no more labour or care, nor cynic laughter, but shall go walking about under shadiest boscage, and enjoy the conversation of Cuchulain[7] and his heroes. A vision of Hy Brazel forebodes national troubles.

Columkille and Rosses are choke-full of ghosts. By bog, road, rath, hill-side, sea-border they gather in all shapes: headless women, men in armour, shadow hares, fire-tongued hounds, whistling seals, and so on. A whistling seal sank a ship the other day. At Drumcliff there is a very ancient graveyard. *The Annals of the Four Masters*[8] have this verse about a soldier named Denadhach, who died in 871: 'A pious soldier of the race of Con[9] lies under hazel crosses at Drumcliff.' Not very long ago an old woman, turning to go into the churchyard at night to pray, saw standing before her a man in armour who asked her where she was going. It was the 'pious soldier of the race of Con', says local wisdom, still keeping watch, with his ancient piety, over the graveyard. Again, the custom is still common hereabouts of sprinkling the doorstep with the blood of a chicken on the death of a very young child, thus (as belief is) drawing into the blood the evil spirits from the too weak soul. Blood is a great gatherer of 'supernaturals'. To cut your hand on a stone on going into a fort is said to be very dangerous.

There is no more curious ghost in Columkille or Rosses than the snipe-ghost. There is a bush behind a house in a village that I know well: for excellent reasons I do not say whether in Columkille or Rosses or on the slopes of Ben Bulben, or even on the plain round Knocknarea. There is a history concerning the house and the bush. A man once lived there who found on the quay of Sligo a package containing three hundred pounds in notes. It was dropped by a foreign sea-captain. This my man knew, but said nothing. It was money for freight, and the sea-captain, not daring to face his owners, committed suicide in mid-ocean. Shortly afterwards my man died. His soul could not rest. At any rate, strange sounds were heard round his house, though that had grown and prospered since the freight money. The wife was often seen by those still alive out in the garden praying at the bush I have spoken of, – the shade of the departed appearing there at times.

The bush remains to this day: once portion of a hedge, it now stands by itself, for no one dare put spade or pruning-knife about it. As to the strange sounds and voices, they did not cease till a few years ago, when, during some repairs, a snipe flew out of the solid plaster and away; the troubled ghost, say the neighbours, of the note-finder was at last dislodged.

Of Sleive-league I know nothing. It was far out of my beat. My forebears and relations have lived near Rosses and Columkille these many years. Northward I am wholly a stranger, and can find nothing. When I ask for stories of the fairies, my answer is some such as was given me by a woman who lives near a white stone fort – one of the few stone ones in Ireland – under the seaward angle of Ben Bulben: 'They always mind their own affairs and I always mind mine': for it is dangerous to talk of the creatures. Only friendship for yourself or knowledge of your forebears will loosen these cautious tongues. My friend, 'the sweet Harp-String' – (I give no more than his Irish name for fear of gaugers[10]) – the best of all our folk-tale hunters – seems to have the science of unpacking the stubbornest heart, but then he supplies the *potheen*-makers with grain from his own fields. Besides, he is descended from a noted Gaelic magician who raised the 'doul' in Great Eliza's century, and he has a kind of prescriptive right to hear tell of all kind of other-world creatures. They are almost relations of his, if all folk say concerning the parentage of magicians be true.

9

'BARDIC IRELAND'

from the *Scots Observer* (1890)

A good deal has been written about the first few centuries of Irish history both for the specialist and the general reader. He who cannot be persuaded to dip into the *Senchus Mor*[1] and *The Book of the Dun Cow*[2] for himself, can turn to the histories of Mr Standish O'Grady,[3] or to Lady Ferguson's[4] *Irish before the Conquest*, or to Mrs Bryant's *Celtic Ireland* (London: Kegan Paul). Sir Samuel Ferguson's[5] ballads and Mr Aubrey de Vere's[6] *Legends of St Patrick*, and the retrospective poems in his *Innisfail* – these more than the *Legends* – are full, too, of the spirit of these stormy centuries. Mrs Bryant runs over what is known of the eleven hundred years from the Nativity to the landing of Strongbow.[7] She does not take it king by king and saint by saint like Lady Ferguson, but picks out facts that seem to her of moment and comments on these. Thus, she has chapters on the influence of ancient Ireland and England on each other, on the bardic order, on St Patrick[8] and his clerics, on the working in precious metals and the missal-painting of the Irish, and so forth; and the general effect is good.

In those ages the genius of the Gael seems to have found its most complete expression. From the monasteries of Ireland Europe learned to illuminate its bibles and psalters, and therewith the manner of working beautifully in metals. Irish music, also, was widely heard of; and some believe that the modern harp came thus from Ireland. Celtic conquest poured out too, one Irish *ard-reigh*[9] meeting his death by lightning as he crossed the Alps; and when St Patrick had Christianised the country another kind of conquest began, and England, Scotland, Iceland, Germany, and France owed their Christianity mainly to the Irish missions. In these first centuries the Celt made himself: later on Fate made him. It is in his early history and literature that you must look for his character: above all in his literature. The bards,[10] kept by the rules of their order apart from war and the common affairs of men, rode hither and thither gathering up the dim feelings of the time, and making them conscious. In the history one sees Ireland ever struggling vainly to attain some kind of unity. In the bardic tales it is ever one, warring within itself, indeed, but always obedient, unless under some great provocation, to its high king. The *Tain Bo*, the greatest of all these epics, is full of this devotion. Later, when things were less plastic, men rose against their *ard-reigh* for any and everything: one because at dinner he was given a hen's egg instead of a duck's.[11]

The bards were the most powerful influence in the land, and all manner of superstitious reverence environed them round. No gift they demanded might be refused them. One king being asked for his eye by a bard in quest of an excuse for rousing the people against him plucked it out and gave it. Their rule was one of fear as much as love. A poem and an incantation were almost the same. A satire could fill a whole country-side with famine. Something of the same feeling still survives, perhaps, in the extreme dread of being 'rhymed up' by some local maker of unkindly verses. This power of the bards was responsible, it may be, for one curious thing in ancient Celtic history: its self-consciousness. The warriors were not simply warriors, the kings simply kings, the smiths simply smiths: they all seem striving to bring something out of the world of thoughts into the world of deeds – a something that always eluded them. When the Fenian[12] militia were established in the second century they were no mere defenders of coastline or quellers of popular tumult. They wanted to revive the kind of life lived in old days when the Chiefs of the Red Branch[13] gathered round Cuchulain. They found themselves in an age when men began to love rich draperies and well-wrought swords, to exult in dominion and the lordship of many flocks. They resolved to live away from these things in the forest, cooking their food by burying it under a fire; and passing such laws as that none of their order should take a dowry with his wife, but marry her for love alone. Nor would they have among them any man who did not understand all the several kinds of poetry. In the end they grew proud and tyrannical, and the people rose and killed them at Gavra.[14] Old Celtic Ireland was full of these conscious strivings – unless her whole history be fiction. Indeed Cuchulain, Fionn, Oisin, St Patrick, the whole ancient world of Erin may well have been sung out of the void by the harps of the great bardic order.

Almost certainly a number of things taken most literally by Mrs Bryant are in no sense history. She supposes it a matter proven and indisputable that the primeval races, Fomorians, Tuatha Dé Dananns, Milesians and the rest mentioned in *The Book of Invasions*,[15] were historic peoples; and Rhys, Joubainville,[16] and others have made it certain that they were merely bardic myths. Their present was not their ancient shape. The monks amused themselves by humanising the old gods, turning them into pious early colonisers, and tracing their descent to Noah. It has been found possible, however, to pick out something of their old significance, and discern in them the gods of light warring on the spirits of darkness – on the Fomorians who had but one leg under them and one arm in the middle of their breasts, and lived under the sea: creatures who turned under the monkish touch into common two-armed and two-legged pirates. Some few of the divine races, indeed – the Tuatha Dé Danann chiefly – preserved a parcel of their ancient dignity, and, becoming the fairies, dwell happily near their deserted altars. The monks were sad spoilers of things pagan. The old warlike centuries bored them. On the margin of a Latin history of the early days of Fionn mac Cumhail, the scribe has written in Gaelic: 'Holy Virgin, when will brother Edmund come home from the meeting?'

Mrs Bryant takes this hurly-burly of gods quite seriously, and tries to identify them with Iberian, Ugrian, Belgae, and other races. She does not seem to have heard even of the mythologic view. Other portions of her book are excellent. Her chapter on the Brehon Laws[17] could scarce be better. She shows how Ireland was above all things democratic and communistic – all lands belonging to the tribe. It was just such a system that a sociable people full of restless energies would make themselves; and, as might be said of Greece, it turned out good for the world, bad for the nation. When other countries were bowed under military despotism, missions poured forth over Europe from the schools of Ireland, but when the day of battle came she could not combine against the invader. Each province had its own assembly and its own king. There was no focus to draw the tribes into one. The national order perished at the moment when other countries like Germany and Iceland were beginning to write out their sagas and epics in deliberate form. The trappings of the warrior ages had not yet passed away, yet modern thought was near enough to give them a certain remoteness, so that the artist could detach himself from his material. The moment had come to write out old tales in *Nibelungenlieds* and *Eddas*;[18] but Ireland was doomed to have no rest, no peace, no leisure for students to labour in: the bees were too hard pressed by the wasps to make any honey. Her passionate bardic inspiration died away, leaving nothing but seeds that never bore stems, stems that never wore flowers, flowers that knew no fruitage. The literature of ancient Ireland is a literature of vast, half-dumb conceptions. The moment when the two worlds, ours and theirs, drew near to speak with each other was wasted in flight. No sooner were the Danes expelled than Strongbow came in. The shaping of bardic tales, the adornment of missals, the working in precious metals, all came to an end. The last-wrought gold shrine was done in 1166, three years before the landing of the Norman. Instead of the well-made poems we might have had, there remains but a wild anarchy of legends – a vast pell-mell of monstrous shapes: huge demons driving swine on the hill-tops; beautiful shadows whose hair has a peculiar life and moves responsive to their thought; and here and there some great hero like Cuchulain, some epic needing only deliberate craft to be scarce less than Homer. There behind the Ireland of to-day, lost in the ages, this chaos murmurs like a dark and stormy sea full of the sounds of lamentation. And through all these throbs one impulse – the persistence of Celtic passion: a man loves or hates until he falls into the grave. Years pass over the head of Conchobar and Fionn: they forget nothing. Quinet[19] has traced the influence of the desert on the Israelitish people. As they were children of the earth, and as the Parsees[20] are of the fire, so do the Celtic Irish seem of the fellowship of the sea: ever changing, ever the same.

10

'TALES FROM THE TWILIGHT'

from the *Scots Observer* (1890)

This new book of Lady Wilde's[1] – *Ancient Cures, Charms, and Usages of Ireland* (London: Ward and Downey) – is a collection of folk-lore mainly from the western islands, the most unpuritan places in Europe. Around and northward of Dublin no small amount of gloom has blown from overseas, though not more than a few miles from Dublin – at Howth, for instance – the old life goes on but little changed. But westward the second century is nearer than the nineteenth, and a pagan memory is more of a power than any modern feeling. On Innismurray,[2] an island near my own district, the people look reverently on the seals as they lie in the warm, shallow water near the shore; for may they not be the spirits of their forebears? Even in their social customs they do not recognise our century; for two peasants, hereditary king and queen of the island, control disputes and deal out laws as occasion demands. From these remote parts Sir William Wilde[3] collected a vast bulk of tales and spells and proverbs. In addition to the peasants he regularly employed to glean the stubble of tradition for him, he got many things from patients at his Dublin hospital; for when grateful patients would offer to send him geese or eggs or butter, he would bargain for a fragment of folk-lore instead. He threw all his gatherings into a big box, and thence it is that Lady Wilde has quarried the materials of her new book: a farrago of spells, cures, fairy-tales, and proverbs – these last beyond price – the districts seldom specified and the dates of discovery never. I heartily wish they had been better and more scientifically treated, but I scarce know whom to blame: Lady Wilde, Sir William Wilde, his collectors, or the big box. However that may be, and in spite of these defects, my author's two volumes of *Ancient Legends* and this new collection are the fullest and most beautiful gathering of Irish folk-lore in existence. Mr Douglas Hyde may some day surpass it – no one else can. In the 'Spells and Cures' section Lady Wilde has lighted on a subject which, so far as Ireland is concerned, has hitherto been almost ignored. Well-nigh all prove with how little gloom the Irish peasant looks on death and decay, but rather turns them to favour and to prettiness. For madness he would give you 'three things not made by the hand of man' – salt and honey and milk, to be drunk out of a sea-shell before sunrise; for the falling sickness he would hang about your neck three hairs of a milk-white greyhound; for almost any minor evil he would prescribe an ointment made of cowslip roots or red berries of rowan, unless indeed you have chanced on one of those desperate ailments that require a plaster of spiders or a draught of water from the skull of a man.

For we too have our horrors, but all are so fancifully self-conscious that they are in no wise burdensome. For instance, if you love and love in vain, all you have to do is to go to a grave-yard at midnight, dig up a corpse, and take a strip of skin off it from head to heel, watch until you catch your mistress sleeping and tie it round her waist, and thereafter she will love you for ever. Even our witches are not so horrible as other peoples.' Sometimes they do things wicked as weird: such, for instance, as burying a sheaf of corn and leaving it to rot away while some hated life rots with it. But the witches themselves are countrywomen of ours, and so we try to forget and forgive. Mostly, too, they are guilty of nothing worse than stealing corn or milk, or making their own fields flourish in unnatural abundance. We have not soured their temper with faggot and stake. Once, it is true, we knocked out a witch's eye with a cabbage-stump, but that was long ago and in the north.[4] Lady Wilde gives a good witch-tale of one of the western islands. There was a man, one Flaherty, who was greatly suspected by his neighbours of foregathering with the Evil One, because with little land he had always much corn. Turns and turns about they watched by night, until one morning a watcher saw something black moving in the field and carrying a grain of corn. That grain the something planted. Then it brought another and did the same, and then another, and yet another, and many hundreds of others; and the man drew near and found it a hideous insect. So he stooped and caught it, and put it in a horn snuff-box, and shut down the lid, and went off home; and presently there was great commotion and excitement, for Flaherty's wife had disappeared. The man happened to mention the black thing in the snuff-box; and 'How do you know,' said his friend, 'but it may be Flaherty's wife?' Flaherty heard the tale, and begged the man to go with him, and carry the snuff-box into the house, and open it in his presence. The man went home with him, and some neighbours likewise; and when the box was opened out crawled a great black insect, and made straight into Mrs Flaherty's room as hard as it could go; and after a little Mrs Flaherty came out, and she was very pale and one finger was bleeding. 'What means the blood?' asked the man of the snuff-box; and says Flaherty: 'When you shut down the lid you snapped off a little bit of the beetle's claw, and so my wife suffers.' After this Flaherty was shunned, and one day he and his wife sailed for another island. There was no trial, no punishing, no 'swimming'. The people did not even throw stones.

Not only witches but the whole demoniac nation is surrounded with fancies that show almost an affection for its terrors: an affection made possible, perhaps, by a sense that he that pays his chapel-dues and has a good heart and does not pull up a sacred hawthorn may get through the world secure, nor find a need for hate. One evil spirit of very murderous habits was accustomed to take the shape of a bag of wool and go rolling along the road; and Death himself at Innisshark[5] comes down and stands by the dying in the form of a black cock, and has been pleased into harmlessness by the blood of a crowing hen. Once by mischance a woman caught not a common barn-door bird but the son of the King of the Cats, who was taking the air in that shape. Then two huge black cats came in and tore her face until they were tired; but her sick child got well, for Death had leave to take but one life, and the son of the King of the Cats was dead. Lady Wilde thinks these stories may be relied on, because the western islanders are an accurate people, who never exaggerate but tell only the simple truth, and are too homely to invent. At Hollandtide[6] they are much troubled by the dead from their graves, who return to ride the sea's white horses, so that no wise fisherman will push out that night. A man once did so, and just as he reached the shore he heard the noise of the breakers behind him, and turning round saw a dead man upon every wave. One came close to him, and he recognised a neighbour drowned the year before; and the neighbour leaned over and bade him hasten home, for the dead were seeking him. He left boat and cargo and fled, and never again put out at Hollandtide . . .

In Ireland this world and the other are not widely sundered; sometimes, indeed, it seems almost as if our earthly chattels were no more than the shadows of things beyond. A lady I knew once saw a village child running about with a long trailing petticoat upon her, and asked the creature why she did not have it cut short. 'It was my grandmother's,' said the child; 'would you have her going about yonder with her petticoat up to her knees, and she dead but four days?' Lady Wilde tells a story of a woman whose ghost haunted her people because they had made her grave-clothes so short that the fires of purgatory burned her knees. And to them the truth is that beyond the grave they will have houses much like their earthly homes, only there the thatch will never grow leaky, nor the white walls lose their lustre, nor shall the dairy be at any time empty of good milk and butter. But now and then a landlord or an agent or a gauger will go by begging his bread, to show how God divides the righteous from the unrighteous.

Irish legends and Irish peasant minds, however, have no lack of melancholy. The accidents of Nature supply good store of it to all men, and in their hearts, too, there dwells a sadness still unfathomed. Yet in the sadness there is no gloom, no darkness, no love of the ugly, no moping. The sadness of a people who hold that 'contention is better than loneliness', it is half a visionary fatalism, a belief that all things rest with God and with His angels or with the demons that beset man's fortunes. 'God is nearer than the door,' they say; 'He waits long; He strikes at last.' They say too that 'Misfortune follows fortune inch by inch'; and again, 'It is better to be lucky than wise', or, 'Every web as it is woven, every nursling as it is nursed.' Shakespeare's witches are born of the Teuton gloom; our Irish sadness grows visible in other shapes. Somewhere I have read a tale that is touched with its very essence. At the grey of dawn an Irish peasant went out to the hills, to shoot curlew or what not. He saw a deer drinking at a pool, and levelled his gun. Now iron dissolves every manner of spell, and the moment he looked along the barrel he saw that the deer was really an old man changed by wizardry; then, knowing him for something wicked, he fired, and the thing fell, and there upon the grass, quite dead, lay the oldest man he ever set eyes on; and while he stood watching a light wind rose, and the appearance crumbled away before his eyes, and not a wrack was left to tell of what had been. The grey of the morning is the Irish witches' hour, when they gather in the shapes of large hares and suck the cattle dry; and the grey morning melancholy runs through all the legends of my people. Then it is that this world and the other draw near, and not at midnight upon Brockens[7] amidst the foul revelry of evil souls and in the light of the torches of hell. At the dawning the wizards come and go and fairy nations play their games of hurley and make their sudden journeys. Nations of gay creatures, having no souls; nothing in their bright bodies but a mouthful of sweet air.[8]

11

'IRISH FAIRIES'

from the *Leisure Hour* (1890)

When I tell people that the Irish peasantry still believe in fairies, I am often doubted. They think that I am merely trying to weave a forlorn piece of gilt thread into the dull grey worsted of this century. They do not imagine it possible that our highly thought of philosophies so soon grow silent outside the walls of the lecture room, or that any kind of ghost or goblin can live within the range of our daily papers. If the papers and the lectures have not done it, they think, surely at any rate the steam-whistle has scared the whole tribe out of the world. They are quite wrong. The ghosts and goblins do still live and rule in the imaginations of innumerable Irish men and women, and not merely in remote places, but close even to big cities.

At Howth,[1] for instance, ten miles from Dublin, there is a 'fairies' path', whereon a great colony of other-world creatures travel nightly from the hill to the sea and home again. There is also a field that ever since a cholera shed stood there for a few months, has broken out in fairies and evil spirits. The last man I have heard of as seeing anything in it is an industrious fisherman of great strength. He is a teetotaller; his sister indeed has told me that his wife and wife's sister often sit and talk of him and wonder 'what he would do if he drank'. They half regret that sobriety should make so strong a man hide his light under a bushel. One night he was coming home through the field, when he saw in front of him a small white cat. While he looked at it the creature began to swell bigger and bigger, and as it grew in size he lost in strength, as though it sucked out his vitality. He stood for a time motionless with terror, but at last turned and fled, and as he got further away his strength came back. It was, a peasant would tell you, a fairy animal, for not all the fairies have human shapes.

Everyone has heard of changelings, how a baby will be taken away and a miserable goblin left in its stead. But animals, it is not generally known, run the same risk. A fine fat calf may be carried off, and one of the fairies of animal shape left in its stead, and no one be the wiser until the butcher tries to kill it; then it will rush away and vanish into some green hillside. The fairy kingdom has everything we have, cats, dogs, horses, carriages, and even fire-arms, for the sounds of unearthly volleys fired by troops of spirits embattled on the winds have been heard by a Munster seer who lived about twenty years ago.

It is, however, further afield than Howth, down westward among the deep bays and mountain valleys of Sligo, that I have heard the best tales and found the most ardent belief. There, many a peasant dreams of growing rich by finding a fairy's crock of gold, and many a peasant's daughter trembles as she passes some famous haunted hillside, and goes over in her mind the names of men and women carried off, as tradition will have it, to the dim kingdom. Only very recently one of these fabled robberies is reported to have been attempted.[2]

There are a number of Gaelic songs and ballads about them, and about the people they have stolen. Some modern Irishmen also have written beautifully on the same matter. An Irish village schoolmaster, named Walsh, wrote the following.[3] It is supposed to be sung by a fairy over a child she has stolen:

Sweet babe! a golden cradle holds thee,
And soft the snow-white fleece enfolds thee;
In airy bower I'll watch thy sleeping,
Where branchy trees to the breeze are sweeping.
Shuheen, sho, lulo, lo!

When mothers languish, broken-hearted,
When young wives are from husbands parted,
Ah, little think the keeners lonely,
They weep some time-worn fairy only.
Shuheen, sho, lulo, lo!

Within our magic halls of brightness
Trips many a foot of snowy whiteness;
Stolen maidens, queens of fairy,
And kings and chiefs *a sluagh shee* airy.
Shuheen, sho, lulo, lo!

Rest thee, babe! I love thee dearly,
And as thy mortal mother, nearly;
Ours is the swiftest steed and proudest,
That moves where the tramp of the host is loudest.
Shuheen, sho, lulo, lo!

Rest thee, babe! for soon thy slumbers
Shall flee at the magic *koel shee's* numbers;
In airy bower I'll watch thy sleeping,
When branchy trees to the breeze are sweeping.
Shuheen, sho, lulo, lo!

The poor schoolmaster has perfectly given the fascination of the mysterious kingdom where the fairies live – a kingdom that has been imagined and endowed with all they know of splendour and riches by a poor peasantry amid their rags. As heaven is the home of their spiritual desires, so fairyland has been for ages the refuge of their earthly ideals. In its shadow kingdom they have piled up all they know of magnificence. Sometimes there is a quaint modernness in the finery. One old man said to me, 'It is full of beautiful drawing-rooms and parlours.'

The fairies are of course not merely feared as robbers, they are looked up to and respected for their great wealth. If a man always speaks respectfully of them, and never digs up one of their sacred thorn bushes, there is no knowing but he may some day dream of a crock of gold and the next day go and find it, and be rich for ever. A man once confessed to me that he had gone at midnight into my uncle's garden and dug for a treasure he had dreamed of, but there was 'a power of earth' in the place, and so he gave up the search and went home . . .[4]

There is one well-known Cork family, all of whose riches are traced back by the people to the days when an old henwife dreamed of a certain field where an iron pot full of gold lay hidden. She is well remembered, because a Celtic poet of the last century, who had come down in the world through the great quantities of whisky he had given away to other Celtic poets, was employed in minding her hens and chickens. He wrote a well-known Gaelic song about her, called 'The Dame of the Slender Wattle'.[5]

I have spoken, so far, entirely of the malice or kindness of the fairies, and said nothing of their mere wantonness. They are as little to be trusted as monkeys and jackdaws. The worst among them may be known, however, by their going about singly or in twos and threes, instead of in tumultuous troops like the more harmless kinds. The best known among the solitary fairies is the Lepracaun. He is something of a dandy, and dresses in a red coat with seven rows of buttons, seven buttons on each row, and wears a cocked-hat, upon whose pointed end he is wont in the north-eastern counties, according to McAnally, to spin like a top when the fit seizes him. His most common pursuit, as everyone knows, is cobbling. The fairies are always wearing out their shoes and setting him to mend them. At night he sometimes rides shepherds' dogs through the country, leaving them muddy and panting at the dawn. He is constantly described as peevish and ill-natured. His mischief, for all that, is much less gruesome than that of the Far Darrig or Red Man, the most unpleasant joker of all the race.[6]

The English peasantry have forgotten their fairies. The Irish peasant remembers and believes – and the Scotch, too, for the matter of that.

We will not too severely judge these creatures of the imagination. There are worse things after all than to believe some pretty piece of unreason, if by so doing you keep yourself from thinking that the earth under your feet is the only god, and that the soul is a little whiff of gas, or some such thing.

The world is, I believe, more full of significance to the Irish peasant than to the English. The fairy populace of hill and lake and woodland have helped to keep it so. It gives a fanciful life to the dead hillsides, and surrounds the peasant as he ploughs and digs with tender shadows of poetry. No wonder that he is gay, and can take man and his destiny without gloom, and make up proverbs like this from the old Gaelic – 'The lake is not burdened by its swan, the steed by its bridle, or a man by the soul that is in him.'[7]

12

'INVOKING THE IRISH FAIRIES'

from the *Irish Theosophist* (1890)

The Occultist and student of Alchemy whom I shall call D.D.[1] and myself sat at opposite sides of the fire one morning, wearied with symbolism and magic. D.D. had put down a kettle to boil. We were accustomed to meet every now and then, that we might summon the invisible powers and gaze into the astral light; for we had learned to see with the internal eyes. But this morning we knew not what to summon, for we had already on other mornings invoked that personal vision of impersonal good which men name Heaven, and that personal vision of impersonal evil, which men name Hell. We had called up likewise, the trees of knowledge and of life, and we had studied the hidden meaning of the Zodiac, and enquired under what groups of stars the various events of the bible story were classified by those dead Occultists who held all things, from the firmament above to the waters under the Earth, to be but symbol and again symbol. We had gone to ancient Egypt, seen the burial of her dead and heard mysterious talk of Isis and Osiris. We had made the invisible powers interpret for us the mystic tablet of Cardinal Bembo,[2] and we had asked of the future and heard words of dread and hope. We had called up the Klippoth[3] and in terror seen them rush by like great black rams, and now we were a little weary of shining colours and sweeping forms. 'We have seen the great and they have tired us,' I said; 'let us call the little for a change. The Irish fairies may be worth the seeing; there is time for them to come and go before the water is boiled.'

I used a lunar invocation and left the seeing mainly to D.D. She saw first a thin cloud as though with the ordinary eyes and then with the interior sight, a barren mountain crest with one ragged tree. The leaves and branches of the tree were all upon one side, as though it had been blighted by the sea winds. The Moon shone through the branches and a white woman stood beneath them. We commanded this woman to show us the fairies of Ireland marshalled in order. Immediately a great multitude of little creatures appeared, with green hair like sea-weed and after them another multitude dragging a car containing an enormous bubble. The white woman, who appeared to be their queen, said the first were the water fairies and the second the fairies of the air. The first were called the Gelki and the second the Gíeri (I have mislaid my notes and am not quite certain if I give their names correctly). They passed on and a troop who were like living flames followed and after them a singular multitude whose bodies were like the stems of flowers and their dresses like the petals. These latter fairies, after a while, stood still under a green bush from which dropped honey like dew and thrust out their tongues, which were so long that they were able to lick the honey-covered ground without stooping. These two troops were the fairies of the fire and the fairies of the earth.

The white woman told us that these were the good fairies and that she would now bring D.D. to the fairies of evil. Soon a great abyss appeared and in the midst was a fat serpent, with forms, half animal, half human, polishing his heavy scales.

The name of this serpent was Grew-grew and he was the chief of the wicked goblins. About him moved quantities of things like pigs, only with shorter legs, and above him in the air flew vast flocks of cherubs and bats. The bats, however, flew with their heads down and the cherubs with their foreheads lower than their winged chins. – I was at the time studying a mystic system that makes this inversion of the form a mark of certain types of evil spirits, giving it much the same significance as is usually given to the inverted pentagram. This system was unknown to D.D., whose mind was possibly, however, overshadowed for the moment by mine; the invoking mind being always more positive than the mind of the seer. – Had she been invoking the conditions would have been reversed.

Presently the bats and cherubs and the forms that a moment

before had been polishing the scales of Grew-grew, rushed high up into the air and from an opposite direction appeared the troops of the good fairies, and the two kingdoms began a most terrible warfare. The evil fairies hurled burning darts but were unable to approach very near to the good fairies, for they seemed unable to bear the neighbourhood of pure spirits. The contest seemed to fill the whole heavens, for as far as the sight could go the clouds of embattled goblins went also. It is that contest of the minor forces of good and evil which knows no hour of peace but goes on everywhere and always. The fairies are the lesser spiritual moods of that universal mind, wherein every mood is a soul and every thought a body.

Their world is very different from ours, and they can but appear in forms borrowed from our limited consciousness, but nevertheless, every form they take and every action they go through, has its significance and can be read by the mind trained in the correspondence of sensuous form and supersensuous meaning.

13

'IRISH FOLK TALES'

from the *National Observer* (1891)

In the notes at the end of *Beside the Fire* (London: Nutt) Dr Hyde contrasts with certain tales of Indian jugglery an old Gaelic account of a magician who threw a rope-ladder into the air and then sent climbing up it all manner of men and beasts. It reads like an allegory to explain the charms of folk- and fairy-tales: a parable to show how man mounts to the infinite by the ladder of the impossible. When our narrow rooms, our short lives, our soon-ended passions and emotions, put us out of conceit with sooty and finite reality, we have only to read some story like Dr Hyde's 'Paudeen O'Kelly and the Weasel', and listen to the witch complaining to the robber, 'Why did you bring away my gold that I was for five hundred years gathering through[1] the hills and hollows of the world?' Here at last is a universe where all is large and intense enough to almost satisfy the emotions of man. Certainly such stories are not a criticism of life[2] but rather an extension, thereby much more closely resembling Homer than that last phase of 'the improving book', a social drama by Henrik Ibsen. They are an existence and not a thought, and make our world of tea-tables seem but a shabby penumbra.

It is perhaps, therefore, by no means strange that the age of 'realism' should be also the harvest-time of folk-lore. We grow tired of tuning our fiddles to the clank of this our heavy chain, and lay them down to listen gladly to one who tells us of men hundreds of years old and endlessly mirthful. Our new-wakened interest in the impossible has been of the greatest service to Irish folk-literature. Until about three years ago the only writers who had dealt with the subject at any length were Crofton Croker,[3] a second-hand bookseller named Kennedy[4] and an anonymous writer in *The Dublin and London Magazine* for 1825 and 1828. Others, it is true, had incorporated (like Gerald Griffin)[5] odd folk-tales in the pages of long novels, or based on them (like Carleton and Lover)[6] stories of peasant-life. Croker was certainly no ideal collector. He altered his materials without word of warning, and could never resist the chance of turning some naïve fairy tale into a drunken peasant's dream. With all his buoyant humour and imagination he was continually guilty of that great sin against art – the sin of rationalism. He tried to take away from his stories the impossibility that makes them dear to us. Nor could he quite desist from dressing his personages in the dirty rags of the stage Irishman. Kennedy, an incomparably worse writer, had one great advantage: he believed in his goblins as sincerely as any peasant. He has explained in his *Legendary Fictions* that he could tell a number of spells for raising the fairies, but he will not – for fear of putting his readers up to mischief. Years went by, and it seemed that we should never have another gathering. Then about three years ago came Lady Wilde's[7] two volumes and David Fitzgerald's[8] contributions to the *Revue Celtique*; with McAnally's[9] inaccurate and ill-written *Irish Wonders* and Curtin's[10] fine collections a little later; and now appears Dr Hyde's incomparable little book. There has been published in three years as much Irish folklore as in the foregoing fifty. Its quality, too, is higher. Dr Hyde's volume is the best written of any. He has caught and faithfully reproduced the peasant idiom and phrase. In becoming scientifically accurate, he has not ceased to be a man of letters. His fifteen translations from traditional Gaelic originals are models of what such translations should be. Unlike Campbell of Islay,[11] he has not been content merely to turn the Gaelic into English; but where the idiom is radically different he has searched out colloquial equivalents from among the English-speaking peasants. The Gaelic is printed side by side with the English, so that the substantial accuracy of his versions can always be tested. The result is many pages in which you can hear in imagination the very voice of the sennachie,[12] and almost smell the smoke of his turf fire.

Now and then Dr Hyde has collected stories which he was compelled to write out in his own Irish through the impossibility, he tells us, of taking them down word for word at the time. He has only printed a half of one story of this kind on the present occasion. One wishes he had not been so rigorous in the matter, especially as it is for this reason, I conclude, that 'Teig O'Kane',[13] still the weirdest of Irish folk-tales, has been omitted. He has printed it elsewhere, but one would gladly have had all his stories under one cover. He is so completely a Gael, alike in thought and literary idiom, that I do not think he could falsify a folk-tale if he tried. At the most he would change it as a few years' passing from sennachie to sennachie must do perforce. Two villages a mile apart will have different versions of the same story; why, then, should Dr Hyde exclude his own reverent adaptions? We cannot all read them in the Gaelic of his *Leabhar Sgeulaighteachta*.[14] Is it the evil communications of that very scientific person, Mr Alfred Nutt (he contributes learned notes), which have robbed us of the latter pages of 'Guleesh na Guss Dhu'?[15] We might at least have had some outline of the final adventures of the young fairy seer and the French princess. After all, imaginative impulse – the quintessence of life – is our great need from folk-lore. When we have banqueted let Learning gather the crumbs into her larder, and welcome. She will serve them up again in time of famine.

Dr Hyde has four tales of hidden treasure, five stories of adventure with a princess or a fortune at the end, a legend of a haunted forest, and a tale of a man who grew very thin and weakly through swallowing a hungry newt, which was only dislodged when made wildly a-thirst by a heavy dinner of salt pork and the allurement of a running stream. Love, fortune, adventure, wonder – the four winds of desire! There is also a chapter of quaint riddles in rhyme. The whole book is full of charming expressions. The French princess is described as 'the loveliest woman on the ridge of the world. The rose and the lily were fighting together in her face, and one could not tell which would get the victory'.[16] Here and there, too, is a piece of delicate observation, as when Guleesh na Guss Dhu waits for the fairies listening to 'the cronawn (hum) of the insects', and watching 'the fadoques and fibeens (golden and green clover) rising and lying, lying and rising, as they do on a fine night'.[17] The riddles also have no lack of poetry. Here is a description of a boreen or little country lane:

From house to house he goes,
A messenger small and slight,
And whether it rains or snows
He sleeps outside in the night.

And here is one of the lintel on a wet day:

There's a poor man at rest
With a stick beneath his breast,
And he breaking his heart a-crying.

These riddles are the possession of children, and have the simple fancifulness of childhood.

It is small wonder that this book should be beautiful, for it is the chronicle of that world of glory and surprise imagined in the unknown by the peasant as he leant painfully over his spade. His spiritual desires ascended into heaven, but all he could dream of material well-being and freedom was lavished upon this world of kings and goblins. We who have less terrible a need dream less splendidly. Mr Hyde bids us know that all this exultant world of fancies is passing away, soon to exist for none but stray scholars and the gentlemen of the sun-myth. He has written on his title-page this motto from an old Gaelic poem: 'They are like a mist on the coming of night that is scattered away by a light breath of wind.' I know that this is the common belief of folk-lorists, but I do not feel certain that it is altogether true. Much, no doubt, will perish – perhaps the whole tribe of folk-tales proper; but the fairy and ghost kingdom is more stubborn than men dream of. It will perhaps, in Ireland at any rate, be always going and never gone. I have talked with men who believe they have seen it. And why should Swedenborg[18] monopolise all the visions? Surely the mantle of Coleridge's 'man of ten centuries'[19] is large enough to cover the witch-doctors also. There is not so much difference between them. Swedenborg's assertion, in the *Spiritual Diary*, that 'the angels do not like butter', would make admirable folk-lore. Dr Hyde finds a sun-myth in one of his most ancient stories. The sun and the revolving seasons have not done helping to draw legends from the right minds. Some time ago a friend of mine talked with an old Irish peasant who had seen a vision of a great tree amid whose branches two animals, one white and one black, pursued each other continually; and wherever the white beast came the branches burst into foliage, and wherever the black one, then all withered away. The changing of the seasons, among the rest, is here very palpable. Only let it be quite plain that the peasant's vision meant much more than the mere atmospheric allegory of the learned. He saw within his tree the birth and death of all things. It cast a light of imagination on his own dull cattle-minding and earth-turning destiny, and gave him heart to repeat the Gaelic proverb: 'The lake is not burdened by its swan, the steed by its bridle, nor a man by the soul that is in him.'[20]

14

'AN IRISH VISIONARY'

from the *National Observer* (1891)

A young man came to see me at my lodgings the other night, and began to talk of the making of the earth and the heavens and much else. I questioned him about his life and his doings. He had written many poems and painted many mystical designs since we met last, but latterly had neither written nor painted, for his whole heart was set upon making his mind strong, vigorous and calm, and the emotional life of the artist was bad for him he feared. He recited his poems readily, however. He had them all in his memory. Some indeed had never been written down. They, with their wild music as of winds blowing in the reeds, seemed to me the very inmost voice of Celtic sadness, and of Celtic longing for infinite things the world has never seen. Suddenly it seemed to me that he was peering about him a little eagerly. 'Do you see anything, X—?' I said. 'A shining, winged woman, covered by her long hair, is standing by the doorway,' he answered, or some such words. 'Is it the influence of some living person who thinks of us and whose thoughts appear to us in that symbolic form?' I said; for I am well instructed in the ways of the visionaries and in the fashion of their speech. 'No,' he replied; 'for if it were the thoughts of a person who is alive I should feel the living influence in my living body, and my heart would beat and my breath would fail. It is a spirit. It is some one who is dead or who has never lived.'

I asked what he was doing, and found he was clerk in a large shop. His pleasure, however, was to wander about upon the hills, talking to half-mad and visionary peasants, or to persuade queer and conscience-stricken persons to deliver up the keeping of their troubles into his care. Another night, when I was with him in his own lodging, more than one turned up to talk over their beliefs and disbeliefs, and sun them as it were in the subtle light of his mind. Sometimes visions come to him as he talks with them, and he is rumoured to have told divers people true matters of their past days and distant friends, and left them hushed with dread of their strange teacher, who seems scarce more than boy and is so much more subtle than the oldest among them.

The poetry he recited me was full of his nature and his visions. Sometimes it told of other lives he believes himself to have lived in other centuries, sometimes of people he had talked to, revealing them to their own minds. I told him I would write an article upon him and it, and was told in turn that I might do so if I did not mention his name, for he wished to be always 'unknown, obscure, impersonal'. Next day a bundle of his poems arrived, and with them a note in these words: 'Here are copies of verses you said you liked. I do not think I could ever write or paint any more. I prepare myself for a cycle of other activities. I will make rigid my roots and branches. It is not now my turn to burst into leaves and flowers.' Among the poems one seemed to me of especial beauty. It is addressed to some girl, and, despite a careless arrangement of the rhymes, has haunted me these three weeks. Surely it is worth preserving in the *National Observer*, safe from the caprices of the gods who rule over a mystic's manuscripts:

I know I could see thro' and thro' you,
  So unconscious, tender, kind,
More than ever was known to you
  Of the pure ways of your mind.

For us who long to rest from strife,
  Yet labour sternly as a duty,
A magic charms us in your life,
  So unknowing of its beauty.

We are pools whose depths are told,
  You are like a mystic fountain
Issuing ever pure and cold
  From the hollows of the mountain.

We are men by anguish taught
  To distinguish false from true;

Higher wisdom we have not,
But a joy within guides you.[1]

One or two others have a like perfection of feeling, but deal with more impalpable matters. There are fine passages in all, but these will often be imbedded in thoughts which have evidently a special value to the writer's mind, but are to other men merely the counters of an unknown coinage. To them they seem merely so much brass or copper or tarnished silver at the best. Sometimes he illustrates his verses with Blake-like drawings, in which rather incomplete anatomy does not altogether hide extreme beauty of feeling. The fairies in whom he believes have given him many subjects, notably Thomas of Ercildoune[2] sitting motionless in the twilight while a young and beautiful creature leans softly out of the shadow and whispers in his ear. He delights above all in strong effects of colour: spirits who have upon their heads instead of hair the feathers of peacocks; a phantom reaching from a swirl of flame towards a star; a spirit passing with a globe of iridescent crystal – symbol of the soul – half shut within his hand. But always under this largess of colour lies some tender homily addressed to man's fragile hopes. This spiritual eagerness draws to him all those who, like himself, seek for illumination or else mourn for some joy that has gone. One of these especially comes to mind. A winter or two ago he spent much of the night walking up and down upon the mountain talking to an old peasant who, dumb to most men, poured out his cares for him. Both were unhappy: X— because he had then first decided that art and poetry were not for him, and the old peasant because his life was ebbing out with no achievement remaining and no hope left him. Both how Celtic! how full of striving after a something never to be completely expressed in word or deed. The peasant was wandering in his mind with prolonged sorrow. Once he burst out with 'God possesses the heavens – God possesses the heavens – but he covets the world'; and once he lamented that his old neighbours were gone, and that all had forgotten him: they used to draw a chair to the fire for him in every cabin, and now they said: 'Who is that old fellow there?' 'The fret (Irish for doom)[3] is over me,' he repeated, and then went on to talk once more of God and heaven. More than once also he said, waving his arm towards the mountain, 'Only myself knows what happened under the thorn tree forty years ago'; and as he said it the tears upon his face glistened in the moonlight.

This old man always rises before me when I think of X—. Both seek, one in wandering sentences, the other in symbolic pictures and subtle allegoric poetry, to express a something that lies beyond the range of expression; and both, if X— will forgive me, have within them the vast and vague extravagance that lies at the bottom of the Celtic heart. The peasant visionaries that are, the landlord duellists that were, and the whole hurly-burly of legends – Cuchulain fighting the sea for two days until the waves pass over him and he dies, Caolte[4] storming the palace of the gods, Oisin seeking in vain for three hundred years to appease his insatiable heart with all the pleasures of fairyland, these two mystics walking up and down upon the mountains uttering the central dreams of their souls in no less dream-laden sentences, and this mind that finds them so interesting – all are a portion of that great Celtic phantasmagoria whose meaning no man has discovered, nor any angel revealed.

15

'AN IRISH STORYTELLER'

the introduction to *Irish Fairy Tales* (1892)

I am often doubted when I say that the Irish peasantry still believe in fairies. People think I am merely trying to bring back a little of the old dead beautiful world of romance into this century of great engines and spinning-jinnies. Surely the hum of wheels and clatter of printing presses, to let alone the lecturers with their black coats and tumblers of water, have driven away the goblin kingdom and made silent the feet of the little dancers.

Old Biddy Hart[1] at any rate does not think so. Our bran-new opinions have never been heard of under her brown-thatched roof tufted with yellow stonecrop. It is not so long since I sat by the turf fire eating her griddle cake in her cottage on the slope of Ben Bulben and asking after her friends, the fairies, who inhabit the green thorn-covered hill up there behind her house. How firmly she believed in them! how greatly she feared offending them! For a long time she would give me no answer but I always mind my own affairs and they always mind theirs. A little talk about my great-grandfather[2] who lived all his life in the valley below, and a few words to remind her how I myself was often under her roof when but seven or eight years old loosened her tongue, however. It would be less dangerous at any rate to talk to me of the fairies than it would be to tell some 'Towrow'[3] of them, as she contemptuously called English tourists, for I had lived under the shadow of their own hillsides. She did not forget, however, to remind me to say after we had finished, 'God bless them, Thursday' (that being the day), and so ward off their displeasure, in case they were angry at our notice, for they love to live and dance unknown of men.

Once started, she talked on freely enough, her face glowing in the firelight as she bent over the griddle or stirred the turf, and told how such a one was stolen away from near Coloney village and made to live seven years among 'the gentry', as she calls the fairies for politeness' sake, and how when she came home she had no toes, for she had danced them off; and how such another was taken from the neighbouring village of Grange and compelled to nurse the child of the queen of the fairies a few months before I came. Her news about the creatures is always quite matter-of-fact and detailed, just as if she dealt with any common occurrence: the late fair, or the dance at Rosses last year, when a bottle of whisky was given to the best man, and a cake tied up in ribbons to the best woman dancer. They are, to her, people not so different from herself, only grander and finer in every way. They have the most beautiful parlours and drawing-rooms, she would tell you, as an old man told me once. She has endowed them with all she knows of splendour, although that is not such a great deal, for her imagination is easily pleased. What does not seem to us so very wonderful is wonderful to her, there, where all is so homely under her wood rafters and her thatched ceiling covered with white-washed canvas. We have pictures and books to help us imagine a splendid fairy world of gold and silver, of crowns and marvellous draperies; but she has only that little picture of St Patrick over the fireplace, the bright-coloured crockery on the dresser, and the sheet of ballads stuffed by her young daughter behind the stone dog on the mantelpiece. Is it strange, then, if her fairies have not the fantastic glories of the fairies you and I are wont to see in picture-books and read of in stories? She will tell you of peasants who met the fairy cavalcade and thought it but a troop of peasants like themselves until it vanished into shadow and night, and of great fairy palaces that were mistaken, until they melted away, for the country seats of rich gentlemen.

Her views of heaven itself have the same homeliness, and she would be quite as naïve about its personages if the chance offered as was the pious Clondalkin[4] laundress who told a friend of mine that she had seen a vision of St Joseph, and that he had 'a lovely shining hat upon him and a shirt-buzzom that was never starched in this world'. She would have mixed some quaint poetry with it, however; for there is a world of difference between Ben Bulben and Dublinised Clondalkin.

Heaven and Fairyland – to these has Biddy Hart given all she dreams of magnificence, and to them her soul goes out – to the one in love and hope, to the other in love and fear – day after day and season after season; saints and angels, fairies and witches, haunted thorn-trees and holy wells, are to her what books, and plays, and pictures are to you and me. Indeed they are far more; for too many among us grow prosaic and commonplace, but she keeps ever a heart full of music. 'I stand here in the doorway,' she said once to me on a fine day, 'and look at the mountain and think of the goodness of God'; and when she talks of the fairies I have noticed a touch of tenderness in her voice. She loves them because they are always young, always making festival, always far off from the old age that is coming upon her and filling her bones with aches, and because, too, they are so like little children.

Do you think the Irish peasant would be so full of poetry if he had not his fairies? Do you think the peasant girls of Donegal, when they are going to service inland, would kneel down as they do and kiss the sea with their lips if both sea and land were not made lovable to them by beautiful legends and wild sad stories? Do you think the old men would take life so cheerily and mutter their proverb, 'The lake is not burdened by its swan, the steed by its bridle, or a man by the soul that is in him,' if the multitude of spirits were not near them?[5]

16

'THE LAST GLEEMAN'

from the *National Observer* (1893)

Michael Moran was born about 1794 in Faddle Abbey, off Black Pitts, in the Liberties of Dublin. A fortnight after birth he went stone blind from illness and became thereby a blessing to his parents, who were soon able to send him to rhyme and beg at street corners and at the bridges over the Liffey. They may well have wished that their quiver were full of such as he, for free from the interruption of sight his mind became a perfect echoing chamber where every movement of the day and every change of public passion whispered itself into rhyme or quaint saying. By the time he had grown to manhood he was the admitted rector of all the ballad-mongers of the Liberties. Madden, the weaver, Kearney, the blind fiddler from Wicklow, Martin from Meath, McBride from heaven knows where, and that McGrane,[1] who in after days when the true Moran was no more, strutted in borrowed plumes, or rather in borrowed rags, and gave out that there had never been any Moran other than himself, and many another did homage before him, and held him chief of all their tribe. Nor despite his blindness did he find any difficulty in getting a wife, but rather was able to pick and choose, for he was just that mixture of ragamuffin and of genius which is dear to the heart of woman, who, perhaps because she is wholly conventional herself, loves the unexpected, the crooked, the bewildering. Nor did he lack despite his rags many excellent things, for it is remembered that he ever loved caper sauce, going so far indeed in his honest indignation at its absence upon one occasion as to fling a leg of mutton at his wife. He was not, however, much to look at, with his coarse frieze coat with its cape and scalloped edge, his old corduroy trousers and great brogues, the stout stick made fast to his wrist by a thong of leather: and he would have been a woeful shock to the gleeman MacConglinne[2] could that friend of kings have beheld him in prophetic vision from the pillar stone at Cork. And yet though the short cloak and the leather wallet were no more, he was a true gleeman, being alike poet, jester and newsman of the people. In the morning when he had finished his breakfast, his wife or some neighbour would read the newspaper to him, and read on and on until he interrupted with, 'that'll do. I have me meditations', and from these meditations would come the day's store of jest and rhyme. He had the whole middle ages under his frieze coat.

He had not, however, MacConglinne's hatred of the Church and clergy, for when the fruit of his meditations did not ripen well, or when the crowd called for something more solid, he would recite or sing some metrical tale or ballad of saint or martyr or of Biblical adventure. He would stand at a street corner, and when a crowd had gathered would begin in some such fashion as follows:– (I copy the record of one who knew him)[3] 'Gather round me, boys, gather round me. Boys, am I standin' in puddle, am I standin' in wet?' Thereon several boys would cry, 'Ah, no! yez, not! yer in a nice dry place. Go on with "St Mary", go on with "Moses"' – each calling for his favourite tale. Then Moran, with a suspicious wriggle of his body and a clutch at his rags, would burst out with 'All me buzzim friends are turned back-biters'; and then with a final 'If yez don't drop your coddin' and deversion I'll lave some of yez a case' by way of warning to the boys, would begin his recitation or perhaps still delay, to ask, 'Is there a crowd around me now? Any blackguard heretic around me?' The best known of his religious tales was 'St Mary', a long poem of exceeding solemnity, condensed from the much longer work of a certain Bishop Coyle. It told how a fast woman of Egypt, Mary by name, followed pilgrims to Jerusalem for no good purpose, and then, turning penitent on finding herself withheld from entering the temple by supernatural interference, fled to the desert and spent the remainder of her life in solitary penance. When at last she was at the point of death, God sent Bishop Zozimus to hear her confession, give her the last sacrament, and with the help of a lion, whom He sent also, dig her grave. The poem has the intolerable cadence of the eighteenth century, but was so popular and so often called for that Moran was soon nicknamed Zozimus, and by that name is he remembered. He had also a poem of his own called 'Moses', which went a little nearer poetry without going very near. But he could ill brook solemnity, and before long parodied his own verses in the following raga-muffin fashion:

In Egypt's land, contagious to the Nile
King Pharaoh's daughter went to bathe in style.
She tuk her dip, then walked unto the land,
To dry her royal pelt she ran along the strand.
A bulrush tripped her, whereupon she saw
A smiling babby in a wad o' straw.
She tuk it up, and said with accents mild,
''Tare-and-agers, girls, which av yer owns the child?'

His humorous rhymes were, however, more often quips and cranks[4] at the expense of his contemporaries. It was his delight, for instance, to remind a certain shoemaker, noted alike for display of wealth and for personal uncleanness, of his inconsiderable origin in a song of which but the first stanza has come down to us:

At the dirty end of Dirty Lane,
Liv'd a dirty cobbler, Dick Maclane;
His wife was in the old king's reign
  A stout brave orange-woman.
On Essex Bridge she strained her throat,
And six-a-penny was her note.
But Dikey wore a bran-new coat,
  He got among the yeomen.
He was a bigot, like his class,
And in the streets he wildly sang,
O Roly, toly, toly raid, with his old jade.

He had troubles of divers kinds, and numerous interlopers to face and put down. Once an officious peeler[5] arrested him as a vaga-bond, but was triumphantly routed amid the laughter of the court, when Moran reminded his worship of the precedent set by Homer, who was also he declared a poet and a blind man and a beggar-man. He had to face a more serious difficulty as his fame grew. Various imitators started up upon all sides. A certain actor, for instance, made as many guineas as Moran did shillings by mimicking his sayings and his songs and his get up upon the stage. One night this actor was at supper with some friends, when dispute arose as to whether his mimicry was overdone or not. It was agreed to settle it by an appeal to the mob. A forty-shilling supper at a famous coffee-house was to be the wager. The actor took up his station at Essex Bridge, a great haunt of Moran's, and soon gathered a small crowd. He had scarce got through 'In Egypt's land, contiguous to the Nile', when Moran himself came up, followed by another crowd. The crowds met in great excitement and laughter. 'Good Christians,' cried the pretender, 'is it possible that any man would mock the poor dark man like that?'

'Who's that? It's some imposhterer,' replied Moran.

'Begone, you wretch! it's you'ze the imposhterer. Don't you fear the light of heaven being struck from your eyes for mocking the poor dark man?'

'Saints and angels, is there no protection against this? You're a most inhuman blaguard[6] to try to deprive me of my honest bread this way,' replied poor Moran.

'And you, you wretch, won't let me go on with the beautiful poem. Christian people, in your charity won't you beat this man away? he's taking advantage of my darkness.'

The pretender, seeing that he was having the best of it, thanked the people for their sympathy and protection, and went on with the poem, Moran listening for a time in bewildered silence. After a while Moran protested again with:

'Is it possible that none of yez can know me? Don't yez see it's myself; and that's some one else?'

'Before I proceed any further in this lovely story,' interrupted the pretender, 'I call on yez to contribute your charitable donations to help me to go on.'

'Have you no sowl to be saved, you mocker of heaven?' cried Moran, put completely besides himself by this last injury. 'Would you rob the poor as well as desave the world? O, was ever such wickedness known?'

'I leave it yourselves my friends,' said the pretender, 'to give to the real dark man, that you all know so well, and save me from that schemer,' and with that he collected some pennies and half pence. While he was doing so, Moran started his 'Mary of Egypt', but the indignant crowd seizing his stick were about to belabour him when they fell back bewildered anew by his close resemblance to himself. The pretender now called to them to 'just give him a grip of that villain' and he'd soon let him know who's that imposhterer was! They led him over to Moran, but instead of closing with him he thrust a few shillings into his hand and turning to the crowd explained to them he was indeed but an actor, and that he had just won a wager and so departed amid much enthusiasm, to eat the supper he had won.

In April 1846 word was sent to the priest that Michael Moran was dying. He found him at 15 (now 14½) Patrick Street on a straw bed in a room full of ragged ballad singers come to cheer his last moments. After his death the ballad-singers, with many fiddles and the like, came again and gave him a fine wake, each adding to the merriment whatever he knew in the way of rann,[7] tale, old saw or quaint rhyme. He had had his day, had said his prayers and made his confession and why should they not give him a hearty send-off? The funeral took place the next day. A good party of his admirers and friends got into the hearse with the coffin for the day was wet and nasty. They had not gone far when one of them burst out with 'It's cruel cowld isn't it'; 'Garra,' replied another, 'we'll all be as stiff as the corpse when we get to the berrin-ground.' 'Bad cess[8] to him,' said a third; 'I wish he'd held out another month until the weather got dacent.' A man called Carroll thereupon produced a half-pint of whiskey and they all drank to the soul of the departed. Unhappily, however, the hearse was over-weighted and they had not reached the cemetery before the spring broke and the bottle with it.

Moran must have felt strange and out of place in that other kingdom he was entering perhaps, while his friends were drinking in his honour. Let us hope that some kindly middle region was found for him where he can call dishevelled angels about him with some new and more rhythmical form of his old

Gather round me boys, will yez
  Gather round me?
And hear what I have to say
  Before ould Salley brings me
My bread and jug of tay,

and fling outrageous quips and cranks at cherubim and seraphim. Perhaps he may have found and gathered, ragamuffin though he be, the Lily of High Truth, the Rose of Far-sight Beauty, for whose lack so many of the writers of Ireland, whether famous or forgotten, have been futile as the blown froth upon the shore.

17

'A LITERARY CAUSERIE'

from the *Speaker* (1893)

In one of his unpublished watercolour illustrations to Young's[1] *Night Thoughts*, William Blake[2] has drawn a numberless host of spirits and fairies affirming the existence of God. Out of every flower and every grass-blade comes a little creature lifting its right hand above its head. It is possible that the books of folk-lore, coming in these later days from almost every country in the world, are bringing the fairies and the spirits to our study tables that we may witness a like affirmation, and see innumerable hands lifted testifying to the ancient supremacy of imagination. Imagination is God in the world of art, and may well desire to have us come to an issue with the atheists who would make us naught but 'realists', 'naturalists', or the like.

Folk-lore is at once the Bible, the Thirty-nine Articles, and the Book of Common Prayer, and well-nigh all the great poets have lived by its light. Homer, Aeschylus, Sophocles, Shakespeare, and even Dante, Goethe, and Keats, were little more than folk-lorists with musical tongues. The root-stories of the Greek poets are told to-day at the cabin fires of Donegal; the Slavonian peasants tell their children now, as they did a thousand years before Shakespeare was born, of the spirit prisoned in the cloven pine; the Swedes had need neither of Dante nor Spenser to tell them of the living trees that cry or bleed if you break off a bough; and through all the long backward and abysm of time,[3] Faust, under many names, has signed the infernal compact, and girls at St Agnes' Eve have waited for visions of their lovers to come to them 'upon the honeyed middle of the night'.[4] It is only in these latter decades that we have refused to learn of the poor and the simple, and turned atheists in our pride. The folk-lore of Greece and Rome lasted us a long time; but having ceased to be a living tradition, it became both worn out and unmanageable, like an old servant. We can now no more get up a great interest in the gods of Olympus than we can in the stories told by the showman of a travelling waxwork company. And for lack of those great typical personages who flung the thunderbolts or had serpents in their hair, we have betaken ourselves in a hurry to the poetry of cigarettes and black coffee, of absinthe, and the skirt dance, or are trying to persuade the lecture and the scientific book to look, at least to the eye, like the old poems and dramas and stories that were in the ages of faith long ago. But the countless little hands are lifted and the affirmation has begun.

There is no passion, no vague desire, no tender longing that cannot find fit type or symbol in the legends of the peasantry or in the traditions of the scalds[5] and the gleemen. And these traditions are now being gathered up or translated by a multitude of writers. The most recent of books upon the subject – *The Ghost World* (Ward & Downey) – is neither a translation nor a collection of tales gathered among the people by its author, but one of those classifications and reviews of already collected facts of which we stand in great need. Its author, Mr T. F. Thistelton Dyer, treats as exhaustively as his four hundred odd pages permit him with the beliefs about ghosts held in every part of the world. The outside of the book is far from comely to look at, and the inside is that mixture of ancient beauty and modern commonplace one has got used to in books by scientific folk-lorists. Mr Dyer collects numbers of the most entirely lovely and sacred, or tragic and terrible, beliefs in the world, and sets them side by side, transfixed with diverse irrelevancies – in much the same fashion that boys stick moths and butterflies side by side upon a door, with long pins in their bodies. At other times he irritates by being hopelessly inadequate, as when he follows a story of priceless beauty with the remark that 'these folktales are interesting as embodying the superstitions of the people among whom they are current'. But then no one expects the scientific folk-lorist to have a tongue of music, and this one gives us a great deal less of himself than the bulk of his tribe, and has the good taste to gird at no man – not even the poor spiritualist.

He deals in thirty-one chapters with such subjects as 'The Soul's Exit', 'The Temporary Exit of the Soul', 'The Nature of the Soul', 'Why Ghosts Wander', 'Phantom Birds', 'Animal Ghosts', 'Phantom Music', and the like. The pages upon the state of the soul after death are particularly interesting and have as much of the heart's blood of poetry as had ever Dis or Hades. Jacob Boehme[6] held that every man was represented by a symbolic beast or bird, and that these beasts and birds varied with the characters of men, and in the folk-lore of almost every country, the ghosts revisit the earth as moths or butterflies, as doves or ravens, or in some other representative shape. Sometimes only voices are heard. The Zulu sorcerer, Mr Dyer says, 'hears the spirits, who speak by whistlings, speaking to him', while the Algonquin Indians of North America 'could hear the shadow souls of the dead chirp like crickets'. In Denmark, he adds, the night ravens are held to be exorcised evil spirits who are for ever flying towards the East, for if they can reach the Holy Sepulchre they will be at rest; and 'In the *Saemund Edda* it is said that in the nether world singed souls fly about like swarms of flies.' He might have quoted here the account in the old Irish romance called *The Voyage of Maeldune*,[7] of that great saint who dwelt upon the wooded island among the flocks of holy birds who were the souls of his relations, awaiting the blare of the last trumpet. Folk-lore often makes the souls of the blessed take upon themselves every evening the shape of white birds,[8] and whether it put them into such charming shape or not, is ever anxious to keep us from troubling their happiness with our grief. Mr Dyer tells, for instance, the story of a girl who heard a voice speaking from the grass-plot of her lover, and saying, 'Every time a tear falls from thine eyes, my shroud is full of blood. Every time thy heart is gay, my shroud is full of rose leaves.'

All these stories are such as to unite man more closely to the woods and hills and waters about him, and to the birds and animals that live in them, and to give him types and symbols for those feelings and passions which find no adequate expression in common life. Could there be any expression of Nature-worship more tender and lovely than that tale of the Indians who lived once by the river Pascajoula, which Mr Dyer tells in his chapter on 'Phantom Music'? Strange musical sounds were said to come out of the river at one place, and close to this place the Indians had set up an idol representing the water spirit who made the music. Every night they gathered about the image and played to it sweet tunes upon many stringed instruments, for they held it to love all music. One day a priest came and tried to convert them from the worship of this spirit, and might have succeeded; but one night the water was convulsed, and the convulsion drew the whole tribe to the edge of the river to hear music more lovely than the spirit ever sang before. They listened until one plunged into the river in his ecstasy and sank for ever, and then men, women and children – the whole tribe – plunged after him, and left a world that had begun to turn from the ancient ways.

The greatest poets of every nation have drawn from stories like this, symbols and events to express the most lyrical, the most subjective moods. In modern days there has been one great poet who tried to express such moods without adequate knowledge of folk-lore. Most of us feel, I think, no matter how greatly we admire him, that there is something of over-much cloud and rainbow in the poetry of Shelley, and is not this simply because he lacked the true symbols and types and stories to express his intense subjective inspiration? Could he have been as full of folk-lore as was Shakespeare, or even Keats, he might have delivered his message and yet kept as close to our hearthstone as did the one in *The Tempest* and *Midsummer Night's Dream*, or as did the other in 'The Eve of St Agnes', but as it is, there is a world of difference between Puck and Peasblossom and the lady who waited for 'The honeyed middle of the night' upon the one hand and the spirits of the hour and the evil voices of Prometheus upon the other.[9] Shakespeare and Keats had the folk-lore of their own day, while Shelley had but mythology;[10] and a mythology which has been passing for long through literary minds without any new influx from living tradition loses all the incalculable instructive and convincing quality of the popular traditions. No conscious invention can take the place of tradition, for he who would write a folk tale, and thereby bring a new life into literature, must have the fatigue of the spade in his hands and the stupors of the fields in his heart. Let us listen humbly to the old people telling their stories, and perhaps God will send the primitive excellent imagination into the midst of us again. Why should we be either 'naturalists' or 'realists'? Are not those little right hands lifted everywhere in affirmation?

18

'OLD GAELIC LOVE SONGS'

from the *Bookman* (1893)

Dr Hyde's volume of translations, *Love Songs of Connacht* (T. Fisher Unwin), is one of those rare books in which art and life are so completely blended that praise or blame become well nigh impossible. It is so entirely a fragment of the life of Ireland in the past that if we praise it we but praise Him who made man and woman, love and fear, and if we blame it we but waste our breath upon the Eternal Adversary who has marred all with incompleteness and imperfection. The men and women who made these love songs were hardly in any sense conscious artists, but merely people very desperately in love, who put their hopes and fears into simple and musical words, or went over and over for their own pleasure the deeds of kindness or the good looks of their sweethearts. One girl praises her lover, who is a tailor, because he tells her such pretty lies, and because he cuts his cloth as prettily as he tells them, and another cannot forget that hers promised her shoes with high heels. Nor is any little incident too slight to be recorded if only it be connected in some way with the sorrow or the hope of the singer. One poor girl remembers how she tossed upon her bed of rushes, and threw the rushes about because of the great heat.

These poems are pieced together by a critical account, which is almost as much a fragment of life as are the poems themselves. Dr Hyde wrote it first in Gaelic, of that simple kind which the writers of the poems must have thought, and talked, and then translated poems and prose together, and now we have both English and Gaelic side by side. Sheer hope and fear, joy and sorrow, made the poems, and not any mortal man or woman, and the veritable genius of Ireland dictated the quaint and lovely prose. The book is but the fourth chapter[1] of a great work called *The Songs of Connacht*. The preceding chapters are still buried in Irish newspapers. The third chapter was about drinking songs, and the present one begins: 'After reading these wild, careless, sporting, airy drinking songs, it is right that a chapter entirely contrary should follow. Not careless and light-hearted alone is the Gaelic nature, there is also beneath the loudest mirth a melancholy spirit, and if they let on (pretend) to be without heed for anything but sport and revelry, there is nothing in it but letting on (pretence). The same man who will today be dancing, sporting, drinking, and shouting, will be soliloquising by himself to-morrow, heavy and sick and sad in his poor lonely little hut, making a croon over departed hopes, lost life, the vanity of this world, and the coming of death. There is for you the Gaelic nature, and that person who would think that they are not the same sort of people who made those loud-tongued, sporting, devil-may-care songs that we have been reading in the last chapter, and who made the truly gentle, smooth, fair, loving poems which we will see in this part, is very much astray. The life of the Gael is so pitiable, so dark and sad and sorrowful, and they are so broken, bruised, and beaten down in their own land and country that their talents and ingenuity find no place for themselves, and no way to let themselves out but in excessive, foolish mirth or in keening and lamentation. We shall see in these poems that follow, more grief and trouble, more melancholy and contrition of heart, than of gaiety or hope. But despite that, it is probably the same men, or the same class of men, who composed the poems which follow and the songs which we have read. We shall not prove that, and we shall not try to prove it, but where is the person who knows the Gaeldom of Erin and will say against (or contradict) us in this? They were men who composed many of the songs in the last chapter, but it is women who made many of the love-songs, and melodious and sorrowful they made them,' and in like fashion the critical account flows on, a mountain stream of sweet waters. Here and there is some quaint or potent verse, like a moss-covered stone or jutting angle of rushes. Thus, for instance, lamented some girl long ago. 'My heart is as black as a sloe, or as a black coal that would be burnt in a forge, as the sole of a shoe upon white halls, and there is great melancholy over my laugh. My heart is bruised, broken, like ice upon the top of water, as it were a cluster of nuts after their breaking, or a young maiden after her marrying. My love is of the colour of the raspberry on a fine sunny day, of the colour of the darkest heath berries of the mountain; and often has there been a black head upon a bright body. Time it is for me to leave this town. The stone is sharp in it, and the mould is cold; it was in it I got a voice (blame) without riches and a heavy word from the band who backbite. I denounce love; woe is she who gave it to the son of yon woman, who never understood it. My heart in my middle, sure he has left it black, and I do not see him on the street or in any place.'

As the mournful sentences accumulate in our ears, we seem to see a heart dissolving away in clouds of sorrow. The whole thing is one of those 'thrusts of power' which Flaubert has declared to be beyond the reach of conscious art.[2] Dr Hyde is wise in giving it to us in prose, and in giving, as he does, prose versions of all the poems, but one would gladly have had a verse version also. He has shown us how well he can write verse by his versions of some of the more elaborate poems, especially of the wonderful 'My love, O, she is my love':

She casts a spell, O, casts a spell,
Which haunts me more than I can tell,
Dearer, because she makes me ill,
Than who would will to make me well.

She is my store, O, she my store,
Whose grey eye wounded me so sore,
Who will not place in mine her palm,
Who will not calm me any more.

She is my pet, O, she my pet,
Whom I can never more forget;
Who would not lose by me one moan,
Nor stone upon my cairn set.

She is my roon, O, she my roon,
Who tells me nothing, leaves me soon;
Who would not lose by me one sigh,
Were death and I within one room.

She is my dear, O, she my dear,
Who cares not whether I be here,
Who would not weep when I am dead,
Who makes me shed the silent tear.

This translation, which is in the curious metre of the original, is, without being exactly a good English poem, very much better than the bulk of Walsh's and beyond all measure better than any of Mangan's[3] in *The Munster Poets*.[4]

I have now given examples of Dr Hyde's critical prose, and of his prose and verse translations, and must leave him to do the rest himself. As for me, I close the book with much sadness. Those poor peasants lived in a beautiful if somewhat inhospitable world, where little had changed since Adam delved and Eve span. Everything was so old that it was steeped in the heart, and every powerful emotion found at once noble types and symbols for its expression. But we – we live in a world of whirling change, where nothing becomes old and sacred, and our powerful emotions, unless we be highly-trained artists, express themselves in vulgar types and symbols. The soul then had but to stretch out its arms to fill them with beauty, but now all manner of heterogeneous ugliness has beset us. A peasant had then but to stand in his own door and think of his sweetheart and of his sorrow, and take from the scene about him and from the common events of his life types and symbols, and behold, if chance was a little kind, he had made a poem to humble generations of the proud. And we – we labour and labour, and spend days over a stanza or a paragraph, and at the end of it have made, likely as not, a mere bundle of phrases. Yet perhaps this very stubborn uncomeliness of life, divorced from hill and field, has made us feel the beauty of these songs in a way the people who made them did not, despite their proverb:

A tune is more lasting than the song of the birds,
A word is more lasting than the riches of the world.

We stand outside the wall of Eden and hear the trees talking together within, and their talk is sweet in our ears.

19

'AN IMPRESSION'

from the *Speaker* (1893)

Away to the north of Ben Bulben and Cope's Mountain lives 'a strong farmer' – a knight of the sheep, they would have called him in the Gaelic days. Proud of his descent from one of the most fighting clans of the Middle Ages, he is a man of force, alike in his words and in his deeds. There is but one man that swears like him, and this man lives far away up on the mountain. 'Father in heaven, what have I done to deserve this?' he says when he has lost his pipe; and no man but he who lives on the mountain can rival his language on a fair-day over a bargain. He is passionate and abrupt in his movements, and when angry tosses his white beard about with his left hand.

One day I was dining with him when the servant-maid announced a certain Mr O'Donnell. A sudden silence fell upon the old man and upon his two daughters. At last the elder daughter said somewhat severely to her father, 'Go and ask him to come in and dine.' The old man went out, and then came in looking greatly relieved, and said, 'He says he will not dine with us.' 'Go out,' said the daughter, 'and ask him into the back parlour, and give him some whisky.' Her father, who had just finished his dinner, obeyed sullenly, and I heard the door of the back parlour – a little room where the daughters sat and sewed during the evening – shut to behind the men. The daughter then turned to me and said, 'Mr O'Donnell is the tax-gatherer, and last year he raised our taxes, and my father was very angry; and when he came, brought him into the dairy, and sent the dairy-woman away on a message, and then swore at him a great deal. "I will teach you, sir," O'Donnell replied, "that the law can protect its officers," but my father reminded him that he had no witness. At last my father got tired, and sorry, too, and said he would show him a short way home. When they were half-way to the main road, they came on a man of my father's who was ploughing, and this somehow brought back remembrances of the wrong. He sent the man away on a message, and began to swear at the tax-gatherer again. When I heard of it, I was disgusted that he should have made such a fuss over a miserable creature like O'Donnell; and when I heard a few weeks ago that O'Donnell's only son had died and left him heart-broken, I resolved to make him be kind to him next time he came.'

She then went out to see a neighbour, and I sauntered towards the back parlour. When I came to the door I heard angry voices inside. The two men were evidently getting on to the tax again, for I could hear them bandying figures to and fro. I opened the door; at sight of my face the farmer was reminded of his peaceful intentions, and asked me if I knew where the whisky was. I had seen him put it into the cupboard, and was able therefore to find it and get it out, looking at the thin, grief-struck face of the old tax-gatherer. He was rather older than my friend, and very much more feeble and worn, and of a very different type. He was not, like him, a robust successful man, but rather one of those whose feet find no resting-place upon the earth. I recognised one of the children of revery, and said, 'You are doubtless of the stock of the old O'Donnells. I know well the hole in the river where their treasure lies buried, under the guard of a serpent with many heads.' 'Yes, sur,' he replied, 'I am the last of a line of princes.'

We then fell to talking of many commonplace things, and my friend did not once toss his beard about with his left hand, but was very friendly. At last the gaunt old tax-gatherer got up to go, and my friend said, 'I hope we will have a glass together next year.' 'No, no,' was the answer, 'I shall be dead next year.' 'I, too, have lost sons,' said the other, in quite a gentle voice. 'But your sons were not like my son.' And then the two men parted, with an angry flush and bitter hearts; and had I not cast between them some common words or other, might not have parted, but have fallen rather into an angry discussion of the value of their dead sons. If I had not pity for all the children of revery I should have let them fight it out, and would now have many a wonderful oath to record.

The knight of the sheep would have had the victory, for no soul that wears this garment of blood and clay can surpass him. He was but once beaten; and this is his tale of how it was. He and some farmhands were playing at cards in a small cabin that stood against the end of a big barn. A wicked woman had once lived in this cabin. Suddenly one of the players threw down an ace and began to swear without any cause. His swearing was so dreadful that the others all stood up, and my friend said, 'All is not right here; there is a spirit in him.' They ran to the door that led into the barn to get away as quickly as possible. The wooden bolt would not move, so the knight of the sheep took a saw which stood against the wall near at hand, and sawed through the bolt, and at once the door flew open with a bang, as though someone had been holding it, and they fled through.

20

'OUR LADY OF THE HILLS'

from the *Speaker* (1893)

When we were children we did not say at such a distance from the post-office, or so far from the butcher's or the grocer's, but measured things by the covered well in the wood, or by the burrow of the fox in the hill. We belonged then to God and to His works, and to things come down from the ancient days. We would not have been greatly surprised had we met the shining feet of an angel among the white mushrooms upon the mountains, for we knew in those days immense despair, unfathomed love – every eternal mood – but now the draw-net is about our feet. A few miles eastward of Lough Gill a young Protestant girl, who was both pretty herself and prettily dressed in blue and white, wandered up among those mountain mushrooms, and I have a letter of hers telling how she met a troop of children, and became a portion of their dream. When they first saw her they threw themselves face down in a bed of rushes, as if in a great fear; but after a little other children came about them, and they got up and followed her almost bravely. She noticed their fear, and presently stood still and held out her arms. A little girl threw herself into them with the cry, 'Ah, you are the Virgin out o' the picture!' 'No,' said another, coming near also, 'she is a sky fairy, for she has the colour of the sky.' 'No,' said a third, 'she is the fairy out of the foxglove grown big.' The other children, however, would have it that she was indeed the Virgin, for she wore the Virgin's colours. Her good Protestant heart was greatly troubled, and she got the children to sit down about her, and tried to explain who she was, but they would have none of her explanation. Finding explanation of no avail, she asked had they ever heard of Christ. 'Yes,' said one; 'but we do not like Him, for He would kill us if it were not for the Virgin.' 'Tell Him to be good to me,' whispered another into her ear. 'He would not let me near Him, for dad says I'm a divil,' burst out a third.

She talked to them a long time about Christ and the apostles, but was finally interrupted by an elderly woman with a stick, who, taking her to be some adventurous hunter for converts, drove the children away, despite their explanation that here was the great Queen of Heaven come to walk upon the mountain and be kind to them. When the children had gone she went on her way, and had walked about half a mile when the child who was called 'a divil' jumped down from the high ditch by the lane, and said she would believe her 'an ordinary lady' if she had 'two skirts', for 'ladies always had two skirts'. The 'two skirts' were shown, and the child went away crestfallen, but a few minutes later jumped down again from the ditch, and cried angrily, 'Dad's a divil, mum's a divil, and I'm a divil, and you are only an ordinary lady,' and having flung a handful of mud and pebbles, ran away sobbing. When my pretty Protestant had come to her own home, she found that she had dropped the tassels of her parasol. A year later she was by chance upon the mountain, but wearing now a plain black dress, and met the child who had first called her the Virgin out o' the picture, and saw the tassels hanging about the child's neck, and said, 'I am the lady you met last year, who told you about Christ.' 'No, you are not! no, you are not! no, you are not!' was the passionate reply. And after all, it was not my pretty Protestant, but Mary Star of the Sea, still walking in sadness and in beauty upon many a mountain and by many a shore, who cast those tassels at the feet of the child. It is indeed fitting that men pray to her who is the mother of peace, the mother of dreams, and the mother of purity, to leave them yet a little hour to do good and evil in, and to watch old Time telling the rosary of the stars.

21

'MICHAEL CLANCY, THE GREAT DHOUL, AND DEATH'

from the *Old Country* (1893)

One July night the tinker, Michael Clancy, was hurrying along under that seaward point of Ben Bulben which juts out like the bow of an overturned ship. He had been mending cans beyond Ballyshannon, and was now hurrying home to mend the pots of his own neighbourhood. The mending of iron pots needed special preparation, and had, therefore, a day set apart for it every summer, and already he knew the neighbours would have brought forty or fifty to his cabin, and his wife would have set them round the wall ready for his return. The moonlight beat down upon the white road, upon his sandy hair and beard, upon the swinging blackthorn in his hand, upon his leather apron of which one corner was tucked up under his belt, and upon the great iron-bound and cloth-covered budget[1] that was strapped to his shoulders, and in which he carried his shears, brazier, punch, lap-anvil, hammers, pewter-sticks, resin, soldering-iron, and much loose tin, beside a bundle of herbs, such as plaintain, mug-wort, self-heal and the like, and a bottle of some unknown mixture to doctor men and cattle when broken cans and porringers fell short, and the coulter of a plough for making red-hot in the hearth when witches and sheogues had made off with some vanathee's[2] butter and a bundle of crimson ribbons for a girl over beyond Calery.

At first he kept smiling to himself, as this or that clever device came up in his memory, how he had cured one Bridget Purcell of the headache by making her say her prayers with a big iron pot on her head, so that, when she took the pot off, her head seemed to be in heaven; and how he had shown one Patrick Bruin a long red worm and made him believe he had taken it out of his bad tooth. Presently, however, he frowned, for he remembered that the apple-tree behind his cabin should now be covered with red apples, but that in all likelihood the boys and girls out of Carney had gone off with the bulk of them, as they had done the year before. 'I've got the betther of many a man an' woman,' he muttered to himself; 'and no woman or man has ever got the betther of me, barrin' the boys an' girls out of Carney, and barrin' thim I fear neither God nor Dhoul.'[3] While thinking these things he came to a place where the road was shaded by big beech trees, and, before he had time to cross himself or mutter a paternoster, or what was much more to his mind, one of the old rhymes against Dhouls and Sheogues which he had picked up in his tramps, he heard something rustle in the leaves over his head, and then fall into his budget with a horrible smoke and odour. He ran as hard as he could go, and did not stop till he was out in the moonlight again. When at last he looked over his shoulder he saw that the budget was bulging and gaping a bit, and that two black things were sticking out through the slit, and swinging about; and that one was long and thin, the other thick and short. One was certainly a forked tongue, and the other a cloven hoof. 'I'm thinkin', sur,' he said, ''tis more aisy you'd be if ye'd come out of that an' walk, for it must be mortial onpleasant to have thim pewtershticks an' thim shears mixin' thimsilves up wid one's inside.' 'Now run, me honey,' a soft voice, like a Corkman's, replied from the budget. ''Tis but a little time I have to be squandherin', and it's not that used I am to aisy livin' and shleepin' that I need mind a pewter shtick or two, or an odd shears in me vitals, wanst in a while.'

'If ye'd be for gettin' out a bit, sur, sure 'tis glad I'd be to light a fire in the brazier, an' maybe it's more at home you'd be feelin' an the top of it nor among them could irons; an' we could tell ould tales for a bit, an' it's mortial bad the boys are beyant an' about Ballyshannon, an' I could tell you things of thim that it behoves ye for to know, for, begor, 'tis the Dhoul himself they'd desaive, bad luck to 'em.'

'Run, run,' said the voice, 'or me an' me ould wife 'ill roast ye this very night'; and the Dhoul made the loose tin rattle horribly. 'Run, for we've got to be in Dublin before mornin'.'

Michael Clancy ran as he was bid, but kept thinking how he

was to get out of this fix. Every now and then he slackened his pace, meaning to try persuasion again, but as soon as the pace grew slack, the voice began to threaten. At last he saw the light of a forge streaming out on the road, and he bethought him what to do. He rushed in, and suddenly unstrapping the budget, flung it on the anvil, and seizing a hammer began to belabour it with all his might, and bade the blacksmith do the same. Then began the most terrible uproar. The yells and oaths that came out of the budget were so loud that it was a wonder they did not shake the stars out of the sky. The budget was so strong that instead of breaking it merely flattened out, and settled down like a concertina, but no sweet music came out of it. The hammers rose and fell, and the most dreadful odour came up from under the blows, and rose up to the rafters, and half-suffocated the cocks, and hens, and chickens, and made them come tumbling down. At last the Dhoul could bear it no longer, and yelled out:

'What'll ye take to let me out of this?'

'Wan thing only will I take; the boys and girls out of Carney does be stealin' me little red apples, and I'm longing to get the betther of thim, for they are the only souls in the worruld, or out of the worruld, that iver got the betther of me. I'll let ye out if y'll grant me that anyone who cames shtalin' me apples 'ill shtick to the three till I comes round an' leathers thim wid me blackthorn, or lets thim go free, as the whim takes me.'

'I'll grant ye that,' says the Dhoul; 'an' now let me out, for all the bones in me body is broke an me.'

They ceased hammering and the Dhoul went away with a rush and took half the roof with him. The blacksmith fell on the floor in a faint, and his face was the colour of a big pullet that lay on the floor beside him where it had fallen from the rafters. He was never the same man after, but sat with his head on his knees, as the people say, to the day of his death. Michael Clancy was not going to be scared at a Dhoul he had got the better of, but went to his own house, thinking of those little red apples, and wondering whether he would find a boy or a girl or two sticking to the leaves or branches. He turned into the fields when he got near home, and went round to the back of his garden, and got over the ditch, and came close up to the tree. Sure enough there was something sticking to it and swinging about, like an old petticoat hung out to dry in a good wind. He came near and poked at it with his blackthorn. It was a little grey figure of some kind with what looked like a skull on it with a few tufts of hair on the top.

'Are ye a gurrl,' he said, 'for if it's a gurrl ye are I'd pull ye're ears an' let yees go; but if so be ye're a boy I'll leather yees.' The only answer was a moan. 'Do ye hear me talkin' to ye now, is it a gurrl or a boy ye are?' he repeated, and still there was no answer but a moan. 'Ye are a boy!' with that he began to beat the figure with the blackthorn. 'What are ye at all at all, for yees rattle like a bag of bones?'

'I am DEATH!' said a voice that was like a rumble of water underground. 'And I have come for your wife. For yesterday when she was putting the pots round the wall, she fell and hit her head on one of them, and now she is near her end. I was slipping in quietly by the back way when I caught sight of a little red apple just ready to fall, and put out my hand for it, and here I am caught by some kind of bird-lime.'

'And there ye'll shtay till I lets ye go.'

'If you will let me go,' said Death, 'I will let your wife live on a bit longer.'

''Tis the blessing of Providence to take the poor woman away from her bargin' an' fightin', an' I'm not the man to interfere with the decrees of the Maker, glory be to God! But whisht, now! an' I'll tell yees how we'll get yees out of that, for I met the ould fellow himself a bit down the road, an' his honour said I might have what I wished, and I, like a glugger-a-bunthaun,[4] axed the weeshiest bit of a thing. But now I've me siven sinses agin, an' I remimber I'm a poor man wid sorra a penny to bless meself, an' a great thirst entirely to satisfy, an' a power of inimies to keep down. Sometimes whin broken cans an' porringers an' ould pots are scarce, I docthor cows an' horses an' pigs an' Christians an' the like; an' sometimes they die an me, an' that's bad for thrade. Now, Death, me honey, just you give me some thrick for knowin' whin Christians an' things is goin' to die, that I mayn't be wastin' me medicine an thim, but keep it an meself out of harm's way. I don't want to be throublin' poor dyin' sowls wid me cures at all.'

'I always sit at the feet of those who are going to get better,' said Death, 'and at the head of them that are going to die.'

'Thank ye kindly,' said Michael Clancy, 'an' now ye may be goin' an' gettin' to your work, for we're all mortial.' And with that he sat down under the apple-tree and began to smoke, while Death went on into the cabin. Presently he saw two black things going through the air together, and shaking the tobacco out of his pipe muttered, 'I wondher now if it's to Hell or Purgatory she's goin' poor sowl!'

He very soon gave up tinkering altogether, and took entirely to doctoring; and, as all his patients recovered, his fame went far and wide, and his purse grew heavy. He spent his money rapidly, however. He bought shawls and ribbons for all the pretty girls, and gave dances with four fiddlers apiece, and lots of whiskey for everybody, in all the villages along his old route. He was thought all the more of because sometimes he would refuse altogether to doctor this or that person, now saying that the fairies had forbidden him, now, that he had to go off to some distant place to doctor a great lord who had been given up by all the doctors of Ireland, Scotland, England and France. He and Death became quite familiar with each other from meeting so often; at last, however, he made Death very angry. A pretty girl up at Roughley O'Byrne fell ill, and her parents sent for him; but when he came he saw Death sitting at the head of the bed. 'Death,' says he, 'ye might let this nice little gurrl get well; an' if ye do I'll show ye where there are two ould aunts of me own with tongues like the clapper of a bell, an' ye can have the two of thim.'

'I don't want any of your relations.'

Made really angry by this, the tinker took the girl up in his arms, and turned her round, so that her feet were to Death. She got well almost at once, and before evening he was able to go home driving a donkey with a keg of good poteen made in the Island of Innismurray (where the souls of the dead come up upon the shore in the shape of seals) in each creel by way of payment from her grateful parents.

When the tinker awoke next morning he saw Death sitting at his own head, perched up on the bedstead. 'Ye've got to come now,' said Death, 'and it's no use trying to turn yourself round, for if ye so much as wriggle, I'll have the soul out of ye in a jiffey'; and with that he put his long, dry fingers close to the tinker's breast.

'Will ye let me say wan Pather-Nosther afore I die for ould friendship's sake, for I've a lot of dhrink an' divilry an me conscience?'

'For ould friendship's sake,' replied Death, 'I won't take you till you have said your Pater-Noster.'

'Then I'll never say another Pather-Nosther as long as I live, but make me sowl an Hail Marys.'

Death got up with a moan, and, looking very old and feeble, went out through the window; but before he disappeared, turned round and cried: 'The mischief take you, ye thief o' the world, that 'ud steal the cross off an ass's back, for I wash my hands of ye for good and all. Do as ye like, do as ye like; an' if ye want me ye'll have to send after me; I'm done with ye. Oh, that I should have lived to see this!' and he went off like a black cloud through the sky.

After this the tinker made a regular practice of turning patients round with their feet to Death, and he let nobody die in the whole country, unless they were very ugly or very cross. He lived on for scores upon scores of years, and began to get tired of things. He had fallen in and out of love dozens of times, and drunk poteen in every still in Connacht, and nothing more remained to be done or seen. He went to the top of Ben Bulben to the pool where Dermod[5] was killed, and sent one of the fairies who lived there to fetch Death, and the fairy led Death to him. Michael Clancy told Death that he wanted to die, and Death took him away through the air until they came to a great grassy road. Death told him that it led from Ireland to Heaven, and Hell, and Purgatory; that it was grass-grown because hardly anyone had passed that way for many a year now. Having said this he left him, and hurried off muttering to himself. The tinker walked on slowly, stopping every now and then to poke with his stick at the glittering things that lay about in the grass. These were the earthly loves and hopes which kings and queens and warriors had flung away there aforetime. Presently he came to a place where the road divided into three, and saw a signboard with three arms, and on the first arm was written 'TO HEAVEN', upon the second 'TO HELL', and upon the third 'TO PURGATORY'.

'I like me whiskey either hot or could, an' I'll keep clear of Purgatory anyhow,' he said. 'I'll thry Heaven for a turn.' He went on until he came to a little door in a big wall, with a square barred hole in the door for talking through. He looked in and saw Death shooting arrows at a butt a good way off among the trees, but could not see St Peter anywhere. He therefore put his mouth to the square hole and crowed like a cock as loud as ever he could. Presently he heard St Peter running up to the gate, calling out 'Whisht! now, whisht!' Michael Clancy stopped crowing, and St Peter whispered through the hole, 'If ye'll shtop that, an' don't be disgracin' me afore the blessed Archangels an' all the Holy Innocents, I'll go straight and bring your case before the authorities.' He went away, but after a little returned and said, 'It's no use at all at all; we've got to make an example of somebody. There are too many the very shpit of ye in the place ye come from. And now begone wid yees, for the sight of ye has given the poor ould gintleman over there a turn. He hasn't been the same this many a day, and keeps practising wid thim arrows of his, for it's a long shot he'll be takin' at the people from this out.'

'Thank ye kindly,' said the tinker; 'it's all wan to me so as I can get a roof over me, and a sate though it 'ud be but a bit of a creepy-stool[6] to sit down on; for it's famished I am for a dhraw of the pipe. I'll thry Hell for I'll be meetin' friends there I'm thinkin'.'

He went back to the cross roads and took the way to Hell. The Great Dhoul was sitting on an iron throne, and his wife, who by her first husband, Adam, who had not then met with Eve, had borne all the fairies, and by her present husband, all the evil spirits in the world, was sitting at his side with their children at their feet. The Dhoul saw Michael Clancy coming, and remembering the anvil, began to rub himself all over; but his wife caught her youngest by the hair, and flung him with all her might at the tinker, and striking him on the mouth, knocked him clean away beyond the grassy road, and down through the air and into the river at Ballisodare; and there her eldest children found him and turned him into a salmon. He still wanders through the water, but, if anyone catch him with a fly, he breaks the tackle or goes off, maybe, with half the rod.

22

PREFACE TO *THE CELTIC TWILIGHT*

from *United Ireland* (1893)

Next to the desire, which every artist feels, to create for himself a little world out of the beautiful, pleasant, and significant things of this marred and clumsy universe, I have desired to show in a vision something of the face of Ireland to any of my own people who care for things of this kind. I have therefore written down accurately and candidly much that I have heard and seen, and, except by way of commentary, nothing that I have merely imagined. I have, however, been at no pains to separate my own beliefs from those of the peasantry, but have rather let my men and women, dhouls and faeries, go their way unoffended or defended by any argument of mine. The things a man has heard and seen are threads of life, and if he pull them carefully from the confused distaff of memory, any who will can weave them into whatever garments of belief please them best. I too have woven my garment like another, but I shall try to keep warm in it, and shall be well content if it do not unbecome me.

Hope and Memory have one daughter and her name is Art, and she has built her dwelling far from the desperate field where men hang out their garments upon forked boughs to be banners of battle. O beloved daughter of Hope and Memory, be with me for a little.[1]

23

'A TELLER OF TALES'

from *The Celtic Twilight* (1893)

Many of the tales in this book were told me by one Paddy Flynn, a little bright-eyed old man, who lived in a leaky and one-roomed cabin in the village of Ballisodare, which is, he was wont to say, 'the most gentle' – whereby he meant fairy – 'place in the whole of County Sligo'. Others hold it, however, but second to Drumcliff and Drumahair. The first time I saw him he was cooking mushrooms for himself; the next time he was asleep under a hedge, smiling in his sleep. He was indeed always cheerful, though I thought I could see in his eyes (swift as the eyes of a rabbit, when they peered out of their wrinkled holes) a melancholy which was well-nigh a portion of their joy; the visionary melancholy of purely instinctive natures and of all animals.

And yet there was much in his life to depress him, for in the triple solitude of age, eccentricity, and deafness, he went about much pestered by children. It was for this very reason perhaps that he ever recommended mirth and hopefulness. He was fond, for instance, of telling how Columcille cheered up his mother. 'How are you to-day, mother?' said the saint. 'Worse,' replied the mother. 'May you be worse to-morrow,' said the saint. The next day Columcille came again, and exactly the same conversation took place, but the third day the mother said, 'Better, thank God.' And the saint replied, 'May you be better to-morrow.' He was fond too of telling how the Judge smiles at the last day alike when he rewards the good and condemns the lost to unceasing flames. He had many strange sights to keep him cheerful or to make him sad. I asked him had he ever seen the faeries, and got the reply, 'Am I not annoyed with them?' I asked too if he had ever seen the banshee. 'I have seen it,' he said, 'down there by the water, batting the river with its hands.'

I have copied this account of Paddy Flynn, with a few verbal alterations, from a note-book which I almost filled with his tales and sayings, shortly after seeing him. I look now at the note-book regretfully, for the blank pages at the end will never be filled up. Paddy Flynn is dead; a friend of mine gave him a large bottle of whiskey, and though a sober man at most times, the sight of so much liquor filled him with a great enthusiasm, and he lived upon it for some days and then died. His body, worn out with old age and hard times, could not bear the drink as in his young days. He was a great teller of tales, and unlike our common romancers, knew how to empty heaven, hell, and purgatory, faeryland and earth, to people his stories. He did not live in a shrunken world, but knew of no less ample circumstance than did Homer himself. Perhaps the Gaelic people shall by his like bring back again the ancient simplicity and amplitude of imagination. What is literature but the expression of moods by the vehicle of symbol and incident?[1] And are there not moods which need heaven, hell, purgatory, and faeryland for their expression, no less than this dilapidated earth? Nay, are there not moods which shall find no expression unless there be men who dare to mix heaven, hell, purgatory, and faeryland together, or even to set the heads of beasts to the bodies of men, or thrust the souls of men into the heart of rocks? Let us go forth, the tellers of tales, and seize whatever prey the heart long for, and have no fear. Everything exists, everything is true, and the earth is only a little dust under our feet.

24

'BELIEF AND UNBELIEF'

from *The Celtic Twilight* (1893)

There are some doubters even in the western villages. One woman told me last Christmas that she did not believe either in hell or in ghosts. Hell she thought was merely an invention got up by the priest to keep people good; and ghosts would not be permitted, she held, to go 'trapsin about the earth' at their own free will; 'but there are faeries,' she added, 'and little lepracauns, and water-horses, and fallen angels.' I have met also a man with a mohawk tattooed upon his arm, who held exactly similar beliefs and unbeliefs. No matter what one doubts one never doubts the faeries, for, as the man with the mohawk on his arm said to me, 'they stand to reason'. Even the official mind does not escape this faith.

A little girl who was at service in the village of Grange, close under the seaward slopes of Ben Bulben, suddenly disappeared one night about three years ago. There was at once great excitement in the neighbourhood, because it was rumoured that the faeries had taken her. A villager was said to have long struggled to hold her from them, but at last they prevailed, and he found nothing in his hands but a broomstick. The local constable was applied to, and he at once instituted a house-to-house search, and at the same time advised the people to burn all the *bucalauns* (ragweed) on the field she vanished from, because *bucalauns* are sacred to the faeries. They spent the whole night burning them, the constable repeating spells the while. In the morning the little girl was found, the story goes, wandering in the field. She said the faeries had taken her away a great distance, riding on a faery horse. At last she saw a big river, and the man who had tried to keep her from being carried off was drifting down it – such are the topsy-turvydoms of faery glamour – in a cockle-shell. On the way her companions had mentioned the names of several people who were about to die shortly in the village.

Perhaps the constable was right. It is better doubtless to believe much unreason and a little truth than to deny for denial's sake truth and unreason alike, for when we do this we have not even a rush candle to guide our steps, not even a poor sowlth[1] to dance before us on the marsh, and must needs fumble our way into the great emptiness where dwell the mis-shapen dhouls. And after all, can we come to so great evil if we keep a little fire on our hearths, and in our souls, and welcome with open hand whatever of excellent come to warm itself, whether it be man or phantom, and do not say too fiercely, even to the dhouls themselves, 'Be ye gone'? When all is said and done, how do we not know but that our own unreason may be better than another's truth? for it has been warmed on our hearths and in our souls, and is ready for the wild bees of truth to hive in it, and make their sweet honey. Come into the world again, wild bees, wild bees!

25

'THE SORCERERS'

from *The Celtic Twilight* (1893)

In Ireland we hear but little of the darker powers,[1] and come across any who have seen them even more rarely, for the imagination of the people dwells rather upon the fantastic and capricious, and fantasy and caprice would lose the freedom which is their breath of life were they to unite them either with evil or with good. And yet the wise are of opinion, that wherever man is, the dark powers, who feel his rapacities; no less than the bright beings, who store their honey in the cells of his heart; and the twilight beings who flit hither and thither; encompass him with their passionate and melancholy multitude. They hold, too, that he who by long desire or through accident of birth possesses the power of piercing into their hidden abode can see them there, those who were once men or women full of a terrible vehemence, and those who have never lived upon the earth, moving slowly and with a subtler malice. The dark powers cling about us, it is said, day and night, like bats upon an old tree; and that we do not hear more of them is merely because the darker kinds of magic have been but little practised. I have indeed come across very few persons in Ireland who try to communicate with evil powers, and the few I have met keep their purpose and practice wholly hidden from the inhabitants of the remote town where they live. It is even possible, though this is perhaps scarcely likely, that their lives will leave no record in the folklore of the district. They are mainly small clerks and the like, and meet for the purpose of their art in a room hung with black hangings. They would not admit me into this room, but finding me not altogether ignorant of the arcane science, showed gladly elsewhere what they would do. 'Come to us,' said their leader, a clerk in a large flour-mill, 'and we will show you spirits who will talk to you face to face, and in shapes as solid and heavy as our own.'

I had been talking of the power of communicating in states of trance with the angelical and faery beings, – the children of the day and of the twilight, – and he had been contending that we should only believe in what we can see and feel when in our ordinary everyday state of mind. 'Yes,' I said, 'I will come to you,' or some such words; 'but I will not permit myself to become entranced, and will therefore know whether these shapes you talk of are any the more to be touched and felt by the ordinary senses than are those I talk of.' I was not denying the power of other beings to take upon themselves a clothing of mortal substance, but only that simple invocations, such as he spoke of, seemed unlikely to do more than cast the mind into trance and thereby bring it into the presence of the powers of day, twilight, and darkness.

'But,' he said, 'we have seen them move the furniture hither and thither, and they go at our bidding, and help or harm people who know nothing of them.' I am not giving the exact words, but as accurately as I can the substance of our talk.

On the night arranged I turned up about eight, and found the leader sitting alone in almost total darkness in a small back room. He was dressed in a black gown, like an inquisitor's dress in an old drawing, that left nothing of him visible except his eyes, which peered out through two small round holes. Upon the table in front of him was a brass dish of burning herbs, a large bowl, a skull covered with painted symbols, two crossed daggers, and certain implements shaped like quern stones, which were used to control the elemental powers in some fashion I did not discover. I also put on a black gown, and remember that it did not fit perfectly, and that it impeded my movements considerably. The sorcerer then took a black cock out of a basket, and cut its throat with one of the daggers, letting the blood fall into the large bowl. He then opened a book and began an invocation, which was certainly not English, and had a deep guttural sound. Before he had finished, another of the sorcerers, a man of about twenty-five, came in, and having put on a black gown also, seated himself at my left hand. I had the invoker directly in front of me, and soon began to find his eyes, which glittered through the small holes in his hood, affecting me in a curious way. I struggled hard against their influence, and my head began to ache. The invocation continued, and nothing happened for the first few minutes. Then the invoker got up and extinguished the light in the hall, so that no glimmer might come through the slit under the door. There was now no light except from the herbs on the brass dish, and no sound except from the deep guttural murmur of the invocation.

Presently the man at my left swayed himself about, and cried out, 'O god! O god!' I asked him what ailed him, but he did not know he had spoken. A moment after he said he could see a great serpent moving about the room, and became considerably excited. I saw nothing with any definite shape, but thought that black clouds were forming about me. I felt I must fall into a trance if I did not struggle against it, and that the influence which was causing this trance was out of harmony with itself, in other words, evil. After a struggle I got rid of the black clouds, and was able to observe with my ordinary senses again. The two sorcerers now began to see black and white columns moving about the room, and finally a man in a monk's habit, and they became greatly puzzled because I did not see these things also, for to them they were as solid as the table before them. The invoker appeared to be gradually increasing in power, and I began to feel as if a tide of darkness was pouring from him and concentrating itself about me; and now too I noticed that the man on my left hand had passed into a death-like trance. With a last great effort I drove off the black clouds, but feeling them to be the only shapes I should see without passing into a trance, and having no great love for them, I asked for lights, and after the needful exorcism returned to the ordinary world.

I said to the more powerful of the two sorcerers – 'What would happen if one of your spirits had overpowered me?' 'You would go out of this room,' he answered, 'with his character added to your own.' I asked about the origin of his sorcery, but got little of importance, except that he had learned it from his father. He would not tell me more, for he had, it appeared, taken a vow of secrecy.

For some days I could not get over the feeling of having a number of deformed and grotesque figures lingering about me. The Bright Powers are always beautiful and desirable, and the Dim Powers are now beautiful, now quaintly grotesque, but the Dark Powers express their unbalanced natures in shapes of ugliness and horror.

26

'REGINA, REGINA PIGMEORUM, VENI'

from *The Celtic Twilight* (1893)

One night a middle-aged man, who had lived all his life far from the noise of cab-wheels, a young girl, a relative of his, who was reported to be enough of a seer to catch a glimpse of unaccountable lights moving over the fields among the cattle, and myself were walking along a far western sandy shore. We talked of the Dinny Math or faery people, and came in the midst of our talk to a notable haunt of theirs, a shallow cave amid black rocks, with its reflection under it in the wet sea sand. I asked the young girl if she could see anything, for I had quite a number of things to ask the Dinny Math. She stood still for a few minutes, and I saw that she was passing into a kind of waking trance, in which the cold sea breeze no longer troubled her, nor the dull boom of the sea distracted her attention. I then called aloud the names of the great faeries, and in a moment or two she said that she could hear music far inside the rocks, and then a sound of confused talking, and of people stamping their feet as if to applaud some unseen performer. Up to this my other friend had been walking to and fro some yards off, but now he passed close to us, and as he did so said suddenly that we were going to be interrupted, for he heard the laughter of children somewhere beyond the rocks. We were however quite alone. The spirits of the place had begun to cast their influence over him also. In a moment he was corroborated by the girl, who said that bursts of laughter had begun to mingle with the music, the confused talking, and the noise of feet. She next saw a bright light streaming out of the cave, which seemed to have grown much deeper, and a quantity of little people,[1] in various coloured dresses, red predominating, dancing to a tune which she did not recognize.

I then bade her call out to the queen of the little people to come and talk with us. There was, however, no answer to her command. I therefore repeated the words aloud myself, and in a moment a very beautiful tall woman came out of the cave. I too had by this time fallen into a kind of trance,[2] in which what we call the unreal had begun to take upon itself a masterful reality, and was able to see the faint gleam of golden ornaments, the shadowy blossom of dim hair. I then bade the girl tell this tall queen to marshal her followers according to their natural divisions, that we might see them. I found as before that I had to repeat the command myself. The creatures then came out of the cave, and drew themselves up, if I remember rightly, in four bands. One of these bands carried quicken boughs in their hands, and another had necklaces made apparently of serpents' scales, but their dress I cannot remember, for I was quite absorbed in that gleaming woman. I asked her to tell the seer whether these caves were the greatest faery haunts in the neighbourhood. Her lips moved, but the answer was inaudible. I bade the seer lay her hand upon the breast of the queen, and after that she heard every word quite distinctly. No, this was not the greatest faery haunt, for there was a greater one a little further ahead. I then asked her whether it was true that she and her people carried away mortals, and if so, whether they put another soul in the place of the one they had taken? 'We change the bodies,' was her answer. 'Are any of you ever born into mortal life?' 'Yes.' 'Do I know any who were among the Dinny Math before birth?' 'You do.' 'Who are they?' 'It would not be lawful for you to know.' I then asked whether she and her people were not 'dramatizations of our moods'? 'She does not understand,' said my friend, 'but says that her people are much like human beings, and do most of the things human beings do.' I asked her other questions, as to her nature, and her purpose in the universe, but only seemed to puzzle her. At last she appeared to lose patience, for she wrote upon the sands – the sands of vision, not the grating sands under our feet – this message for me – 'Be careful, and do not seek to know too much about us.' Seeing that I had offended her, I thanked her for what she had shown and told, and let her depart again into her cave. In a little while the young girl awoke out of her trance, and felt again the cold wind of the world, and began to shiver.

I tell these things as accurately as I can, and with no theories to blur the record.[3] Theories are poor things at the best, and the bulk of mine have perished long ago. I love better than any theory the sound of the Gate of Horn swinging upon its hinges, and hold that he alone who has passed the rose-strewn threshold can catch the far glimmer of the Ivory Gate. It were perhaps well for us all if we would but raise the cry Lilly the astrologer raised in Windsor Forest, 'Regina, Regina Pigmeorum, Veni,' and remember with him, that God visiteth His children in dreams. Tall, glimmering queen, come near, and let me see again the shadowy blossom of thy dim hair.

27

'THE UNTIRING ONES'

from *The Celtic Twilight* (1893)

It is one of the great troubles of life that we cannot have any unmixed emotions. There is always something in our enemy that we like, and something in our sweetheart that we dislike. It is this entanglement of moods which makes us old, and puckers our brows and deepens the furrows about our eyes. If we could love and hate with as good heart as the faeries do, we might grow to be long-lived like them. But until that day their untiring joys and sorrows must ever be one-half of their fascination. Love with them never grows weary, nor can the circles of the stars tire out their dancing feet. The Donegal peasants remember this when they bend over the spade, or sit full of the heaviness of the fields beside the griddle at nightfall, and tell stories about it that it may not be forgotten. A short while ago, they say, two faeries, little creatures, one like a young man, one like a young woman, came to a farmer's house, and spent the night sweeping the hearth and setting all tidy. The next night they came again, and while the farmer was away, brought all the furniture up-stairs into one room, and having arranged it round the walls, for the greater grandeur it seems, they began to dance. They danced on and on, and days and days went by, and all the countryside came to look at them, but still their feet never tired. The farmer did not dare to live at home the while; and after three months he made up his mind to stand it no more, and went and told them that the priest was coming. The little creatures when they heard this went back to their own country, and there their joy shall last as long as the points of the rushes are brown, the people say, and that is until God shall burn up the world with a kiss.[1]

But it is not merely faeries who know untiring days, for there have been men and women who, falling under their enchantment, have attained, perhaps by the right of their God-given spirits, an even more than faery abundance of life and feeling. It seems that when mortals have gone amid those poor happy leaves of the Imperishable Rose of Beauty,[2] blown hither and thither by the winds that awakened the stars, the dim kingdom has acknowledged their birthright, perhaps a little sadly, and given them of its best. Such a mortal was born long ago at a village in the south of Ireland. She lay asleep in a cradle, and her mother sat by rocking her, when a woman of the sidhe (the faeries) came in, and said that the child was chosen to be the bride of the prince of the dim kingdom, but that as it would never do for his wife to grow old and die while he was still in the first ardour of his love, she would be gifted with a faery life. The mother was to take the glowing log out of the fire and bury it in the garden, and her child would live as long as it remained unconsumed. The mother buried the log, and the child grew up, became a beauty, and married the prince of the faeries, who came to her at nightfall. After seven hundred years the prince died, and another prince ruled in his stead and married the beautiful peasant girl in his turn; and after another seven hundred years he died also, and another prince and another husband came in his stead, and so on until she had had seven husbands. At last one day the priest of the parish called upon her, and told her that she was a scandal to the whole neighbourhood with her seven husbands and her long life. She was very sorry, she said, but she was not to blame, and then she told him about the log, and he went straight out and dug until he found it, and then they burned it, and she died, and was buried like a Christian, and everybody was pleased. Such a mortal too was Clooth-na-bare,[3] who went all over the world seeking a lake deep enough to drown her faery life, of which she had grown weary, leaping from hill to lake and lake to hill, and setting up a cairn of stones wherever her feet lighted, until at last she found the deepest water in the world in little Lough Ia, on the top of the Bird's Mountain at Sligo.

The two little creatures may well dance on, and the woman of the log and Clooth-na-bare sleep in peace, for they have known untrammelled hate and unmixed love, and have never wearied themselves with 'yes' and 'no', or entangled their feet with the sorry net of 'maybe' and 'perhaps'. The great winds came and took them up into themselves.

28

'THE MAN AND HIS BOOTS'

from *The Celtic Twilight* (1893)

There was a doubter in Donegal, and he would not hear of ghosts or sheogues, and there was a house in Donegal that had been haunted as long as man could remember, and this is the story of how the house got the better of the man. The man came into the house and lighted a fire in the room under the haunted one, and took off his boots and set them on the hearth, and stretched out his feet and warmed himself. For a time he prospered in his unbelief; but a little while after the night had fallen, and everything had got very dark, one of his boots began to move. It got up off the floor and gave a kind of slow jump towards the door, and then the other boot did the same, and after that the first boot jumped again. It thereupon dawned upon the man that an invisible being had got into his boots, and was now going away in them. When the boots reached the door they went upstairs slowly, and then the man heard them go tramp, tramp round the haunted room over his head. A few minutes passed, and he could hear them again upon the stairs, and after that in the passage outside, and then one of them came in at the door, and the other gave a jump past it and came in too. They jumped along towards him, and then one got up and hit him, and afterwards the other hit him, then again the first hit him, and so on, until they drove him out of the room, and finally out of the house. In this way he was kicked out by his own boots, and Donegal was avenged upon its doubter. It is not recorded whether the invisible being was a ghost or a sheogue, but the fantastic nature of the vengeance is like the work of the sidhe who live in the heart of fantasy.

29

'A COWARD'

from *The Celtic Twilight* (1893)

One day I was at the house of my friend the strong farmer,[1] who lives beyond Ben Bulben and Cope's mountain, and met there a young lad who seemed to be disliked by the two daughters. I asked why they disliked him, and was told he was a coward. This interested me, for some whom robust children of nature take to be cowards are but men and women with a nervous system too finely made for their life and work. I looked at the lad; but no, that pink-and-white face and strong body had nothing of undue sensibility. After a little he told me his story. He had lived a wild and reckless life, until one day, two years before, he was coming home late at night, and suddenly felt himself sinking in, as it were, upon the ghostly world. For a moment he saw the face of a dead brother rise up before him, and then he turned and ran. He did not stop till he came to a cottage nearly a mile down the road. He flung himself against the door with so much of violence that he broke the thick wooden bolt and fell upon the floor. From that day he gave up his wild life, but was a hopeless coward. Nothing could ever bring him to look, either by day or night, upon the spot where he had seen the face, and he often went two miles round to avoid it; nor could, he said, 'the prettiest girl in the country' persuade him to see her home after a party if he were alone. He feared everything, for he had looked at the face no man can see unchanged – the imponderable face of a spirit.

30

'THE THREE O'BYRNES AND THE EVIL FAERIES'

from *The Celtic Twilight* (1893)

In the dim kingdom there is a great abundance of all excellent things. There is more love there than upon the earth; there is more dancing there than upon the earth; and there is more treasure there than upon the earth. In the beginning the earth was perhaps made to fulfil the desire of man, but now it has got old and fallen into decay. What wonder if we try and pilfer the treasures of that other kingdom!

A friend was once at a village near Slieve League. One day he was straying about a rath called 'Cashel Nore'. A man with a haggard face and unkempt hair, and clothes falling in pieces, came into the rath and began digging. My friend turned to a peasant who was working near and asked who the man was. 'That is the third O'Byrne,' was the answer. A few days after he learned this story: A great quantity of treasure had been buried in the rath in pagan times, and a number of evil faeries set to guard it; but some day it was to be found and belong to the family of the O'Byrnes. Before that day three O'Byrnes must find it and die. Two had already done so. The first had dug and dug until at last he got a glimpse of the stone coffin that contained it, but immediately a thing like a huge hairy dog came down the mountain and tore him to pieces. The next morning the treasure had again vanished deep into the earth. The second O'Byrne came and dug and dug until he found the coffer, and lifted the lid and saw the gold shining within. He saw some horrible sight the next moment, and went raving mad and soon died. The treasure again sank out of sight. The third O'Byrne is now digging. He believes that he will die in some terrible way the moment he finds the treasure, but that the spell will be broken, and the O'Byrne family made rich for ever, and become again a great people, as they were of old.

A peasant of the neighbourhood once saw the treasure. He found the shin-bone of a hare lying on the grass. He took it up; there was a hole in it; he looked through the hole, and saw the gold heaped up under the ground. He hurried home to bring a spade, but when he got to the rath again he could not find the spot where he had seen it.

31

'THE THICK SKULL OF THE FORTUNATE'

from *The Celtic Twilight* (1893)

Once a number of Icelandic peasantry found a very thick skull in the cemetery where the poet Egil[1] was buried. Its great thickness made them feel certain it was the skull of a great man, doubtless of Egil himself. To be doubly sure they put it on a wall and hit it hard blows with a hammer. It got white where the blows fell but did not break, and they were convinced that it was in truth the skull of the poet, and worthy of every honour. In Ireland we have much kinship with the Icelanders, or 'Danes' as we call them and all other dwellers in the Scandinavian countries. In some of our mountainous and barren places, and in our seaboard villages, we still test each other in much the same way the Icelanders tested the head of Egil. We may have acquired the custom from those ancient Danish pirates, whose descendants the people of Rosses tell me still remember every field and hillock in Ireland which once belonged to their forebears, and are able to describe Rosses itself as well as any native. There is one seaboard district known as Roughley O'Byrne, where the men are never known to shave or trim their wild red beards, and where there is a fight ever on foot. I have seen them at a boat-race fall foul of each other, and after much loud Gaelic, strike each other with oars. The first boat had gone aground, and by dint of hitting out with the long oars kept the second boat from passing, only to give the victory to the third. One day the Sligo people say a man from Roughley O'Byrne was tried in Sligo for breaking a skull in a row, and made the defence not unknown in Ireland, that some heads are so thin you cannot be responsible for them. Having turned with a look of passionate contempt towards the solicitor who was prosecuting, and cried, 'that little fellow's skull if ye were to hit it would go like an egg-shell', he beamed upon the judge, and said in a wheedling voice, 'but a man might wallop away at your lordship's for a fortnight'.[2]

32

'THE RELIGION OF A SAILOR'

from *The Celtic Twilight* (1893)

A sea captain when he stands upon the bridge, or looks out from his deck-house, thinks much about God and about the world. Away in the valley yonder among the corn and the poppies men may well forget all things except the warmth of the sun upon the face, and the kind shadow under the hedge; but he who journeys through storm and darkness must needs think and think. One July a couple of years ago I took my supper with a Captain Moran on board the S.S. *Margaret*, then put into a western river from I know not where. I found him a man of many notions all flavoured with personality, as is the way with sailors. He talked in his queer sea manner of God and the world, and up through all his words broke the hard energy of the man of action.

'Sur,' said he, 'did you ever hear tell of the sea captain's prayer?'

'No,' said I; 'what is it?'

'It is,' he replied, '"O Lord, give me a stiff upper lip."'

'And what does that mean?'

'It means,' he said, 'that when they come to me some night and wake me up, and say, "Captain, we're going down," that I won't make a fool o' meself. Why, sur, we war in mid Atlantic, and I standin' on the bridge, when the third mate comes up to me lookin' mortial bad. Says he, "Captain, all's up with us." Says I, "Didn't you know when you joined that a certain percentage go down every year?" "Yes, sur," says he; and says I, "Arn't you paid to go down?" "Yes, sur," says he; and says I, "Then go down like a man, and be damned to you!"'

He told this tale of himself quietly, simply, as if he talked of the bubbling of the tar between the deck planks in the hot sun, the gathering of barnacles along the keel, or of any other part of the daily circumstance of his calling. Let us look upon him with wonder, for his mind has not fallen into a net of complexity, nor his will melted into thought and dream. Our journey is through other storms and other darkness.

33

'CONCERNING THE NEARNESS TOGETHER OF HEAVEN, EARTH, AND PURGATORY'

from *The Celtic Twilight* (1893)

In Ireland this world and the other are not widely sundered; sometimes, indeed, it seems almost as if our earthly chattels were no more than the shadows of things beyond. A lady I knew once saw a village child running about with a long trailing petticoat upon her, and asked the creature why she did not have it cut short. 'It was my grandmother's,' said the child; 'would you have her going about yonder with her petticoat up to her knees, and she dead but four days?' I have read a story of a woman whose ghost haunted her people because they had made her grave-clothes so short that the fires of purgatory burned her knees. The peasantry expect to have beyond the grave houses much like their earthly homes, only there the thatch will never grow leaky, nor the white walls lose their lustre, nor shall the dairy be at any time empty of good milk and butter. But now and then a landlord or an agent or a gauger will go by begging his bread, to show how God divides the righteous from the unrighteous.

34

'THE EATERS OF PRECIOUS STONES'

from *The Celtic Twilight* (1893)

Sometimes when I have been shut off from common interests, and have for a little forgotten to be restless, I get waking dreams, now faint and shadow-like, now vivid and solid-looking, like the material world under my feet. Whether they be faint or vivid, they are ever beyond the power of my will to alter in any way. They have their own will, and sweep hither and thither, and change according to its commands. One day I saw faintly an immense pit of blackness, round which went a circular parapet, and on this parapet sat innumerable apes eating precious stones out of the palms of their hands. The stones glittered green and crimson, and the apes devoured them with an insatiable hunger. I knew that I saw the Celtic Hell, and my own Hell, the Hell of the artist, and that all who sought after beautiful and wonderful things with too avid a thirst, lost peace and form and became shapeless and common. I have seen into other people's Hells also, and saw in one an infernal Peter, who had a black face and white lips, and who weighed on a curious double scales not only the evil deeds committed, but the good deeds left undone, of certain invisible shades. I could see the scales go up and down, but I could not see the shades who were, I knew, crowding about him. I saw on another occasion a quantity of demons of all kinds of shapes – fish-like, serpent-like, ape-like, and dog-like – sitting about a black pit such as that in my own Hell, and looking at a moon-like reflection of the Heavens which shone up from the depths of the pit.

35

'THE GOLDEN AGE'

from *The Celtic Twilight* (1893)

A while ago I was in the train, and getting near Sligo. The last time I had been there something was troubling me, and I had longed for a message from those beings or bodiless moods, or whatever they be, who inhabit the world of spirits. The message came, for one night I saw with blinding distinctness a black animal, half weasel half dog, moving along the top of a stone wall, and presently the black animal vanished, and from the other side came a white weasel-like dog, his pink flesh shining through his white hair and all in a blaze of light; and I remembered a peasant belief about two faery dogs who go about representing day and night, good and evil, and was comforted by the excellent omen. But now I longed for a message of another kind, and chance, if chance there is, brought it, for a man got into the carriage and began to play on a fiddle made apparently of an old blacking-box, and though I am quite unmusical the sounds filled me with the strangest emotions. I seemed to hear a voice of lamentation out of the Golden Age. It told me that we are imperfect, incomplete, and no more like a beautiful woven web, but like a bundle of cords knotted together and flung into a corner. It said that the world was once all perfect and kindly, and that still the kindly and perfect world existed, but buried like a mass of roses under many spadefuls of earth. The faeries and the more innocent of the spirits dwelt within it, and lamented over our fallen world in the lamentation of the wind-tossed reeds, in the song of the birds, in the moan of the waves, and in the sweet cry of the fiddle. It said that with us the beautiful are not clever and the clever are not beautiful, and that the best of our moments are marred by a little vulgarity, or by a pin-prick out of sad recollection, and that the fiddle must ever lament about it all. It said that if only they who live in the Golden Age could die we might be happy, for the sad voices would be still; but alas! alas! they must sing and we must weep until the Eternal gates swing open.

We were now getting into the big glass-roofed terminus, and the fiddler put away his old blacking-box and held out his hat for a copper, and then opened the door and was gone.

36

'THE EVANGEL OF FOLK-LORE'

from the *Bookman* (1894)

The recent revival of Irish literature has been very largely a folk-lore revival, an awakening of interest in the wisdom and ways of the poor, and in the poems and legends handed down among the cabins. Past Irish literary movements were given overmuch to argument and oratory; their poems, with beautiful exceptions, were noisy and rhetorical, and their prose, their stories even, ever too ready to flare out in expostulation and exposition. So manifest were these things that many had come to think the Irish nation essentially rhetorical and unpoetical, essentially a nation of public speakers and journalists, for only the careful student could separate the real voice of Ireland, the song which has never been hushed since history began, from all this din and bombast. But now the din and bombast are passing away, or, at any rate, no longer mistaken for serious literature, and life is being studied and passion sung not for what can be proved or disproved, not for what men can be made do or not do, but for the sake of Beauty 'and Time's old daughter Truth'. Let us be just to this din and bombast; they did good in their day, helped many an excellent cause, made the young more patriotic, and set the crooked straight in many ways, but they were of practical and not poetical importance. Compare the method of the older writers[1] with the method of the new, and lay the difference at the door of the folk-lorist, for it is practically with his eyes that Miss Barlow,[2] Miss Lawless,[3] Mr Standish O'Grady, and Mrs Hinkson[4] in her later work, look at Irish life and manners, and it is he who has taught them to love the wisdom and ways of the poor, the events which have shaped those ways and that wisdom, and the kings and heroes of the phantasies of the cabin with so simple a love, such a quiet sincerity.

There is indeed no school for literary Ireland just now like the school of folk-lore; and, lest the school should lack teachers, every year brings us some new collection.

Mr Curtin, Lady Wilde, Dr Hyde, Mr McAnally, Mr Fitzgerald[5] have already given us a goodly parcel of the ancient romance, and now comes Mr Larminie with as fine a book as the best that has been.

Is not the evangel of folk-lore needed in England also? For is not England likewise unduly fond of the story and the poem which have a moral in their scorpion tale. These little stories of Mr Larminie's have no moral, and yet, perhaps, they and their like are the only things really immortal, for they were told in some shape or other, by old men at the fire before Nebuchadnezzar ate grass, and they will still linger in some odd crannie or crevice of the world when the pyramids have crumbled into sand. Their appeal is to the heart and not to the intellect. They take our emotions and fashion them into forms of beauty as a goldsmith fashions gold, as a silversmith fashions silver. Our love for woman's beauty is for ever a little more subtle once we have felt the marvel of that tale of a boy who, finding on the road a little box containing a lock of hair which shone with a light like many candles, travelled through numberless perils to find her from whose head it had been shorn;[6] our sense of pity is ever a little more poignant once we have understood the charm of that tale of the woman who dwelt seven years in hell to save her husband's soul, keeping – for such was her appointed work – the ever-bobbing souls of the lost from getting out of a great boiler, and then another seven years that she might have the right to take all she could carry, and bring the souls away clinging to her dress.[7] Nor can our power of wonder be other than a little more transcendent when we have dreamed that dream of 'the place where were seals, whales, crawling, creeping things, little beasts of the sea with red mouths, rising on the sole and palm of the oar, making faery music and melody for themselves, till the sea arose in strong waves, hushed with magic, hushed with wondrous voices';[8] or of the magical adventurer[9] who became for a year a grey flagstone covered with heaps of ice and snow, and yet died not wholly, but awoke again and turned to his adventures as before.

And there are a plenty of such things in Mr Larminie's book, more, perhaps, than in any book of Irish folk-lore since Lady Wilde's *Ancient Legends*. Dr Hyde is by far the best Irish folk-lorist by the right of his incomparable skill as a translator from the Gaelic, and among the first of Irish story-tellers by the right of 'Teig O'Kane', well nigh as memorable a masterpiece as 'Wandering Willie's Tale';[10] but his *Beside the Fire* is no such heaped-up bushel of primeval romance and wisdom as *West Irish Folk Tales*. Mr Larminie gathered his store in remote parts of Donegal, Roscommon and Galway, and his book has the extravagance and tumultuous movement as of waves in a storm, which Mr Curtin had already taught us to expect from the folk tale of the extreme west. When such tales are well understood; when the secret of their immortality is mastered; when writers have begun to draw on them as copiously as did Homer, and Dante, and Shakespeare, and Spenser, then will the rhetorician begin to wither and the romance maker awake from a sleep as of a grey flagstone, and shake off the ice and snow and weave immortal woofs again.

37

'THE TRIBES OF DANU[1]'

from the *New Review* (1897)

I. *The Lands of the Tribes of Danu*

The poet is happy, as Homer was happy, who can see from his door mountains, where the heroes and beautiful women of old times were happy or unhappy, and quiet places not yet forsaken by the gods. If a poet cannot find immortal and mysterious things in his own country, he must write of far-off countries oftener than of his own country, or of a vague country that is not far off or near at hand, for even the most fleeting and intelligible passions of poetry live among immortal and mysterious things; and when he does not write of his own country the waters and mountains about him, and the lives that are lived amongst them, are less beautiful than they might be. He will be more solitary too, for people will find little in their lives to remind them of him, and he will find little in his writings to remind him of them, and the world and poetry will forget one another. The more he has of spiritual passion the more solitary he will be, for who would not think *Prometheus Unbound* better to read and better to remember if its legends and its scenery were the legends and the scenery they had known from childhood, or that Shelley had known from childhood and filled with the passion of many memories? Indeed, I am certain that the writers of a spiritual literature, if it is not a literature of simple prayers and cries, must make the land about them a Holy Land; and now that literature which is not spiritual literature is, perhaps, passing away, we must begin making our lands Holy Lands, as the Jews made Palestine, as the Indians made Northern India, as the Greeks made the lands about the Ionian Sea. I think that my own people, the people of a Celtic habit of thought, if genius which cannot be whistled for blow their way, can best begin, for they have a passion for their lands, and the waters and mountains of their lands remind them of old love tales, old battle tales, and the exultant hidden multitudes. There is no place in Ireland where they will not point to some mountain where Grania slept beside her lover, or where the mis-shapen Fomor[2] were routed, or to some waters where the Sacred Hazel[3] once grew and fattened the Salmon of Wisdom with its crimson nuts; nor is there I think, a place outside the big towns where they do not believe that the Fairies, the Tribes of the goddess Danu, are stealing their bodies and their souls, or putting unearthly strength into their bodies, and always hearing all that they say. Nothing shows more how blind educated Ireland – I am not certain that I should call so unimaginative a thing education – is about peasant Ireland, than that it does not understand how the old religion which made of the coming and going of the greenness of the woods and of the fruitfulness of the fields a part of its worship, lives side by side with the new religion which would trample nature as a serpent under its feet; nor is that old religion faded to a meaningless repetition of old customs, for the ecstatic who has seen the red light and white light of God smite themselves into the bread and wine at the Mass, has seen the exultant hidden multitudes among the winds of May, and if he were philosophical would cry with the painter, Calvert:– 'I go inward to God, outward to the gods.'[4]

II. *The Persons of the Tribes of Danu*

The old poets thought that the tribes of the goddess Danu were of a perfect beauty, and the creators of beautiful people and beautiful arts. The hero Fiachna[5] sang when he came from among them:–

> They march among blue lances,
> Those troops of white warriors with knotted hair,
> Their strength, great as it is, cannot be less.
> They are sons of queens and kings,
> On the heads of all a comely
> Harvest of hair yellow like gold.
> Their bodies are graceful and majestic,
> Their eyes have looks of power and blue pupils,

Their teeth shine like glass,
Their lips are red and thin.

And 'every artist harmonious and musical' is described in an old book by one Duald mac Firbis,[6] of Laccan, as of the Tribes of the goddess Danu, that is to say, inspired by the Tribes of the goddess Danu. It took me a long time to find out that they still kept their beauty, for the peasant visionaries have never been from their own countrysides, and can only compare what they have seen to commonplace things and tell you that they have seen rooms 'grander' than some commonplace room 'up at the Lodge', or marching people, who looked (as a poteen-maker, who had praised their magnificence, said to me) 'for all the world like policemen'. But now I ask careful questions, and am told, as I was told the other day by a woman, who was telling of a sight one Martin Roland saw in a bog, that 'their women had their hair wound round their heads, and had a wild look, and there were wreaths of flowers upon their horses'; or, as I was told when I asked an old man who has seen them, and whose uncle used to be away among them, if their great people had crowns of one shape:– 'O no, their crowns have all kinds of shapes, and they have dresses of all kinds of colours'; or, as I was told by the same old man, when the friend who was with me held up a sapphire ring and made it flash, and asked if their dresses were as beautiful:– 'O, they are far grander than that, far grander than that'; or, as I was told by a blind piper, when I asked if he had any of their music:– 'I have no music like theirs, for there is no music in the world like theirs.'

Many have thought that the Tribes of the goddess Danu have become little, like the fairies in the *Midsummer Night's Dream*, and some have built a theory on their littleness; but they are indeed tall and noble, as many have told me. They have among them monsters and grotesque persons who are now big and now little; but these are their old enemies, the Fomor, the Caetchen, the Laighin, the Gailioin, the Goborchin, the Fir Morca, the Luchorpain, the Firbolg, and the Tribes of Domnu, divinities of darkness and death and ugliness and winter cold and evil passion;[7] and they can take shapes and sizes that are not their true shapes and sizes, as they and the Druids do in the poems, and become 'very small and go into one another, so that all you see might be a sort of a little bundle'; or become 'like a clutch of hens', or become like 'a flock of wool by the road', or become like a tar-barrel 'flaming and rolling', 'or look like a cow and then like a woman'; but all the while 'they are death on handsome people because they are handsome themselves'. The Country of the Young, as the poets call their country, is indeed the country of bodiless beauty that was among the Celtic races and of which (if D'Arbois de Jubainville[8] has written correctly) the Greek mythology and all that came of it were but the beautiful embodiment; and it still lives, forgotten by proud and learned people, among simple and poor people. When the Irish peasant passes into a sudden trance and, sleeping, is yet awake and awake is yet sleeping, it is still that bough of golden apples, whose rustling cast Cormac, son of Art,[9] into a Druid sleep, whose rustling has overcome him; and its beauty is not the less beautiful because Christianity has forbidden its rustling, and made Eve's apple grow among its golden apples.

III. *The Houses of the Tribes of Danu*

Although a man has told me that 'the others', as the Galway peasant, like the Greek peasant, has named the gods, can build up 'in ten minutes and in the middle of a field a house ten times more beautiful than any house in the world', and although some have told me that they live everywhere, they are held by most to live in forts or 'forths', the little fields surrounded by clay ditches that were the places of the houses of the ancient people. Every countryside is full of stories of the evils that have fallen upon the reckless or unbelieving people, who have broken down the ditches of the forts, or cut the bushes that are in them. A man, who has a mill and a farm near Gort, in Galway County, showed me where a fort on his farm had been cut through to make a road, and said:– 'The engineer must have been a foreigner or an idolater, but he did not live long anyway'; and the people of a neighbouring townland tell how an old man, who is not long dead, cut a bush from one behind his house, and 'next morning he had not a blade of hair on his head – not one blade, and he had to buy a wig and wear it all the rest of his life'. A distant relation of my own bid his labourers cut down some bushes in a fort in Sligo, and the next morning they saw a black lamb among his sheep, and said it was a warning, and would not cut the bushes; and the lamb had gone the morning after that. A great number of the people of every countryside have seen some fort lighted up, with lights which they describe sometimes as like torches, and sometimes as like bonfires; but once, when I questioned a man who described them as like a bonfire, I found that he had seen a long thin flame, going up for thirty feet and whirling about at the top. A man, who lives near the fort where the old man lost his hair, sees a woman lighting a fire under a bush in the fort; but I do not know what the fire is like, as I have not been able to question him; but a girl says the fires come with a sudden blaze 'like a man lighting his pipe'. Somebody in almost every family that lives near a fort has heard or seen lights or shadows, or figures that wail or dance, or fight or play at hurling, which was a game among the Tribes of Danu in old days, or ride upon horseback, or drive in strange carriages that make a muffled sound. I know one fort where they hear the galloping of horses, as if from underground, but 'the others' are generally supposed to live in the forts, as the ancient people lived in them and are indeed sometimes said to be the ancient people doomed to await the end of the world for their redemption, because they had (as a man said to me) 'Freemasons and all sorts of magicians among them', or, as another said to me, 'because they used to be able to put souls into rocks and to make birds and fishes speak, and everybody who has read about the old times knows that fishes and birds used to speak'.

Certain queerly-shaped bushes, not near forts and often alone in the middle of fields, and certain trees, are also frequented and protected. The people say that you must not hurt these bushes and trees, because 'the others' have houses near them; but sometimes it seems that, if you hurt one of them, you hurt one of 'the others', for I have been told of a man who went to cut a bush on the road to Kinvara, in Galway County, 'and at the first blow he heard something like a groan coming from beneath it; but he would not leave off, and his mouth was drawn to one side all of a sudden, and two days after he died'. A man has told me that he and another went in their boyhood to catch a horse in a certain field full of boulders and bushes of hazel and rock roses and creeping juniper that is by Coole Lake; and he said to the boy who was with him:– 'I bet a button that if I fling a pebble on to that bush, it will stay on it', meaning that the bush was so matted that the pebble would not be able to pass through it. So he 'took up a pebble of cow-dung, and as soon as it hit the bush, there came out of it the most beautiful music that ever was heard'. They ran away and, when they had gone about two hundred yards, they looked back, and saw a woman dressed in white walking round and round the bush:– 'First it had the form of a woman and then of a man, and it going round the bush.' He said that some time afterwards 'the master sent men to cut down the bushes in that part of the field, and a boy was cutting them near the matted bush, and a thorn ran into his eye and blinded him'. There is an old big elm at the corner of a road a couple of miles from the field; and a boy, who was passing before daylight with a load of hay, fell from his cart, and was killed just beside it, and people say that the horse was standing quite still by him when he was found, and that a shower of rain, which fell just after he was taken away, wet everything except the dust where he had lain. Many places have bad names, because people have fallen from their carts at them, and 'the others' are said to have these people among them. The old big elm has not altogether a bad name, because it is said that one day a man was passing by it, who had come from Galway with 'a ton weight in his cart', and 'the lynching of his wheel came out, and the cart fell down, and a little man about two and a half feet high came out of the wall, and lifted up the cart, and held it up until he had the lynching put up again, and never said a word, but went away as he came'. This may be a story come out of old times; but it may not, for simple people live so close to trance that the lynching may never have come off, and the carter may have seen it all awake and yet asleep or asleep and yet awake; or the lynching may have come off, and the carter may have put it on with his own hands, and not have known that he put it on. There is a plantation of younger trees near the big old elm which they protected also; and when a man called Connellan went a while ago to cut trees there, 'he was prevented, and never could get the hand-saw near a tree, nor the man that was with him' (but I have not been able to find out how he was prevented); and there is a whole wood bordering on the field where the matted bush used to be, which Biddy Early,[10] a famous wise woman, used to call a 'very bad place'; and many see sights in it, and many go astray in it, and wander about for hours in a twilight of the senses. Souls are sometimes said to be put into the trees for a penance; for there was a woman who was 'for seven years in a tree at Kinadyfe, and seven years after that in the little bridge beyond Kilcreest, below the arch with the water running under her; and while she was in the tree, whether there was frost or snow or storm, she hadn't so much as the size of a leaf to shelter her'.

A woman has told me that people only see 'the others' in the forts and by the bushes and trees, because 'they are thinking of them there', but that 'they are everywhere like the blades of the grass'; and she showed me a corner of a road, where there was neither a fort nor a bush nor a tree, and said that they had put her brother 'into a faint' there, and that the young men were afraid to come home at night from card playing till there were a number of them together. She herself has seen something far from a fort or a bush or a tree:– 'I was walking with another girl, and I looked up, and saw a tall woman dressed in black, with a mantle of some sort, a wide one, over her head, and the waves of the wind were blowing it off her, so that I could hear the noise of it. All her clothes were black and had the appearance of being new.' She asked the other if she could see the woman, but she could not:– 'For two that are together can never see such things, but only one of them.' They ran away then, and the woman followed them until she came to a running stream. They thought the woman was one who had been 'taken', for they were coming from 'a house of the Kearneys, where the father and mother had died, but it was well known they often came back to look after the children'. She is confident, however, that you must not question a dead person till you come to a bush, showing, as indeed everything shows, that half the dead are believed to have gone to the houses of 'the others', lured thither by sweet music or by the promise of unearthly love, or taken captive by their marching host.

They live also in certain hills like the hill behind Corcamroe Abbey, in which they have 'a town', and they are very plentiful under waters. A woman at Coole, in Galway, says:– 'They are in the sea as well as on the land. That is well known by those that are out fishing by the coast. When the weather is calm, they can look down sometimes, and see cattle and pigs and all such things as we have ourselves. And at night their boats come out and they can be seen fishing; but they never last out after one o'clock.'

IV. *The Friends of the Tribes of Danu*

Though hundreds in every countryside that I know in Ireland have seen them, and think of seeing them as but a common chance, the most are afraid to see them, because they may not wish to be seen. The people about Inchy, at Coole, point out an old blind man, and say that he was not blind when he was a boy; but one day he heard the coach of 'the others', the coach-a-bower, or deaf coach, as it is called, because it makes a deaf or muffled sound, and stood up to look at them instead of sitting still and looking another way. He had only time to see beautiful ladies, with flowers about them, sitting in the coach before he was smitten blind. Some of the old books call Midir[11] the king of the fairies; and one of the old books says that three herons stand before his door, and when they see anybody coming, the first heron cries:– 'Do not come, do not come'; and the second heron cries:– 'Go away'; and the third heron cries:– 'Go by the house, by the house'. There are, however, people that the gods favour, and permit to look upon them and go among them. A young man in the Burren Hills told me that he remembers an old poet, who made his poems in Irish, and who met, when he was young, one who called herself Maive, and said she was a queen among them, and asked him if he would have money or pleasure. He said he would have pleasure, and she gave him her love for a time, and then went from him, and ever after he was very sad. The young man had often heard him sing the poem of lamentation that he made, but could only remember that it was 'very mournful', and that it called her 'beauty of all beauties'. 'The others' are often said to be very good to many people, and to make their crops abundant, and to do them many services. I have been told 'there was a family at Tirneevan, and they were having a wedding there; and when it was going on the wine ran short, and the spirits; and they didn't know what to do to get more, Gort being two miles away; and two or three strange people came in, that they never had seen before, but they made them welcome; and when they heard what was wanting they said they would get it, and in a few minutes they were back with the spirits and the wine, and no place to get it nearer than Gort!' But the people they let look upon them often live in poor and tumble-down houses. I asked a man once if a neighbour of his, who could see things, had the cure that is made out of seven common things, and can end 'all the evils that are in the world'; and he answered:– 'She has the scenery for it, but I do not know that she has it' – meaning that his neighbour's house was a poor and tumble-down house.[12]

There was an old Martin Roland, who lived near a bog a little out of Gort, who saw them often from his young days, and always towards the end of his life. He told me a few months before his death that 'they' would not let him sleep at night with crying things at him in Irish and with playing their pipes. He had asked a friend of his what he should do, and the friend had told him to buy a flute, and play on it when they began to shout or to play on their pipes, and maybe they would give up annoying him, and he did, and they always went out into the field when he began to play. He showed me the flute, and blew through it, and made a noise, but he did not know how to play; and then he showed me where he had pulled his chimney down, because one of them used to sit up on it and play on the pipes. A friend of his and mine went to see him a little time ago, for she heard that 'three of them' had told him he was to die. He said they had gone away after warning him, and that the children (children they had 'taken', I suppose) who used to come with them, and play about the house with them, had 'gone to some other place', because 'they found the house too cold for them, maybe'; and he died a week after he said these things. His neighbours were not certain that he really saw anything in his old age, but they were all certain that he saw things when he was a young man. His brother said:– 'Old he is, and it's all in his brain the things he sees. If he was a young man we might believe in him.' But he was improvident and never got on with his brothers. A neighbour said:– 'The poor man! they say they are mostly in his head now, but sure he was a fine fresh man twenty years ago, the night he saw them linked in two lots, like young slips of girls walking together. It was the night they took away Fallon's little girl'; and she told how Fallon's little girl had met a woman 'with red hair that was as bright as silver' who took her away. Another neighbour, who was herself 'clouted over the ear' by one of them for going into a fort where they were, said:– 'I believe it's mostly in his head they are, and when he stood in the door last night I said:– "The wind does be always in my ears and the sound of it never stops," to make him think it was the same with him; but he says:– "I hear them singing and making music all the time, and one of them is after bringing out a little flute, and it's on it he's playing to them." And this I know, that when he pulled down the chimney where he said the piper used to be sitting and playing, he lifted up stones, and he an old man, that I could not have lifted when I was young and strong.' The people often tell one, as a proof that somebody is in communication with 'the others', that nobody can do so much work as he does, or that nobody can lift such weights as he does, or that nobody can play so well at the hurling as he does. The Country of the Gods is called 'the Country of the Young', and the strength of their youth is believed to fall about those they love just as it fell about Cuchulain and the other heroes in the poems, and as the strength of Apollo was believed to fall about his priests at Hylae,[13] so that they could leap down steep places and tear up trees by the roots, and carry them upon their backs over narrow and high places. When one has crossed the threshold of trance, it may be that one comes to the secret Waters of Life, where Maeldun[14] saw the dishevelled eagle bathing till it had grown young again, and that their drifting spray can put strength into our bodies.

Those who can see 'the others' as easily as Martin Roland saw them, look on them very much as we look on people from another townland; and indeed many among those who have seen them but seldom, think of their coming and going as of a simple and natural thing and not a thing to surprise anybody. I have often been told in Galway that the people in the North of Ireland see them easily; and a friend[15] has written for me an account of a talk she had with an old woman in Tyrone, who considers their coming and going a very small and natural thing. It is quite accurate, for my friend, who had heard the old woman's story some time before I heard of it, got her to tell it over again, and wrote it out at once. She began by telling the old woman that she did not like being in the house alone because of the ghosts and fairies; and the old woman said:– 'There's nothing to be frightened about in fairies, Miss. Many's the time I talked to a woman myself that was a fairy or something of the sort, and no less and more than mortal anyhow. She used to come about your grandfather's house, your mother's grandfather that is, in my young days. But you'll have heard all about her.' My friend said that she had heard about her, but a long time before, and she wanted to hear about her again; and the old woman went on:– 'Well, dear, the very first time ever I heard word of her coming about was when your uncle, that is, your mother's uncle, Joseph, was married, and building a house for his wife, for he brought her first to his father's, up at the house by the Lough. The foundations were marked out, and the building stones lying about, but the masons had not come yet, and one day I was standing with my mother fornent[16] the house, when we sees a smart Wee Woman coming up the field over the burn to us. I was a bit of a girl at the time, playing about and sporting myself, but I mind her as well as if I saw her there now!' My friend asked how the woman was dressed, and the old woman said:– 'It was a grey cloak she had on, with a green cashmere skirt and a black silk handkerchief tied round her head, like the countrywomen did use to wear in them times.' My friend asked:– 'How wee was she?' And the old woman said:– 'Well, now, she wasn't wee at all when I think of it, for all we called her the Wee Woman she was bigger than many a one, and yet not tall as you would say. She was like a woman about thirty, brown-haired, and round in the face. She was like Miss Betty, your grandmother's sister, and Betty was like none of the rest, not like your grandmother nor any of them. She was round and fresh in the face, and she never was married, and she never would take any man, and we used to say that the Wee Woman, her being like Betty, was maybe one of their own people that had been took off before she grew to her full height, and for that she was always following us and warning and foretelling. This time she walks straight over to where my mother was standing:– "Go over to the Lough this minute" – ordering her like that! – "go over to the Lough, and tell Joseph that he must change the foundation of this house to where I'll show you forenenst[17] the thorn bush. That is where it is to be built, if he is to have luck and prosperity, so do what I'm telling ye this minute." My mother goes over to the Lough, and brings Joseph down and shows him, and he changes the foundations, the way he was bid, but didn't bring it exactly to where was pointed, and the end of that was, when he come to the house, his own wife lost her life with an accident that come to a horse that hadn't room to turn right with a harrow between the bush and the wall. The Wee Woman was queer and angry when next she come, and says to us:– "He didn't do as I bid him, but he'll see what he'll see."' My friend asked where the woman came from this time, and if she was dressed as before, and the woman said:– 'Always the same way, up the field beyant the burn. It was a thin sort of shawl she had about her in summer, and a cloak about her in winter, and many and many a time she came, and always it was good advice she was giving to my mother, and warning her what not to do if she would have good luck. There was none of the other children of us ever seen her unless me, but I used to be glad when I seen her coming up the burn, and would run out and catch her by the hand and the cloak, and call to my mother:– "Here's the Wee Woman!" No man body ever seen her. My father used to be wanting to, and was angry with my mother and me, thinking we were telling lies and talking foolish-like. And so one day when she had come, and was sitting by the fireside talking to my mother, I slips out to the field where he was digging, and "Come up," says

I, "if ye want to see her. She's sitting at the fireside now talking to mother." So in he comes with me and looks round angry-like and sees nothing, and he up with a broom that was near hand and hits me a crig[18] with it, and "Take that now," says he, "for making a fool of me," and away with him as fast as he could, and queer and angry with me. The Wee Woman says to me then:– "Ye got that now for bringing people to see me. No man body ever seen me and none ever will." There was one day, though, she gave him a queer fright anyway, whether he seen her or not. He was in among the cattle when it happened, and he comes up to the house all trembling-like. "Don't let me hear you say another word of your Wee Woman. I have got enough of her this time." Another time all the same he was up Gortin to sell horses, and, before he went off, in steps the Wee Woman, and says she to my mother, holding out a sort of a weed:– "Your man is gone up by Gortin, and there's a bad fright waiting him coming home, but take this and sew it in his coat, and he'll get no harm by it." My mother takes the herb but thinks to herself:– "Shure there's nothing in it," and throws it on the floor, and lo and behold and sure enough! coming home from Gortin, my father got as bad a fright as ever he got in his life. What it was I don't right mind, but anyway he was badly damaged by it. My mother was in a queer way, frightened by the Wee Woman, after what she done, and sure enough the next time she was angry. "Ye didn't believe me," she said, "and ye threw the herb I gave ye in the fire, and I went far enough for it. Ye'll believe me when I tell ye this now."' She then told them of a time they were in Edinburgh and of a countrywoman that came up and talked to them. They did not remember at first, but when she told them what they had talked about, they remembered.

'There was another time she came and told how William Hearn was dead in America. "Go over," she says, "to the Lough, and say that William is dead, and he died happy, and this was the last Bible chapter ever he read," and with that she gave the verse and chapter. "Go," she says, "and tell them to read them at the next class-meeting, and that I held his head while he died." And sure enough word came after that how William had died on the day she named. And, doing as she bid about the chapter and hymn, they never had such a prayer meeting as that. One day she and me and my mother was standing talking, and she was warning her about something, when she says of a sudden:– "Here comes Miss Letty in all her finery, and it's time for me to be off." And with that she gave a swirl round on her feet, and raises up in the air, and round and round she goes, and up and up, as if it was a winding stairs she went up, only far swifter. She went up and up, till she was no bigger nor a bird up against the clouds, singing and singing the whole time the loveliest music I ever heard in my life from that day to this. It wasn't a hymn she was singing, but poetry, lovely poetry, and me and my mother stands gaping up, and all of a tremble. "What is she at all, mother?" said I. "Is it an angel she is or a fairy woman, or what?" With that up come Miss Letty, that was your grandmother, dear, but Miss Letty she was then, and no word of her being anything else, and she wondered to see us gaping up that way, till me and my mother told her of it. She went on gay dressed then, and was lovely looking. She was up the lane where none of us could see her coming forward when the Wee Woman rose up in that queer way, saying:– "Here comes Miss Letty in all her finery." Who knows to what far country she went or to see who dying?

'It was never after dark she came, but daylight always as far as I mind, but wanst, and that was on a Hallow Eve night. My mother was by the fire, making ready the supper, she had a duck down and some apples. In slips the Wee Woman. "I'm come to pass my Hallow Eve with you," says she. "That's right," says my mother, and thinks to herself:– "I can give her supper nicely." Down she sits by the fire awhile. "Now I'll tell you where you'll bring my supper," says she. "In the room beyond there beside the loom, set a chair in and a plate." "When ye're spending the night, mayn't ye as well sit by the table and ate with the rest of us?" "Do what you're bid, and set whatever you give me in the room beyant. I'll eat there and nowhere else." So my mother sets her a plate of duck and some apples, whatever was going, in where she bid, and we got to our supper and she to hers; and when we rose I went in, and there, lo and behold ye, was her supper plate a bit ate of each portion, and she clean gone!'[19]

The old woman went on to tell how her mother made the Wee Woman angry 'off and on like she did about the herb, and asking questions that way. The Wee Woman said one day:– "You're in trouble now, but it is in thicker trouble you will be, and you'll mind this warning, and believe what I tell you." And after this she quit coming.' But the old woman saw her once more, and before the 'thick trouble' came, as it did:– 'One night I was over on some errand to your uncle's people's place. Rightly I mind it was a basket of praties we were carrying, me and a girl called Rosanna McLaren, and coming over the stile by the haggard, I leaped over first, the better to help with the basket, and what do I see across the burn, over by a haystack, but the Wee Woman with all her hair hanging about her, lovely long brown hair, and she combing away at it; and I gives a screech, startled like, and Rosanna drops the basket, and all the praties spilt, but when I turned my head back, she was clean gone, while you would take time to wink, and the two of us took to our heels as hard as we could, and round the end of the house. I don't know what came over me to be scared that way at seeing her, but maybe she was angered, for from that day to this I never seen or heard tell of her, but once that she came to my mother in Belfast. She was always friendly with me, and I was always glad to see her, and I would run out to meet her; but none of the children ever seen her except myself, only my mother and me, and no man body at all at all, as I have told ye.'

'Uncle Joseph's' house had to be moved, one has no doubt, because it was 'on the path'; for there are stories everywhere of houses that had to be pulled down, because they were 'on the path' or 'in the way', or were pulled down by the whirling winds that are 'the others' journeying in their ways. There is a house in Gort, for instance, on which, people say, it is impossible to keep a roof, although the roofs keep on the houses beside it. I have no doubt either that the old woman's mother threw the herb away, because she was afraid of it, for the gifts of 'the others' are often believed to bring ill-luck in the end. The people say:– 'O, yes, it is best to be without them anyway.' If the 'Wee Woman' was, as I think she was, one of the dead, she came on Hallow Eve because it was the beginning of the old Celtic winter,[20] and the time when many old nations held a festival of the dead amid the dropping leaves and gathering cold. In Brittany a table covered with food and a warm fire are left for them even now on 'All Souls Night', which is but two days from Hallow Eve. 'The others', however, are said also to be busier, on Hallow Eve and on the first of November, than at any other time, except the first of May, the beginning of the old Celtic summer. The Wee Woman ate by herself, because 'the others', and the dead, and even the living, that are among them, may not eat while mortal eyes are looking. The people put potatoes on the doorstep for them, often night after night throughout the year, and these potatoes must not have been 'put on the table', for they would not eat them if they had been 'put before any common person'; and there is a young man near Gort who is believed to go out of our world at night, and it is said, though not correctly, that he will not let anybody see him eating. All ancient peoples set food for the dead, and believed that they could eat as we do, and about this and about the possibility of them and of 'the others' bringing and taking away solid things I have much to say, but at present I hold a clean mirror to tradition. They often go away as the Wee Woman did by going up and round and round in the air. A woman who lives by Kiltartan bog says:– 'I often saw a light in the wood at Derreen. It would rise high over the trees going round and round. I'd see it maybe for fifteen minutes at a time, and then it would fall like a lamp'; and the whirling winds that are their winds, but were called the dance of the daughters of Herodias[21] in the middle ages, show how much their way is a whirling way.

All of us are said to have a great many friends among them – relations and forebears snatched away; and they are said to come at times like the Wee Woman to warn us and protect us, and lament over us. I have been told that nobody can tell how many have been snatched away, for that two or three years ago 'eighteen or nineteen young men and young girls' were taken out of one village. The Country of 'the others', 'the Country of the Young', is in truth the heaven of the ancient peoples, and I can discover, and will show in the stories told of it, the ancient thoughts, plausible and complex thoughts, about life and death. It has been the Celt's great charge to remember it with ancient things, among forgetful peoples; and it may be his charge to speak of it and of ancient sanctities to peoples who have only new things. It was perhaps for this that the Roman went by him afar off, and that the Englishman is beating in vain upon his doors and wondering how doors of dreams can be so greatly harder than doors of iron; and that his days pass among grey stones and grey clouds and grey seas, among things too faint and seemingly frail to awaken him from the sleep, in which the ancient peoples dreamed the world and the glory of it, and were content to dream.

38

'THE PRISONERS OF THE GODS'

from the *Nineteenth Century* (1898)

None among people visiting Ireland, and few among the people living in Ireland, except peasants, understand that the peasants believe in their ancient gods, and that to them, as to their forebears, everything is inhabited and mysterious. The gods gather in the raths or forts, and about the twisted thorn trees, and appear in many shapes, now little and grotesque, now tall, fair-haired and noble, and seem busy and real in the world, like the people in the markets or at the crossroads. The peasants remember their old name, the *sheagh sidhe*,[1] though they fear mostly to call them by any name lest they be angry, unless it be by some vague words, 'the gentry', or 'the royal gentry', or 'the army', or 'the spirits', or 'the others', as the Greek peasant calls his Nereids;[2] and they believe, after twelve Christian centuries, that the most and the best of their dead are among them.

A man close by the bog of Kiltartan said to the present writer: 'I don't think the old go among them when they die, but, believe me, it's not many of the young they spare, but bring them away till such time as God sends for them'; and a woman at Spiddal, in north-western Galway, where the most talk nothing but Gaelic, said: 'There are but few in these days that die right. The priests know all about them, more than we do, but they don't like to be talking of them, because they might be too big in our minds.' Halloran[3] of Inchy, who has told me and told a friend of mine many stories, says: 'All that die are brought away among them, except an odd old person.' And a man at Spiddal says: 'Is it only the young go there? Ah, how do we know what use they may have for the old as well as for the young?' A fisher woman among the Burren Hills says: 'It's the good and the handsome they take, and those that are of use, or whose name is up for some good action. Idlers they don't like; but who would like idlers?' An old man near Gort has no fear of being taken, but says: 'What would they want with the like of me? It's the good and the pious they come for.' And an old woman living on a bog near Tuam says: 'I would hardly believe they'd take the old, but we can't know what they might want of them. And it's well to have a friend among them, and it's always said you have a right not to fret if you lose your children, for it's well to have them there before you. They don't want cross people, and they won't bring you away if you say so much as one cross word. It's only the good and the pious they want; now, isn't that very good of them?'

There are countless stories told of people who meet 'the others' and meet friends and neighbours among them. This old woman tells of 'a man living over at Caramina, Rick Moran was his name, and one night he was walking over the little green hill that's near his house, and when he got to the top of it he found it like a fair green, just like the fair of Abbey with all the people that were in it, and a great many of them were neighbours he used to know when they were alive, and they were all buying and selling just like ourselves. And they did him no harm, but they put a basket of cakes into his hand and kept him selling them all through the night. And when he got home he told the story, and the neighbours, when they heard it, gave him the name of the cakes, and to the day of his death he was called nothing but Richard Crackers.'

A Spiddal man says: 'There was a man told me he was passing the road one night, near Cruach-na-Sheogue, where they are often seen dancing in the moonlight, and the walls on each side of the road were all crowded with people sitting on them, and he walked between, and they said nothing to him. And he knew many among them that were dead before that time.' And a weatherbound boatman from Roundstone had a friend who was 'out visiting one night, and coming home across the fields he came into a great crowd of them. They did him no harm, and among them he saw a great many that he knew that were dead, five or six out of our own village. And he was in his bed for two months after that. He said he couldn't understand their talk, it was like the hissing of geese, and there was one very big man that seemed the master of them, and his talk was like a barrel when it is being rolled.' Halloran of Inchy knew a man that was walking along the road near the corner where Mr Burke and the soldier who was with him were shot in the time of the land troubles,[4] and he saw 'in the big field that's near the corner a big fire and a lot of people round about it, and among them a girl he used to know that had died'.

The old inhabitants of the forts dug caves under the forts, in which they kept their precious things, one supposes, and these caves, though shallow enough, are often believed to go miles. They are thought pathways into the country of the dead, and I doubt not that many who have gone down into them shaking with fear, have fallen into a sudden trance, and have had visions, and have thought they had walked a great way. The fisher woman among the Burren Hills tells this story, that has doubtless come of such a trance, and would be like the visions of St Patrick's Purgatory[5] if it were at all Christian:

'There's a forth away in the county Clare, and they say it's so long that it has no end. And there was a pensioner, one Rippingham, came back from the army, and a soldier has more courage than another and he said he'd go try what was in it, and he got another man to go with him, and they went a long, long way and saw nothing, and then they came to where there was the sound of a woman beetling.[6] And then they began to meet people they knew before, that had died out of the village, and they all told them to go back, but still they went on. And then they met the parish priest of Ballyvaughan, Father Ruane, that was dead, and he told them to go back, and so they turned and went. They were just beginning to come to the grandeur when they were turned away.'

The dead do not merely live among their captors as we might among a strange people, but have the customs and power which they have, and change their shapes and become birds and beasts when they will. A Mrs Sheridan said to me, 'Never shoot a hare, for you wouldn't know what might be in it. There were two women I knew, mother and daughter, and they died, and one day I was out by the wood and I saw two hares sitting by the wall, and the minute I saw them I knew well who they were. And the mother made as though she'd kill me, but the daughter stopped her. Bad they must have been to be put into that shape, and indeed I knew that they were not too good. I saw the mother another time come up near the door as if to see me, and when she got near she turned herself into a big red hare.' The witches are believed to take the shape of hares, and so the hare's is a bad shape. Another time she saw 'the old Captain standing near the road, she knew well it was him, and while she was looking at him he was changed into the shape of an ass'.

Young children are believed to be in greater danger than anybody else, and the number of those whose cries are heard in the wind shows how much 'the others' have to do with the wind. A man called Martin, who lives by Kiltartan bog, says: 'Flann told me he was by the hedge up there by Mr Gerald's farm one evening, and a blast came, and as it passed he heard something crying, crying, and he knew by the sound it was a child that they were carrying away.'

All the young are in danger, however, because of the long lives they have before them, and the desire of 'the others' to have their lives devoted to them and to their purposes. When I was staying with a friend in Galway a little time ago, an old woman came from the Burren Hills to ask for help to put a thatch on her cottage, and told us, crying and bemoaning herself, of the snatching away of her five children. One of us asked her about a certain place upon the road where a boy had fallen from his cart and been killed, and she said:

'It's a bad piece of the road. There's a forth near it, and it's in that forth my five children are that were swept from me. I went and I told Father Lally I knew they were there, and he said, "Say your prayers, my poor woman, that's all you can do." When they were young they were small and thin enough, and they grew up like a bunch of rushes, but then they got strong and stout and good-looking. Too good-looking they were, so that everybody would remark them and would say, "Oh! look at Ellen Joyce, look at Catherine, look at Martin! So good to work and so handsome and so loyal to their mother!" And they were all taken from me; all gone now but one. Consumption they were said to get, but it never was in my family or in the father's, and how would they get it without some privication? Four of them died with that, and Martin was drowned. One of the little girls was in America and the other at home, and they both got sick at the one time, and at the end of nine months the both of them died.

'Only twice they got a warning. Michael, that was the first to go, was out one morning very early to bring a letter to Mr Blake. And he met on the road a small little woman, and she came across him again and again, and then again, as if to humbug him. And he got afraid, and he told me about her when he got home. And not long after that he died.

'And Ellen used to be going to milk the cow for the nuns morning and evening, and there was a place she had to pass, a sort of an enchanted place, I forget the name of it. And when she came home one evening she said she would go there no more, for when she was passing that place she saw a small little woman with a little cloak about her, and her face not the size of a doll's face. And with the one look of her she got, she got a fright and ran as fast as she could and sat down to milk the cow. And when she was milking she looked up and there was the small little woman coming along by the wall. And she said she'd never go there again. So to move the thought out of her mind I said, "Sure that's the little woman is stopping up at Shemus Mor's house." "Oh, it's not, mother," says she. "I know well by her look she was no right person." "Then, my poor girl, you're lost," says I, for I knew it was the same woman that Michael saw. And sure enough, it was but a few weeks after that she died.

'And Martin, the last that went, was stout and strong and nothing ailed him, but he was drowned. He'd go down sometimes to bathe in the sea, and one day he said he was going, and I said, "Do not, for you have no swim." But a boy of the neighbour's came after that and called to him, and I was making the little dinner for him, and I didn't see him pass the door. And I never knew he was gone till when I went out of the house the girl from next door looked at me some way strange, and then she told me two boys were drowned, and then she told me one of them was my own. Held down, they said he was, by something underneath. They had him followed there.

'It wasn't long after he died I woke one night, and I felt some one near, and I struck the light, and there I saw his shadow. He was wearing his little cap, but under it I knew his face and the colour of his hair. And he never spoke, and he was going out the door and I called to him and said, "O Martin, come back to me, and I'll always be watching for you!" And every night after that I'd hear things thrown about the house outside, and noises. So I got afraid to stop in it, and I went to live in another house, and I told the priest I knew Martin was not dead, but that he was still living.

'And about eight weeks after Catherine dying I had what I thought was a dream. I thought I dreamt that I saw her sweeping out the floor of the room. And I said, "Catherine, why are you sweeping? Sure you know I sweep the floor clean and the hearth every night." And I said, "Tell me where are you now?" and she said, "I'm in the forth beyond." And she said, "I have a great deal of things to tell you, but I must look out and see are they watching me." Now, wasn't that very sharp for a dream? And she went to look out the door, but she never came back again.

'And in the morning, when I told it to a few respectable people they said, "Take care but it might have been no dream but herself that came back and talked to you." And I think it was, and that she came back to see me and to keep the place well swept.

'Sure we know there were some in the forth in the old times, for my aunt's husband was brought away into it, and why wouldn't they be there now? He was sent back out of it again, a girl led him back and told him he was brought away because he answered to the first call, and that he had a right only to answer to the third. But he didn't want to come home. He said he saw more people in it than he ever saw at a hurling, and that he'd ask no better place than it in high heaven.'

Mystics believe that sicknesses and the elements do the will of spiritual powers, but Mrs Joyce had not heard this, and so could only deny that her children had died of consumption or were drowned by the unaided waters. Her aunt's husband was doubtless called by a voice into the fort, and he went at the first call, instead of waiting, as the country people say all should, for the third call, which it seems cannot be called except by the living; and doubtless wandered about there in a dream and a sleep until it seemed in his dream that a girl of 'the others' led him out of the fort and he awoke.

Next to young children women after childbirth are held to be in most danger. I hear often of a year in which many were taken out of South Galway. A man about Tillyra said to me: 'It's about fourteen years since so many young women were brought away after their child being born. Peter Regan's wife of Peterswell, and James Jordan's wife of Derreen, and Loughlin's wife of Lissatunna – hundreds were carried off in that year. They didn't bring so many since then; I suppose they brought enough then to last them a good while.' And a man near Gort says: 'And it's not many years ago that such a lot of fine women were taken from Gort very sudden after childbirth – fine women. I knew them all myself.'

These women are taken, it is believed, to suckle children who have been made captive or have been born from the loves of spirits for mortals. Another man from near Gort says: 'Linsky the slater's mother was taken away, it's always said. The way it's known is, it was not long after her baby was born, but she was doing well. And one morning very early a man and his wife were going in a cart to Loughrea one Thursday for the market, and they met some of those people, and they asked the woman that had her child with her, would she give a drink to their child that was with them. And while she was doing it they said, "We won't be in want of a nurse to-night; we'll have Mrs Linsky of Gort." And when they got back in the evening, Mrs Linsky was dead before them.'

A fisherman from Aasleagh showed a correspondent, who was sailing along by the Killeries, a spot on the side of Muel Rae where there was a castle 'haunted by evil spirits' who were often heard 'making a noise like screeching and crying and howling and singing', and 'Peter's brother's wife' was there; 'she was taken in her labour. It was an evil spirit that was in her, she couldn't bring it to the birth alive. In the morning when her crying was done they went to see her. There wasn't a bit of her there.' Evil spirits had 'fetched her away, and they took the sack of potatoes to put her in, and the potatoes were running all over the road even down to the water. She's there shut up to nurse the queen's child. A fine creature she was.' The tales of fishermen are full of the evil powers of the world.

The old woman who lives on the bog near Tuam says: 'There are many young women taken by them in childbirth. I lost a sister of my own in that way. There's a place in the river at Newtown where there's stones in the middle you can get over by, and one day she was crossing, and there in the middle of the river, and she standing on a stone, she felt a blow on the face. And she looked round to see who gave it, and there was no one there, so then she knew what had happened, and she came to my mother's house, and she carrying at the time. I was but a little slip at that time, with my books in my hand coming from the school, and I ran in and said, "Here's Biddy coming," and my mother said, "What would bring her at this time of the day?" But she came in and sat down on a chair, and she opened the whole story. And my mother, seeing she got a fright, said to quiet her, "It was only a pain you got in the ear, and you thought it was a blow." "Ah," she said, "I never got a blow that hurted me like that did."

'And the next day and every day after that, the ear would swell a little in the afternoon, and then she began to eat nothing, and at the last her baby wasn't born five minutes when she died. And my mother used to watch for her for three or four years after, thinking she'd come back, but she never did.'

Many women are taken, it is believed, on their marriage day, and many before their babies are born, that they may be born among 'the others'. A woman from the shore about Duras says: 'At Aughanish there were two couples came to the shore to be married, and one of the new-married women was in the boat with the priest, and they going back to the island. And a sudden blast of wind came, and the priest said some blessed words that were able to save himself, but the girl was swept.'

This woman was drowned, doubtless. Every woman who dies about her marriage day is believed to die, I think, because a man of 'the others' wants her for himself. Next after a young child and a woman in childbirth, a young, handsome and strong man is thought in most danger. When he dies about his marriage day he is believed to die, I think, because a woman of 'the others' wants him for herself. A man living near Coole says: 'My father? Yes, indeed, he saw many things, and I'll tell you a thing he told me, and there's no doubt in the earthly world about it. It was when they lived in Inchy they came over here one time to settle a marriage for Peter Quin's aunt. And when they had the marriage settled they were going home at dead of night. And a wedding had taken place that day, of one Merrick from beyond Turloughmore, and the drag was after passing the road with him and his party going home. And in a minute the road was filled with men on horses riding along, so that my father had to take shelter in Carthy's big haggard. And the horsemen were calling on Merrick's name. And twenty-one days after he lay dead. There's no doubt at all about the truth of that, and they were no riders belonging to this world that were on those horses.'

The hurling was the game of the gods in old times, and 'the others' are held everywhere to-day to delight in good hurlers and to carry them away. A man by the sea-shore near the Connemara hills in western Galway says: 'There was a man lived about a mile beyond Spiddal, and he was one day at a play, and he was the best at the hurling and the throwing and at every game. And a woman in the crowd called out to him, "You're the strongest man that's in it." And twice after that a man that was beside him and that heard that said, saw him pass by, with his coat on, before sunrise. And on the fifth day after he was dead. He left four or five sons, and some of them went to America, and the eldest of them married and was living in the place with his wife. And he was going to Galway for a fair, and his wife was on a visit to her father and her mother on the road to Galway, and she bid him to come early, that she'd have commands for him. So it was before sunrise when he set out, and he was going up a little side road through the fields to make a short cut, and he came on the biggest fair he ever saw, and the most people in it, and they made a way for him to pass through. And a man with a big coat and a tall hat came out from them and said, "Do you know me?" And he said, "Are you my father?" And he said, "I am, and but for me you'd be sorry for coming here, but I saved you; but don't be coming out so early in the morning again." And he said, "It was a year ago that Jimmy went to America." And that was true enough. And then he said, "And it was you that drove your sister away, and gave her no peace or ease, because you wanted the place for yourself." And he said, "That is true." And he asked the father, "Were you all these years here?" And he said, "I was. But in the next week I'll be moved to the west part of Kerry, and four years after that my time will come to die." It was the son himself told me all this.'

This man was taken according to the traditional philosophy because someone praised him and did not say 'God bless him', for the admiration of a sinner may, it says, become the admiration of 'the others', who do many works through our emotions, and become as a rope to drag us out of the world.

They take the good dancers too, for they love the dance. Old Langan, a witch doctor on the borders of Clare, says: 'There was a boy was a splendid dancer. Well, one night he was going to a house where there was a dance. And when he was about half way to it, he came to another house where there was music and dancing going on. So he turned in, and there was a room all done up with curtains and with screens, and a room inside where the people were sitting, and it was only those that were dancing sets that came to the outside room. So he danced two or three sets and then he saw that it was a house they had built up where there was no house before for him to come into. So he went out, but there was a big flagstone at the door, and he stumbled on it and fell down. And in a fortnight after he was dead.'

I know a doctor who met one day among the Burren Hills the funeral of a young man he had been attending some time before. He stopped and asked the sister why he had not been sent for of late, and she said, 'Sure you could do nothing for him, doctor. It's well known what happened, him such a grand dancer, never home from a wedding or a wake till three o'clock in the morning, and living as he did beside a forth. It's *they* that have him swept.'

All the able-bodied, however, should fear the love of the gods. A man who lives by Derrykeel, on the Clare border, says of a friend and neighbour of fifty years ago: 'We were working together, myself and him, making that trench you see beyond to drain the wood. And it was contract work, and he was doing the work of two men, and was near ready to take another piece. And some of the boys began to say to him, "It's a shame for you to be working like that, and taking the bread out of the mouth of another," and I standing there. And he said he didn't care what they said, and he took the spade and sent the scraws[7] out flying to the right and to the left. And he never put a spade into the ground again, for that night he was taken ill and died shortly after. Watched he was and taken by *them*.'

Even the old and feeble should not feel altogether safe. I have been told at Coole that 'there was a man on this estate, and he sixty years, and he took to his bed and the wife went to Biddy Early, a famous wise woman of whom I have many stories, and said, "It can't be by *them* he's taken. What use would he be to them, being so old?" And Biddy Early is the one that should know, and she said, "Wouldn't he be of use to them to drive their cattle?"'

But all are not sad to go. I have heard 'there were two men went with poteen to the island of Aran. And when they were on the shore they saw a ship coming as if to land, and they said, "We'll have the bottle ready for those that are coming." But when the ship came close to land it vanished. And presently they got their boat ready and put to sea. And a sudden blast came and swept one of them off. And the other saw him come up again, and put out the oar across his breast for him to take hold of it. But he would not take it, but said, "I'm all right now," and sank down again, and was seen no more.'

There is indeed no great cause why any should fear anything except in the parting, for they expect to find there things like the things they have about them in the world, only better and more plentiful. A man at Derrykeel says: 'There was a woman walking in the road that had a young child at home, and she met a very old man having a baby in his arms. And he asked would she give it a drop of breast milk. So she did, and gave it a drink. And the old man said, "It's well for you you did that, for you saved your cow by it; but to-morrow look over the wall into the field of the rich man that lives beyond the boundary, and you'll see that one of his was taken in the place of yours." And so it happened.'

Mrs Colahan of Kiltartan says: 'There was a woman living on the road that goes to Scahanagh, and one day a carriage stopped at her door and a grand lady came out of it, and asked would she come and give the breast to her child. And she said she wouldn't leave her own children, but the lady said no harm would happen them, and brought her away to a big house, but when she got there she wouldn't stop, but went home again. And in the morning the woman's cow was dead.'

And because it is thought 'the others' and the dead may need the milk for the children that are among them, it is thought wrong to 'begrudge' the cows. An old farmer at Coole says: 'The way the bad luck came to Tommy Glyn was when his cow fell sick and lay for dead. He had a right to leave it or to kill it himself. But his father-in-law was covetous, and he cut a bit of the lug[8] off it, and it rose again, and he sold it for seven pound at the fair of Tubber. But he never had luck since then, and lost four or five bullocks, near all he owned.' To 'cut a bit of the lug off it' is, it seems, a recognised way of breaking the enchantment.

A man at Gortaveha says: 'There was a drunkard in Scariff, and one night he had drink taken he couldn't get home, and fell asleep by the roadside near the bridge. And in the night he woke and heard them at work, with cars and horses, and one said to another, "This work is too heavy; we'll take the white horse belonging to Whelan" (that was the name of a rich man in the town). So, as soon as it was light, he went to this rich man, and told him what he heard them say. But he would only laugh at him and said, "I'll pay no attention to what a drunkard dreams." But when he went out after to the stable, the white horse was dead.' A woman near Spiddal says: 'We had a mare, the grandest from this to Galway, had a foal there on that floor, and before long both mare and foal died. And I often hear them galloping round the house, both mare and foal, and I not the only one, but many in the village can hear them too.'

Roots and plants are taken too. I have heard of their pulling the nuts in the woods about Coole, and a woman who lives on the side of the road between Gort and Ardrahan says: 'There was a girl used to come with me every year to pick water grass, and one year I couldn't go and she went by herself. And when she looked up from picking it she saw a strange woman standing by her with a red petticoat about her head and a very clean white apron. And she took some of the water in her hand and threw it in the girl's face and gave her a blow and told her never to come there again. Vexed they were the water grass to be taken away; they wanted it left to themselves.'

A Galway lady tells of great noises that she and her household heard coming out of the apple room, and I asked a friend's gardener if he ever heard noises of the kind, and he said, 'For all the twelve nights I slept in the apple house I never saw anything, and I never went to bed or stripped off my clothes all the time, but I kept up a good turf fire all the night. But every night I could hear the sound of eating and of knives and forks, I don't know, was it the apples they were eating or some dinner they brought with them. And one night one of them jumped down from the granary over the bed, I could hear him scraping with his hands, and I went out and never came in again that night, and ever since that time I am a bit deaf.' Once he was in the grape house and there came a great wind and shook the house, and when it had gone by one of the bunches had been 'swept'. He has often heard that the pookas, a kind of mischievous spirits that come mostly in the shape of animals and are associated with November, take away the blackberries in the month of November, and he says: 'Anyway, we know that when the potatoes are taken it's by "the gentry", and surely this year they have put their fancy on them.'

Kirwan, the faery man of a place opposite Aran, under the Connemara hills, who learns many things from his sister who is away among them, says: 'Last year I was digging potatoes, and a boy came by, one of *them*, and one that I knew well before. And he said, "They're yours this year, and the next two years they will be ours." And you know the potatoes were good last year, and you see how bad they are this year, and how they have been made away with. And the sister told me that half the food in Ireland goes to them, but that if they like they can make out of cow dung all they want, and they can come into a house and use what they like, and it will never be missed in the morning.'

The woman on the bog near Tuam says: 'There's a very loughy[9] woman living up that boreen beyond, is married to a man of the Gillanes, and last year she told me that a strange woman came into her house and sat down, and asked her had she good potatoes, and she said she had. And the woman said, "You have them this year, but we'll have them next year." And she said, "When you go out of the house it's your enemy you'll see standing outside." And when she went away the woman went to the door to see what way did she go, but she could see her nowhere. And sure enough there was a man standing outside that was a near neighbour and was her most enemy.' A correspondent found a man on the Killeries cutting oats with a scissors, and was told that they had seen his scythe the year before, and to keep him from taking the oats they 'came in the middle of the night and trampled it all down, so he was cutting it quietly this year'.

It is, I think, a plausible inference that, just as people who are taken grow old among them, so unripe grain and fruits and plants that are taken grow ripe among them. Everything, according to this complex faith, seems to have a certain power of life it must wear out, a certain length of life it must live out, in either world, and the worlds war on one another for its possession.

A sound of fighting is often heard about dying persons, and this is thought to come of fighting between their dead friends who would prevent their being taken, and those who would take them. An old man died lately near Coole, and some of the neighbours heard fighting about his house, though one neighbour of his own age will not believe it was for him, because he was 'too cross and too old' to be taken; and last year I met a man on the big island of

Aran who heard fighting when two of his children died. I did not write his story down at the time, and so cannot give his very words. One night he heard a sound of fighting in the room. He lit the light, but everything became silent at once and he could see nothing. He put out the light and the room was full of the sound of fighting as before. In the morning he saw blood in a box he had to keep fish in, and his child was very ill. I do not remember if his child died that day, but it died soon. He heard fighting another night, and he tried to throw the quilt on the people who were fighting, but he could not find anybody. In the morning he found blood scattered about and his second child dead. A man he knew was in love with a girl who lived near and used to sleep with her at night, and he was going home that morning and saw a troop of them, and the child in the middle of them. Once, while he was telling this story, he thought I was not believing him, and he got greatly excited and stood up and said he was an old man and might die before he got to his house and he would not tell me a lie, before God he would not tell me a lie.

A man near Cahir-glissane says: 'As to fighting for those that are dying, I'd believe in that. There was a girl died not far from here, and the night of her death there was heard in the air the sound of an army marching and the drums beating, and it stopped over her house where she was lying sick. And they could see no one, but could hear the drums and the marching plain enough, and there was like little flames of lightning playing about it.'

A woman at Kiltartan says: 'There does often be fighting heard when a person is dying. John King's wife that lived in this house before I came to it, the night she died there was a noise heard, that all the village thought that every wall of every garden round about was falling down. But in the morning there was no sign of any of them being fallen.'

A woman at Spiddal says: 'There are more of them in America than what there are here, and more of other sort of spirits. There was a man came from there told me that one night in America he had brought his wife's niece that was sick back from the hospital, and had put her in an upper room. And in the evening they heard a scream from her, and she called out, "The room is full of them, and my father is with them and my aunt." And he drove them away, and used the devil's name and cursed them. And she was left quiet that night, but the next day she said, "I'll be destroyed altogether to-night with them." And he said he'd keep them out, and he locked the door of the house. And towards midnight he heard them coming to the door and trying to get in, but he kept it locked and he called to them by way of the keyhole to keep away out of that. And there was talking among them, and the girl that was upstairs said she could hear the laugh of her father and of her aunt. And they heard the greatest fighting among them that ever was, and after that they went away, and the girl got well. That's what often happens, crying and fighting for one that's sick or going to die.'

A woman at Coole says: 'There was an old woman the other day was telling me of a little girl was put to bake a cake, for her mother was sick in the room. And when she turned away her head for a minute the cake was gone. And that happened the second day and the third, and the mother was vexed when she heard it, thinking some of the neighbours had come in and taken it away. But the next day an old man appeared, and they knew he was the grandfather, and he said, "It's by me the cake was taken, for I was watching the house these three nights, where I knew there was one sick in it. And you never knew such a fight as there was for her last night, and they would have brought her away but for me that had my shoulder to the door." And the woman began to recover from that time.'

The woman on the bog near Tuam says: 'It's said to be a very good place, with coaches and all such things, but a person would sooner be in this world, for all that. And when a man or a woman is dying, the friends and the others among them will often gather about the house and will give a great challenge for him.'

And Langan, the faery man on the borders of Clare and Galway, says: 'Everyone has friends among them, and the friends would try to save when others would be trying to bring you away.'

Sometimes those they are trying to take seem to have a part in the fight, for they tell about Kiltartan of a woman who seemed dying, and suddenly she sat up and said, 'I have had a hard fight for it,' and got well after; and they understood her words to mean that she was fighting with the host of 'the others'.

Sometimes, too, the friends and neighbours and relations who are among them are thought to help, instead of hindering, the taking away. The fisherwoman from Burren says: 'There was my own uncle that lived on the road between Kinvara and Burren, where the shoemaker's shop is now, and two of his children were brought away from him. And the third he was determined he would keep, and he put it to sleep between himself and the wife in the bed. And one night a hand came in at the window and tried to take the child, and he knew who the hand belonged to, and he saw it was a woman of the village that was dead. So he drove her away and held the child, and he was never troubled again after that.'

And Kirwan the faery man says: 'One night I was in the bed with the wife beside me, and the child near me, next the fire. And I turned and saw a woman sitting by the fire, and she made a snap at the child, and I was too quick for her and got hold of it, and she was at the door and out of it before I could get hold of her.' The woman was his sister, who is among them and has taught him his unearthly knowledge.

In November, 'the others' are said to fight for the harvest, and I may find, when I know more, that this fight is between the friends of the living among the dead, and those among the dead who would carry it away. The shadow of battle was over all Celtic mythology, for the gods established themselves and the fruitfulness of the world, in battle against the Fomor, or powers of darkness and barrenness: and the children of Mill,[10] or the living, and perhaps the friends of the living, established themselves in battle against the gods and made them hide in the green hills and in the barrows of the dead, and they still wage an endless battle against the gods and against the dead.

39

'THE BROKEN GATES OF DEATH'

from the *Fortnightly Review* (1898)

The most of the Irish country people believe that only people who die of old age go straight to some distant Hell or Heaven or Purgatory. All who are young enough for any use, for begetting or mothering children, for dancing or hurling, or even for driving cattle, are taken, I have been told over and over again, by 'the others', as the country people call the fairies; and live, until they die a second time, in the green 'forts', the remnants of the houses of the old inhabitants of Ireland, or under the roots of hills, or in the woods, or in the deep of lakes. It is not wonderful, when one remembers this nearness of the dead to the living, that the country people should sometimes go on half-hoping for years, that their dead might walk in at the door, as ruddy and warm as ever, and live with them again. They keep their hopes half-living with many stories, but I think only half-living, for these stories begin mostly: 'There was an old man on the road', or 'There was one time a tailor', or in some like way; and not with the confident, 'There was a sister of Mick Morans, that is your own neighbour', or 'It happened to a young brother of my own', of the mere fairy tales. I once heard them called in the partly Elizabethan speech of Galway, 'Maybe all vanities', and have heard many sayings like this of a woman at Inchy, 'Did I know anyone that was taken by them? Well, I never knew one that was brought back again.' Such stories have the pathos of many doubts. Numbers of those said to have been brought back, were children. A fisherwoman among the Burren Hills says: 'There was an old man on the road one night near Burren, and he heard a cry in the air over his head, the cry of a child that was being carried away. And he called out some words, and the child was let down into his arms and he brought it home, and when he got there he was told that it was dead. So he brought in the live child, and you may be sure it was some sort of a thing that was good-for-nothing that was put in its place.'

And another woman among the Burren Hills says: 'There was one time a tailor, and was a wild card, always going to sprees. And one night he was passing by a house, and he heard a voice saying, "Who'll take the child." And he saw a little baby held out, and the hands that were holding it, but he could see no more than that. So he took it and he brought it to the next house, and asked the woman there to take it in for the night. Well, in the morning, the woman in the first house found a dead child in the bed beside her. And she was crying and wailing, and called all the people. And when the woman from the neighbouring house came, there in her arms was the child she thought was dead. But if it wasn't for the tailor that chanced to be passing by, and to take it, we may know well what would have happened to it.'

Sometimes a spell, like the spell of fire, even where used by accident, is thought to have brought the dead home, as in this tale, another Burren woman told a friend of mine:–

'There was a man lived beyond on the Kinvara road, and his child died and he buried it. But he was passing the place after, and he'd asked a light for his pipe in some house, and after lighting it, he threw the sod, and it glowing, over the wall where he had buried the child. And what do you think, but it came back to him again, and he brought it to its mother. For they can't bear fire.'

Most of the stories are about women who are brought back by their husbands, but almost always against their will, because their will is under enchantment.

An old man at Lisadell, in county Sligo, who told me also a number of tradition tales of the kind that are told generation after generation in the same words and in the same chanting voice, told me one tale, full of that courtesy between 'the others' and the living which endures through all the bitterness of their continuous battles.

His father had told him 'never to refuse a night's lodging to any poor travelling person', and one night 'a travelling woman' or beggar woman, told him that in her place, a woman died, and was taken by 'the gentry', and her husband often saw her after she was dead, and was afraid to speak to her. He told his brother, and his brother said he would come and speak to her, and he came, and at night lay on a settle at the foot of the bed. When she came in, he laid hold of her and would not let her go, although she begged him to let her go because 'she was nursing the child of the King'. Twelve messengers came in one after the other, and begged him to let her go, but he would not; and at last the King came himself, and said that she had been always well treated, and let come and nurse her own child, and that if she might stay until his child was weaned, he would send her home again, and leave, where they could find it, money to pay a debt of some forty pounds that 'was over' her husband.[1] The man said, 'Do you promise this on your honour as a King?' and the King said, 'I do,' and so the man let her go, and all happened as the King had promised.

They are brought back more violently in most of the stories, as in this story told to a friend of mine by a man at Coole: 'And I'll tell you a thing I heard of in the country. There was a woman died and left her child. And every night at twelve o'clock she'd come back, and bring it out of the bed to the fire, and she'd comb it and wash it. And at last six men came and watched and stopped her at the door, and she went very near to tear them all asunder. But they got the priest, and he took it off her. Well, the husband had got another wife, and the priest came and asked him, "Would he put her away and take the first wife again?" And so he did, and brought her to the chapel to be married to her again, and the whole congregation saw her there.' When my friend asked if that was not rather hard on the second wife, he said: 'Well, but wasn't it a great thing for the first poor creature to be brought back. Sure there's many of those poor souls wandering about.'

Those who are brought back are sometimes thought to bring with them unholy knowledge. A woman at Kiltartan says: 'There's a man in Kildare that lost his wife. And it was known that she would come back at twelve o'clock every night to look at her baby. And it was told the husband that if he had twelve men with him with forks, when she came in, they would be able to keep her from going out again. So the next night he was there and all his friends with forks, and when she came in they shut the door, and when she saw she could not get out, she sat down and was quiet. And one night as she sat by the hearth with them all, she said to her husband: "It's a strange thing that Leuchar would be sitting there so quiet with the bottom after bein' knocked out of his churn." And her husband went to Leuchar's house, and he found it was true as she had said. But after that he left her, and would not go back to her any more.'

Sometimes the women themselves tell how they are to be brought back, but they have sometimes to be seized and held before they will speak, as though a human touch broke the enchantment, as in this story told by a woman at Gort. 'There was a woman beyond at Rua died, and she came back one night, and her husband saw her at the dresser looking for something to eat. And she slipped away from him that time, but the next time she came he got hold of her, and she bid him come for her to the fair at Eserkelly, and watch for her at the Custom Gap, and she'd be on the last horse that would pass through. And then she said: "It's best for you not to come yourself, but send your brother." So the brother came, and she dropped down to him, and he brought her to the house. But in a week after he was dead and buried. And she lived a long time; and she never would speak three words to anyone that would come into the house, but working, working all the day. I wouldn't have liked to live in the house with her after her being away like that.'

I heard a story from a man at Doneraile, in county Cork, of a woman who bade a man go and look for her in a certain fort, and told him to hold her, even though she would struggle to escape, and scream out, either because the enchantment would have returned again, or because she would not have 'the others' think her willing to leave them. I have only heard one story of a woman who came back of her own will, and without the help of anybody. A woman at Kiltartan says: 'Mick Foley was here the other day telling us newses, and he told the strangest thing ever I heard that happened to his own first cousin. She died and was buried, and a year after, her husband was sitting by the fire, and she came back and walked in. He gave a start, for she said, "Have no fear of me,

I was never in the coffin and never buried, but I was kept away for the year." So he took her again, and they reared four children after that. She was Mick Foley's own first cousin, and he saw the four children himself.'

The dead body was but an appearance made by the enchantment of 'the others', according to the country faith.

If the country people sometimes doubt that those they have seen die can come and live with them as before, they never doubt that those they have seen die constantly visit them for a little while. A woman at Kiltartan says: 'It's well known that a mother that's taken from her child will come back to it at night, and that's why a light is kept burning all night for a good while after a woman dying that has left young children in the house.' And I have even been told that a mother always comes to her children; and because of the greater power of the dead, a dead mother is sometimes thought better than a living one.

Another woman at Kiltartan says: 'Did the mother come to care them? Sure an' certain she did, an' I'm the one that can tell that. For I slept in the room with my sister's child after she dyin' – and as sure as I stand here talkin' to you, she was back in the room that night. An' a friend o' mine told me the same thing. His wife was taken away in childbirth, an' the five children she left that did be always ailin' an' sickly, from that day there never was a ha'porth ailed them.'

And another woman at Kiltartan says: 'My own sister was taken away, she an' her husband within twenty-four hours, an' not a thing upon them, an' she with a baby a week old. Well, the care of that child fell upon me, an' sick or sorry it never was, but thrivin' always.'

Sometimes nothing but a chance is believed to prevent the dead being kept in the world for good. A woman at Sligo knew a Mayo man who was told to wait for his wife in a certain yard at night, and that she would come riding on a white horse, and would stay with him if he would snatch her from her horse, but the owner of the yard laughed at him and would not give him the key; while the terror of the husband did the mischief in a story told by an old man at Gortavena. 'There was a man and he a cousin of my own, lost his wife. And one night he heard her come into the room where he was in the bed with the child beside him. And he let on to be asleep, and she took the child and brought her out to the kitchen fire, and sat down beside it, and suckled it. And she put it back then into the bed again, and he lay still and said nothing. The second night she came again, and he had more courage and he said, "Why are you without your boots?" for he saw that her feet were bare. And she said, "Because there's nails in them." So he said, "Give them to me," and he got up and drew all the nails out of them, and she brought them away. The third night she came again, and when she was suckling the child, he saw she was still barefoot, and he asked why didn't she wear the boots? "Because," said she, "you left one sprig in them, between the upper and the lower sole. But if you have courage," says she, "you can do more than that for me. Come to-morrow night to the gap up there beyond the hill, and you'll see the riders going through, and I'll be the one you'll see on the last horse. And bring with you some fowl droppings and urine, and throw them at me as I pass, and you'll get me again." Well, he got so far as to go to the gap, and to bring what she told him, but when they came riding through the gap he saw her on the last horse, but his courage failed him, and he let what he had in his hand drop, and he never got the chance to see her again. Why she wanted the nails out of the boots? Because it's well known they will have nothing to do with iron. And I remember when every child would have an old horse-nail hung round its neck with a bit of string, but I don't see it done now.'

The mother comes sometimes out of hate of the second wife or the second wife's children. A man near Gort says: 'There was a little girl I knew, not five years of age, and whenever the second wife would bid her rock the cradle or do anything for her children, she'd just get as far as the bed, and lie down asleep. It was the mother put that on her, she wouldn't have her attending to the children of the second wife.'

A woman at Kiltartan says: 'There was a man had buried his wife, and she left three children; and when he took a second wife she did away with the children, hurried them off to America and the like. But the first wife used to be seen up in the loft, and she making a plan of revenge against the other wife. The second one had one son and three daughters. And one day the son was out digging in the field, and presently he went into what is called a fairy hole. And there a woman came before him, and, says she, "What are you doing here, trespassing on my ground?" And with that she took a stone and hit him in the head, and he died with the blow of the stone she gave him. And all the people said, it was by the fairies he was taken.'

And a woman at Inchy says: 'There was a woman in Ballyderreen died after her baby being born. And the husband took another wife, and she was very young, that everybody wondered she'd like to go into the house. And every night the first wife came in the loft, and looked down at her baby, and they couldn't see her, but they knew she was there by the child looking up and smiling at her. So at last someone said that if they'd go up in the loft after the cock crowing three times, they'd see her. And so they did, and there she was, with her own dress on, a plaid shawl she had brought from America, and a cotton skirt with some edging at the bottom. So they went to the priest, and he said mass in the house, and they didn't see so much of her after that. But after a year the new wife had a baby, and one day she bid the first child to rock the cradle. But when she sat down to do it, a sort of a sickness came over her, and she could do nothing, and the same thing always happened, for her mother didn't like to see her caring the second wife's baby. And one day the wife herself fell in the fire and got a great many burns, and they said that it was she did it. So they went to the blessed well of Tubber Macduagh; and they were told to go there every Friday for twelve weeks, and they said seven prayers and gathered seven stones every time. And since then she doesn't come to the house, but the little girl goes out and meets her mother at a fairy bush. And sometimes she speaks to her there, and sometimes in her dreams. But no one else but her own little girl has seen her of late.'

People indeed come back for all kinds of purposes. I was told at Sligo about four years ago of a man who was being constantly beaten by a dead person. Sometimes it was said you could hear the blows as he came along the road, and sometimes he would be dragged out of bed at night and his wife would hear the blows, but you could never see anything. He had thought to escape the dead person by going to a distant place, Bundoran I think, but he had been followed there. Nobody seemed to give him any pity, for it was 'an old uncle of his own that was beating him'.

Sometimes people come back out of mere friendliness, though the sight of them is often an unwholesome sight to the living. A man on the coast opposite Aran, in Western Galway, told a friend and me this tale as we were coming from a witch-doctor's. 'There was a boy going to America, and when he was going, he said to the girl next door, "Wherever I am when you're married, I'll come back to the wedding." And not long after he went to America he died. And when the girl was married and all the friends and neighbours in the house, he appeared in the room, but no one saw him but his comrade he used to have here; and the girl's brother saw him too, but no one else. And the comrade followed him and went close to him, and said, "Is it you indeed?" And he said, "It is, and from America I came to-night." And he asked how long did that journey take, and he said "three-quarters of an hour", and then he went away. And the comrade was never the better of it; either he got the touch, or the other called him, being such friends as they were, and soon he died. But the girl is now middle-aged, and is living in that house we're just after passing, and is married to one Bruen.'

Many and many are believed to come back to pay some debt, for, as a woman at Gort says: 'When some one goes that owes money, the weight of the soul is more than the weight of the body, and can't get away till someone has courage to question it.'

A man who lives close to the witch-doctor says: 'There was a man had come back from Boston, and one day he was out in the bay, going to Aran with £3 worth of cable he was after getting at McDonough's store, in Galway. And he was steering the boat, and there were two turf boats along with him, and all in a minute the men in them saw he was gone, swept off the boat with a wave, and it a dead calm. And they saw him come up once, straight up as if he was pushed, and then he was brought down again and rose no more. And it was some time after that a friend of his in Boston, and that was coming home to this place, was in a crowd of people out there. And he saw him coming to him, and he said, "I heard you were drowned." And the man said, "I am not dead, but I was brought here, and when you go home bring these three guineas in Michael McDonough, in Galway, for it's owed him for the cable I got from him." And he put the three guineas in his hand and vanished away.'

Only those the living retake in their continuous battle against 'the others', and those 'the others' permit to return for an hour, are thought to come in their own shape; but all the captives of 'the others', according to some tellers of tales, return in a strange shape at the end of their unearthly lives. I have been told about Gort that nobody is permitted to die among 'the others', but everybody, when the moment of their death is coming, is changed into the shape of some young person, who is taken in their stead, and put into the world to die, and to receive the sacraments.

A woman at Kiltartan says: 'When a person is taken, the body is taken as well as the spirit, and some good-for-nothing thing left in its place. What they take them for is to work for them and to do things they can't do themselves. You might notice it's always the good they take. That's why when we see a child that's good-for-nothing we say "Ah, you little fairy."'

A woman near Gort says: 'There was a woman with her husband passing by Eserkelly, and she had left her child at home. And a man came and called her in, and promised to leave her on the road where she was before. So she went, and there was a baby in the place where she was brought to, and they asked her to suckle it. And when she was come out again, she said, "One question I'll ask, what were those two old women sitting by the fire?" And the man said, "We took the child to-day and we'll have the mother to-night, and one of those will be out in her place, and the other in the place of some other person, and then he left her where she was before. But there's no harm in them, no harm at all."'

She said 'there's no harm in them' because they might be listening to her.

Death among 'the others' seems not less grievous than among us, for another woman near Gort says: 'There was a woman going to Loughrea with a bundle of flannel on her head, was brought into the castle outside Roxborough gate to give the breast to a child, and she saw an old woman beside the fire, and an old man behind the door, who had eyes red with crying. They were going to be put in the place of people who were to be taken that night. "The others" gave her a bottle, and when she'd put a drop of what was in it on her eyes, she'd see them hurling, or whatever they were doing. But they didn't like her to be seeing so much, and after a little time the sight of one of her eyes was taken away from her.'

A man who lives near Gort was coming home from a fair. 'And there were two men with him, and when three persons are together, there's no fear of anything, and they can say what they like.' One of the men pointed out a place they were passing: 'And it was a fairy place, and many strange things had happened there,' and the other 'told him how there was a woman lived close by had a baby. And before it was a week old her husband had to leave her because of his brother having died. And no sooner was she left alone than she was taken, and they sent for the priest to say mass in the house, but she was calling out every sort of thing they couldn't understand, and within a few days she was dead. And after death the body began to change, and first it looked like an old woman and then like an old man, and they had to bury it the next day. And before a week was over, she began to appear. They always appear when they leave a child like that. And surely she was taken to nurse the fairy children, just like poor Mrs Gleeson was last year.'

And a woman from Kiltartan says: 'My sister told me that near Cloughballymore, there was a man walking home one night late, and he had to pass by a smiths' forge, where one Kenealy used to work. And when he came near he heard the noise of the anvil and he wondered Kenealy would be working so late in the night. But when he went in he saw they were strange men that were in it. So he asked them the time and they told him, and he said, "I won't be home this long time yet." And one of the men said, "You'll be home sooner than what you think," and another said, "There's a man on a grey horse gone the road, you'll get a lift from him." And he wondered that they'd know the road he was going to his own house. But sure enough, as he was walking, he came up with a man on a grey horse and he gave him a lift. But when he got home his wife saw he looked strange-like, and she asked what ailed him, and he told her all that had happened. And when she looked at him, she saw that he was taken. So he went into the bed, and the next evening he was dead. And all the people that came in knew by the appearance of the body that it was an old man that had been put in his place, and that he was taken when he got on the grey horse. For there's something not right about a grey or a white horse, or about a red-haired woman. And as to forges, there's some can hear working and hammering in them all the night.'

Forges and smiths have always been magical in Ireland. St Patrick prayed against the spells of women and smiths, and the old romances are loud with the doings of Goibnui, the god of the smiths, who is remembered in folk-tale as the Mason Goban, for he works in stone as in metal.[2]

Another woman from Kiltartan says: 'Near Tyrone there was a girl went out one day to get nuts near the wood. And she heard music inside the wood, and when she went home she told her mother. But the next day she went again, and the next, and she stopped so long away that her mother sent the other little girl to look for her, but she could see no one. She came in after a while, and she went inside in to the room, but, when the girl came out, she said she heard nothing. But the next day after that she died. The neighbours all came in to the wake, and there was tobacco and snuff there, but not much, for it's the custom not to have so much when a young person dies. But when they looked at the bed, it was no young person in it, but an old woman with long teeth, that you'd be frightened, and the face wrinkled and the hands. So they didn't stop, but went away, and she was buried the next day. And in the night the mother could hear music all about the house, and lights of all colours flashing about the windows. She was never seen again, except by a boy that was working about the place; he met her one evening at the end of the house, dressed in her own clothes. But he couldn't question her where she was, for it's only when you meet them by a bush you can question them there. I'll gather more stories for you, and I'll tell them some time when the old woman isn't in the house, for she's that bigoted, she'd think she'd be carried off there and then.'

Tyrone is a little headland in the south of Galway Bay.

Sometimes the 'old person' lives a good time in the likeness of the person who has been taken, as in this tale, told by a woman at Ardrahan: 'My mother told me that when she was a young girl, and before the time of side-cars, a man that lived in Duras married a girl from Ardrahan side. And it was the custom then, for a newly-married girl to ride home on a horse behind her next of kin. And she was on the pillion behind her uncle. And when they passed Ardrahan churchyard, he felt her to shiver and nearly to slip off the horse. And he put his hand behind for to support her, and all he could feel was like a piece of tow. And he asked her what ailed her, and she said she thought of her mother when she was passing the churchyard. And a year after her baby was born, and then she died. And everyone said, the night she was taken was her wedding night.'

An old woman in the Burren Hills says: 'Surely there are many taken. My own sister that lived in the house beyond, and her husband and her three children, all in one year. Strong they were, and handsome and good and best, and that's the sort that are taken. They got in the priest when first it came on the husband, and soon after a fine cow died, and a calf. But he didn't begrudge that if he'd get his health, but it didn't save him after. Sure Father Leraghty said, not long ago in the chapel, that no one had gone to heaven for the last ten years.

'But whatever life God has granted them, when it's at an end, go they must, whether they're among them or not. And they'd sooner be among them than go to Purgatory.

'There was a little one of my own taken. Till he was a year old, he was the stoutest and the best, and the finest of all my children, and then he began to pine, till he wasn't thicker than a straw, but he lived for about four years. How did it come on him? I know that well. He was the grandest ever you saw, and I proud of him, and I brought him to a ball in this house, and he was able to drink punch. And soon after I stopped one day at a house beyond, and a neighbouring woman came in with her child, and she says: "If he's not the stoutest, he's the longest." And she took off her apron and the string of it to measure them both. I had no right to let her do that, but I thought no harm of it at the time. But it was that night he began to screech, and from that time he did no good. He'd get stronger through the winter, but about the Pentecost, in the month of May, he'd always fall back again, for at that time they're at the worst. I didn't have the priest in, it does them no good but harm, to have a priest take notice of them when they're like that. It was in the month of May, at the Pentecost, he went at last. He was always pining, but I didn't think he'd go so soon. At the end of the bed he was lying with the other children, and he called to me and put up his arms. But I didn't want to take too much notice of him, or to have him always after me, so I only put down my foot to where he was. And he began to pick straws out of the bed, and to throw them over the little sister that was beside him till he had thrown as much as would thatch a goose. And when I got up, there he was, dead, and the little sister asleep, and all covered with straws.'

She believed him to fall under the power of 'the others', because of the envy of the woman who measured him, for 'the others' can only take their prey through 'the eye of a sinner'. She dwelt upon his getting worse, and at last dying, in May, because 'the others' are believed to come and go a great deal in May.

Sometimes 'the old person' is recognised by the living, as in this tale told by another woman in the Burren Hills: 'There were three women living at Ballindeereen: Mary Flaherty, the mother, and Mary Grady, the daughter, and Ellen Grady, that was a by-child[3] of hers. And they had a little dog, called Floss, that was like a child to them. And the grandmother went first, and then the little dog, and then Mary Grady, within a half-year. And there was a boy wanted to marry Ellen Grady that was left alone. But his father and mother wouldn't have her, because of her being a by-child. And the priest wouldn't marry them not to give the father and mother offence. So it wasn't long before she was taken too, and those that saw her after death knew it was the mother that was there in place of her. And when the priest was called the day before she died, he said, "She's gone since twelve o'clock this morning, and she'll die between the two masses to-morrow." For he was Father Hynes that had understanding of these things. And so she did.'

Sometimes 'the old person' is said to melt away before burial. A woman near Cork says:– 'There were two brothers, Mullallys, in Ballineen. And when one got home one night and got into the bed, he found the brother cold and dead before him. And not a ha'porth on him when he went out. Taken by them he surely was. And when he was being buried in Kiltartan, the brother looked into the coffin, finding it so light, and there was nothing in it but the clothes that were around him. Sure if he'd been a year in the grave he couldn't have melted away like that.'

A woman from Kiltartan says:– 'There was a girl buried in Kiltartan, one of the Joyces, and when she was laid out on the bed, a woman that went in to look at her saw that she opened her eyes, and made a sort of a face at her. But she said nothing but sat down by the hearth. But another woman came in after that and the same thing happened, and she told the mother, and she began to cry and roar that they'd say such a thing of her poor little girl. But it wasn't the little girl that was in it at all, but some old person. And the man that nailed down the coffin left the nails loose, and when they came to Kiltartan churchyard he looked in, and not one they saw inside but the sheet and a bundle of shavings.'

'The others' sometimes it seems take this shape; a woman in the Burren Hills tells of their passing her in the shape of shavings driven by the wind. She knew they were not really shavings, because there was no place for shavings to come from.

Even when cattle are taken, something or someone is put in their place. A man at Doneraile told me a story of a man who had a bullock that got sick, and that it might be of some use, he killed it and skinned it, and when it was in a trough being washed it got up and ran away. He ran after it and knocked it down and cut it up, and after he and his family had eaten it, a woman, that was passing by, said: 'You don't know what you have eaten. It is your own grandmother that you have eaten.'

A man in the Burren Hills says: 'When anyone is taken something is put in his place, even when a cow or the like goes. There was one of the Nestors used to be going about the country skinning cattle, and killing them, even for the country people if they were sick. One day he was skinning a cow that was after dying by the roadside, and another man with him. And Nestor said, "It's a pity we couldn't sell the meat to some butcher, we might get something for it." But the other man made a ring of his fingers, like this, and looked through it, and then bade Nestor to look, and what he saw was an old piper that had died some time before, and when he thought he was skinning the cow, what he was doing was cutting the leather breeches off the piper. So it's very dangerous to eat beef you buy from any of those sort of common butchers. You don't know what might have been put in its place.'

And sometimes cattle are put in the place of men and women, and Mrs Sheridan, a handsome old woman who believes herself to have been among 'the others', and to have suckled their children, tells many stories of the kind; she says: 'There was a woman, Mrs Keevan, killed near the big tree at Raheen, and her husband was after that with Biddy Early,[4] and she said it was not the woman that died at all, but a cow that died and was put in her place.'

Biddy Early was a famous wise woman, and the big tree at Raheen is a great elm tree where many mischiefs and some good fortunes have happened to many people. Few know as much as Mrs Sheridan about 'the others', and if she were minded to tell her knowledge and use the cure they have given her for all the mischiefs they work, she would be a famous wise woman herself, and be sought out, perhaps, by pilgrims from neighbouring counties. She is, however, silent, and it was only when we had won her confidence, that she came of her self, with some fear of the anger of 'the others', and told a friend and myself certain of the marvels she had seen. She had hitherto but told us tales that other people had told her, but now she began:

'One time when I was living at Cloughauish, there were two

little boys drowned in the river there. One was eight years and the other eleven years. And I was out in the fields and the people looking in the river for their bodies, and I saw a man coming over the fields and the two little boys with him, he holding a hand of each and leading them away. And he saw me stop and look at them, and he said: "Take care, would you bring them from me (for he knew I had power to do it), for you have only one in your house, and if you take these from me, she'll never go home to you again." And one of the boys broke from his hand and came running to me, but the other cried out to him, "O Pat, will you leave me!" So then he went back, and the man led them away. And then I saw another man, very tall he was, and crooked, and watching me like this, with head down; and he was leading two dogs, and I knew well where he was going and what he was going to do with the dogs. And when I heard the bodies were laid out, I went to the house to have a look at them, and those were never the two boys that were lying there, but the two dogs that were put in their place. I knew them by a sort of stripes on the bodies, such as you'd see on the covering of a mattress. And I knew the boys couldn't be in it, after me seeing them led. And it was at that time I lost my eye, something came on it, and I never got the sight of it again.'

'The others' are often described as having striped clothes like the striped hair of the dogs.

The stories of the country people, about men and women taken by 'the others', throw a clear light on many things in the old Celtic poems and romances, and when more stories have been collected and compared, we shall probably alter certain of our theories about the Celtic mythology. The old Celtic poets and romance writers had beautiful symbols and comparisons that have passed away, but they wrote of the same things that the country men and country women talk of about the fire, – the country man or country woman who falls into a swoon, and sees in a swoon a wiser and stronger people than the people of the world, but goes with less of beautiful circumstance upon the same journey Etain went when she passed with Midir into the enchanted hills; and Oisin when he rode with Niamh on her white horse over the sea;

and Conla when he sailed with a divine woman in a ship of glass to 'the ever-living, living ones'; and Cuchulain when he sailed in a ship of bronze to a divine woman; and Bran, the son of Feval, when a spirit came through the closed door of his house holding an apple-bough of silver, and called him to 'the white-silver plain'; and Cormac, the son of Art, when his house faded into mist, and a great plain, and a great house, and a tall man, and a crowned woman, and many marvels came in its stead. And when the country men and country women tell of people taken by 'the others', who come into the world again, they tell the same tales the old Celtic poets and romance writers told when they made the companions of Fionn compel, with threats, the goddess Miluchra to deliver Fionn out of the Grey Lake on the Mountain of Fuad; and when they made Cormac, the son of Art, get his wife and children again from Mananan, the son of Lir; and, perhaps, when they made Oisin sit with Patrick and his clergy and tell of his life among the gods, and of the goddess he had loved.[5]

40

'THE CELTIC ELEMENT IN LITERATURE'

from *Cosmopolis* (1898)

I

Ernest Renan[1] described what he held to be Celtic characteristics in *The Poetry of the Celtic Races*. 'No race communed so intimately as the Celtic race with the lower creation, or believed it to have so big a share of moral life.' The Celtic race had 'a realistic naturalism', 'a love of nature for herself, a vivid feeling for her magic, commingled with the melancholy a man knows when he is face to face with her, and thinks he hears her communing with him about his origin and his destiny'. 'It has worn itself out in mistaking dreams for realities', and 'compared with the classical imagination the Celtic imagination is indeed the infinite contrasted with the finite'. 'Its history is one long lament, it still recalls its exiles, its flights across the seas.' 'If at times it seems to be cheerful, its tear is not slow to glisten behind the smile. Its songs of joy end as elegies; there is nothing to equal the delightful sadness of its national melodies.' Matthew Arnold,[2] in *The Study of Celtic Literature*, has accepted this passion for nature, this imaginativeness, this melancholy, as Celtic characteristics, but has described them more elaborately. The Celtic passion for nature comes almost more from a sense of her 'mystery' than of her 'beauty', and it adds 'charm and magic' to nature, and the Celtic imaginativeness and melancholy are alike 'a passionate, turbulent, indomitable reaction against the despotism of fact'. The Celt is not melancholy, as Faust or Werther[3] are melancholy, from 'a perfectly definitive motive', but because of something about him 'unaccountable, defiant and titanic'. How well one knows these sentences, and how well one knows the passages of prose and verse which he uses to prove that wherever English literature has the qualities these sentences describe, it has them from a Celtic source. Though I do not think any of us who write about Celtic things have built any argument upon them, it is well to consider them a little, and see where they are helpful and where they are hurtful. If we do not, we may go mad some day, and the enemy of Celtic things root up our rose garden and plant a cabbage garden instead.

I am going to make a claim for the Celt, but I am not going to make quite the same claim that Ernest Renan and Matthew Arnold made. Matthew Arnold, and still more Ernest Renan, wrote before the activity in the study of folk-lore and of folk literature of our own day had begun to give us so many new ideas about old things. When we talk to-day about the delight in nature, about the imaginativeness, about the melancholy of the Celt, we cannot help thinking of the delight in nature, of the imaginativeness, of the melancholy of the makers of the Icelandic *Eddas*, and of the *Kalavala*,[4] and of many other folk literatures, and we soon grow persuaded that much that Matthew Arnold and Ernest Renan thought wholly or almost wholly Celtic is of the substance of the minds of the ancient farmers and herdsmen. One comes to think of the Celt as an ancient farmer or herdsman, who sits bowed with the dreams of his unnumbered years, in the gates of the rich races, talking of forgotten things. Is the Celt's feeling for nature, and for the 'lower creation', one of those forgotten things? Because we have come to associate the ancient beliefs about nature with 'savage customs' and with books written by men of science, we have almost forgotten that they are still worth dreaming about and talking about. It is only when we describe them in some language, which is not the language of science, that we discover they are beautiful.

II

Once every people in the world believed that trees were divine, and could take a human or grotesque shape and dance among the shadows of the woods; and deer, and ravens and foxes, and wolves and bears, and clouds and pools, almost all things under the sun and moon, and the sun and moon, not less divine and changeable: they saw in the rainbow the still bent bow of a god thrown down in his negligence; they heard in the thunder the sound of his beaten water-jar, or the tumult of his chariot wheels; and when a sudden flight of wild duck, or of crows, passed over their heads, they thought they were gazing at the dead hastening to their rest; while they dreamed of so great a mystery in little things that they believed the waving of a hand, or of a sacred bough, enough to trouble far-off hearts, or hood the moon with darkness. All old literatures are full of this way of looking at things, and all the poets of races, who have not lost this way of looking at things, could have said of themselves, as the poet of the *Kalavala* said of himself, 'I have learned my songs from the music of many birds, and from the music of many waters.' When a mother in the *Kalavala* weeps for a daughter, who was drowned flying from an old suitor, she weeps so greatly that her tears become three rivers, and cast up three rocks, on which grow three birch trees, where three cuckoos sit and sing, the one 'love, love', the one 'suitor, suitor', the one 'consolation, consolation'. And the makers of the sagas made the squirrel run up and down the sacred ash tree carrying words of hatred from the eagle to the worm, and from the worm to the eagle; although they had less of the old way than the makers of the *Kalavala*, for they lived in a more crowded and complicated world, and were learning the abstract meditation which lures men from visible beauty, and were unlearning, it may be, the impassioned meditation which brings men beyond the edge of trance and makes trees, and beasts, and dead things talk with human voices.

The Celts, though they had less of the old way than the makers of the *Kalavala*, had more of it than the makers of the sagas, and it is this that distinguishes the examples Matthew Arnold quotes of the Celts' 'natural magic', of their sense of 'the mystery' more than of 'the beauty' of nature. When Matthew Arnold thought he was criticising the Celts, he was really criticising the ancient religion of the world, the ancient worship of nature and the troubled ecstasy before her, the belief that all beautiful places are haunted, which it brought into men's minds. The ancient religion is in that marvellous passage from the *Mabinogion*[5] about the making of 'Flower Aspect'. Gwydion and Math made her 'by charms and illusions' 'out of flowers'. 'They took the blossoms of the oak, and the blossoms of the broom, and the blossoms of the meadow-sweet, and produced from them a maiden the fairest and most graceful that man ever saw; and they baptized her, and called her Flower Aspect'; and one finds it in the not less beautiful passage about the burning Tree, that has half its beauty from calling up a fancy of leaves so living and beautiful, they can be of no less living and beautiful a thing than flame: 'They saw a tall tree by the side of the river, one half of which was in flames from the root to the top, and the other half was green and in full leaf.' And one finds it very certainly in the quotations he makes from English poets to prove a Celtic influence in English poetry; in Keats's 'magic casements, opening on the foam of perilous seas in faerylands forlorn'; in his 'moving waters at their priest-like task of pure oblations round earth's human shore';[6] in Shakespeare's 'floor of heaven', 'inlaid with patens of bright gold'; and in his Dido standing 'on the wild sea banks', 'a willow in her hand', and waving it in the ritual of the old worship of nature and the spirits of nature, to wave 'her love to come again to Carthage'.[7] And his other examples have the delight and wonder of devout worshippers among the haunts of their divinities. Is there not such delight and wonder in the description of Olwen in the *Mabinogion*: 'More yellow was her hair than the flower of the broom, and her skin was whiter than the foam of the wave, and fairer were her hands and her fingers than the blossoms of the wood-anemony amidst the spray of the meadow fountains.' And is there not such delight and wonder in –

> Meet we on hill, in dale, forest or mead,
> By paved fountain or by rushy brook,
> Or on the beached margent of the sea?[8]

If men had never dreamed that maidens could be made out of flowers, or rise up out of meadow fountains and paved fountains, neither passage could have been written. Certainly, the descriptions of nature made in what Matthew Arnold calls 'the faithful way', or in what he calls 'the Greek way', would have lost nothing if all the meadow fountains or paved fountains were nothing but meadow fountains and paved fountains.[9] When Keats wrote, in the Greek way, which adds lightness and brightness to nature:

What little town by river or sea-shore
Or mountain built with quiet citadel,
Is emptied of its folk, this pious morn;[10]

When Shakespeare wrote in the Greek way:

I know a bank whereon the wild thyme blows,
Where oxlips and the nodding violet grows;[11]

When Virgil wrote in the Greek way:

Muscosi fontes et somno mollior herba,

and

Pallentes violas et summa papavera carpens
Narcissum et florem jungit bene olentis anethi;[12]

they looked at nature without ecstasy, but with the affection a man feels for the garden where he has walked daily and thought pleasant thoughts. They looked at nature in the modern way, the way of people who are poetical, but are more interested in one another than in a nature which has faded to be but friendly and pleasant.

III

Men who lived in a world where anything might flow and change, and become any other thing; and among great gods whose passions were in the flaming sunset, and in the thunder and the thunder-shower, had not our thoughts of weight and measure. They worshipped nature and the abundance of nature, and had always, as it seems, for a supreme ritual that tumultuous dance among the hills or in the depths of the woods, where unearthly ecstasy fell upon the dancers, until they seemed the gods or the god-like beasts, and felt their souls overtopping the moon; and, as some think, imagined for the first time in the world the blessed country of the gods and of the happy dead. They had imaginative passions because they did not live within our own straight limits, and were nearer to ancient chaos, every man's desire, and had immortal models about them. The hare that ran by among the dew might have sat upon his haunches when the first man was made, and the poor bunch of rushes under their feet might have been a goddess laughing among the stars; and with but a little magic, a little waving of the hands, a little murmuring of the lips, they too could become a hare or a bunch of rushes, and know immortal love and immortal hatred.

All folk literature, and all literature that keeps the folk tradition, delights in unbounded and immortal things. The *Kalavala* delights in the seven hundred years that Luonaton wanders in the depths of the sea with Wäinämöinen in her womb, and the Mahomedan king in the *Song of Roland*,[13] pondering upon the greatness of Charlemaine, repeats over and over, 'He is three hundred years old, when will he weary of war?' Cuchulain in the Irish folk tale had the passion of victory, and he overcame all men, and died warring upon the waves, because they alone had the strength to overcome him; and Caolte, in his sorrow for his companions, dead upon the plain of Gabra, stormed the house of the Gods at Asseroe, and drove them out and lives there in their stead. The lover in the Irish folk song bids his beloved come with him into the woods, and see the salmon leap in the rivers, and hear the cuckoo sing, because death will never find them in the heart of the woods.[14] Oisin, new come from his three hundred years of faeryland, and of the love that is in faeryland, bids St Patrick cease his prayers a while and listen to the blackbird, because it is the blackbird of Darrycarn that Fionn brought from Norway, three hundred years before, and set its nest upon the oak tree with his own hands.[15] Surely if one goes far enough into the woods, there one will find all that one is seeking? Who knows how many centuries the birds of the woods have been singing?

All folk literature has indeed a passion whose like is not in modern literature and music and art, except where it has come by some straight or crooked way out of ancient times. Love was held to be a fatal sickness in ancient Ireland, and there is a love-poem in *The Songs of Connacht* that is like a death cry: 'My love, O she is my love, the woman who is most for destroying me, dearer is she for making me ill than the woman who would be for making me well. She is my treasure, O she is my treasure, the woman of the grey eyes . . . a woman who would not lay a hand under my head . . . She is my love, O she is my love, the woman who left no strength in me; a woman who would not breathe a sigh after me, a woman who would not raise a stone at my tomb . . . She is my secret love, O she is my secret love. A woman who tells me nothing . . . a woman who does not remember me to be out . . . She is my choice, O she is my choice, the woman who would not look back at me, the woman who would not make peace with me . . . She is my desire, O she is my desire: a woman dearest to me under the sun, a woman who would not pay me heed, if I were to sit by her side. It is she ruined my heart and left a sigh for ever in me.'[16] There is another song that ends, 'The Erne shall be in strong flood, the hills shall be torn down, and the sea shall have red waves, and blood shall be spilled, and every mountain valley and every moor shall be on high, before you shall perish, my little black rose.'[17] Nor does the Celt weigh and measure his hatred. The nurse of O'Sullivan Bere in the folk song prays that the bed of his betrayer may be the red hearthstone of hell for ever.[18] And an Elizabethan Irish poet cries (I quote him from memory, but I can hardly have forgotten the bitterest curse in literature): 'Three things are waiting for my death. The devil, who is waiting for my soul and cares nothing for my body or my wealth; the worms, who are waiting for my body but care nothing for my soul or my wealth; my children, who are waiting for my wealth and care nothing for my body or my soul. O Christ, hang all three in the one noose.'[19] Such love and hatred seek no mortal thing but their own infinity, and such love and hatred soon become love and hatred of the idea. The lover who loves so passionately can soon sing to his beloved like the lover in the poem by AE, an exquisite Irish poet of our days, 'A vast desire awakes and grows into forgetfulness of thee.'[20] When an early Irish poet calls the Irishman famous for much loving and a proverb, a friend[21] has heard in the Highlands of Scotland, talks of the lovelessness of the Irishman, they may say but the same thing, for if your passion is but great enough it leads you to a country where there are many cloisters. The hater who hates with too good a heart soon comes also to hate the idea only; and from this idealism in love and hatred comes, as I think, a certain power of saying and forgetting things, especially a power of saying and forgetting things in politics, which others do not say and forget. The ancient farmers and herdsmen were full of love and hatred, and made their friends gods, and their enemies the enemies of gods, and those who keep their tradition are not less mythological. From this 'mistaking dreams', which are perhaps essences, for 'realities' which are perhaps accidents, from this 'passionate, turbulent reaction against the despotism of fact', comes, it may be, that melancholy which made all ancient peoples delight in tales that end in death and parting, as modern peoples delight in tales that end in marriage bells; and made all ancient peoples who like the Celts had a nature more lyrical than dramatic, delight in wild and beautiful lamentations. Life was so weighed down by the emptiness of the great forests and by the mystery of all things, and by the greatness of its own desires, and, as I think, by the loneliness of much beauty; and seemed so little and so fragile and so brief, that nothing could be more sweet in the memory than a tale that ended in death and parting, and than a wild and beautiful lamentation. Men did not mourn because their beloved was married to another, or because learning was bitter in the mouth, for such mourning believes that life might be happy were it different, and is therefore the less mourning; but because they had been born and must die with their great thirst unslaked. And so it is that all the august sorrowful persons of literature, Cassandra and Helen and Brunhilda, and Lear and Tristram, have come out of legends and are indeed but the images of the primitive imagination mirrored in the little looking-glass of the modern and classic imagination. This is that 'melancholy a man knows when he is face to face' with nature, and thinks 'he hears her communing with him about' the mournfulness of being born and of dying; and how can it do otherwise than call into his mind 'its exiles, its flights across the seas', that it may stir the ever-smouldering ashes?[22] No Gaelic poetry is so popular in Gaelic-speaking places as the lamentations of Oisin, old and miserable, remembering the companions and the loves of his youth, and his three hundred years in faeryland, and faery love: all dreams withering in the winds of time lament in his lamentations: 'The clouds are long above me this night; last night was a long night to me; although I find this day long, yesterday was still longer. Every day that comes to me is long . . . No one in this great world is like me – a poor old man dragging stones. The clouds are long above me this night. I am the last man of the Fianna, the great Oisin, the son of Fionn, listening to the sound of bells. The clouds are long above me this night.'[23] Almost more beautiful is the lamentation of Leyrach Hen, which Matthew Arnold quotes as a type of the Celtic melancholy, and which I prefer to quote as a type of the primitive melancholy: 'O my crutch, is it not autumn when the fern is red and the water flag yellow? Have I not hated that which I love?. . . Behold, old age, which makes sport of me, from the hair of my head and my teeth, to my eyes which women loved. The four things I have all my life most hated fall upon me together – coughing and old age, sickness and sorrow. I am old, I am alone, shapeliness and warmth are gone from me, the couch of honour shall be no more mine; I am miserable, I am bent on my crutch. How evil was the lot allotted to Leyrach, the night he was brought forth! Sorrows without end and no deliverance from his burden.'[24] There are an Oisin and a Leyrach Hen still in the hearts of the Irish peasantry. 'The same man,' writes Dr Hyde in the beautiful prose which he first writes in Gaelic, 'who will to-day be dancing, sporting, drinking, and shouting, will be soliloquising by himself to-morrow, heavy and sick and sad in his own lonely little hut, making a croon over departed hopes, lost life, the vanity of this world, and the coming of death.'[25]

IV

Matthew Arnold asks how much of the Celt must one imagine in the ideal man of genius. I prefer to say, how much of the ancient hunters and fishers and of the ecstatic dancers among hills and woods must one imagine in the ideal man of genius. Certainly a thirst for unbounded emotion and a wild melancholy are troublesome things in the world, and do not make its life more easy or orderly, but it may be the arts are founded on the life beyond the world, and that they must cry in the ears of our penury until the world has been consumed and become a vision. Certainly, as

Samuel Palmer wrote, 'Excess is the vivifying spirit of the finest art, and we must always seek to make excess more abundantly excessive.'[26] Matthew Arnold has said that if he were asked 'where English got its turn for melancholy and its turn for natural magic,' he 'would answer with little doubt that it got much of its melancholy from a Celtic source, with no doubt at all that from a Celtic source is got nearly all its natural magic.' I will put this differently and say that literature dwindles to a mere chronicle of circumstance, or passionless phantasies, and passionless meditations, unless it is constantly flooded with the passions and beliefs of ancient times,[27] and that of all the fountains of the passions and beliefs of ancient times in Europe, the Slavonic, the Finnish, the Scandinavian, and the Celtic, the Celtic alone has been for centuries close to the main river of European literature. It has again and again brought 'the vivifying spirit' 'of excess' into the arts of Europe. Ernest Renan has told how the visions of purgatory seen by pilgrims to Lough Derg – once visions of the pagan underworld, as the hollow tree that bore the pilgrim to the holy island was alone enough to prove – gave European thought new symbols of a more abundant penitence; and had so great an influence that he has written, 'It cannot be doubted for a moment that to the number of poetical themes Europe owes to the genius of the Celt is to be added the framework of the divine comedy.' A little later the legends of Arthur and his table, and of the Holy Grail, once the cauldron of the Irish god, the Dagda,[28] changed the literature of Europe, and it may be changed, as it were, the very roots of man's emotions by their influence on the spirit of chivalry and on the spirit of romance; and later still Shakespeare found his Puck and his Mab, and one knows not how much else of his faery kingdom, in Celtic legend; and Spenser, living in Celtic Ireland where the faeries were part of men's daily lives, set the faery kingdom over all the kingdoms of romance; while at the beginning of our own day Sir Walter Scott gave Highland legends and Highland excitability so great a mastery over all romance that they seem romance herself.[29] In our own time Scandinavian tradition, thanks to the imagination of Richard Wagner[30] and of William Morris, whose *Sigurd the Volsung* is surely the most epical of modern poems, and of the earlier and, as I think, greater Dr Ibsen, has created a new romance, and through the imagination of Richard Wagner, become the most passionate element in the arts of the modern world. There is indeed but one other element that is almost as passionate, the still unfaded legends of Arthur and of the Holy Grail; and now a new fountain of legends, and, as scholars have said, a more abundant fountain than any in Europe, is being opened, the great fountain of Gaelic legends; the tale of Deirdre,[31] who alone among the women who have set men mad was at once the white flame and the red flame, wisdom and loveliness; the tale of the Sons of Turran,[32] with its unintelligible mysteries, an old Grail Quest as I think; the tale of the four children changed into four swans, and lamenting over many waters;[33] the tale of the love of Cuchulain for an immortal goddess,[34] and his coming home to a mortal woman in the end; the tale of his many battles at the ford with that dear friend, he kissed before the battles, and over whose dead body he wept when he had killed him; the tale of the flight of Grainne with Diarmaid, strangest of all tales of the fickleness of woman;[35] and the tale of the coming of Oisin out of faeryland, and of his memories and lamentations. 'The Celtic movement', as I understand it, is principally the opening of this fountain, and none can measure of how great importance it may be to coming times, for every new fountain of legends is a new intoxication for the imagination of the world. It comes at a time when the imagination of the world is as ready, as it was at the coming of the tales of Arthur and of the Grail, for a new intoxication. The reaction against the rationalism of the eighteenth century has mingled with a reaction against the materialism of the nineteenth century, and the symbolical movement, which has come to perfection in Germany in Wagner, in England in the Pre-Raphaelites,[36] and in France in Villiers de l'Isle-Adam,[37] and Mallarmé[38] and Maeterlinck,[39] and has stirred the imagination of Ibsen and D'Annunzio,[40] is certainly the only movement that is saying new things. The arts by brooding upon their own intensity have become religious, and are seeking, as some French critic[41] has said, to create a sacred book. They must, as religious thought has always done, utter themselves through legends; and the Slavonic and Finnish legends tell of strange woods and seas, and the Scandinavian legends are held by a great master, and tell also of strange woods and seas, and the Welsh legends are held by almost as many great masters as the Greek legends; while the Irish legends move among known woods and seas, and have so much of a new beauty, that they may well give the opening century its most memorable symbols.[42]

41

'CELTIC BELIEFS ABOUT THE SOUL'

from the *Bookman* (1898)

Celtic legends are, according to certain scholars, our principal way to an understanding of the beliefs out of which the beliefs of the Greeks and other European races arose. Mr Nutt has written a masterly book upon the most important of all old beliefs – the beliefs about the destiny of the soul and the light Celtic legends have thrown upon it. His book is indeed so masterly that I have no doubt that D'Arbois De Joubainville's *Mythologie Irlandais*,[1] Professor Rhys' *Celtic Heathendom*,[2] and it are the three books without which there is no understanding of Celtic legends. Mr Nutt published the first volume in 1895 as a commentary on *The Voyage of Bran*, an old Celtic poem translated and annotated by Kuno Meyer for the purpose; and described with much detail 'the happy other world' in Celtic and Greek and Anglo-Saxon and Jewish and Scandinavian and Indian literature. He showed 'that Greek and Irish alone have preserved the early stages of the happy other world conception with any fulness', and that Ireland has preserved them 'with greater fulness and precision' than the Greeks. He describes in *The Voyage of Bran*, vol. 2, the Celtic and Greek doctrine of the rebirth of the soul, of its coming out of the happy other world of the dead, and living once more, and of its power of changing its shape as it desires. By comparing the Greek cult of Dionysius and the Irish cult of the fairies, he concludes that its rebirth and its many changes are because 'the happy other world' is the country of the powers of life and increase, of the powers that can never lay aside the flame-like variability of life. He describes the old orgiac dances, in which the worshippers of the powers of life and increase believed themselves to take the shapes of gods and divine beasts, and first, he thinks, imagined 'the happy other world', in which their momentary and artificial ecstasy was a continual and natural ecstasy. If the fairy legends of the Irish peasants were better collected, he would have even more copious evidence to prove the association of continual change and of the continual making of new things with the inhabitants of the other world, with the dead as well as with the fairies. I have been often told that 'the fairies' change their shapes and colours every moment, and that they can build their houses in a moment and that they can make the fields fruitful and make the milk abundant, and that they can make food or money out of cow dung, and change apples into eggs, or anything into any other thing; and all that is told of the fairies is told of the dead who are among them. The traditional explanation of the battle fought by the fairies in autumn for the harvest is probably less allegorical and less simple than Mr Nutt's, who explains it as a battle between the powers of life and increase against the powers of death and decay. The peasants are very positive – I have given their words in the January *Nineteenth Century*[3] – that a bad harvest with us is a good harvest among the fairies, and the analogy of a battle fought about the dying makes one inclined to believe that the battle is between the guardians of the living who would leave the harvest for the living, and the fairies and the dead who would take the harvest for themselves. The main argument of Mr Nutt's book is the argument of Mr Frazer's *Golden Bough*[4] applied to Celtic legends and belief, and being itself a deduction from peasant custom and belief, and not, like the solar myth theory, from the mythology of cultivated races, it must look always for the bulk of its proofs and illustrations to peasant custom and belief. Mr Nutt seems to imply in a foot-note that the solar myth mythology is a later development and is based upon the harvest mythology, and this shows an accommodating spirit not to be found in Mr Lang[5] and Mr Frazer. Mr Nutt is indeed so tolerant that I am filled with wonder when I find him writing, like other folklorists, as if you had necessarily discovered the cause of a thing when you had discovered its history. Man may have first perceived 'the happy other world' in the orgiac dance or in some other ecstasy, but to show that he has done so, though important and interesting, is not to make a point in the great argument about the mystery of man's origin and destiny.

42

'THE ACADEMIC CLASS AND THE AGRARIAN REVOLUTION'

from the *Daily Express* (1899)

There are opinions and manners so memorable as indications of movements of thought that one longs to put them into some shape in which they may be read after the discussion that gave them birth is forgotten. I would gladly give such permanence to certain literary opinions of Dr Atkinson and to a certain violence of manner in his expression of them. He has said 'All folk-lore is essentially abominable', and of Dr Hyde's imaginative and often beautiful stories 'they are so very low', and of 'the whole range of Irish literature' (including those tales of Cuchulain which 'made an epoch' in the life of Burne-Jones,[1] and many tales that are the foundation of much in contemporary Irish literature), that it has 'very little of the ideal, and very little imagination'; and, in what one must conclude to have been a paroxysm of political excitement, that there was a book of Irish tales 'with translations' published the other day which 'no human being could read without being absolutely degraded by contact with it, of the filth which I won't even demean myself to mention' – a book which every folklorist knows to have no existence outside the imagination of Dr Atkinson. 'All folk-lore is essentially abominable.' If a Professor at an English University were to say these things in any conspicuous place, above all before a Commission which he hoped would give his opinion an expression in action, he would not be reasoned with, but his opinion would be repeated with a not ill-humoured raillery and his name remembered at times with a little laughter. Dr Hyde has understood, however, and perhaps rightly understood, that the conditions of Ireland are so peculiar that it is necessary to answer Dr Atkinson, lest, as I should imagine, some imperfectly educated priest in some country parish might believe that Irish literature was 'abominable', or 'indecent' – to use another favourite word of Dr Atkinson's – and raise a cry against the movement for the preservation of the Irish language. I prefer principally to inquire how a philologist and archaeologist of eminence comes to hold and to express violently such opinions upon matters that are neither philological nor archaeological, and which he would under ordinary circumstances have approached with some modesty and timidity. I remember repeating to William Morris[2] some twelve years ago an opinion of Dr Atkinson's about Irish literature very like his present opinions, and William Morris answering: 'People who talk that way' – or some such words – 'know nothing of the root thoughts of literature.' I do not think this is the explanation; for a certain lack of fine literary instinct, a certain lack of real understanding of the ideas and passions that give a literature importance, is common among men who spend their lives with words rather than ideas, with facts rather than emotions; and yet I do not think there is a Professor of any eminence at any English University who would not be as incapable of Dr Atkinson's intemperate opinions as of his quaint manner of expressing them.

The true explanation is that Dr Atkinson, like most people on both sides in politics of the generation which had to endure the bitterness of the agrarian revolution, is still in a fume of political excitement, and cannot consider any Irish matter without this excitement. If I remember my Bible correctly, the children of Israel had to wander forty years in the wilderness that all who had sinned a particular sin might die there; and Ireland will have no dispassionate opinion on any literary or political matter till that generation has died or has fallen into discredit. One watches with an irritation, that sometimes changes to pity, members of Parliament, Professors, eminent legal persons, officials of all kinds, men often of great natural power, who cannot talk, whether in public or private, of any Irish matter in which any living affection or enthusiasm has a part without becoming bitter with the passion of old controversies in which nobody is any longer interested. When the ideality of the National movement, as 'Young Ireland' shaped it, faded before the inevitably imperfect ideals of the agrarian revolution, those streams of fruitful thought, which had begun to flow in Nationalist Ireland under 'Young Ireland', became muddy; but the class, among whom Dr Atkinson lives and from whom he takes his emotions, dried up the springs of all streams that had any sweet water for human thirst. The academic class in Ireland, because the visible enthusiasm of the time threatened its interests or the interests of the classes among whom it dined and married, set its face against all Irish enthusiasms in the first instance, and then, by perhaps slow degrees, against all the great intellectual passions. An academic class is always a little dead and deadening; and our political rancours may long have made our academic class even quicker in denial than its association with undeveloped minds, and its preoccupation with words rather than ideas, with facts rather than emotions, made unavoidable; but I am persuaded, from much that I have heard and read, that it only came to its full maturity of bitterness in the agrarian revolution.

One would be content to wait in silence the change that must already have begun within itself, had it not in part destroyed, and was it not still destroying, the imaginative life of the minds that have come under its influence. An American publisher of great experience said to me the other day: 'I have noticed that quite a number of young men, who have come to the States from your Dublin University, try literature or art, but that they always take to commerce in the end. They are very clever – smart, we say – and they make a pot of money; but why do they do it?' I answered, so far as I remember, 'Trinity College, Dublin, makes excellent scholars, but it does not make men with any real love for ideal things or with any fine taste in the arts. One does not meet really cultivated Trinity College men as one meets really cultivated Oxford and Cambridge men. The atmosphere of what is called educated Dublin is an atmosphere of cynicism – a cynicism without ideas which expresses itself at the best in a wit without charm.' I might have said that our academic class has had the educating of the great majority of Irishmen who are educated at all, and yet that almost all Irishmen who have any fine taste in the arts, any gift for imaginative writing, any mastery over style, have come from beyond its influence, or have a fierce or smouldering anger waiting to thrust it to its fall. It might have opposed the often narrow enthusiasm of nationalism with the great intellectual passions of the world, as I think Professor Dowden[3] would have preferred; but it chose the easier way, that brings the death of imagination and at last the death of character.

'All folk-lore is essentially abominable': in that mood it has lived and worked, and of that mood its influence is dying. Fortunately for its country it has raised up powerful enemies, perhaps the most powerful of all enemies. 'Imagination', as an old theologian has written, 'cannot be hindered because it creates and substantiates as it goes.' Imagination and style are the only things that can, as it were, root and uproot the heart and give men what loves and hates they will; and our academic class understands in some dim way that its influence is passing into the hands of men who are seeking to create a criticism of life which will weigh all Irish interests, and bind rich and poor into one brotherhood; and a literature which will bring together, as Homer and Dante and Shakespeare and all religions have brought together, the arranging and comparing powers of the man of books, and the dreams and idealisms of the man of legends. Our academic class has worked against imagination and character, against the mover and sustainer of manhood; and eternity is putting forth its flaming fingers to bring its work to nothing. It understands that a movement which has published and sold in seven years more books about Ireland and of all kinds than were published and sold during the thirty years before it began, and that has published and sold fifty thousand Gaelic text books in a single year, must be taking away the attention and perhaps the respect of all young minds that have a little literature and a little ideality. Our academic class has hated enthusiasm, and Irish enthusiasm above all, and it has scorned the Irish poor; and here is a movement which has made a religion of the arts, which would make our hills and rivers beautiful with memories, and which finds its foundations in the thoughts and the traditions of the Irish poor. Hence that angry voice, sounding so strange in the modern world, and crying that 'all folk-lore is essentially abominable', that a charming and admired book 'is so very low', that an old literature, which has inspired many poets, has very 'little of the ideal and very little imagination', and that a book of folk tales, which no folklorist has ever heard of, is full of 'filth', which he will not 'even demean himself to mention'. Nor is this a solitary voice, for one finds the same violence of petulance, or a brawling or chuckling cynicism, which is perhaps worse, at many tables and in the mouths of Judges, Professors, and politicians. Until the young have pushed these men from their stools or have come to think of them as many, younger than I, do already, and as I perhaps am too deep in the argument to do with the good-humoured indifference with which one remembers Jacobins and Jacobites, we shall not have a natural and simple intellectual life in Ireland.

43

'A NOTE ON "THE HOSTING OF THE SIDHE"'

from *The Wind Among the Reeds* (1899)

The powerful and wealthy called the gods of ancient Ireland the Tuatha Dé Danaan, or the Tribes of the goddess Danu, but the poor called them, and still sometimes call them, the sidhe, from aes sidhe or sluagh sidhe, the people of the Faery Hills, as these words are usually explained. Sidhe is also Gaelic for wind, and certainly the sidhe have much to do with the wind. They journey in whirling winds, the winds that were called the dance of the daughters of Herodias[1] in the Middle Ages, Herodias doubtless taking the place of some old goddess. When the country people see the leaves whirling on the road they bless themselves, because they believe the sidhe to be passing by. They are almost always said to wear no covering upon their heads, and to let their hair stream out; and the great among them, for they have great and simple, go much on horseback. If any one becomes too much interested in them, and sees them over much, he loses all interest in ordinary things. I shall write a great deal elsewhere about such enchanted persons, and can give but an example or two now.[2]

A woman near Gort, in Galway says: 'There is a boy, now, of the Cloran's; but I wouldn't for the world let them think I spoke of him; it's two years since he came from America, and since that time he never went to Mass, or to Church, or to fairs, or to market, or to stand on the cross roads, or to hurling, or to nothing. And if anyone comes into the house, it's into the room he'll slip, not to see them; and as to work, he has the garden dug to bits, and the whole place smeared with cow dung; and such a crop as was never seen; and the alders all plaited till they look grand. One day he went as far as the chapel; but as soon as he got to the door he turned straight round again, as if he hadn't power to pass it. I wonder he wouldn't get the priest to read a Mass for him, or something; but the crop he has is grand, and you may know well he has some to help him.' One hears many stories of the kind; and a man whose son is believed to go out riding among them at night tells me that he is careless about everything, and lies in bed until it is late in the day. A doctor believes this boy to be mad. Those that are at times 'away', as it is called, know all things, but are afraid to speak.[3] A countryman at Kiltartan says, 'There was one of the Lydons – John – was away for seven years, lying in his bed, but brought away at nights, and he knew everything; and one, Kearney, up in the mountains, a cousin of his own, lost two hoggets, and came and told him, and he knew the very spot where they were, and told him, and he got them back again. But *they* were vexed at that, and took away the power, so that he never knew anything again, no more than another.' This wisdom is the wisdom of the fools of the Celtic stories, that was above all the wisdom of the wise. Lomna, the fool of Fionn, had so great wisdom that his head, cut from his body, was still able to sing and prophesy; and a writer in the *Encyclopaedia Britannica* writes that Tristram, in the oldest form of the tale of Tristram and Iseult, drank wisdom, and madness the shadow of wisdom, and not love, out of the magic cup.

The great of the old times are among the Tribes of Danu, and are kings and queens among them. Caolte was a companion of Fionn; and years after his death he appeared to a king in a forest, and was a flaming man, that he might lead him in the darkness. When the king asked him who he was, he said, 'I am your candlestick.' I do not remember where I have read this story, and I have, maybe, half forgotten it.[4] Niam was a beautiful woman of the Tribes of Danu, that led Oisin to the Country of the Young, as their country is called; I have written about her in *The Wanderings of Oisin*; and he came back, at last, to bitterness and weariness.

Knocknarea is in Sligo, and the country people say that Maeve, still a great queen of the western sidhe, is buried in the cairn of stones upon it. I have written of Clooth-na-Bare in *The Celtic Twilight*.[5] She 'went all over the world, seeking a lake deep enough to drown her faery life, of which she had grown weary, leaping from hill to hill, and setting up a cairn of stones wherever her feet lighted, until, at last, she found the deepest water in the world in little Lough Ia, on the top of the bird mountain, in Sligo.' I forget, now, where I heard this story, but it may have been from a priest at Collooney.[6] Clooth-na-Bare would mean the old woman of Bare, but is evidently a corruption of Cailleac Bare, the old woman Bare, who, under the names Bare, and Berah, and Beri, and Verah, and Dera, and Dhira, appears in the legends of many places. Mr O' Grady found her haunting Lough Liath high up on the top of a mountain of the Fews, the Slieve Fuadh, or Slieve Gullion of old times, under the name of the Cailleac Buillia. He describes Lough Liath as a desolate moon-shaped lake, with made wells and sunken passages upon its borders, and beset by marsh and heather and gray boulders, and closes his *Flight of the Eagle*[7] with a long rhapsody upon mountain and lake, because of the heroic tales and beautiful old myths that have hung about them always. He identifies the Cailleac Buillia with that Meluchra[8] who persuaded Fionn to go to her amid the waters of Lough Liath, and so changed him with her enchantments, that, though she had to free him because of the threats of the Fianna, his hair was ever afterwards as white as snow. To this day, the Tribes of the Goddess Danu that are in the waters beckon to men, and drown them in the waters; and Bare, or Dhira, or Meluchra, or whatever name one likes the best, is, doubtless, the name of a mistress among them. Meluchra was daughter of Cullain; and Cullain Mr O'Grady calls, upon I know not what authority, a form of Lir,[9] the master of waters. The people of the waters have been in all ages beautiful and changeable and lascivious, or beautiful and wise and lonely, for water is everywhere the signature of the fruitfulness of the body and of the fruitfulness of dreams. The white hair of Fionn may be but another of the troubles of those that come to unearthly wisdom and earthly trouble, and the threats and violence of the Fianna against her, a different form of the threats and violence the country people use, to make the Tribes of Danu give up those that are 'away'. Bare is now often called an ugly old woman; but Dr Joyce says that one of her old names was Aebhin, which means beautiful. Aebhen was the goddess of the tribes of northern Leinster; and the lover she had made immortal, and who loved her perfectly, left her, and put on mortality, to fight among them against the stranger, and died on the strand of Clontarf.[10]

44

'A NOTE ON "THE HOST OF THE AIR"'

from *The Wind Among the Reeds* (1899)

Some writers distinguish between the Sluagh Gaoith, the host of the air, and Sluagh Sidhe, the host of the sidhe, and describe the host of the air of a peculiar malignancy. Dr Joyce[1] says, 'of all the different kinds of goblins . . . air demons were most dreaded by the people. They lived among clouds, and mists, and rocks, and hated the human race with the utmost malignity.' A very old Aran charm, which contains the words 'Send God, by his strength, between us and the host of the sidhe, between us and the host of the air', seems also to distinguish among them. I am inclined, however, to think that the distinction came in with Christianity and its belief about the prince of the air,[2] for the host of the sidhe, as I have already explained, are closely associated with the wind.

They are said to steal brides just after their marriage, and sometimes in a blast of wind. A man in Galway says, 'At Aughanish[3] there were two couples came to the shore to be married, and one of the newly married women was in the boat with the priest, and they going back to the island; and a sudden blast of wind came, and the priest said some blessed words that were able to save himself, but the girl was swept.'

This woman was drowned; but more often the persons who are taken 'get the touch', as it is called, and fall into a half dream, and grow indifferent to all things, for their true life has gone out of the world, and is among the hills and the forts of the sidhe. A faery doctor has told me that his wife 'got the touch' at her marriage because there was one of them wanted her; and the way he knew for certain was, that when he took a pitchfork out of the rafters, and told her it was a broom, she said, 'It is a broom.'[4] She was, the truth is, in the magical sleep to which people have given a new name lately,[5] that makes the imagination so passive that it can be moulded by any voice in any world into any shape. A mere likeness of some old woman, or even old animal, some one or some thing the sidhe have no longer a use for, is believed to be left instead of the person who is 'away'; this some one or some thing can, it is thought, be driven away by threats, or by violence (though I have heard country women say that violence is wrong), which perhaps awakes the soul out of the magical sleep. The story in the poem is founded on an old Gaelic ballad that was sung and translated for me by a woman at Ballisodare in County Sligo; but in the ballad the husband found the keeners keening his wife when he got to his house. She was 'swept' at once; but the sidhe are said to value those the most whom they but cast into a half dream, which may last for years, for they need the help of a living person in most of the things they do. There are many stories of people who seem to die and be buried – though the country people will tell you it is but some one or some thing put in their place that dies and is buried – and yet are brought back afterwards. These tales are perhaps memories of true awakenings out of the magical sleep, moulded by the imagination, under the influence of a mystical doctrine which it understands too literally, into the shape of some well-known traditional tale. One does not hear them as one hears the others, from the persons who are 'away', or from their wives or husbands; and one old man, who had often seen the sidhe, began one of them with 'Maybe it is all vanity.'

Here is a tale that a friend of mine[6] heard in the Burren Hills, and it is a type of all:

'There was a girl to be married, and she didn't like the man, and she cried when the day was coming, and said she wouldn't go along with him. And the mother said, "Get into the bed, then, and I'll say that you're sick." And so she did. And when the man came the mother said to him, "You can't get her, she's sick in the bed." And he looked in and said, "That's not my wife that's in the bed, it's some old hag." And the mother began to cry and to roar. And he went out and got two hampers of turf and made a fire, that they thought he was going to burn the house down. And when the fire was kindled, "Come out now," says he, "and we'll see who you are, when I'll put you on the fire." And when she heard that, she gave one leap, and was out of the house, and they saw, then, it was an old hag she was. Well, the man asked the advice of an old woman, and she bid him to go to a faery-bush that was near, and he might get some word of her. So he went there at night, and saw all sorts of grand people, and they in carriages or riding on horses, and among them he could see the girl he came to look for. So he went again to the old woman, and she said, "If you can get the three bits of blackthorn out of her hair, you'll get her again." So that night he went back again, and that time he only got hold of a bit of her hair. But the old woman told him that he was no use, and that he was put back now, and it might be twelve nights before he'd get her. But on the fourth night he got the third bit of blackthorn, and he took her, and she came away with him. He never told the mother he had got her; but one day she saw her at a fair, and, says she, "That's my daughter; I know her by the smile and by the laugh of her," and she with a shawl about her head. So the husband said, "You're right there, and hard I worked to get her." She spoke often of the grand things she saw underground, and how she used to have wine to drink, and to drive out in a carriage with four horses every night. And she used to be able to see her husband when he came to look for her, and she was greatly afraid he'd get a drop of the wine, for then he would have come underground and never left it again. And she was glad herself to come to earth again, and not to be left there.'

The old Gaelic literature is full of the appeals of the Tribes of the goddess Danu to mortals whom they would bring into their country; but the song of Midir to the beautiful Etain, the wife of the king who was called Echaid the ploughman, is the type of all.[7]

'O beautiful woman, come with me to the marvellous land where one listens to a sweet music, where one has spring flowers in one's hair, where the body is like snow from head to foot, where no one is sad or silent, where teeth are white and eyebrows are black . . . cheeks red like foxglove in flower . . . Ireland is beautiful, but not so beautiful as the Great Plain I call you to. The beer of Ireland is heady, but the beer of the Great Plain is much more heady. How marvellous is the country I am speaking of! Youth does not grow old there. Streams with warm flood flow there; sometimes mead, sometimes wine. Men are charming and without a blot there, and love is not forbidden there. O woman, when you come into my powerful country you will wear a crown of gold upon your head. I will give you the flesh of swine, and you will have beer and milk to drink. O beautiful woman. O beautiful woman, come with me!'[8]

45

'A NOTE ON "THE VALLEY OF THE BLACK PIG"'

from *The Wind Among the Reeds* (1899)

All over Ireland there are prophecies of the coming rout of the enemies of Ireland, in a certain Valley of the Black Pig,[1] and these prophecies are, no doubt, now, as they were in the Fenian[2] days, a political force. I have heard of one man who would not give any money to the Land League[3] because the Battle could not be until the close of the century; but, as a rule, periods of trouble bring prophecies of its near coming. A few years before my time, an old man who lived at Lisadell, in Sligo, used to fall down in a fit and rave out descriptions of the Battle; and a man in Sligo has told me that it will be so great a battle that the horses shall go up to their fetlocks in blood, and that their girths, when it is over, will rot from their bellies for lack of a hand to unbuckle them. The battle is a mythological battle, and the black pig is one with the bristleless boar, that killed Dearmod, in November, upon the western end of Ben Bulben; Misroide MacDatha's sow, whose carving brought on so great a battle;[4] 'the croppy black sow', and 'the cutty black sow' of Welsh November rhymes (*Celtic Heathendom*,[5] 509–516); the boar that killed Adonis; the bear that killed Attis; and the pig embodiment of Typhon[6] (*Golden Bough*,[7] II. 26, 31). The pig seems to have been originally a genius of the corn, and seemingly because the too great power of their divinity makes divine things dangerous to mortals, its flesh was forbidden to many eastern nations; but as the meaning of the prohibition was forgotten, abhorrence took the place of reverence, pigs and boars grew into types of evil, and were described as the enemies of the very gods they once typified (*Golden Bough*, II. 26–31, 56–7). The Pig would, therefore, become the Black Pig, a type of cold and of winter that awake in November, the old beginning of winter, to do battle with the summer, and with the fruit and leaves, and finally, as I suggest; and as I believe, for the purposes of poetry; of the darkness that will at last destroy the gods and the world. The country people say there is no shape for a spirit to take so dangerous as the shape of a pig; and a Galway blacksmith – and blacksmiths are thought to be especially protected – says he would be afraid to meet a pig on the road at night; and another Galway man tells this story: 'There was a man coming the road from Gort to Garryland one night, and he had a drop taken; and before him, on the road, he saw a pig walking; and having a drop in, he gave a shout, and made a kick at it, and bid it get out of that. And by the time he got home, his arm was swelled from the shoulder to be as big as a bag, and he couldn't use his hand with the pain of it. And his wife brought him, after a few days, to a woman that used to do cures at Rahasane. And on the road all she could do would hardly keep him from lying down to sleep on the grass. And when they got to the woman she knew all that happened; and, says she, it's well for you that your wife didn't let you fall asleep on the grass, for if you had done that but even for one instant, you'd be a lost man.'

It is possible that bristles were associated with fertility, as the tail certainly was, for a pig's tail is stuck into the ground in Courland, that the corn may grow abundantly, and the tails of pigs, and other animal embodiments of the corn genius, are dragged over the ground to make it fertile in different countries. Professor Rhys,[8] who considers the bristleless boar a symbol of darkness and cold, rather than of winter and cold, thinks it was without bristles because the darkness is shorn away by the sun. It may have had different meanings, just as the scourging of the man god has had different though not contradictory meanings in different epochs of the world.

The Battle should, I believe, be compared with three other battles; a battle the sidhe are said to fight when a person is being taken away by them; a battle they are said to fight in November for the harvest; the great battle the Tribes of the goddess Danu fought, according to the Gaelic chroniclers, with the Fomor at Moytirra, or the Towery Plain.[9]

I have heard of the battle over the dying both in County Galway and in the Isles of Aran, an old Aran fisherman having told me that it was fought over two of his children, and that he found blood in a box he had for keeping fish, when it was over; and I have written about it, and given examples elsewhere.[10] A faery doctor, on the borders of Galway and Clare, explained it as a battle between the friends and enemies of the dying, the one party trying to take them, the other trying to save them from being taken. It may once, when the land of the sidhe was the only other world, and when every man who died was carried thither, have always accompanied death. I suggest that the battle between the Tribes of the goddess Danu, the powers of light, and warmth, and fruitfulness, and goodness, and the Fomor, the powers of darkness, and cold, and barrenness, and badness upon the Towery Plain, was the establishment of the habitable world, the rout of the ancestral darkness; that the battle among the sidhe for the harvest is the annual battle of summer and winter; that the battle among the sidhe at a man's death is the battle between the manifest world and the ancestral darkness at the end of all things; and that all these battles are one, the battle of all things with shadowy decay. Once a symbolism has possessed the imagination of large numbers of men, it becomes, as I believe, an embodiment of disembodied powers, and repeats itself in dreams and visions, age after age.

46

'IRELAND BEWITCHED'

from the *Contemporary Review* (1899)

When one talks to the people of the West of Ireland, and wins their confidence, one soon finds that they live in a very ancient world, and are surrounded by dreams that make the little round fields that were the foundations of ancient houses (forts or forths as they call them), a great boulder up above on the hillside, the more twisted or matted thorn trees, all unusual things and places, and the common crafts of the country always mysterious and often beautiful. One finds the old witches and wisemen still busy, and even the crafts of the smith and of the miller touched with a shadow of old faiths, that gives them a brotherhood with magic. The principal crafts were once everywhere, it seems, associated with magic, and had their rites and their gods; and smith-craft, of which one hears much from Galway story-tellers, that was once the distinguishing craft of races that had broken many battles upon races whose weapons were of stone, was certainly associated with a very powerful magic. A man on the borders of Clare and Galway tells how his house was enchanted and filled with smoke that was like the smoke of a forge, and a man living by the sea in North Galway says: 'This is a fairy stream we're passing; there were some used to see them by the side of it, and washing themselves in it. And there used to be heard a fairy forge here every night, and the hammering on the iron could be heard and the blast of the furnace.' A man at Kiltartan says: 'Blacksmiths are safe from these things,' meaning fairy mischiefs, 'and if a blacksmith was to turn his anvil upside down and say malicious words he could do you great injury.' A man in the Burren Hills says: 'Yes, they say blacksmiths have something about them. And if there's a seventh blacksmith in succession from seven generations, he can do many strange things, and if he gave you his curse you wouldn't be the better of it. There was one at Belharbour, Jamsie Finucane, but he did no harm to any one, but was as quiet as another. He is dead now and his son's a blacksmith, too.' A woman near Coole says: 'A seventh son has the power to cure the ringworm, and if there is a seventh blacksmith in a family he can do his choice thing.'[1] And an old man near Kiltartan says: 'Blacksmiths have power, and if you could steal the water from the trough in the forge, it would cure all things.' And a woman from Ardrahan says: 'A blacksmith can do all things. When my little boy was sick I was told to go to a forge before sunrise and to collect some of the dust from the anvil. But I didn't after, he was too far gone.' A drunken blacksmith at a village in the county of Clare, when asked by a friend who has collected many of these and other stories for me, if he had ever been to the famous wise woman, Biddy Early, answered: 'I never went to Biddy Early for a cure myself, for you should know that no ill or harm ever comes to a blacksmith.'

Iron is believed to be the great dissolver of all charms, and one hears stories of enchanted people and creatures that take their right shape when you point a gun at them and look along the iron of the barrel. It seems to be this property of iron that makes blacksmiths invulnerable. A woman from near Feakle says: 'There was a man one time that was a blacksmith, and he used to go every night playing cards. And for all his wife could say he wouldn't leave off doing it. So one night she got a boy to go stand in the old churchyard he'd have to pass, and to frighten him.

'So the boy did so, and began to groan and to try to frighten him when he came near. But it's well-known that nothing of that kind can do any harm to a blacksmith. So he went in and got hold of the boy, and told him he had a mind to choke him, and went his way.

'But no sooner was the boy left alone than there came about him something in the shape of a dog, and then a great troop of cats. And they surrounded him, and he tried to get away home, but he had no power to go the way he wanted, but had to go with them. And at last they came to an old forth and a fairy bush, and he knelt down and made the sign of the cross and said a great many Our Fathers. And after a time they went into the fairy bush and left him.

'And he was going away and a woman came out of the bush, and called to him three times to make him look back. And he saw it was a woman he knew before, that was dead, and so he knew she was among the fairies. And she said to him, "It's well for you I was here, and worked hard for you, or you would have been brought in among them, and be like me." So he got home.

'And the blacksmith got home, too, and his wife was surprised to see he was no way frightened. But he said, "You might know that there's nothing of the sort that could harm me."

'For a blacksmith is safe from all, and when he goes out in the night he keeps always in his pocket a small bit of iron, and they know him by that.

'So he went on card playing, and they grew very poor after.'

Millers, too, have knowledge and power. An old man I knew, who believed himself to be haunted, went to the nearest miller for a cure; and a woman among the Slieve Echtge Hills says that 'a miller can bring any one he likes to misfortune by working his mill backwards', and adds, 'just as the blacksmith can put his anvil upside down'.

The people who have most knowledge, however, are not thought to have it from a craft, but because it has been told them, revealed to them, as it might be told or revealed to anybody. Once everybody almost had it, for as an old man in Kiltartan says: 'Enchanters and magicians they were in the old times, and could make the birds sing and the stones and the fishes speak.' But now only a few have it. One hears comparatively little of magic of the old wonder-working kind, but one does hear something of it. An old woman from the borders of Sligo and Mayo says that she remembers seeing, when she was a child, 'a wild old man in flannel who came from Erris'. He and the men used to sit up late at night sometimes, playing cards in a big barn. She was not allowed to go into the barn because children kneel down and look up under the cards, and a player has bad luck if anybody kneels when he is playing, but her father often told her that when they had been playing a long time 'the wild old man' would take up the cards and move them about and a hare would leap out of the cards, and then a hound would leap out after the hare and chase it round and round the barn and away.[2]

One hears sometimes of people who can see what is happening at a distance, or what is happening among 'the others' (the fairies), or what is going to happen among us. A woman at Coole says: 'There was a man at Ardrahan used to see many things. But he lost his eyesight after. That often happens, that those who see those things lose their earthly sight.'

A man of the large island of Aran says: 'There was a strange woman came to the island one day and told some of the women down below what would happen them. And they didn't believe, she being a stranger, but since that time it's all been coming true.' And it is sometimes said that if you have the habit of walking straight on the road, and not of wavering a little from side to side, you are more likely to 'see things' than another, which means, I suppose, that you should be in good health and strength if you are 'to see things'. The gift most valued seems to be the power of bringing back people who are in the power of 'the others', or of curing the many illnesses that 'the others' are believed to give us, that they may take us into their world. It is possible that all illness was once believed to come from them, but I am not sure, because a distinction is now made between the illnesses they make and ordinary illnesses. A man on one of the Aran Islands told my friend, with many other stories which I have, how he got a little of the knowledge and the use he made of it. He has not, however, the whole of the knowledge, for the people are at this moment looking out for a 'knowledgeable' man or woman, to use their own words, as at present they have to go to Roundstone in Galway. The man says: 'There are many can do cures because they have something walking with them, what we may call a ghost, from among the sheogue (the fairies). A few cures I can do myself, and this is how I got them. I told you I was for five quarters[3] in Manchester, and where I lodged were two old women in the house, from the farthest side of Mayo, for they were running from Mayo at that time because of the hunger. And I knew they were likely to have a cure, for St Patrick blessed the places he was not in more than the places he was in, and with the cure he left, and the fallen angels, there are many in Mayo, can do them.

'Now it's the custom in England never to clear the table but once in the week, and that on a Saturday night. And in that night all is set out clean, and all the crusts of bread and bits of meat and the like are gathered together in a tin can and thrown out in the street. And women that have no other way of living come round with a bag that would hold two stone, and they pick up all that's thrown out, and live on it for a week. But often I didn't eat the half of what was before me, and I wouldn't throw it out, but I'd bring it to the two old women that were in the house, so they grew very fond of me.

'Well, when the time came that I thought I'd draw towards home, I brought them one day to a public-house, and made a drop of punch for them, and then I picked the cure out of them, for I was wise in those days. There was a neighbour's child was sick and I got word of it, and I went to the house, for the woman there had showed me kindness, and I went in to the cradle and I lifted the quilt off the child's face, and you could see by it, and I saw the signs, that there was some of their work there. And I said, "You're not likely to have the child long with you, ma'am." And she said, "Indeed, I know I won't have him long." So I said nothing, but I went out, and whatever I did and whatever I got there, I brought it in again and gave it to the child, and he began to get better. And the next day I brought the same thing again and gave it to the child, and I looked at him and I said to the mother, "He'll live to comb his hair grey." And from that time he got better, and now there's no stronger child in the island, and he the youngest in the house.

'After that the husband got sick, and the woman said to me one day: "If there's anything you can do to cure him, have pity on me and my children, and I'll give you what you'll ask." But I said, "I'll do what I can for you, but I'll take nothing from you, except maybe a grain of tea or a glass of porter, for I wouldn't take money for this, and I refused £2 one time for a cure I did." So I went and brought back the cure, and I mixed it with flour and made it into three little pills that it couldn't be lost, and gave them to him, and from that time he got well.

'There was a woman lived down the road there, and one day I went into the house when she was after coming from Galway town, and I asked charity of her. And it was in the month of August when the bream fishing was going on, and she said, "There's no one need be in want now, with fresh fish in the sea and potatoes in the gardens," and she gave me nothing. But when I was out the door, she said, "Well, come back here." And I said, "If you were to offer me all you brought from Galway I wouldn't take it from you now."

'And from that time she began to pine and to wear away and to lose her health. And at the end of three years she walked outside her house one day, and when she was two yards from her own threshold she fell on the ground, and the neighbours came and lifted her up on a door and brought her into the house, and she died.

'I think I could have saved her then – I *think* I could. But when I saw her lying there I remembered that day, and I didn't stretch out a hand and I spoke no word.

'I'm going to rise out of the cures and not to do much more of them, for *they* have given me a touch here in the right leg, so that it's the same as dead; and a woman in my village that does cures, she is after being struck with a pain in the hand. Down by the path at the top of the slip, from there to the hill, that is the way they go most nights, hundreds and thousands of them some nights; sleeping in that little cabin of mine I heard them ride past, and I could hear by the feet of the horses that there was a long line of them there.'

Of all who have had this gift in recent years in the south-west of Ireland, the most famous was Biddy Early, who had most other fairy gifts likewise. She is dead some twenty years, but her cottage is pointed out at Feakle in Clare. It is a little rough-built cottage by the roadside, and is always full of turf-smoke, like many others of the cottages, but once it was sought out by the sick and the troubled of all the south-west of Ireland. My friend[4] went to Feakle for me a while back, and found it full of memories of

Biddy Early's greatness. Nobody there denies her power, but some of the better off think her power unholy, and one woman says: 'It is against our religion to go to fortune-tellers. She did not get her power from God, so it must have been from demons.' The poor think better of her, and one man says: 'She was as good to the poor as to the rich. Any poor person she'd see passing the road she'd call in and give them a cup of tea or a glass of whisky and bread and all they wanted. She had a big chest within in that room, and it was full of pounds of tea and bottles of wine and of whisky and of claret and all things in the world.' 'I knew her well,' says one, 'a nice fresh-looking woman she was. It's to her the people used to be flocking, to the door and even to the window, and if they'd come late in the day they'd have no chance of getting to her, they'd have to take lodgings for the night in the town. She was a great woman. If any of the men that came into the house had a drop too much drink taken, and said an unruly word, she'd turn them out. And if any of them were disputing or fighting or going to law, she'd say, "Be at one and you can rule the world." The priests were against her, and used to be taking the cloaks and the baskets from the country people to keep them from going to her.' An old pensioner at Kiltartan says: 'When I was in the army, whenever a Clare man joined, we were sure to hear of Biddy Early'; and another man says that people came to her 'from the whole country round, and from Limerick and Loughrea, and even from England and Wales. She had four or five husbands, and they all died of drink, one after another. They had the temptation, for maybe twenty or thirty people would be there in the day looking for cures, and every one of them would bring a bottle of whisky. Wild cards they were or they wouldn't have married her.' Everybody tells of her many husbands, though not always of the same number. A man in Burren says: 'She had three husbands; I saw one of them the day I was there, but I knew by the look of him he wouldn't live long.' She is believed to have journeyed all over the country with the fairies, and she seems to have first seen and thrown her enchantment on one of the men she married, when on one of these journeys.

A woman near Roxborough says: 'There was a Clare woman

with me when I went there, and she told me there was a boy from a village near her brought tied in a cart to Biddy Early, and she said: "If I cure you, will you be willing to marry me"; and he said he would. So she cured him and married him; I saw him there at her house. It might be that she had the illness put on him first.' One man at Feakle seems to think that she had a lover or a husband among 'the others' also, for he says: 'Surely she was away herself, and as to her son, she brought him with her when she came back, and for eight or nine years he was lying on the bed. And he'd never stir as long as she was in it, but no sooner was she gone away anywhere then he'd be out down the village among the people, and then back again before she'd get to the house.' Some, however, say that this boy was not her son but her brother. Most of the country people think she got her knowledge from this boy, though a witch doctor in Clare, whom I have described elsewhere, says that she told him her knowledge came to her from a child she met when she was at service. A woman at Burren says: 'He was a little chap that was astray. And one day when he was lying sick in the bed, he said: "There's a woman in such a house has a hen down in the pot, and if I had the soup of the hen I think it would cure me." So Biddy Early went to the house, and when she got there, sure enough there was a hen in the pot on the fire. But she was ashamed to tell what she came for, and she let on to have only come for a visit, and so she sat down. But presently in the heat of talking she told what the little chap had said. "Well," says the woman, "take the soup and welcome, and the hen too, if it'll do him any good." So she brought them with her, and when the boy saw the soup, "It can't save me," says he, "for no earthly thing can do that. But since I see how kind and how willing you are, and did your best for me all these years, I'll leave you a way of living." And so he did, and taught her the cure. That's what's said at any rate.'

But others say that after his death she was always crying and lamenting for the loss of him, and that she had no way of earning her bread, till at last he appeared to her and gave her the gift. One man who was cured by her thinks that she got her knowledge through having been among the fairies herself, and says: 'She was away for seven years; she didn't tell it to me, but she told it to others'; and adds, 'any how it is certain that when the case was a bad one, she would go into a stable, and there she would meet her people and consult with them.' An old man near Coole says: 'Biddy Early surely did thousands of cures; out in the stable she used to go, there her friends met her, and they told her all things.' Another says: 'She used to go out into a field and talk with her friends through the holes in the walls.' Many tell, too, of a bottle in which she looked and found out whatever she wanted to know. A young man at Feakle, too young to remember her, says: 'The people do be full of stories of all the cures she did. It was by the bottle she did all. She would shake it, and she'd see everything when she looked at it.' She would say at once whether the sickness she was asked to cure was a common sickness or one of those mysterious sicknesses the people lay at the door of the fairies. A woman at Kiltartan says: 'It's I was with this woman here to Biddy Early. And when she saw me she knew it was for my husband I came, and she looked in her bottle, and said: "It's nothing put upon him by my people that's wrong with him." And she bid me give him cold vinegar and some other things – herbs. He got better after. And sometimes she would see in the bottle that the case was beyond her power, and then she would do nothing.' An old woman near Feakle says: 'I went there but once myself, when my little girl that was married was bad after her second baby being born. I went to the house and told her about it. And she took the bottle and shook it and looked in it, and then she turned and said something to himself (her husband) that I didn't hear, and she just waved her hand to me like that, and bid me go home, and she would take nothing from me. But himself came out and told me that what she was after seeing in the bottle was the face of my little girl and her coffin standing beside her. So I went home, and sure enough on the tenth day after she was dead.' Another woman tells a like story, but does not mention the bottle: 'Often I heard of Biddy Early, and I know of a little girl was sick, and the brother went to Biddy Early to ask would she get well. And she said: "They have a place ready for her, it's room for her they have." So he knew she would die, and so she did.'

A woman at Feakle says: 'I knew a man went to Biddy Early about his wife, and as soon as she saw him she said, "On the fourth day a discarded priest will call in and cure your wife." And so he did, one Father Ford.' A woman at Burren says: 'I went up to Biddy Early one time with another woman. A fine stout woman she was, sitting straight up in her chair. She looked at me, and she told me my son was worse than what I was, and for myself she bid me to take what I was taking before, and that's dandelions. Five leaves she bid me lay out on the table, with three pinches of salt on the three middle ones. As for my son, she gave me a bottle for him, but he wouldn't take it; and he got better without.' One does not know whether this was a common illness, but in most of the stories the illness is from the fairies. Somebody has been 'overlooked' – that is, looked at with envy or with unbridled admiration by some one who would not say, or forgot to say, 'God bless him', or its like; and because this emotion has given the persons looked at into the power of the fairies, who can only take people 'away' 'through the eye of a sinner', he has been given 'the touch' or 'the stroke' that is the definite beginning of their power. I have been told that only those who have been or are themselves 'away' – that is, in the world of fairy, a changeling taking their place upon the earth – can cure those who are 'away', though many can cure 'the touch' or 'the stroke'. There are, however, stories of cures that contradict this. A woman near Gort says: 'There was a boy of the Brennans in Gort was out at Kiltartan thatching Heniff's house. And a woman passed by, and she looked up at him, but she never said, "God bless the work." And Brennan's mother was on the road to Gort, and the woman met her, and said, "Where did your son learn thatching?" And that day he had a great fall, and was brought home hurt. And the mother went to Biddy Early, and she said, "Didn't a red-haired woman meet you one day going into Gort, and ask where did your son learn thatching; and didn't she look up at him as she passed? It was then it was done." And she gave a bottle, and he got well after a time.' 'The touch' or 'the stroke' often show themselves by a fall. A red-haired woman is always unlucky, and a woman near Gort who had told a friend and neighbour about an old man who lost his hair all at once in a fairy fort after he had cut down some bushes says: 'The old man here that lost his hair went to Biddy Early, but he didn't want to go, and we forced him and persuaded him. And when he got to the house she said, "It wasn't of your own free will you came here," and at the first she wouldn't do anything for him. And then she said, "Why did you go to cut down the phillibine (magpie) bush[5] – that bush you see out of the window?" And she told him an old woman in the village had overlooked him – Daly's sister – and she gave him a bottle to sprinkle about her house. I suppose it was the bush being interfered with she didn't like.' Another woman near Gort says: 'There was a man I knew sick, and he sent to Biddy Early, and she said, "Was Andy in the house?" And they said he was, "Well," says she, "the next time he comes in ask him his name and his Christian name three times." And so they did, and the third time he turned and went out. And the man got better, but Andy's stock all went from him, and he never throve from that time.'

The asking the name is, no doubt, connected with the belief that if you know a person's name you have power over him. I have a story of a Tipperary woman who was tormented by fairies, who were always trying to get her name from her that they might have power over her.

A woman near Coole says: 'It was my son was thatching Heniff's house when he got the touch, and he came back with a pain in his back and his shoulders, and took to the bed. And a few nights after that, I was asleep, and the little girl came and woke me, and said, "There's none of us can sleep with all the cars and carriages rattling round the house." But, though I woke and heard that said, I fell into a sound sleep again, and never woke till morning. And one night there came two taps to the window, one after another, and we all heard it, and no one there. And at last I sent the other boy to Biddy Early, and he found her in the house; she was then married to her fourth man. And she said he came a day too soon, and would do nothing for him; and he had to walk away in the rain. And the next day he went back, and she said, "Three days later and you'd have been too late." And she gave him two bottles; the one he was to bring to boundary water[6] and to fill it up, and that was to be rubbed to the back, and the other was to drink. And the minute he got them he began to get well; and he left the bed, and could walk, but he was always delicate. When he rubbed the back we saw a black mark, like the bite of a dog, and as to his face, it was as white as a sheet. I have the bottle here yet, though it's thirty year ago I got it. She bid the boy to bring whatever was left of it to a river, and to pour it away with the running water. But when he got well I did nothing with it and said nothing about it, and here it is now for you to see, and you the first I ever showed it to. I never let on to Father Curran that I went to her, but one time the bishop came. I knew he was a rough man, and I went to him and made a confession, and I said, "Do what you like with me, but I'd walk the world for my son when he was sick." And all he said was, "I wouldn't have wondered if your messenger had had the two feet cut off from him." And he said no more.'

An old man near Coole says: 'I got cured by her myself one time. Look at this thumb. I got it hurted, and I went out into the field after, and was ploughing all the day, I was that greedy for work. And when I went in, I had to lie on the bed with the pain of it, and it swelled, and the arm with it, to the size of a horse's thigh. I stopped two or three days in the bed, and then my wife went to see Biddy Early; and she came home; and the next day it burst, and you never saw anything like all the stuff that came away from it. A good bit after I went to her myself, where it wasn't quite healed, and she said, "You'd have lost it altogether if your wife hadn't been so quick to come." She brought me into a small room, and said good words and sprinkled water from a bottle, and told me to believe. The priests were against her, but they were wrong. How could that be evil doing that was all charity and kindness and healing? She was a decent-looking woman, no different from any other woman of the country. The boy she was married to at the time was lying on the bed drunk. There were side cars and common cars and gentry and country people at the door, just like Gort market, and dinner for all that came. And every one would bring her something, but she didn't care what it was. Rich farmers would bring her the whole side of a pig. Myself I brought a bottle of whisky and a shilling's worth of bread, and a quarter of sugar, and a quarter pound of tea. She was very rich, for there wasn't a farmer but would give her the grass of a couple of bullocks or a filly – she had the full of a field of fillies if they'd all been gathered together.

'She died a good many years ago. I didn't go to the wake myself, but I heard that her death was natural.'

A well-to-do man near Kilchreest says: 'It was all you could do to get to Biddy Early with your skin whole, the priests were so set against her. I went to her one time myself, and it was hard when you got near to know the way, for all the people were afraid to tell it.

'It was about a little chap of my own I went, that some strange thing had been put upon. When I got to her house there were about fifty to be attended to before me, and when my turn came, she looked in her bottle, a sort of a common greenish one that seemed to have nothing in it, and she told me where I came from, and the shape of the house and the appearance of it, and of the little lake you see there, and everything round about. And she told me of a limekiln that was near, and then she said the harm that came to him came from the forth beyond that. And I never knew of there being a forth there; but after I came home I went to look, and there, sure enough, it was.

'And she told me how it had come on him, and bid me remember a day that a certain gentleman stopped and spoke to me when I was out working in the hayfield, and the child with me playing about. And I remembered it well; it was old John Lydon, of Carrig, that was riding past, and stopped and talked, and was praising the child. And it was close by that forth beyond that John Lydon was born.

'I remembered it was soon after that day that the mother and I went to Loughrea, and when we came back the child had slipped on the threshold of the house and got a fall, and he was screeching and calling out that his knee was hurt, and from that time he did no good, and pined away and had the pain in his knee always.

'And Biddy Early said: "While you're talking to me now the child lies dying." And that was at twelve o'clock in the day. And she made up a bottle for me, herbs, I believe, it was made of, and she said, "Take care of it going home, and whatever may happen, don't drop it," and she wrapped it in all the folds of my handkerchief. So when I was coming home and got near Tillyra, I heard voices, and the man that was with me said, "Did you see all the people beyond the wall?" And I saw nothing, but I kept a tight hold on the bottle. And when we got to the Roxborough gate, there were many people talking and coming to where we were. I could hear them and see them, and so could the man that was with me; but when I heard them I remembered what she had said, and I took the bottle in my two hands and held it, and so I brought it home safely. And when I got home they told me the child was worse, and that at twelve o'clock the day before he lay, as they thought, dying. And when I brought in the bottle to him he pulled the bed-clothes up over his head, and we had the work of the world to make him swallow it. But from the time he took it the pain in his knee left him and he began to get better. And Biddy Early had told me not to let May Day pass without coming to her again when she gave me the bottle. But seeing him so well, I thought it no use to go again, and he got bad again, and it was not on May Day, but was in the month of May he died. He took to the bed before that, and he'd be always calling to me to come inside the bed where he was, and if I went in he'd hardly let me go. But I got afraid, and I didn't like to be too much with him.

'He was not eight years old when he died, but Mark Spelman, that used to live beyond there at that time, told me privately that when I'd be out of the house and he'd come in, the little chap would ask for the pipe and smoke it, but he'd never let me see him doing it. And queer chat he had, and he was old-fashioned in all his ways.' The child was evidently 'away', and a changeling believed to have taken his place. May Day, Midsummer Day, and November Eve, which are old Celtic festivals, are thought times of great activity among the fairies, and that is why he was to bring the child to Biddy Early before May Day. One story tells how she offered to show a mother the child the fairies had taken from her and whom she thought dead. A woman from Kiltartan says: 'My mother got crippled in her bed one night, God save the hearers!

And it was a long time before she could walk again with the pain in her back, and my father was always telling her to go to Biddy Early, and so at last she went. But she would do nothing for her, for, she said, "What ails you is nothing to do with my business." And she said, "You have lost three, and one was a grand little fair-haired one, and if you'd like to see her again I'll show her to you." And when she said that, my mother had no courage to look and to see the child she lost, but fainted then and there. And then she said, "There's a field with corn beyond your house, and a field with hay, and it's not long since the little fellow that wears a Lanberis[7] cap fell asleep there on a cock of hay. And before the stooks of corn are in stacks he'll be taken from you, but I'll save him if I can." And it was true enough what she said; my little brother that was wearing a Lanberis cap had gone to the field and fallen asleep on the hay a few days before. But no harm happened him, and he's all the brother I have living now. And it was Bruen from Gort went with my mother where his sister was sick. And she turned to him and she said, "When you get home, the coffin will be level with the door before you." And sure enough when he got home the sister had died, and the coffin had been brought and left at the door.'

The people always believed, I think, that whenever she saved anyone the fairies were trying to take, somebody or something was taken instead. She would sometimes ask people who came to her if they were ready to pay the penalty, and there is a story of one man who refused to lose a cow to save the wife he had come about, and when he got home she was dead before him. A well-to-do farmer near Gort, says, however: – 'It was Donovan gave his life for my sister that was his wife. When she fell sick he said he'd go to an old woman, one Biddy Early, that lived in the mountains beyond, and that did a great deal of cures, but the priests didn't like any one to be going to her. So he brought her there and she cured her the first time, but she says, "If you bring her again you'll pay the penalty."

'But when she fell sick again, he brought her the second time, but he stopped a mile from the house himself. But she knew it well and told the wife where he was, but she cured her, and that time the horse died. And the third time she fell sick he went again, knowing full well he'd pay the penalty. And so he did and died. But she married again, one O'Mara, and lives over there towards Kinvara.'

A cow or a horse or a fowl was generally sufficient. A man at Corcomroe says: 'Did I ever hear of Biddy Early? There's not a man in this countryside over forty years of age that hasn't been with her some time or other.

'There's a man living in that house over there was sick one time, and he went to her and she cured him, but, says she, "You'll have to lose something, and whatever it is, don't fret after it." So he had a grey mare and she was going to foal, and one morning when he went out he saw that the foal was born and was lying by the side of the wall. So he remembered what she had said to him, and he didn't fret.' Sometimes, however, the people believed that many lives were given instead of one. A man at Burren whom she cured says: 'I didn't lose anything at the time, but sometimes I thought afterwards it came on my family, when I lost so many of my children. A grand stout girl went from me, stout and broad, what else would ail her to go?'

One often hears of the difficulty of bringing the bottle Biddy Early gave safe home, because of the endeavours of the fairies to break it. A man near Gort says: 'Sometimes she'd give a bottle of some cure to people that came, but if she'd say to them, you'll never bring it home, break it they must on the way back with all the care they'd take of it.'

A man near Gort says: 'There was a boy I knew went to Biddy Early and she gave him a bottle, and she told him it would cure him if he did not lose it in the crossing of some road. And when he came to that place, for all he could do, the bottle was broke.'

A woman in Burren says: 'Himself went one time to Biddy Early, for his uncle Donoghue that was sick, and he found her, and her fingers all covered with gold rings, and she gave him a bottle, and she said, "Go into no house on the way home, or stop nowhere, or you'll lose it."

'But going home he had a thirst on him, and he came to a

public-house, and he wouldn't go in, but he stopped and bid the boy bring him a drink. But a little farther on the road the horse got a fall and the bottle was broke.'

And one story implies that the bottle was likely to be broken if you went 'too late'. A man from between Gort and Kiltartan says: 'Biddy Early didn't like you to go too late. Brien's sister was sick a long time, and when the brother went to her at the last she gave him a bottle with a cure. But on the way home the bottle broke, and the car and the horse got a fright and ran away. And when Dr Nolan was sent for to see her, he was led astray, and it's beyond Ballylee he found himself. And surely she was *taken* if ever any one was.'

Her 'second sight' seems to have been even more remarkable than her cures, and every one who ever went to her speaks of it with wonder. A very old woman in Kiltartan says: 'I went to Biddy Early one time myself, about my little boy that's now in America, that was lying sick in the house. But on the way to her I met a sergeant of police, and he asked where I was going, and when I told him, to joke like he said, "Biddy Early's after dying." "Then the devil die with her," said I. Well, when I got to the house, what do you think, if she didn't know that, and what I said. And she was vexed, and at the first she would do nothing for me. I had a pound for her here in my bosom, but when I held it out she wouldn't take it, but she turned the rings on her fingers, for she had a ring for every one, and she said, "A shilling for one, sixpence for another." But all she told me was that the boy was nervous, and so he was, she was right in that, and that he'd get well, and so he did.

'There was a man beyond, one Coen, was walking near the gate the same day, and he turned his foot and hurt it, and she knew that. She told me she slept in Ballylee Mill last night, and that there was a cure for all things in the world between the two wheels there.'

The witch doctor Kerwin says that 'the cure for all ills' was the moss on the stones, but that it cured evils done by the fairies and not common evils. When Biddy Early spoke of sleeping in Ballylee Mill, which is a great many miles from Feakle, she meant that she had been 'away' the night before and journeyed about where she would. A woman near Derrykeil in the Slieve Echtge Hills, says: 'I went to her myself one time to get a cure for myself where I was hurt with a fall I got coming down that hill over there. And she gave me what cured me, and she told me all about the whole place, and that there was a bowl broken in the house, and so there was.' A fall is often believed to be the work of the fairies. A woman at Tillyra says: 'There was a boy of the Saggartons in the house beyond went to Biddy Early, and she told him the name of the girl he would marry, and he did marry her after. And she cured him of a weakness he had and cured many, but it was seldom the bottle she'd give could be brought home without being spilled. I wonder did she go to *them* when she died? She got the cure among them anyway.'

A woman in Gort says: 'There was a man went to Biddy Early, and she told him that the woman he'd marry would have her husband killed by her brother. And it happened, for the woman he married was sitting by the fire with her husband and the brother came in having a drop of drink taken, and threw a pint pot at him that hit him in the head and killed him. It was the man that married her that told me this. One time she called in a man that was passing, and gave him a glass of whisky, and then she said to him, "The road you were going home by, don't go by it." So he asked why not, and she took the bottle, a long shaped bottle it was, and looked at it, holding it up, and then she bid him look through it and he'd see what would happen. But her husband said: "Don't show it to him, it might give him a fright he wouldn't get over." So she only said: "Well, go home by another way," and so he did and got home safe, for in the bottle she had seen a party of men that wouldn't have let him pass alive.

'She got the rites of the Church when she died, but first she was made to break the bottle.'

A man at Corcomroe says: 'There was a man, one Flaherty, came to his brother-in-law's house one day to borrow a horse. And the next day the horse was sent back, but he didn't come himself. And after a few days more they went to ask for him, but he had never come back at all. So the brother-in-law came to

Biddy Early's. And she and some others were drinking whisky, and they were sorry that they were at the bottom of the bottle. And she said, "That's no matter; there's a man on his way now, there soon will be more." And sure enough there was; for he brought a bottle with him. So when he came in he told her about Flaherty having disappeared. And she described to him a corner of a garden at the back of a house, and she said, "Go look for him there and you'll find him." And so they did, dead and buried.

'Another time a man's cattle was dying, and he went to her and she said: "Is there such a place as Benburb?" naming a forth up on the hill beyond there, "for it's there they're gone." And sure enough it was toward that forth they were straying before they died.' The cattle were in Benburb 'forth' or rath, for cattle are taken by the fairies as often as are women.

She was consulted about all kinds of things, for she knew all fairy things. A man at Doneraile, Co. Cork, tells how a man asked her to help him to find a buried treasure, but the story is vague, and he did not know the name of the man. He indeed knows much about her, but it is all vague, and he thinks that she is still living. He says: 'A man dreamed there was treasure in a certain "forth", and he went to her and asked what he should do. She said it must not be more than four that would dig for it. He and she and two others went, and they dug until they came to the lid of a big earthen pot, and she killed a black cock. A thing like a big ox came at them, and she said it was no use and that they must go home, because five and not four had come. They found a man watching behind the ditch, and they beat him before they went home. The next day the hole they had dug was filled up.'

The priests tried vainly to keep the people from going to her.

An old man on the beach at Duras says: 'The priests were greatly against Biddy Early, and there's no doubt at all it was from the fairies she got her knowledge. But who wouldn't go to hell for a cure when one of his own is sick?'

An old woman at Feakle says: 'There was a man I knew, living near the sea, and he set out to go to her at one time. And on the way he went into his brother-in-law's house, and a priest came in there and bid him not to go. "Well, Father," says he, "cure me yourself if you won't let me go to her to be cured." And when the priest wouldn't do that, he said: "Go on I will," and he went to her. And the minute he came in: "Well," says she, "you made a great fight for me on the way." For though it's against our creed to believe it, she could hear every earthly thing that was said in every part, miles off. But she had two red eyes, and some used to say, "If she can cure so much, why can't she cure her own eyes?"'

When she spoke of the red eyes, an old man who was listening said: 'She had no red eyes, but was a nice clean-looking woman. Any one might have red eyes at a time they'd have a cold, or the like'; this man had been to see her. A woman at Burren says: 'There was one Casey, in Kinvara, and he went to her one time for a cure. And Father Xavier came to the house and was mad with him for going, and, says he, "You take the cure out of the hand of God." And Mrs Casey said, "Your reverence, none of us can do that." "Well," says Father Xavier, "then I'll see what the devil can do, and I'll send my horse to-morrow that has a sore on his leg this long time, and try will she be able to cure him."

'So next day he sent a man with his horse, and when he got to Biddy Early's house she came out, and she told him every word Father Xavier had said, and she cured the sore. So after that he left the people alone. But before it he'd be dressed in a frieze coat, and a whip in his hand, driving away the people from going to her.'

A woman near Coole says: 'The priests took the bottle from Biddy Early before she died, and they found some sort of black things in it.' The bottle was of course merely a bottle of some kind of liquid in which she looked as 'crystal gazers' look into their crystals. She was surrounded all her life by a great deal of terror and reverence, but perhaps the terror was the greatest. She seems to have known how greatly she was feared, for a man who lived by the roadside near Tillyra says: 'I was with her myself one time and got a cure from her for my little girl that was sick. A bottle of whisky I brought her, and the first thing she did was to give me a glass out of it, "For," says she, "you'll maybe want it, my poor man." But I had plenty of courage in those days.'

A little while ago I met in Dublin a young man not at all of the people, and he told me that an uncle of his had once been her landlord, but had evicted her because of the scandal of seeing such great crowds drawn to her by what he held superstition, or diabolical power, I am not sure which. She cursed him, and in a very little time a house he was visiting at was burned to the ground and he was burned to death.

The 'knowledgeable' men and women may leave their knowledge to some one before they die, but few believe that Biddy Early left her knowledge to any one. One woman said to my friend, 'It's said that at a hurling the other day, there was a small little man seen, and that he was a friend of hers, and that she had left him the gift'; but the woman's husband said, 'No; the bottle was broken, and, anyhow, she had no power to pass it on; it was given to her for the term of her life.'

47

'DUST HATH CLOSED HELEN'S EYE'[1]

from the *Dome* (1899)

I have been lately to a little group of houses, not many enough to be called a village, in the barony of Kiltartan in County Galway, whose name, Baile-laoi,[2] is known through all the west of Ireland. There is the old square castle, Baile-laoi, inhabited by a farmer and his wife, and a cottage where their daughter and their son-in-law live, and a little mill with an old miller, and old ash trees throwing green shadows upon a little river and great stepping-stones. I went there two or three times last year to talk to the miller about Biddy Early,[3] a wise woman that lived in Clare some years ago, and about her saying, 'There is a cure for all evil between the two mill wheels of Baile-laoi,' and to find out from him or another whether she meant the moss between the running waters or some other herb. I have been there this summer, and I shall be there again before it is autumn, because Mary Hynes, a beautiful woman whose name is still a wonder by turf fires, died there sixty years ago; for our feet would linger where beauty has lived its life of sorrow to make us understand that it is not of the world. An old man brought me a little way from the mill and the castle, and down a long narrow boreen that was nearly lost in brambles and sloe bushes, and he said, 'That is the little old foundation of the house, but the most of it is taken for building walls, and the goats have ate those bushes that are growing over it till they've got cranky[4] and they won't grow any more. They say she was the handsomest girl in Ireland, her skin was like dribbled snow – he meant driven snow, perhaps, – and she had blushes in her cheeks. She had five handsome brothers, but all are gone now!' I talked to him about a poem in Irish, Raftery,[5] a famous poet, made about her, and how it said 'there is a strong cellar in

Baile-laoi'. He said the strong cellar was the great hole where the river sank under ground, and he brought me to a deep pool, where an otter hurried away under a grey boulder, and told me that many fish came up out of the dark water at early morning 'to taste the fresh water coming down from the hills'.

I first heard of the poem[6] from an old woman who lives about two miles further up the river and who remembers Raftery and Mary Hynes. She says, 'I never saw anybody so handsome as she was, and I never will till I die,' and that he was nearly blind and had 'no way of living but to go round and to mark some house to go to, and then all the neighbours would gather to hear. If you treated him well he'd praise you, but if you did not, he'd fault you in Irish. He was the greatest poet in Ireland, and he'd make a song about that bush if he chanced to stand under it. There was a bush he stood under from the rain, and he made verses praising it, and then when the water came through he made verses dispraising it.'[7] She sang the poem to a friend[8] and to myself in Irish, and every word was audible and expressive, as the words in a song were always, as I think, before music grew too proud to be the garment of words, flowing and changing with the flowing and changing of their energies. The poem is not as natural as the Irish poetry of the last century, for the thoughts are arranged in a too obviously traditional form, so that the old poor half blind man who made it, has to speak as if he were a rich farmer offering the best of everything to the woman he loves, but it has naïve and tender phrases. The friend that was with me has made some of the translation, but some of it has been made by the country people themselves. I think it has more of the simplicity of the Irish verses than one finds in most translations.

Going to Mass by the will of God,
The day came wet and the wind rose;
I met Mary Hynes at the cross of Kiltartan,
And I fell in love with her then and there.

I spoke to her kind and mannerly,
As by report was her own way;
And she said, Raftery, my mind is easy,
You may come to-day to Baile-laoi.

When I heard her offer I did not linger,
When her talk went to my heart my heart rose.
We had only to go across the three fields,
We had daylight with us to Baile-laoi.

The table was laid with glasses and a quart measure;
She had fair hair and she sitting beside me;
And she said, 'Drink, Raftery, and a hundred welcomes,
There is a strong cellar in Baile-laoi.'

O star of light and O sun in harvest,
O amber hair, O my share of the world,
Will you come with me upon Sunday
Till we agree together before all the people?

I would not grudge you a song every Sunday evening,
Punch on the table or wine if you would drink it.
But O King of Glory, dry the roads before me,
Till I find the way to Baile-laoi.

There is sweet air on the side of the hill
When you are looking down upon Baile-laoi;
When you are walking in the valley picking nuts and blackberries,
There is music of the birds in it and music of the Sidhe.

What is the worth of greatness till you have the light
Of the flower of the branch that is by your side?
There is no good to deny it or to try and hide it,
She is the sun in the heavens who wounded my heart.

There was no part of Ireland I did not travel,
From the rivers to the tops of the mountains,
To the edge of Lough Greine whose mouth is hidden
And I saw no beauty but was behind hers.

Her hair was shining and her brows were shining too;
Her face was like herself, her mouth pleasant and sweet.
She is the pride, and I give her the branch,
She is the shining flower of Baile-laoi.

It is Mary Hynes, the calm and easy woman,
Has beauty in her mind and in her face.
If a hundred clerks were gathered together,
They could not write down a half of her ways.

An old weaver, whose son is supposed to go away among the sidhe (the fairies) at night, says:– 'Mary Hynes was the most beautiful thing ever made. My mother used to tell me about her, for she'd be at every hurling, and wherever she was she was dressed in white. As many as eleven men asked her in marriage in one day, but she wouldn't have any of them. There was a lot of men up beyond Kilbecanty one night sitting together, drinking and talking of her, and one of them got up and set out to go to Baile-laoi and see her, but Cloon bog was open then, and when he came to it he fell into the water, and they found him dead there in the morning. She died of the fever that was before the famine.' Another old man says he was only a child when he saw her, but he remembered that 'the strongest man that was among us, one John Madden, got his death on the head of her, cold he got crossing rivers in the night time to get to Baile-laoi'. This is perhaps the man the other remembered, for tradition gives the one thing many shapes. There is an old woman who remembers her, at Derrybrien among the Echtge Hills, a vast desolate place, which has changed little since the old poem said 'the stag upon the cold summit of Echtge hears the cry of the wolves',[9] but still mindful of many poems and of the dignity of ancient speech. She says, 'The sun and the moon never shone on anybody so handsome, and her skin was so white that it looked blue and she had two little blushes on her cheeks.' And an old wrinkled woman who lives close by Baile-laoi and has told me many tales of the sidhe, says, 'I often saw Mary Hynes, she was handsome indeed. She had two bunches of curls beside her cheeks, and they were the colour of silver. I saw Mary Molloy that was drowned in the river beyond, and Mary Guthrie that was in Ardrahan, but she took the sway of them both, a very comely creature. I was at her wake too – she had seen too much of the world. She was a kind creature. One day I was coming home through the field beyond and I was tired, and who should come out but the *Poisin Glegeal*[10] (the shining flower), and she gave me a glass of new milk.' This old woman meant no more than some beautiful bright colour by the colour of silver, for though I knew an old man, he is dead now who thought she might know 'the cure for all the evils in the world', that the sidhe know. She has seen too little gold to know its colour. But a man by the shore of Kinvara, who is too young to remember Mary Hynes, says, 'Everybody says there is no one at all to be seen now so handsome, it is said she had beautiful hair the colour of gold. She was poor, but her clothes every day were the same as Sunday, she had such neatness. And if she went to any kind of a meeting, they would all be killing one another for a sight of her, and there was a great many in love with her, but she died young. It is said that no one that has a song made about them will ever live long.'

Those who are much admired are, it is held, taken by the sidhe, who can use ungoverned feeling for their own ends, so that a father, as an old herb doctor told me once, may give his child into their hands, or a husband his wife. The admired and desired are only safe if one says 'God bless them' when one's eyes are upon them. The old woman that sang the song thinks too that Mary Hynes was 'taken', as the phrase is, 'for they have taken many that are not handsome and why would they not take her, and people came from all parts to look at her, and maybe there were some that did not say God bless her'. An old man, who lives by the sea at Duras, has as little doubt that she was taken, 'for there are some living yet can remember her coming to the pattern[11] there beyond, and she was said to be the handsomest girl in Ireland'. She died young because the gods loved her, for the sidhe are the gods, and it may be that the old saying, which we forget to understand literally, meant her manner of death in old times. These poor countrymen and countrywomen in their beliefs and in their emotions are many years nearer to that old Greek world, that set beauty beside the fountain of things, than are our men of learning. She 'had seen too much of the world', but these old men and women when they tell of her blame another and not her, and though they can be hard they grow gentle as the old men of Troy grew gentle when Helen passed by on the walls.

The poet who helped her to so much fame has himself a great fame throughout the west of Ireland. Some think that Raftery was half blind and say, 'I saw Raftery, a dark man, but he had sight enough to see her,' or the like, but some think he was wholly blind, as he may have been at the end of his life. Fable makes all things perfect in their kind, and her blind people must never look on the world and the sun. I asked a man I met one day, when I was looking for a pool *na mna sidhe*[12] where women of faery have been seen, how Raftery could have admired Mary Hynes so much if he had been altogether blind. He said, 'I think Raftery was altogether blind, but those that are blind have a way of seeing things, and have the power to know more, and to feel more, and to do more, and to guess more than those who have their sight, and a certain wit and a certain wisdom is given to them.' Everybody indeed will tell you that he was very wise for was he not only blind but a poet? The weaver whose words about Mary Hynes I have already given, says, 'His poetry was the gift of the Almighty, for there are three things that are the gift of the Almighty, poetry and dancing and principles. That is why in the old times an ignorant man coming down from the hillside would be better behaved and have better learning than a man with education you'd meet now, for they got it from God'; and a man at Coole says 'when he put his finger to one part of his head everything would come to him as if it was written in a book'; and an old pensioner at Kiltartan says 'he was standing under a bush one time and he talked to it and it answered him back in Irish. Some say it was the bush that spoke, but it must have been an enchanted voice in it, and it gave him the knowledge of all the things of the world. The bush withered up afterwards, and it is to be seen on the roadside now between this and Rahasane.' There is a poem of his about a bush, which I have never seen, and it may have come out of the cauldron of fable in this shape. A friend of mine met a man once who had been with him when he died, but the people say that he died alone, and one Maurteen Gillane told Dr Hyde[13] that all night long a light was seen streaming up to heaven from the roof of the house where he lay, and 'that was the angels who were with him'; and all night long there was a great light in the hovel, 'and that was the angels who were waking him. They gave that honour to him because he was so good a poet and sang such religious songs.' It may be that in a few years Fable, who changes mortalities to immortalities in her cauldron, will have changed Mary Hynes and Raftery to perfect symbols of the sorrow and beauty and of the magnificence and penury of dreams.[14]

48

'*MAEVE* AND CERTAIN IRISH BELIEFS'

from *Beltaine* (1900)

I think I remember Mr Martyn[1] telling me that he knew nothing, or next to nothing, about the belief in such women as Peg Inerny among the Irish peasants. Unless the imagination has a means of knowledge peculiar to itself, he must have heard of this belief as a child and remembered it in that unconscious and instinctive memory on which imagination builds. Biddy Early,[2] who journeyed with the people of faery when night fell, and who cured multitudes of all kinds of sickness, if the tales that one hears from her patients are not all fancy, is, I think, the origin of his Peg Inerny; but there were, and are, many like her. Sometimes, as it seems, they wander from place to place begging their bread, but living all the while a noble second life in faery. They are sometimes called 'women from the North', because witchcraft, and spirits, and faeries come from the North. A Kiltartan woman said to a friend who has got me many tales: 'One time a woman from the North came to our house, and she said a great deal of people are kept below there in the lisses. She had been there herself, and in the night-time, in one moment, they'd be all away at Cruachma, wherever that may be – down in the North, I believe. And she knew everything that was in the house, and told us about my sister being sick, and that there was a hurling match going on that day, and that it was at the Isabella Wood. I'd have picked a lot of stories out of her, but my mother got nervous when she heard the truth coming out, and told me to be quiet. She had a red petticoat on her, the same as any country woman, and she offered to cure me, for it was that time I was delicate, and her ladyship sent me to the salt water. But she asked a shilling, and my mother said she hadn't got it. "You have," said she, "and heavier metal than that you have in the house." So then my mother gave her the shilling, and she put it in the fire and melted it, and, says she, "after two days you'll see your shilling again"; but we never did. And the cure she left, I never took it; it's not safe, and the priests forbid us to take their cures. No doubt at all she was one of the ingentry (I have never heard this word for the faeries from anybody else) that can take the form of a woman by day and another form by night.' Another woman in the same neighbourhood said: 'I saw myself, when I was but a child, a woman come to the door that had been seven years with the good people, and I remember her telling us that in that seven years she'd often been glad to come outside the houses and pick the bits that were thrown into the trough for the pigs; and she told us always to leave a bit about the house for those that could not come and ask for it: and though my father was a cross man, and didn't believe in such things, to the day of his death we never went up to bed without leaving a bit of food outside the door!' Sometimes, however, one hears of their being fed with supernatural food, so that they need little or none of our food.

I have two or three stories of women who were queens when in faery; I have many stories of men and women, and have even talked with some four or five among them, who believed that they had had supernatural lovers. I met a young man once in the Burren Hills who remembered an old Gaelic poet, who had loved Maive, and was always very sorrowful because she had deserted him. He had made lamentation for her, but the young man could only remember that it was sorrowful, and that it called her 'beauty of all beauty';[3] a phrase that makes one think that she had become a symbol of ideal beauty, as the supernatural lover is in Mr Martyn's play. One of the most lovely of old Gaelic poems is the appeal of such a lover to his beloved. Midir,[4] who is called King of the sidhe (the faeries), sang to the beautiful Etain, wife of the King who was called Eochaid the ploughman.[5] 'O beautiful woman, come with me to the marvellous land where one listens to a sweet music, where one has spring flowers in one's hair, where the body is like snow from head to foot, where no one is sad or silent, where teeth are white and eyebrows are black . . . cheeks red, like foxglove in flower . . . Ireland is beautiful, but not so beautiful as the Great Plain I call you to. The beer of Ireland is heady, but the beer of the Great Plain is much more heady. How marvellous is the country I am speaking of: Youth does not grow old there; streams of warm blood flow there, sometimes meed, sometimes wine. Men are charming, and without a blot there. O woman, when you come into my powerful country, you will wear a crown of gold upon your head. I will give you the flesh of swine, and you will have beer and milk to drink, O beautiful woman. O beautiful woman, come with me!'

Maive (Medb is the Irish spelling) is continually described as the queen of all western faeries, and it was probably some memory of her lingering in western England, or brought home by adventurers from Ireland, that gave Shakespeare his Queen Mab. But neither Maive, nor any of our Irish faeries are like the fairies of Shakespeare; for our fairies are never very little, and are sometimes taller and more beautiful than mortals. The greatest among them were the gods and goddesses of ancient Ireland, and men have not yet forgotten their glory.

49

'IRISH FAIRY BELIEFS'

from the *Speaker* (1900)

Some ten or eleven years ago, when I was compiling a little anthology of Irish fairy and folk tales,[1] somebody asked an eminent authority to advise me. He replied that there was little Irish folklore in print, that could be trusted as one could trust the books of Scottish folklore, and went on to moralise over the defects of Irish character. A couple of years ago this eminent authority described the works of the Irish folklorists as more exhaustive and valuable than the works of the Scottish folklorists. The truth is that moralising over defects and virtues of national character is for the most part foolish, for the world is shaped by habits of thought and habits of expression, and these, in young nations at any rate, can change with extreme swiftness. Ireland learned to do in about five years the work she had neglected for a century, and the intellectual awakening, which has given us so much, gave us Mr Larminie, Mr Curtin, Dr Hyde,[2] the most admirable of all that have translated out of the Gaelic of the country people, and some whose work is in magazines and newspapers. But because these writers, with the exception of Mr Curtin in one little book,[3] have devoted themselves to the traditional tales and rather neglected the traditional beliefs one has a quite unworn welcome for Mr Daniel Deeney, a National school teacher of Spiddal, in Western Galway, and a Gaelic speaker, who has got together a little bundle of tales of omens and charms and apparitions. He follows his masters wisely too, though here and there he shows a defect of the evil days of Croker and Lover,[4] and, while making some little incident vivid with characteristic dialogue, uses a word or phrase which has not come out of the life he is describing, but out of the life of some other place, or out of books.

He should know the English dialect of Galway as few know it, and yet I am certain that 'indade' is out of some novelist. The Irish countrypeople do not mispronounce, but rather over pronounce, the sound of the 'ees' in 'indeed', and surely 'till' for 'to' belongs to the north of Ireland, where Mr Deeney was born, I believe, and not to Galway. He has heard many of his stories in Irish, I should imagine, for the countrypeople where he lives talk Irish principally, and, concluding very rightly that literary English is not a natural equivalent for the Irish of the countrypeople, has translated them into a dialect which even those who know it perfectly must continue to write imperfectly until it is classified and examined by learned men, as English and Scottish dialect has been. No merely instinctive knowledge can quite overcome a convention which innumerable novelists and journalists have imposed upon the imagination. A safer equivalent would have been that English, as full of Gaelic constructions as the English of the countrypeople but without a special pronunciation, which Dr Hyde has adopted in *Beside the Fire*,[5] the one quite perfect book of Irish folklore. Once, too, in telling a very wild and curious story of the Cladagh of Galway, he allows himself to look through the clouds of a literary convention. Lily-white fingers and flowing golden hair cannot be typical of the Cladagh, though they are typical of the heroines of forty years ago.

I point out these faults because Mr Deeney, living in the middle of a primitive people and with a real knack in story and dialogue and a perfect knowledge of Gaelic, has only to work carefully at his craft to be of great importance to the intellectual awakening of Ireland. As it is he has made a book which makes one understand better than any book I know of the continual communion of the Irish countrypeople with supernatural beings of all kinds. A man who lives not far from Mr Deeney once said to me, 'There is no man mowing a meadow but sees them one time or another.' These country people have seen what a king might give his crown and the world its wealth to have seen, and the doubts and speculations, that are in our eyes so great a part of the progress of the world, would be in their eyes, could they understand them, but dust in the hollow of a hand. Already some that have devoted themselves to the study of the visions and the beliefs of such people are asking whether it is we, still but very few, or primitive and barbaric people, still a countless multitude, who are the exceptions in the order of nature, and whether the seer of visions and hearer of voices is not the normal and healthy man. It may be that but a few years shall pass before many thousands have come to think that men like these mowers and fishers of Mr Deeney's, who live a simple and natural life, possess more of the experience on which a true philosophy can be founded than we who live a hurried, troubled, unhealthy life. I am convinced, as I am convinced by no other thing, that this change will come; and it may be that this change will make us look to men like Mr Deeney, who are at the gates of primitive and barbaric life, for a great deal of the foundations of our thought.

50

'IRISH WITCH DOCTORS'

from the *Fortnightly Review* (1900)

The Irish countryman certainly believes that a spiritual race lives all about him, having horses and cattle, and living much the same life that he does, and that this race snatches out of our life whatever horse or cow, or man or woman it sets its heart on; and this belief, harmonised with Christianity by certain ingenious doctrines, lives side by side with Christianity and has its own priesthood. This priesthood, sometimes called 'faery doctors', sometimes 'knowledgeable men', and sometimes 'cow doctors', from its curing cows that have been 'swept', as the word is, has secrets which no folklorist may ever perhaps wholly discover, for it lives in terror of the spiritual race who are, it believes, the makers and transmitters of its secrets. I have questioned these men, and some of them have talked to me pretty freely, so freely, indeed, that they were afraid for themselves afterwards, but I feel that there is more to be known about them, and that I know less about them than about anything else in Irish folklore. I met one man, whom I will call Kirwan, on the Galway coast last year. I cannot tell his whereabouts more freely, for he is afraid of the priests, and has made me promise to tell nobody where he lives. A friend of mine, who knew I was curious in these matters, had asked some of the coast people if there was anyone who did cures through the power of the faeries, as I wanted a cure for a weakness of the eyes that had been troubling me. A man I will call Daly said, 'There's a man beyond is a great warrior in this business, and no man within miles of the place will build a house or a cabin or any other thing without going there to ask if it's a right place. He cured me of a pain in my arm I couldn't get rid of. He gave me something to drink, and he bid me to go to a quarry and to touch some of the stones that were lying outside it, and not to touch others of them. Anyway, I got well.'

The country people are always afraid of building upon a path of 'the others', as they call the spirits, and one sometimes hears of houses being deserted because of their being 'in the way', as the phrase is. The pain in the arm was doubtless believed to be what is called 'the touch', an ailment that is thought to come from 'the others', and to be the beginning of being carried away. The man went on to give another example of Kirwan's power, a story of a horse that seemed possessed, as we would say, or 'away' and something else put in its place, as he would say. 'One time down by the pier we were gathering in the red seaweed; and there was a boy there was leading a young horse the same way he had been leading him a year or more. But this day, of a sudden, he made a snap to bite him; and, secondly, he reared and made as if to jump on top of him; and, thirdly, he turned round and made at him with the hoofs. And the boy threw himself on one side and escaped, but with the fright he got he went into the bed and stopped there. And the next day Kirwan came, and told him everything that had happened, and he said, "I saw thousands on the strand near where it happened last night."'

The next day my friend went to see the wife of 'the great warrior in this business', to find out if he would cure my eyes. She found her in a very small cottage, built of very big stones, and of a three-cornered shape that it might fit into a crevice in the rocks. The old woman was very cautious at first, but presently drew her stool over to where my friend was sitting, and said, 'Are you *right*? you are? then you are my friend. Come close and tell me is there anything Himself can do for you?' She was told about my eyes, and went on, 'Himself has cured many, but sometimes *they* are vexed with him for some cure he has done, when he interferes with the herb with some person they are meaning to bring away, and many's the good beating they gave him in the field for doing that. Myself they gave a touch to here in the thigh, so that I lost my walk; vexed they are with me for giving up the throwing of the cup.' She had been accustomed to tell fortunes with tea-leaves. 'I do the fortunes no more, since I got great abuse from the priest for it. Himself got great abuse from the priest, too, Father Peter, and he gave him plaster of Paris. I mean by that he spoke soft and humbugged him, but he does the cures all the same, and Father Maginn gave him leave when he was here.' She asked for my Christian names, and when she heard them went on, 'I'll keep that, for Himself will want it when he goes on his knees. And when he gathers the herb, if it's for a man, he must call on the name of some other man, and call him a King, *Righ*. And if it's for a woman, he must call on the name of some other woman, and call her a Queen. That is calling on the king or the queen of the plant.' My friend asked where her husband had got the knowledge and she answered, 'It was from his sister he got the cure. Taken she was. We didn't tell John of it, where he was away caring horses. But he knew of it before he came home, for she followed him there one day he was out in the field, and when he didn't know her, she said, "I'm your sister Kate." And she said, "I bring you a cure that you may cure both yourself and others." And she told him of the herb, and the field he'd find it growing, and he must choose a plant with seven branches, the half of them above the clay and the half of them covered up. And she told him how to use it. Twenty years she's gone, but she's not dead yet, but the last time he saw her he said she was getting grey. Every May and November he sees her; he'll be seeing her soon now. When her time comes to die, she'll be put in the place of some other one that's taken, and so she'll get absolution. A nurse she has been all the time among them.'

May and November, the beginning and end of the old Celtic year, are always times of supernatural activity in Ireland. She is to be put back as a changeling to get absolution when she is too old to be any more use among 'the others'. All, one is almost always told, are put back in this way. I had been told near Gort that 'the others' had no children of their own, but only children they stole from our world. My friend, hearing her say that Kirwan's sister was a nurse, asked her about this. She said, 'Don't believe those that say they have no children. A boy among them is as clever as any boy here, but he must be matched with a woman from earth; and the same way with their women, they must get a husband here. And they never can give the breast to a child, but must get a nurse from here.' She was asked if she had herself seen 'the others', and if 'Himself' saw them often. She said, 'One time I saw them myself in a field, and they hurling. Bracket caps they wore, and bracket clothes of all colours. Some were the same size as ourselves, and some looked like gossoons that didn't grow well But Himself has the second sight, and can see them in every place There's as many of them in the sea as on the land, and sometimes they fly like birds across the bay. There is always a mistress among them. When one goes among them they would be al laughing and jesting, but when that tall mistress you heard o would tap her stick on the ground, they'd all draw to silence.'

The clothes of 'the others' are always described as 'bracket' which is the Irish for variegated, but is explained to mean striped by the country people when talking of 'the others'. The old inhabitants of Ireland who have become 'the others', the people say, because they were magicians, and cannot die till the last day, wore striped clothes. The famous story of *The Quest of the Bull of Cualgne*,[1] preserved in a manuscript of the eleventh cen tury, makes its personages wear 'striped' and 'streaked' and 'vari egated' jackets of many colours.

It was arranged that I should go to Daly's house, and tha Kirwan should go there to meet me after dark, that our meeting might not be noticed. We went to Daly's next evening, but found that Kirwan had been there earlier in the day to leave a bunch o herbs, which a botanist has since identified as the dog violet, fo me to drink in boiled milk, which was to be brought to the boi three times; and to say that he could do nothing more for me, fo what was wrong with my eyes 'had nothing to do with tha business', meaning that it was not the work of spirits. We left an urgent message asking Kirwan to come and talk to us, and nex day Daly, who had been very doubtful if he would come, brough us word that he would come as soon as it was dark. We reached the cottage amid a storm of wind, and the door was cautiously opened, and we were let in. Kirwan was sitting on a low stool in a corner of a wide hearth, beside a bright turf fire. He was shor and broad, with regular features, and had extraordinary dark and bright eyes, and though an old man, had, as is common among these sea people, thick dark hair. He wore a flannel-sleeved waistcoat, cloth trousers, patched on the knees with darker stuff, and held a soft felt hat in his hands, which he kept turning and squeezing constantly. Unlike his wife he spoke nothing but Irish. Daly sat down near us with a guttering candle in his hands, and interpreted. A reddish cat and a dog lay beside the fire, and sometimes the dog growled, and sometimes the woman of the house clutched her baby uneasily and looked frightened. Kirwan said, stopping every now and then for Daly to interpret, 'It's not from *them* the harm came to your eyes. There's one of the eyes worse than the other' (which was true) 'and it's not in the eyes that the trouble began' (which was true). I tried to persuade him that it might be 'from them', to find out why he thought it was not, and I told him of a certain vision I had once, to make him feel that I was not a mere prying unbeliever. He said my eyes would get well, and gave me some more of the herb, but insisted that the harm was not 'from *them*'. He took the vision as a matter of course, and asked if I was ever accustomed to sleep out at night, but added that some might sleep out night after night and never fall into their power, or even see them. I asked if it was his friends among them who told what was wrong with anybody, and he said, 'Yes, when it has to do with their business, but in this case they had nothing to do with it.' My friend asked how he got his knowledge first, and he said, 'It was when I was in the field one day a woman came beside me, and I went on to a gap in the wall, and she was in it before me. And then she stopped me, and she said, "I'm your sister that was taken, and don't you remember how I got the fever first and you tended me, and then you got it yourself, and one had to be taken, and I was the one?" And she taught me the cure and the way to use it. And she told me she was in the best of places, and told me many things that she bound me not to tell. And I asked was it here she was kept ever since, and she said it was, but, she said, in six months I'll have to move to another place, and others will come where I am now, and it would be better for you if we stopped here, for the most of us here now are your neighbours and your friends. And it was she gave me the second sight.'

I asked if he saw 'them' often, and he said: 'I see them in all places, and there's no man mowing a meadow that doesn't see them at some time or other. As to what they look like, they'll change colour and shape and clothes while you look round. Bracket caps they always wear. There is a king and a queen and a fool in each house of them, that is true enough, but they would do you no harm. The king and the queen are kind and gentle, and whatever you'll ask them for they will give it. They'll do no harm at all, if you don't injure them. You might speak to them if you'd meet them on the road, and they'd answer you, if you'd speak civil and quiet, and not be laughing or humbugging – they wouldn't like that.'

He told a story about a woman he knew, who had been taken away among them to nurse their children, and how she had come back after – a story that I am constantly hearing – and then suddenly stopped talking and stooped to the hearth, and took up a handful of hot ashes in his hand, and put them into the pocket of his waistcoat, and said he'd be afraid going home, because he'd 'have to tell what errand he had been on'. I gave him some whisky out of my flask, and we left him.

The next day we saw Daly again, and he said, 'I walked home with the old man last night, he was afraid to go by himself. He pointed out to me on the way home a graveyard where he got a great beating from them one night. He had a drop too much taken, after a funeral, and he went there to gather the plant, and gathered it wrong, and they came and punished him, that his head is not the better of it ever since. He told me the way he knows, in the gathering of the plant, what is wrong with the person that is looking for a cure. He has to go on his knees and to say a prayer to the king and the queen and to the gentle and the simple among them, and then he gathers it; and if there are black leaves about it, or white (withered) ones, but chiefly a black leaf folded down, he knows the illness is some of their doing. But for this young man the plant came fresh and clean and green. He has been among them himself, and has seen the king and the queen, and he says they are no bigger than the others, but the queen wears a wide cap, and the others have bracket caps. He never would allow me to build a shed beside the house here, though I never saw anything there myself.'

We found an old man on the borders of Clare and Galway who knew English, and was less afraid of talking to us, from whom we heard a great deal. We went through a stony country, a good way from any town, and came at last to the group of poor cottages which had been described to us. We found his wife, a big, smiling woman, who told us that her husband was haymaking with their children. We went to the hay-field, and he came, very well pleased, for he knew my friend, to the stone wall beside the road. He was very square and gaunt, and one saw the great width of his chest through his open shirt, and recognised the great physical strength, supposed constantly to mark those who are in the service of 'the others'. We talked of some relations of his, who were in good circumstances and tenants of my friend, and I think I told him some visionary experiences of my own. It was evident that he lived in great terror of 'the others', but gradually he began to talk. We asked him where he got his power to work cures, and he replied, 'My uncle left me the power, and I was able to do them, and did many, but my stock was all dying, and what could I do? So I gave a part of the power to Mrs Merrick, who lives in Gort, and she can do a great many things.'

His stock died because of the anger of 'the others', or because some other life had to be given for every life saved. We asked about his uncle, and he said, 'My uncle used to go away amongst them. When I was a young chap, I'd be out in the field working with him, and he'd bid me to go away on some message, and when I'd come back it might be in a faint I'd find him. It was he himself was taken, it was but his shadow or something in his likeness was left behind. He was a very strong man. You might remember Ger Kelly, what a strong man he was, and stout, and six feet two inches in height. Well, he and my uncle had a dispute one time, and he made as though to strike at him, and my uncle, without so much as taking off his coat, gave one blow that stretched him on the floor. And at the barn at Bunnahow he and my father could throw a hundredweight over the collar beam, what no other man could do. My father had no notion at all of managing things. He lived to be eighty years, and all his life he looked as innocent as that little chap turning the hay. My uncle had the same innocent look. I think they died quite happy.'

He pointed out to us where there was a lake, and said, 'My uncle one time told, by name, of a man that would be drowned there that day at 12 o'clock; and so it happened.' We asked him if his uncle's knowledge was the same kind of knowledge as the knowledge of a famous wise woman called Biddy Early;[2] and he said, 'Surely I knew Biddy Early, and my uncle was a friend of hers. It was from the same they got the cures. Biddy Early told me herself that where she got it was, when she was a servant-girl in a house, there was a baby lying in the cradle, and he went on living for a few years. But he was friendly to her, and used to play tunes for her, and when he went away he gave her the bottle and the power. She had but to look in the bottle and she'd see all that had happened and all that was going to happen. But he made her give a promise that she'd never take more than a shilling for any cure she did, and she wouldn't have taken £50 if you had offered it to her, though she might take presents of bread and wine, and such things. The cure for all things in the world? Surely she had it, and knew where it was, and I knew it myself, too, but I could not tell you of it. Seven parts I used to make it with, and one of them's a thing that's in every house.'

He only told us of one spirit he had himself seen. He was walking with another man on the road to Galway, and he saw 'a very small woman in a field beside the road, walking down towards us, and she smiling and carrying a can of water on her head, and she dressed in a blue spencer',[3] and he asked the other man if he saw her, 'but he did not, and when I came up to the wall she was gone'. I have since heard, however, that he was 'away' among them himself. He would only talk of what his uncle or somebody else had seen. I showed him some water-colour drawings of men and women of great beauty, and with very singular haloes about their heads, which had been drawn and painted from visions by a certain Irish poet who, if he lives, will have seen as many wonders as Swedenborg;[4] and rather to my surprise, for I had thought the paintings too idealised for a peasant to understand, he became evidently excited. 'They have crowns like that and of other shapes,' he said, pointing to the halo. I asked if they ever made their crowns out of light, and he said, 'They can do that.' He said one of the paintings was of a queen, and that they had 'different queens, not always the same, and clothes of all colours they wear'. My friend held up a sapphire ring, and made it flash, and asked if their clothes were as beautiful. He said, 'Oh, they are far grander than that, far grander than that. They have wine from foreign parts, and cargoes of gold coming in to them. The houses are ten times more beautiful and ten times grander than any house in this world, and they could build one of them up in that field in ten minutes. Coaches they make up when they want to go out driving, with wheels and all, but they want no horses. There might be twenty going out together sometimes, and all full of them. Youngsters they take mostly to do work for them, and they are death on handsome people, for they are handsome themselves. To all sorts of work they put them, digging potatoes, and the like. The people they bring away must die some day, but as to themselves they were living from past ages, and can never die till the time when God has his mind made up to redeem them. And those they bring away are always glad to be brought back again. If you were to bring a heifer from those mountains beyond and to put it into a meadow, it would be glad to get back again to the mountain, because it's the place it knows.'

And he showed us a sign with the thumb that we were never to tell to anybody, but that we were to make if we ever felt 'a sort of a shivering in the skin when we were walking out, for that shows that something is near'. If we held our hand like that we might go 'into a forth itself' and get no harm, but we were not to neglect that, 'for if they are glad to get one of us they'd be seven times better pleased to get the like of you. And they are everywhere around us, and now they may be within a yard of us on this grass. But if I ask you, What day's to-morrow? and you said Thursday, they wouldn't be able to overhear us. They have the power to go in every place, even on the book the priest is reading!'

To say, 'What day is to-morrow?' and be answered 'Thursday', or to say, 'What day is this?' and be answered 'Thursday', or to say, 'God bless them Thursday', is a common spell against being overheard, but in some places the countrypeople think that it is enough to be told what day the next day, or that day, really is. There is no doubt some old pagan mystery in Thursday,[5] and if we knew more about the old Celtic week[6] of nine nights we might understand it.

We went to see old Langan, as I will call him, another day, and found him hay-making as before, but he went with us into his house, where he gave us tea and home-made bread, both very good. He would take no money either that time or the time before, and his manner was very courteous and dignified. He told much more about 'the Others', this time. He said: 'There are two classes, the Dundonians, that are like ourselves, and another race more wicked and more spiteful. Very small they are and wide, and their belly sticks out in front, so that what they carry, they don't carry it on the back, but in front, on the belly, in a bag.'

The Dundonians are undoubtedly the Tuatha Dé Danaan, and Folk of the Goddess Danu, the old gods of Ireland, and the men with the bags on their stomachs undoubtedly the Firbolg, or Bag Men, as it is commonly translated, who are thought by M. de Jubainville[7] an inferior Divine race, and by Prof. Rhys[8] an inferior human race conquered by the Celts. The old Irish epic tales associate the Megalithic ruins upon Aran with the Firbolg, and a friend, Mr Synge,[9] tells me that the people of Aran call the builders of the ruins belly-men. Bolg in Irish means bag or belly.

He went on: 'There are fools among them, dressed in strange clothes like mummers, but it may be the fools are wisest after all. There is a queen in every regiment or house of them. It is of those they steal away they make queens for as long as they live, or that they are satisfied with them. There were two women fighting at a spring of water, and one hit the other on the head with a can and killed her. And after that her children began to die. And the husband went to Biddy Early, and as soon as she saw him she said, "There's nothing I can do for you. Your wife was a wicked woman, and the one she hit was a queen among them, and she is taking your children one by one, and you must suffer till twenty-one years are up." And so he did.'

We asked him if he ever knew anybody 'the others' had given money to, and he said, 'As to their treasure, it's best be without it. There was a man living by a forth, and where his house touched the forth he built a little room and left it for them, clean and in good order, the way they'd like it. And whenever he'd want money, for a fair or the like, he'd find it laid on the table in the morning. But when he had it again, he'd leave it there, and it would be taken away in the night. But after that going on for a time, he lost his son.

'There was a room at Cregg where things used to be thrown about, and every one could hear the noises there. They had a right to clear it out and settle it the way they'd like it.' Then he turned to my friend and said, 'You should do that in your own big house. Set out a little room for them with spring water in it always, and wine you might leave – no, not flowers, they wouldn't want so much as that, but just what will show your good will.'

A man at Kiltartan had told us that Biddy Early had said to him, 'There is a cure for all the evil in the world between the two millwheels at Ballylee,' and I asked what cure that could be. He said, 'Biddy Early's cure that you heard of, between the two wheels of Ballylee, it was the moss on the water of the millstream. It can cure all things brought about by *them*, but not any common ailment. But there is no cure for the stroke given by a queen or a fool.'

We told him of an old man who had died a little time before, and how fighting was heard by the neighbours before he died. He said, 'They were fighting when Stephen Gorham died, that is what often happens. Everyone has friends among them, and the friends would try to save, when the others would be trying to bring you away. Youngsters they pick up here and there, to help them in their fighting or in their work. They have cattle and horses, but all of them have only three legs. The handsome they like, and the good dancers, and the straight and firm; they don't like those that go to right and left as they walk. And if they get a boy amongst them, the first to touch him, he belongs to her. They don't have children themselves, only the women that are brought away among them have children, but those don't live for ever like the Dundonians. They can only take a child, or a horse, or such thing, through the eye of a sinner. If his eye falls on it, and he speaks and doesn't say, "God bless it," they can bring it away then. But if you say it yourself in your heart, it will do as well. They take a child through the eye of its father, a wife through the eye of her husband.' The meaning was that if you look at anybody or anything with envy or desire or admiration, it may be used by 'the others', as a link between them and the thing or person they are coveting. One finds this thought all over Ireland, and it is probably the origin of the belief in the evil eye. Blake thought that everything is 'the work of spirits, no less than digestion and sleep';[10] and this thought means, I think, that every emotion, which is not governed by our will, or suffused with some holy feeling, is the emotion of spirits who are always ready to bring us under their power. Langan had himself been accused once of giving a chicken into the power of 'the others'. 'One time myself, when I went to look for a wife, I went to the house, and there was a hen and a brood of small chickens before the door. Well, after I went home, one of the chickens died. And what do you think they said, but that it was I overlooked it.'

This seems to have broken off the marriage for a time, but he married her in the end, and has had to suffer all kinds of misfortunes because of her. 'The others' tried to take her first, the day after her marriage using, as I understand, his feelings about her as their link between her and them. 'My wife got a touch from them, and they have a watch on her ever since. It was the day after I married, and I went to the fair of Clarenbridge. And when I came back the house was full of smoke, but there was nothing on the hearth but cinders, and the smoke was more like the smoke of a forge. And she was within lying on the bed, and her brother was sitting outside the door crying. And I took down a fork from the rafters, and asked her was it a broom, and she said it was. So then I went to the mother and asked her to come in, and she was crying too, and she knew well what had happened, but she didn't tell me, but she sent for the priest. And when he came, he sent me for Geoghagan, and that was only an excuse to get me away, and what he and the mother tried was to get her to face death. But the wife was very stout, and she wouldn't give in to them. So the priest read mass, and he asked me, would I be willing to lose something. And I said, so far as a cow or a calf, I wouldn't mind losing that.'

Smiths are often associated with 'the others', and with magic in Ireland, and so the room filled 'with the smoke of a forge'. St Patrick prayed against the spells of smiths. The question about the fork was to find out if she was in what we would call an hypnotic state, receptive to every suggestion. 'Well, she partly recovered, but from that day no year went by, but I lost ten lambs maybe, or other things. And twice they took my children out of the bed, two of them I have lost. And the others they gave a touch to. That girl there, see the way she is, and she is not able to walk. In one minute it came on her, out in the field, with the fall of a wall.' He told the girl to come out from where she sat in the corner of the chimney, with the dazed vacant look that one saw on the faces of the other children. She staggered for a foot or two, and then sat down again. From our point of view, her body was paralysed and her mind gone. She was tall and gentle-looking, and should have been a strong, comely, country girl. The old man went on: 'Another time the wife got a touch, and she got it again, and the third time she got up in the morning, and went out of the house and never said where she was going. But I had her watched, and I told the boy to follow her, and never to lose sight of her. And I gave him the sign to make if he'd meet any bad thing. So he followed her, and she kept before him, and while he was going along the road, something was up on top of the wall with one leg. A red-haired man it was, with a thin face and no legs. But the boy got hold of him and made the sign, and carried him till he came to the bridge. At first he could not lift him, but after he had made the sign he was quite light. And the woman turned home again, and never had a touch after. It's a good job the boy had been taught the sign. It was one among them that wanted the wife. A woman and a boy we often saw coming to the door, and she was the matchmaker. And when we would go out, they would have vanished.'

He told us some other little odds and ends about a warning his uncle had given against cutting down a certain bush before his house, and how, when it was cut down twenty years after his uncle's death, a bullock died; and that 'Danes hate Irishmen to this day', and that 'when there is a marriage in Denmark', he has been told, 'the estates they owned in Ireland are handed down' (I have heard something like this in Sligo also); and then, evidently feeling that he was telling us a great mystery, he said, 'The cure I made with seven parts, and I took three parts of each, and I said, Father, Son, and Holy Spirit be on it, and with that I could go into a forth or any place. But as to the ingredients, you could get them in any house.'

We did not ask him for the ingredients, nor do I believe that any threat or any bribes would ever get them from him. When we were going, he said, and we were both struck by his dignity as he said it, 'Now I've told you more than ever I told my wife. And I could tell you more, but I'd suffer in my skin for it. But if ever you, or one belonging to you, should be in trouble, come to me, and what I can do to relieve you, I'll do it.'

Kirwan spoke of seeing his spirits, and Langan his, while in their ordinary state; but only those who are at times 'away', that is, who are believed to go away among the spirits, while their bodies are in a trance, are thought to be able to bring back those who are 'away'. In ancient Ireland it was only a *file* who had the knowledge of a certain ritual called the *imbas forosna*, or great science which enlightens, whereby he could pass as many as nine days in trance, who had the full knowledge of his order.[11] It was long before we could find anyone who was 'away' and would tell us what it was like, for almost all who are 'away' believe that they must be silent. At last an old woman, whom I will call Mrs Sheridan, after telling many lesser things, told us what it was like. My friend had gone to see her one day, and been told a few curious things, but cautiously, for her daughter, who was afraid of such things, was there. She had said, 'Come here close, and I'll tell you what I saw at the old castle there below. I was passing there in the evening, and I saw a great house and a grand one, with screens at the end of it, and windows open. Coole House[12] is nothing to what it was for size or grandeur. And there were people inside, and a lady leaning out of the window, and her hair turned back, and she made a sign to me, and ladies walking about, and a bridge over the river. For they can build up such things all in a minute. And two coaches came driving up and across the bridge to the house, and in one of them I saw two gentlemen, and I knew them both well, and both of them had died long before. One was Redmond Joyce, and the other was the master's own father. As to the coach and horses, I didn't take much notice of them, for I was too much taken up with looking at the gentlemen. And a man came and called out to me and asked, would I come across the bridge, and I said I would not. And he said it would be better for you if you did; you'd go back heavier than you came. I suppose by that he meant they'd give me some good thing. And then two men took up the bridge and laid it against the wall. Twice I've seen that same thing, the house and the coaches, and the bridge, and I know well I'll see it a third time before I die.'

This woman had never seen a drawbridge, and she had not read about one, for she cannot read. 'It would have cost a penny a week to go to school,' she explains, and it is most unlikely that she has ever seen a picture of one. The peasants continually see in their visions the things and costumes of past times, and this can hardly be tradition, for they have forgotten the names of their own great-grandfathers, and know so little about ancient customs that they will tell you about Finn mac Cumhail flinging a man over a haystack on his way to the assizes in Cork.

They had met another day on the road, and as they came opposite to a very big twisted thorn-tree, the old woman had curtsied very low to the bush, and said, 'And that's a grand bush we're passing by – whether it's a bush belonging to them I don't know, but wherever they get shelter, there they might be, but anyway it's a fine bush, God bless it.' But she had not said anything about being 'away'. At last, one day she came and sat with us and talked and seemed very glad to talk. She is one of the handsomest old country-women I have ever seen, and though an old woman, is vigorous in mind and body. She does not seem to know the cures that Kirwan and Langan know, and has not, I think, any reputation for doing cures. She says, however – 'I know the cure for anything *they* can do to you, but it's few I'd tell it to. It was a strange woman came in and told it to me, and I never saw her again. She bid me to spit and to use the spittle, or to take a graineen of dust from the navel, and that's what you should do if anyone you care for gets a cold or a shivering, or they put anything upon him.

'All my life I've seen them, and enough of them. One day I was with John Cuniff by the big hole near his house, and we saw a man and a woman coming from it, and a great troop of children, little boys they seemed to be, and they went through the gate into Coole, and there we could see them running and running along by the wall. And I said to John Cuniff, "It may be a call for one of us," and he said, "Maybe it's for some other one it is." But on that day next week he was dead.'

She has seen the coach-a-baur,[13] or deaf coach, as it is called from the deaf or rumbling sound it makes, in which they drive about.

'I saw the coach one night near the chapel. Long it was, and black, and I saw no one in it. But I saw who was sitting up driving it, and I knew it to be one of the Fardys that was taken some time before. I never saw them on horses, but when I came to live at Martin Macallum's, he used to bring in those red flowers that grow by the road, when their stalks were withered, to make the fire. And one day I was out in the road, and two men came over to me, and one was wearing a long grey dress, and he said to me, "We have no horses to ride on, and we have to go on foot, because you have too much fire." So then I knew it was their horses we were burning.'

She seems to confuse red and yellow, and to have meant the yellow *bucalauns* or ragweeds, believed to be the horses of 'the others'. Ragweed is given as a medicine to horses, and it may have got its association with the horses of 'the others' through its use in witch medicine.

'One day I saw a field full of them, some were picking up stones to clear it, and some were ploughing it up. But the next day, when I went by, there was no sign of it being ploughed up at all. They can do nothing without some live person is looking at them, that's why they were always so much after me.'

One is constantly hearing that 'the others' must have a mortal among them, for almost everything they do, and one reads as constantly in the old Irish epic tales of mortals summoned by the gods to help them in battles. The tradition seems to be that, though wisdom comes to us from among spirits, the spirits must get physical power from among us. One finds a modification of the same idea in the spiritualistic theory of mediumship. Mrs Sheridan went on: 'One time I went up to a forth to pick up a few sticks for the fire, and I was breaking one of the sticks on the ground, and a voice said from below, "Is it to break down the house you want?" and a thing appeared that was like a cat, but bigger than any cat ever was. And one time I was led astray in Coole, where I went to gather sticks for the fire. I was making a bundle of them, and I saw a boy beside me and a little dogeen with me, a grey one. And at first I thought it was Andrew Healy, and then I saw it was not. And he walked along with me, and I asked him did he want any of the sticks, and he said he did not, and as we were walking he seemed to grow bigger. And when we came to where the caves go underground he stopped, and I asked him his name, and he said, "You should know me, for you've seen me often enough." And then he was gone, and I knew he was no living thing.

'One day I was following the goat, to get a sup of milk from her, and she turned into the field and up into the castle of Lydican, and went up from step to step up the stairs to the top, and I followed, and on the stairs a woman passed me, and I knew her to be Ryan's wife that died. And when I got to the top I looked up, and there standing on the wall was a woman looking down at me, long-faced and tall, and with bracket clothes, and on her head something yellow and slippery, not hair, but like marble. And I called out to ask her wasn't she afraid to be up there, and she said she was not. And a herd that used to live below in the castle saw the same woman one night he went up to the top, and a room and a fire, and she sitting at it, but when he went there again there was no sign of her or of the room.[14]

'I know that I used to be away with them myself, but how they brought me I don't know; but when I'd come back, I'd be cross with my husband and with all; and I believe that I was cross with *them* when they wouldn't let me go. I met a man on the road one time, he had striped clothes like the others, and he told me why they didn't keep me altogether was because they didn't like cross people to be with them. The husband would ask me where I was, and why I stopped so long away; but I think he knew I was taken, and it fretted him; but he never spoke much about it. But my mother knew it well, but she'd try to hide it. The neighbours would come in and ask where was I, and she'd say I was sick in the bed, for whatever was put there in place of me would have the head in under the clothes. And when a neighbour would bring me in a drink of milk, my mother would put it by, and say, "Leave her now, maybe she'll drink it to-morrow." And, maybe, in a day or two I'd meet a friend, and she'd say, "Why wouldn't you speak to me when I went into the house to see you?" And I was a young, fresh woman at that time. Where they brought me to I don't know; nor how I got there; but I'd be in a very big house, and it round, the walls far away that you'd hardly see them, and a great many people all round about. I would see there neighbours and friends that I knew, and they in their own clothing, and with their own appearance, but they wouldn't speak to me, nor I to them, and when I'd meet them again, I'd never say to them that I saw them there. But the others had all long faces, and striped (bracket) clothes of blue and all colours, and they'd be laughing and talking and moving about. What language did they speak? Irish, of course; what else would they speak? And there was one woman of them, very tall, and with a long face, standing in the middle, taller than anyone you ever saw in this world, and a tall stick in her hand: she was the Mistress. She had a high yellow thing on her head – not hair – her hair was turned back under it, like the woman I saw at the window of the castle, and she had a long yellow cloak hanging down behind, and down to her feet.'

I showed her a picture of a spirit, by the seer I have already spoken of, and made her look at the halo, which is made up of rods of light, with balls of gold light upon their ends, and asked if she had anything like that on her head. She answered, 'It was not on her head, it was lower down here about the body'; and by body she seemed to mean the waist. The old epic tales talk constantly of golden apples being used as ornaments. She looked at the brooch in the picture, a great wheel brooch, and said, 'She had a brooch like that in the picture, but hanging low down like the other.' I took up a different picture, a picture of a gigantic spirit, with the same rod-like headdress, leaning over a sleeping man. It was painted in dull blue and grey, and very queer. She did not wait for me to question her, but said, 'And that picture you have there in your hand, I saw one like it on the wall. It was a very big place and very grand, and a long, long table set out, and grand food offered me, and wine, but I never would touch it. And sometimes I had to give the breast to a child; and there were cradles in the room. I didn't want to stop there, and I began crying to get home, and the tall woman touched me here on the breast with the stick in her hand; she was vexed to see me wanting to go away.

'They have never brought me away since the husband died, but it was they took him from me.' She has much fear of 'the others', and tells of many mischiefs they have done her. She went on to tell of her husband's death. 'It was in the night, and he lying beside me, and I woke and heard him move, and I thought I heard someone with him. And I put out my hand, and what I touched was an iron hand, like knitting needles it felt. And I heard the bones of his neck crack, and he gave a sort of a choked laugh; and I got out of the bed and struck a light, and saw nothing, but I thought I heard someone go through the door. And I called to Honor, and she didn't come, and I called again, and she came; and she said she struck a light when she heard me calling, and was coming, and someone came and struck the light from her hand. And when we looked in the bed he was dead, and not a mark on him.'

They have taken also two of her children. 'There was a child of my own, and he but a year and a-half old, and he got a quinsy and a choking in the throat, and I was holding him in my arms beside the fire, and all in a minute he died. And the men were working down by the river washing sheep, and they heard the crying of a child pass over in the air, and they said, "That's Sheridan's child that's brought away." So I know, sure enough, that he was taken.'

Another fell under their power through being brought to Biddy Early by a neighbour. 'There was a woman, Mrs Merrick, had something wrong with her, and she went to Biddy Early, and nothing would do her but to bring my son along with her. And I was vexed – what call had she to bring him there? And when Biddy Early saw him she said, "You'll travel far, but wherever you go, you'll not escape." The woman he went up with died about six months after; but he went to America, and he wasn't long there, when what was said came true and he died. They followed him sure enough as far as he went. And one day since then I was on the road to Gort, and Macan said to me, "Your son is on the road before you." And I said, "How can that be and he dead?" But for all that, I hurried on. And on the road I met a little boy, and I asked did he see anyone, and he said, "You know well who I saw." But I got no sight of him at all myself.'

They have injured her and annoyed her in all kinds of ways. 'Even when I was a child I could see them, and once they took my walk from me and gave me a bad foot. And my father cured me, and if he did, in five days after he died. But there's not much harm at all in them, not much harm.' She said there was not much harm in them for fear they might be listening. 'Three times when I went for water to the well the water was spilled over me, and I told Honor after that, they must bring the water themselves, I'd go for it no more. And the third time it was done there was a boy – one of the Healys – was near, and when he heard what happened me, he said, "It must have been the woman that was at the well along with you that did that." And I said, "There was no woman at the well along with me." "There was," he said; "I saw her there beside you, and she with two tin cans in her hand." One time after I came to live here, a strange woman came into the house, and I asked what was her name; and she said, "I was in it before you were in it"; and she went into the room inside, and I saw her no more. But Honor and Martin saw her coming in the door, and they asked me who was she, for they never saw her before. And in the night, where I was sleeping at the foot of the bed, she came and threw me out on the floor, that the joint of my arm has a mark on it yet. And every night she'd come, and she'd spite and annoy me in some way. And at last we got Father Boyle to come and to drive her out. And as soon as he began to read, there went out of the house a great blast, and there was a sound as loud as thunder. And Father Boyle said, "It's well for you she didn't have you killed before she went."'

And another time a man said to her in a forth, "Here's gold for you, but don't look at it till you go home." And I looked and saw horse-dung, and I said, "Keep it yourself, much good may it do you." They never gave me anything did me good, but a good deal of torment I had from them.' She is afraid that the cat by her hearth may be one of *them* in disguise, come to work her some evil. 'There's something that's not right about an old cat, and it's well not to annoy them. I was in the house one night, and one came in, and he tried to bring away the candle that was lighting in the candlestick, and it standing on the table. And I had a little rod beside me, and I made a hit at him with it, and with that he dropped the candle, and made at me, as if to kill me. And I went on my two knees, and I asked his pardon three times, and when I asked it the third time he got quiet all of a minute, and went out the door. But when you speak of them, you should always say the day of the week. Maybe you didn't notice that I said, "This is Friday," just as we passed the gate.'

I did not see her again, but last winter my friend heard she was ill, and went to see her. She said: 'It's very weak I am, and took to my bed since yesterday. *They* have changed now out of where they were, near the castle, and it's inside the demesne they are. It was an old man told me that; I met him on the road there below. First I thought he was a young man, and then I saw he was old, and he grew very nice-looking after, and he had plaid clothes. "We've moved out of that now," he said, "and it's strangers will be coming in it. And you ought to know me," he said.

'It's about a week ago, one night someone came in the room, in the dark, and I knew it was my son that I lost, he that went to

America – Mike. He didn't die; he was whipped away. I knew he wasn't dead, for I saw him one day on the road to Gort on a coach, and he looked down and he said, "That's my poor mother." And when he came in here I couldn't see him, but I knew him by his talk. And he said, "It's asleep she is," and he put his two hands on my face, and I never stirred. And he said, "I'm not far from you now." For he is with the others, inside Coole, near where the river goes down.[15] To see me he came, and I think he'll be apt to come again before long. And last night there was a light about my head all the night, and no candle in the room at all.'

51

'TO D. P. MORAN'S *LEADER*'

(1900)

Dear Sir,

I look upon the appearance of *The Leader* as of importance, for it will express, I understand, and for the first time, the loves and hates, the hopes and fears, the thoughts and ideals of the men who have made the Irish language a political power. *Claideamh Soluis* and *Fainne an Lae,*[1] because of their preoccupation with the language itself, have been unable to make that free comment on the life about them, which the times require, if illusions that were, perhaps, truths in their day are not to cling about us and drown us. Ireland is at the close of a long period of hesitation, and must set out before long under a new policy, and it is right that any man who has anything to say should speak clearly and candidly while she is still hesitating. I myself believe that unless a great foreign war comes to re-make everything, we must be prepared to turn from a purely political nationalism with the land question as its lever, to a partly intellectual and historical nationalism like that of Norway, with the language question as its lever. The partial settlement of the land question has so limited the number of men on whom misrule presses with an immediate pressure, and ten years of recrimination have so tarnished the glory that once surrounded politics as a mere game, that the people of Ireland will not in our time give a full trust to any man who has not made some great spectacular sacrifice for his convictions, or that small continual sacrifice which enables a man to become himself Irish, to become himself an embodiment of some little of the national hope. We will always have politics of some kind, and we may have to send members of Parliament to England for a long time to come, but our politics and our members of

Parliament will be moved, as I think, by a power beyond themselves, though by one which they will gladly obey, as they were moved by a power beyond themselves, which they gladly obeyed, in the recent debate on the report of the Commissioners of Education.[2] We need not feel anxious because the new movement has taken a firmer hold in the towns than in the country places, for very many of the priesthood are coming to understand that the Irish language is the only barrier against the growing atheism of England, just as we men of letters have come to understand that it is the only barrier against the growing vulgarity of England; and the priesthood can do what they like with the country places. In ten years or in fifteen years or in twenty years the new movement will be strong enough to shake governments, and, unlike previous movements that have shaken governments, it will give continuity to public life in Ireland, and make all other righteous movements the more easy.

I do not think that I am likely to differ very seriously from you and from your readers about this movement, and for the very reason that it is a national movement, a movement that can include the most different minds. I must now, however, discuss another matter, about which I have differed and may still differ from you and from many of your readers. Side by side with the spread of the Irish language, and with much writing in the Irish language, must go on much expression of Irish emotion and Irish thought, much writing about Irish things and people, in the English language, for no man can write well except in the language he has been born and bred to, and no man, as I think, becomes perfectly cultivated except through the influence of that language; and this writing must for a long time to come be the chief influence in shaping the opinions and the emotions of the leisured classes in Ireland in so far as they are concerned with Irish things, and the more sincere it is, the more lofty it is, the more beautiful it is, the more will the general life of Ireland be sweetened by its influence, through its influence over a few governing minds. It will always be too separate from the general life of Ireland to influence it directly, and it was chiefly because I believed this that I differed so strongly in 1892 and 1893 from Sir Charles Gavan Duffy and his supporters, who wished to give such writing an accidental and fleeting popularity by uniting it with politics and economics.[3] I believe that Ireland cannot have a Burns or a Dickens, because the mass of the people cease to understand any poetry when they cease to understand the Irish language, which is the language of their imagination, and because the middle class is the great supporter and originator of the more popular kind of novels, and we have no middle class to speak of; but I believe that we may have a poetry like that of Wordsworth and Shelley and Keats, and a prose like that of Meredith and Pater and Ruskin. There will be a few of all classes who will read this kind of literature, but the rest will read and listen to the songs of some wandering Raftery,[4] or of some poet like Dr Hyde,[5] who has himself high culture, but makes his songs out of the thoughts and emotions he finds everywhere about him, and out of the circumstances of a life that is kept poetical by a still useful language, or they will go to perdition with their minds stuffed full of English vulgarity; till perhaps a time has come when no Irishman need write in any but his own language.

We can bring that day the nearer by not quarrelling about names, and by not bringing to literary discussion, which needs a delicate and careful temper, the exasperated and violent temper we have learned from a century of political discussion. You have decided, and rightly, considering your purpose, to call all 'literature concerning Ireland written in English', 'Anglo-Irish literature', and I shall certainly do the same when I would persuade a man that nothing written in English can unite him perfectly to the past and future of his country, but I will certainly call it Irish literature, for short, when I would persuade him that 'Farewell to Ballyshannon and the Winding Banks of Erne' should be more to him than 'The Absent-Minded Beggar',[6] or when I am out of temper with all hyphenated words, or with all names that are a mixture of Latin and English. Such things are governed by usage and convenience, and I do not foresee a day when there will not be Englishmen who will call Walt Whitman English literature, and merely because they like him, and Englishmen who will call him American literature, and merely because they dislike him. And I would be sorry to see a day when I should not find a certain beautiful sermon of

St Columbanus,[7] which compares life to a roadway on which we journey for a little while, and to the rising and falling of smoke, in accounts of Irish literature, as well as in accounts of the Latin literature of the Early Church.

Whether we dispute about names or not, the temper of our dispute is perhaps of more importance than the subject, and it is certainly of especial importance when we discuss those among our writers who have any rank, however small, in that great household I have spoken of. Ruskin, Meredith, Pater, Shelley, Keats, Wordsworth, had all to face misunderstanding and misrepresentation, and sometimes contumely, for they spoke to an evil time out of the depths of the heart, and if England had been accustomed to use in literary discussion the coarse methods of political discussion, instead of descending to them in rare moments of excitement, she would not now have that remnant which alone unites her to the England of Shakespeare and Milton. In Ireland, too, it may be those very men, who have made a subtle personal way of expressing themselves, instead of being content with English as it is understood in the newspapers, or who see all things reflected in their own souls, which are from the parent fountain of their race, instead of filling their work with the circumstance of a life which is dominated by England, who may be recognised in the future as most Irish, though their own time entangled in the surfaces of things may often think them lacking in everything that is Irish. The delicate, obscure, mysterious song of my friend, 'AE', which has, as I know, comforted the wise and beautiful when dying, but has hardly come into the hands of the middle class – I use the word to describe an attitude of mind more than an accident of birth – and has no obviously Irish characteristics, may be, or rather must be, more Irish than any of those books of stories or of verses which reflect so many obviously Irish characteristics that every newspaper calls them, in the trying phrase of 1845, 'racy of the soil'![8]

Now, sir, you and I have paid each other a very pretty compliment, for when you wrote to me for a letter, you must have thought that I would not be influenced by the many attacks you have made upon me and upon the movement I represent,[9] while I, on my side, have written this letter because I am convinced from what I have read of your writings, that you are one of the few in Ireland who try to go down to the root of public events and who seek the truth with earnestness and sincerity. For you and me, as for all others, it may be wholesome to dispute about a real issue, but if we dispute about misunderstandings or about names we can only destroy that clear ardour of life which is as necessary to your cause as to mine, and never long exists without precision and lucidity. I have, therefore, dealt at length with the public issues which lie between us, and must say some few words on a purely personal issue. You have been misled, doubtless, by reading what some indiscreet friend or careless opponent has written, into supposing that I have ever used the phrases 'Celtic note' and 'Celtic renaissance' except as a quotation from others, if even then, or that I have quoted Matthew Arnold's essay on Celtic literature 'on a hundred platforms' or elsewhere in support of the ideas behind these phrases, or that I have changed my opinions about the revival of the Irish language since a certain speech in Galway. I have avoided 'Celtic note' and 'Celtic renaissance' partly because both are vague and one is grandiloquent, and partly because the journalist has laid his ugly hands upon them, and all I have said or written about Matthew Arnold since I was a boy is an essay in *Cosmopolis*,[10] in which I have argued that the characteristics he has called Celtic, mark all races just in so far as they preserve the qualities of the early races of the world. And I think I need not say, after the first part of this letter, that I still believe what I believed when I made that speech in Galway; but none of these matters are likely to interest your readers. I will, therefore, close this long letter with a hope that *The Leader* may enable you to complete the powerful analysis of Irish life which you have begun in the *New Ireland Review*.

52

'THE FOOL OF FAERY'

from the *Kensington* (1901)

I have heard one Hearne a witch doctor, who is on the border of Clare and Galway, say that in 'every household' of faery 'there is a queen and a fool', and that if you are 'touched' by either you never recover, though you may from the touch of any other in faery. He said of the fool that he was 'maybe the wisest of all', and spoke of him as dressed like one of 'the mummers that used to be going about the country'. Since then a friend has gathered me some few stories of him, and I have heard that he is known, too, in the highlands. I remember seeing a long, lank, ragged man sitting by the hearth in the cottage of an old miller not far from where I am now writing, and being told that he was a fool; and I find from the stories that my friend has gathered that he is believed to go to faery in his sleep; but whether he becomes an *Amadán-na-Breena*, a fool of the forth, and is attached to a household there, I cannot tell. It was an old woman that I know well, and who has been in faery herself, that spoke of him. She said, 'There are fools amongst them, and the fools we see, like that *Amadán of Ballylee,* go away with them at night, and so do the woman fools that we call *Oinseachs* (apes).' A woman who is related to the witch doctor on the border of Clare, and who can cure people and cattle by spells, said, 'There are some cures I can't do. I can't help anyone that has got a stroke from the queen or the fool of the forth. I knew of a woman that saw the queen one time, and she looked like any Christian. I never heard of any that saw the fool but one woman that was walking near Gort, and she called out, "There's the fool of the forth coming after me." So her friends that were with her called out, though they could see nothing, and I suppose he went away at that, for she got no harm. He was like a big strong man, she said, and half naked, and that is all she said about him. I have never seen any myself, but I am a cousin of Hearne and my uncle was away twenty-one years.' The wife of the old miller said, 'It is said they are mostly good neighbours, but the stroke of the fool is what there is no cure for; anyone that gets that is gone. The *Amadán-na-Breena* we call him!' And an old woman who lives in the Bog of Kiltartan, and is very poor, said: 'It is true enough, there is no cure for the stroke of the *Amadán-na-Breena*. There was an old man I knew long ago, he had a tape, and he could tell what diseases you had with measuring you; and he knew many things. And he said to me one time, "What month of the year is the worst?" and I said "The month of May, of course." "It is not," he said; "but the month of June, for that's the month that the Amadan gives his stroke!" They say he looks like any other man, but he's leathan (wide), and not smart. I knew a boy one time got a great fright, for a lamb looked over the wall at him with a beard on it, and he knew it was the *Amadan*, for it was the month of June. And they brought him to that man I was telling about, that had the tape, and when he saw him he said, "Send for the priest and get a Mass said over him." And so they did, and what would you say but he's living yet and has a family! A certain Regan said, "They, the other sort of people, might be passing you close here and they might touch you. But any that gets the touch of the *Amadán-na-Breena* is done for." It's true enough that it's in the month of June he's most likely to give the touch. I knew one that got it, and he told me about it himself. He was a boy I knew well, and he told me that one night a gentleman came to him, that had been his landlord, and that was dead. And he told him to come along with him, for he wanted him to fight another man. And when he went he found two great troops of them, and the other troop had a living man with them too, and he was put to fight him. And they had a great fight, and he got the better of the other man, and then the troop on his side gave a great shout, and he was left home again. But about three years after that he was cutting bushes in a wood and he saw the *Amadan* coming at him. He had a big vessel in his arms, and it was shining, so that the boy could see nothing else; but he put it behind his back then and came running, and he said he looked wild and wide, like the side of the hill. And the boy ran, and he threw the vessel after him, and it broke with a great noise, and whatever came out of it, his head was gone there and then. He lived for a while after, and used to tell us many things, but his wits were gone. He thought they mightn't have liked him to beat the other man, and he used to be afraid something would come on him.'

The country of faery has taken its form from old Irish life, and old Celtic legends show one many a fool that was terrible or wise. The head of Fionn's fool[1] prophesied and sang after it had been cut from his body, like the head of Bran[2] in the Welsh story, and was perhaps at one time as holy as the head on a dish, that is in place of the Grail in another Welsh story.

Cairbre loved the wife of Fionn, and because Lomna the fool got to know of it, Cairbre killed him, and fled with the head upon a spear. Presently he thought himself safe, and began to cook fish upon a stone, with the head beside him and his men about him. He should have put a piece of the fish in the mouth of the head if he would have escaped ill luck, but did not, and the head began to sing something hard to understand about the fish. Cairbre cooked another fish, and still did not put a piece in the mouth of the head, and the head sang about the ill dividing of the food and of the coming vengeance of Fionn; and Cairbre bade his men put the head outside the house, though he knew that this would make his luck the worse. The head sang a third time outside the house, and while it was singing Fionn came with all his men about him.

I knew a man who was trying to bring before his mind's eye an image of Aengus, the old Irish god of love and poetry and ecstasy, who changed four of his kisses into birds and suddenly the image of a man with a cap and bells rushed before his mind's eye, and grew vivid and spoke and called itself 'Aengus' messenger'.[3] And I knew another man, a truly great seer, who saw a white fool in a visionary garden, where there was a tree with peacocks' feathers instead of leaves, and flowers that opened to show little human faces when the white fool had touched them with his coxcomb, and he saw at another time a white fool sitting by a pool and smiling and watching the images of many fair women floating up from the pool. All ancient peoples have thought that death was the beginning of wisdom and power and beauty; and that foolishness was a kind of death. It is therefore natural that many should see a fool with a shining vessel of some enchantment or wisdom or dream too powerful for mortal brains in 'every household of them'. It is natural, too, that there should be a queen to every household of them, and that one should hear little of their kings, for women come more easily than men to that wisdom which ancient peoples, and all wild peoples even now, think the only wisdom. The self, which is the foundation of our knowledge, is broken in pieces by foolishness, and is forgotten in the sudden emotions of women, and therefore fools may get, and women certainly get, glimpses of much that sanctity finds at the end of its painful journey. The man who saw the white fool said of a certain woman, not a peasant woman, 'If I had her power of vision I would know all the wisdom of the gods, and her visions do not interest her.' And I know of another woman, also not a peasant woman, who would pass in sleep into countries of an unearthly beauty and who never cared for anything but to be busy about her house and her children; and presently an herb doctor cured her, as he called it. Wisdom and beauty and power may sometimes come to those who die every day they live, though their dying may not be like the dying Shakespeare spoke of. There is a war between the living and the dead, and the Irish legends keep harping upon it. They will have it that when the potatoes or the wheat or any other of the fruits of the earth decay, they ripen in faery, and that our dreams lose their wisdom when the sap rises in the trees, and that our dreams can make the trees wither, and that one hears the bleating of the lambs of faery in November, and that blind eyes can see more than other eyes. Because the soul always believes in these, or in like things, the cell and the wilderness shall never be long empty, or lovers come into the world who will not understand Shelley's verse –

> Heardst thou not sweet words among
> That heaven resounding minstrelsy?
> Heardst thou not that those who die
> Awake in a world of ecstasy?

How love, when limbs are interwoven,
And sleep, when the night of life is cloven,
And thought to the world's dim boundaries clinging,
And music when one's beloved is singing,
Is death?[4]

53

'BY THE ROADSIDE'

from *An Claidheamh Soluis* (1901)

Last night I went to a wide place on the Kiltartan road to listen to some Irish songs. While I waited for the singers an old man sang the 'Pósaidh Glégeal,'[1] the praise of that country beauty who died so many years ago and is still remembered, and spoke of a singer he had known who sang so beautifully that no horse would pass him, but must turn its head and cock its ears to listen. Presently a score of men and boys, and girls, with shawls over their heads, gathered under the trees to listen. Somebody sang 'Sa Mhuirnín Dílis', and then somebody else 'Jimmy Mo Mhíle Stor', mournful songs of separation, of death, and of exile. Then some of the men stood up and began to dance, while another lilted the measure they danced to, and then somebody sang 'Eibhlín a Rúin', that glad song of meeting which has always moved me more than other songs, because the lover who made it so long ago sang it to his sweetheart under the shadow of a mountain I looked at every day in my childhood. The voices melted into the twilight, and were mixed into the trees, and when I thought of the words they too melted away, and were mixed with the generations of men. Now it was a phrase, now it was an attitude of mind, an emotional form, that had carried my memory to older verses, or even to forgotten mythologies. I was carried so far that it was as though I came to one of the four rivers, and followed it under the wall of Paradise to the roots of the trees of knowledge and of life. There is no song or story handed down among the cottages that has not words and thoughts to carry one as far, for though one can but know a little of their ascent, one knows that they ascend like those old genealogies through unbroken dignities to the beginning of the world. Folk art is indeed the oldest of the aristocracies of thought, and because it refuses what is passing, trivial, the merely clever and pretty, as certainly as the vulgar and insincere, and because it has gathered into itself the simplest and most unforgettable thoughts of the generations it is the soil where all great art is rooted. It gave to the Cathedral of Chartres and to Cormac's Chapel[2] their ornament and something of their form, and to Homer and Shakespeare their stories and half their images, and to the painters of Italy a thousand beautiful details; and wherever it is spoken by the fireside, or sung by the roadside, or carved upon the lintel, appreciation of the arts that a single mind gives unity and design to, spreads quickly amongst everybody when its hour is come.

Some years ago I was at a Masonic concert in a Connacht town. A man from London, where he had lived, perhaps, in some coterie where good taste protested against modern taste, sang a couple of old English folk-songs, but all the other songs were vulgar and modern. Instead of an ancient tradition, one found the short-lived conventions of this age, the insincerity, the shallow cleverness, the reeking vulgarity. I had never been at a concert of this kind before, and listened in astonishment. I knew many of the people there, but it had never occurred to me that they had tastes harder to forgive than any vice. Presently somebody sang about whiskey and shillelaghs and Donnybrook fair, and all those Irish men and women applauded. I waited till my voice could be heard, and hissed loudly. No matter how little one hopes for a change, no matter even if one think that this vulgarity is to overrun the world to the end, one can protest and keep one's integrity. To protest against it in one form is to protest against it in all, for vulgarity is uninventive, and the architecture those people admired, the books they read, the windows they set up in the churches, the sermons they listened to, their conversation about the fire, though I, like another, had come to take all these for matters of course, had been moulded in the same workshop with the songs that gave them pleasure.

In a society that has cast out imaginative tradition, only a few people – three or four thousand out of millions – favoured by their own characters and by happy circumstances, and only then after much labour, have understanding of imaginative things, and yet 'the imagination is the man himself'. The churches in the middle ages won all the arts into their service because men understood that when imagination is impoverished, a principal voice – some would say the only voice – for the awakening of wise hope and durable faith, and understanding charity, can speak but in broken words, if it does not fall silent. And so it has always seemed to me that we, who would re-awaken imaginative tradition by making old songs live again, or by gathering old stories into books, or by learning Irish, take part in the quarrel of Galilee. Those who are Irish and would spread English ways, which, for all but a few, are ways of vulgarity, take part also. Their part is with those who were of Jewry, and yet cried out, 'If thou let this man go thou art not Caesar's friend.'[3]

54

'NEW CHAPTERS OF THE CELTIC TWILIGHT', I

from the *Speaker* (1902)

Enchanted Woods

Of late, whenever I had finished my day's work, I used to go wandering in what I have called the seven woods,[1] and there I would often meet an old countryman, and talk to him about his work and about the woods, and sometimes a friend would come with me to whom he would open his heart more readily than to me. He had spent all his life lopping away the wild elm and the hazel and the privet and the hornbeam from the paths, and he had thought much about the natural and supernatural creatures of the wood. He has heard the hedgehog – 'grainne oge',[2] he calls it 'grunting like a Christian', and is certain that it steals apples by rolling about under an apple tree until there is an apple sticking to every quill; and he is certain that cats, of whom there are many in the woods, have a language of their own – some kind of old Irish, he thinks – and that they were all serpents once upon a time. Sometimes they change into wild cats, and then a nail grows on the end of their tails; but these wild cats are not the same as the martin cats, who have been always in the woods. The foxes were once tame, as the cats are now, but they ran away and became wild. He talks of all wild creatures except squirrels – whom he hates – with what seems an affectionate interest, though at times his eyes will twinkle with pleasure as he remembers how he made hedgehogs unroll themselves when he was a boy, by putting a wisp of straw under them.

I am not certain that he distinguishes between the natural and supernatural very clearly. He told me the other day that foxes and cats like greatly to be in the 'forths' and lisses[3] after nightfall; and he will certainly pass from some story about a fox to a story about a spirit with less change of voice than when he is going to speak about a martin cat, a rare beast nowadays. Many years ago he used to work in the garden, and once they put him to sleep in a garden-house where there was a loft full of apples, and all night he could hear people rattling plates and knives and forks over his head in the loft. Once, at any rate, he has seen an unearthly sight in the woods. He says: 'One time I was out cutting timber over in Inchy,[4] and about eight o'clock one morning when I got there I saw a girl picking nuts, with her hair hanging down over her shoulders, brown hair, and she had a good, clean face, and she was tall and nothing on her head, and her dress no way gaudy but simple, and when she felt me coming she gathered herself up and was gone as if the earth had swallowed her up. And I followed her and looked for her, but I never could see her again from that day to this, never again.' He meant by the word clean what we would mean by words like fresh or comely.

There have been others who have seen like things among the woods. There is a path which winds by the limekiln, now deserted and overgrown with bushes, where somebody has seen a short broad man who vanished of a sudden, and there is another path where a countrywoman met a woman who spat in her face and vanished; and a man has seen two women rise up out of a certain deep pool in the river and mount through the air, whirling round and round, and many have seen or believed they have seen a strange sort of dragon in the lake that borders the woods by a mile or two; and there is one wood where there are many little twisted paths whereon people lose their way, and it is thought to be full of wicked spirits.

I often entangle myself in arguments more complicated than even these paths of Inchy as to what is the true nature of apparitions, but at other times I say as Socrates said when they told him a learned opinion about a nymph of the Illssus, 'The common opinion is enough for me.'[5] I believe, generally, that all nature is full of people whom we cannot often see, and that some of these are ugly or grotesque, and some wicked or foolish, but very many beautiful beyond any one in our world, and that these beautiful ones are not far away when we are walking in pleasant and quiet places. Even when I was a boy I could never walk in a wood without feeling that at any moment I might find somebody or something I had long looked for without knowing what I looked for. And now I will at times explore every little nook of some poor coppice with almost anxious footsteps, so deep a hold has this imagination upon me. You have a like imagination, doubtless, somewhere, wherever your ruling stars decide, Saturn driving you to the woods, or the moon, it may be, to the edges of the sea. I will not of a certainty believe that there is nothing in the sunset, where our forefathers imagined the dead following their shepherd the sun, or nothing but some vague presence as little moving as nothing. If beauty is not a gateway out of the net we were taken in at our birth, it will not long be beauty, and we will find it better to sit at home by the fire and fatten a lazy body or to run hither and thither in some foolish sport than to look at the finest show that light and shadow ever made among green leaves. I say to myself, when I am well out of that thicket of argument, that they are surely there, the divine people, for only we who have neither simplicity nor wisdom have denied them, and the simple of all times and the wise men of ancient times have seen them and even spoken to them. They live out their passionate lives not far off, as I think, and we shall be among them when we die if we but keep our natures simple and passionate.

May it not even be that death shall unite us to all romance, and that some day we shall fight dragons among blue hills, or come to that whereof all romance is but

> Foreshadowings mingled with the images
> Of man's misdeeds in greater days than these,

as the old men thought in *The Earthly Paradise*[6] when they were in good spirits?

55

'NEW CHAPTERS OF THE CELTIC TWILIGHT', II

from the *Speaker* (1902)

Happy and Unhappy Theologians

A Mayo woman[1] once said to me 'I knew a servant girl who hung herself for the love of God. She was lonely for the priest and her society,[2] and hung herself to the banisters with a scarf. She was no sooner dead than she became as white as a lily, and if it had been murder or suicide she would have become as black as black. They gave her a Christian burial, and the priest said she was no sooner dead than she was with the Lord. So nothing matters that you do for the love of God.' I do not wonder at the pleasure she has in telling this story, for she herself loves all holy things with an ardour that brings them greatly into her life. She told me once that she never hears anything described in a sermon that she does not see afterwards with her eyes. She has described the gates of Purgatory to me, but I remember nothing of the description except that she could not see the souls in trouble, but only the gates. Her mind continually dwells on what is pleasant and beautiful. One day she asked me what month and what flower were the most beautiful. When I answered that I did not know she said, 'The month of May, because of the Virgin, and the lily of the valley because it never sinned, but came pure out of the rock,' and then she added, 'What is the cause of the three cold months of winter?' I did not know even that, and so she said, 'The sin of man and the vengeance of God.' Christ Himself was, in her eyes, not only blessed, but perfect in all manly proportions, so much do beauty and holiness go together as she thinks. He alone of men was exactly six feet high; all others are a little more or a little less.

Her thoughts and her sights of the people of faery are pleasant and beautiful too, and I have never known her call them the

Fallen Angels. They are people like ourselves, only better looking, and many and many a time she has gone to the window to watch them drive their waggons through the sky, waggon behind waggon in a long line, or to the door to hear them singing and dancing in the Forth. They sing chiefly, it seems, a song called the 'The Distant Waterfall', and though they once knocked her down she never thinks badly of them. She saw them most easily when she was in service in King's County, and one morning a little while ago she said to me: 'Last night I was waiting up for the master and it was a quarter past eleven. I heard a bang right down on the table. "King's County all over," says I, and I laughed till I was near dead. It was a warning I was staying too long. They wanted the place to themselves!' I told her once of somebody who saw a faery and fainted, and she said, 'It could not have been a faery, but some bad thing; nobody would faint at a faery; it was a demon. I was not afraid when they near put me and the bed under me out through the roof. I wasn't afraid either when you were at some work and I heard a thing come flop, flop up the stairs like an eel and it squealing. It went to all the doors; it could not get in where I was. I would have sent it through the universe like a flash of fire. There was a man in my place, a tearing fellow, and he put one of them down. He went out to meet it on the road, but he must have been told the words. But the faeries are the best neighbours. If you do good to them they will do good to you, but they don't like you to be on their path.' Another time she said to me, 'They are always good to the poor.'

There is, however, a man in a Galway village who can see nothing but wickedness. Some think him holy, and others think him a little crazed, but some of his talk reminds one of those old Irish visions[3] of the three worlds, which are supposed to have given Dante the plan of *The Divine Comedy*. But I could not imagine this man seeing Paradise. He is especially angry with the people of faery, and describes the fawn-like feet that are so common among them, who are, indeed, children of Pan, to prove them children of Satan. He will not grant that 'they carry away women, though there are many that say so', but he is certain that 'they are as thick as the sands of the sea about us, and they tempt poor mortals'. He says, 'There is a priest I heard of was looking along the ground as if he was hunting for something, and a voice said to him, "If you want to see them, you'll see enough of them," and his eyes were opened and he saw the ground thick with them. Singing, they do be sometimes and dancing, but all the time they have cloven feet.' Yet he was so scornful of unchristened things, for all their dancing and singing, that he thinks that 'you have only to bid them begone and they will go!' 'I was one night,' he says, 'after walking back from Kinvara and down by the wood beyond, I felt one coming beside me, and I could feel the horse he was riding on, and the way it lifted its legs, but they did not make a sound like the hoofs of a horse. So I stopped and turned around, and said out loud, "Be off!" and he went and never troubled me after. And I knew a man that was dying, and one came up on his bed, and he cried out to it, "Get out of that, you unnatural animal!" and it left him. Fallen Angels they are, and after the fall God said, "Let there be Hell," and there it was in a moment!' An old woman sitting by the fire joined in as he said this with 'God save us. It's a pity He said the word and there might have been no Hell the day,' but the seer did not notice her words. He went on, 'And then He asked the Devil what would he take for the souls of all the people. And the Devil said nothing would satisfy him but the blood of a virgin's son, so he got that and then the gates of Hell were opened.' He understood the story, it seems, as if it were some riddling old folk tale.

He went on. 'I have seen Hell myself. I had a sight of it one time in a vision. It had a very high wall around it, all of metal, and an archway and a straight walk into it, just like what would be leading into a gentleman's orchard, but the edges were not trimmed with box but with red hot metal. And inside the wall there were cross walks, and I'm not sure what there was to the right, but to the left there was five great furnaces, and they full of souls kept there with great chains. So I turned short and went away, and in turning I looked again at the wall, and I could see no end to it.

'Another time I saw Purgatory. It seemed to be in a level place and no walls around it, but it all one bright blaze, and the souls standing in it. And they suffer near as much as in Hell, only there are no devils with them there, and they have the hope of Heaven.

'And I heard a call to me from there. "Help us to come out o' this!" and when I looked it was a man I used to know in the army, an Irishman and from this country, and I believe him to be a descendant of King O'Connor[4] of Athenry.

'So I stretched out my hand first, but then I called out "I'd be burned in the flames before I could get within three yards of you." So then he said, "Well help me with your prayers," and so I do.

'And Father Connellan says the same thing, to help the dead with your prayers; and he's a very clever man to make a sermon, and has a great deal of cures made with the Holy Water he brought back from Lourdes.'

56

'NEW CHAPTERS OF THE CELTIC TWILIGHT', III

from the *Speaker* (1902)

The Old Town

I fell, one night some fifteen years ago, into what seemed the power of faery.

I had gone with a young man and his sister – friends and relatives of my own – to pick stories out of an old countryman; and we were coming home talking over what he had told us. It was dark, and our imaginations were excited by his stories of apparitions, and this may have brought us, unknowing, to the threshold between sleep and waking, where sphinxes and chimæras sit open-eyed, and where there are always murmurings and whisperings. I cannot think that what we saw was an imagination of the waking mind. We had come under some trees that made the road very dark when the girl saw a bright light moving slowly across the road. Her brother and myself saw nothing, and did not see anything until we had walked for about half an hour along the edge of the river and down a narrow lane to some fields where there was a ruined church covered with ivy, and the foundations of what was called the old town, burnt, it was said, in Cromwell's time. We had stood for some few minutes, as far as I can recollect, looking over the fields full of stones and brambles when I saw a small, bright light, on the horizon as it seemed, mounting up slowly towards the sky. Then we saw faint lights for a moment or two, and at last a very bright light, like the light of a torch, moving rapidly over the river. We saw it all in such a dream, and it seemed all so unreal to me that I have never written of it until now, and hardly ever spoken of it, and even when thinking of it – because of an unreasoning impulse – I have avoided giving it weight in the argument. Perhaps I have felt that my recollection of things seen when the sense of reality was weakened must be unreliable. A few months ago, however, I talked it over with my two friends, and compared their somewhat vague recollections with my own. That sense of unreality was all the more wonderful because the next day I heard sounds as unaccountable as were those lights and without any emotion of unreality, and I remember them with perfect distinctness and confidence. The girl was sitting reading under a large old-fashioned mirror, and I was reading or writing a couple of yards away, when I heard a sound, as if a shower of peas had been thrown against the mirror, and while I was looking at it I heard the sound again; and presently, while I was alone in the room, I heard a sound as if something much bigger than a pea had struck the wainscoting beside my head. And after that for some days came other sights and sounds, not to me, but to the girl's brother and to the servants. Now it was a bright light, now it was letters of fire that vanished before they could be read, now it was a heavy foot moving about in the seemingly empty house. One wonders whether creatures who live, as the country people believe, wherever men and women have lived in earlier times, followed us from the ruins of the old town? Or did they come from the banks of the river where the first light had shone for a moment under the trees?

War

When there was a rumour of war with France a while ago I met a poor Sligo woman, a soldier's widow, that I knew. I read her a sentence out of a letter I had just had from London. 'The people here are mad for war, but France seems inclined to take things peacefully.' Her mind ran a good deal on war, which she imagined partly from what she had heard from soldiers, and partly from traditions, of the rebellion of '98;[1] but the word London doubled her interest. She knew that there were a great many people in London, and she herself had lived in 'a congested district'.[2] She said, 'There are too many over one another in London. They are getting tired of the world. It is killed they want to be. It will be no matter. And sure the French want nothing but peace and quietness. The people here don't mind the war coming. They could not be worse than they are. They may as well die soldierly before God. Sure, they will get quarters in heaven.' Then she began to say it would be a hard thing to see children tossed about on bayonets, and I knew her mind was running on traditions of the great rebellion. She said presently, 'I never knew a man that was in a battle that liked to speak of it after. They'd sooner be throwing hay down from a haycock.' She told me how she and her neighbours used to be sitting over the fire when she was a girl talking of the war that was coming; now she was afraid it was coming again, for she had dreamed that all the bay was 'stranded and covered with sea-weed'! I asked her if it was in Fenian times she had been so much afraid of war coming. She cried out, 'Never had I such fun and pleasure as in Fenian times.[3] I was in a house where some of the officers used to be staying, and in the daytime I would be walking after the soldiers' band, and at night I'd be going down to the end of the garden watching a soldier, with his red coat on him, drilling the Fenians in the field behind the house. One night the boys tied the liver of an old horse that had been dead three weeks to the knocker, and I found it when I opened the door in the morning.' And presently our talk of war shifted, as it had a way of doing, to the battle of the Black Pig,[4] which seems to her a battle between Ireland and England, but to me an Armageddon which shall quench all things in the ancestral darkness again; and shifted from that to sayings about war and vengeance. 'Do you know,' she said, 'what the curse of the Four Fathers is? They put the man-child on the spear, and somebody said to them, "You will be cursed in the fourth generation after you," and that is why disease or anything always comes in the fourth generation.'

Earth, Fire, and Water

Some French writer, that I read when I was a boy, said that the desert went into the heart of the Jews in their wandering and made them what they are.[5] I cannot remember by what argument he proved them to be even yet the indestructible children of earth, but it may well be that the elements have their children. If we knew the fire worshippers[6] better we might find that their centuries of pious observance have been rewarded, and that the fire has given them a little of its nature; and I am certain that the water, the water of the sea, and of lakes, and of mist and rain, has all but made us Irish after its image. Images form themselves in our minds perpetually, as if they were reflected in some pool. In the old times we gave ourselves up to mythology and saw the gods everywhere. We talked to them face to face, and the stories of that communion are so many that I think they outnumber all the like stories of all the rest of Europe. Even to-day our country people speak with the dead and with some who perhaps have never died as we understand death; and even our educated people pass without great difficulty into the condition of quiet that is the condition of vision. We can make our minds so like still water that beings gather about us that they may see, it may be, their own images, and so live for a moment with a clearer, perhaps even with a fiercer, life because of our quiet. Did not the wise Porphyry[7] think all souls come to be born because of water, and that 'even the generation of images in the mind is from water'?

57

'NEW CHAPTERS OF THE CELTIC TWILIGHT', IV

from the *Speaker* (1902)

A Voice

One day I was walking over a bit of marshy ground close to Inchy Wood[1] when I felt, all of a sudden, and only for a second, an emotion which I said to myself was the root of Christian mysticism. There had swept over me a sense of weakness, of dependence on a great personal Being somewhere far off yet near at hand. No thought of mine had prepared me for this emotion, for I had been pre-occupied with Ængus[2] and Edain, and with Mannanan, Son of the Sea. That night I awoke lying upon my back and hearing a voice speaking above me and saying, 'No human soul is like any other human soul, and therefore the love of God for any human soul is infinite, for no other soul can satisfy the same need in God.' A few nights after this I awoke to see the loveliest people I have ever seen. A young man and a young girl dressed in olive-green raiment, cut like old Greek raiment, were standing at my bedside. I looked at the girl and noticed that her dress was gathered about her neck into a kind of chain, or perhaps some kind of stiff embroidery which represented ivy leaves. But what filled me with wonder was the miraculous mildness of her face. There are no such faces now. It was beautiful, as few faces are beautiful, but it had neither, one would think, the light that is in desire or in hope or in fear or in speculation. It was peaceful like the faces of animals, or like mountain pools at evening, so peaceful that it was a little sad. I thought for a moment that she might be the beloved of Ængus; but how could that hunted, alluring, happy, immortal wretch have a face like this! Doubtless she was from among the children of the Moon, but who among them I shall never know.

The Swine of the Gods

A few years ago a friend of mine told me of something that happened to him when he was a young man and out drilling with some Connacht Fenians. They were but a carful, and drove along a hillside until they came to a quiet place. They left the car and went further up the hill with their rifles, and drilled for a while. As they were coming down again they saw a very thin, long-legged pig of the old Irish sort, and the pig began to follow them. One of them cried out as a joke that it was a fairy pig, and they all began to run to keep up the joke. The pig ran too, and presently, how nobody knew, this mock terror became real terror, and they ran as for their lives. When they got to the car they made the horse gallop as fast as possible, but the pig still followed. Then one of them put up his rifle to fire, but when he looked along the barrel he could see nothing. Presently they turned a corner and came to a village. They told the people of the village what had happened, and the people of the village took pitchforks and spades and the like, and went along the road with them to drive the pig away. When they turned the corner they could not find anything.

The Devil

My old Mayo woman told me one day that something very bad had come down the road and gone into the house opposite, and, though she would not say what it was, I knew quite well. Another day she told me of two friends of hers who had been made love to by one whom they believed to be the devil. One of them was standing by the roadside when he came by on horseback, and asked her to mount up behind him and go riding. When she would not he vanished. The other was out on the road late at night waiting for her young man, when something came flapping and rolling along the road up to her feet. It had the likeness of a newspaper, and presently it flapped up into her face, and she knew by the size of it that it was the *Irish Times*. All of a sudden it changed into a young man, who asked her to go walking with him. She would not, and he vanished.

I know of an old man, too, on the slopes of Ben Bulben, who found the devil ringing a bell under his bed, and he went off and stole the chapel bell and rang him out. It may be that this, like the others, was not the devil at all, but some poor wood spirit whose cloven feet had got him into trouble.

'And Fair, Fierce Women'

One day a woman that I know came face to face with heroic beauty, that highest beauty which Blake[3] says changes least from youth to age, a beauty which has been fading out of the arts since that decadence we call progress set voluptuous beauty in its place. She was standing at the window, looking over to Knocknarea, where Queen Maive is thought to be buried, when she saw, as she has told me, 'the finest woman you ever saw travelling right across from the mountain and straight to her'. The woman had a sword by her side and a dagger lifted up in her hand, and was dressed in white, with bare arms and feet. She looked 'very strong, but not wicked', that is, not cruel. The old woman had seen the Irish giant, and 'though he was a fine man', he was nothing to this woman, 'for he was round, and could not have stepped out so soldierly'; 'she was like Mrs —', a stately lady of the neighbourhood, 'but she had no stomach on her, and was slight and broad in the shoulders, and was handsomer than anyone you ever saw; she looked about thirty'. The old woman covered her eyes with her hands, and when she uncovered them the apparition had vanished. The neighbours were 'wild with her', she told me, because she did not wait to find out if there was a message, for they were sure it was Queen Maive, who often shows herself to the pilots. I asked the old woman if she had seen others like Queen Maive, and she said, 'Some of them have their hair down, but they look quite different, like the sleepy-looking ladies one sees in the papers. Those with their hair up are like this one. The others have long white dresses, but those with their hair up have short dresses, so that you can see their legs right up to their calf.' After some careful questioning I found that they wore what might very well be a kind of buskin; she went on, 'They are fine and dashing looking, like the men one sees riding their horses in twos and threes on the slopes of the mountains with their swords swinging.' She repeated over and over, 'There is no such race living now, none so finely proportioned,' or the like, and then said, 'The present Queen[4] is a nice, pleasant-looking woman, but she is not like her. What makes me think so little of the ladies is that I see none as they be,' meaning as the spirits. 'When I think of her and of the ladies now, they are like little children running about without knowing how to put their clothes on right. Is it the ladies? Why I would not call them women at all.' The other day a friend of mine questioned an old woman in a Galway workhouse about Queen Maive, and was told that 'Queen Maive was handsome, and overcame all her enemies with a hazel stick, for the hazel is blessed, and the best weapon that can be got. You might walk the world with it,' but she grew 'very disagreeable in the end – oh, very disagreeable. Best not to be talking about it. Best leave it between the book and the hearer.' My friend thought the old woman had got some scandal about Fergus son of Roy[5] and Maive in her head.

And I myself met once with a young man in the Burren Hills who remembered an old poet who made his poems in Irish, who had met when he was young, the young man said, one who called herself Maive, and said she was a queen 'among them', and asked him if he would have money or pleasure. He said he would have pleasure, and she gave him her love for a time, and then went from him, and ever after he was very mournful. The young man had often heard him sing the poem of lamentation that he made, but could only remember that it was 'very mournful', and that he called her 'beauty of all beauties'.

Mortal Help

One hears in the old poems of men taken away to help the gods in their battles, of Cuchulain who won the Goddess Fand for a while, by helping her married sister and her sister's husband to overthrow another nation of the Land of Promise. I have been told, too, that the people of faery cannot ever play at hurling unless they have on either side some mortal whose body, or whatever has been put in its place, as the story-teller would say, is asleep at home. Without mortal help they are shadows, and cannot even strike the balls. One day I was walking over some marshy land in Galway with a friend when we found an old hard-featured man digging a drain. My friend had heard that this man had seen a wonderful sight of some kind, and at last we got the story out of him. When he was a boy he was working one day with about thirty men and women and boys. They were beyond Tuam, and not far from Knock-na-gar. Presently they saw, all thirty of them, and at a distance of about half a mile, some hundred and fifty of the people of faery. There were two of them, he said, in dark clothes like people of our own time, and they stood about one hundred and fifty yards from one another, but the others were in clothes of all colours, some 'bracket' and some chequered, and some with red waistcoats. He could not see what they were doing, but all might have been playing hurley, for they looked as if it was that! Sometimes they would vanish, and then he would almost swear they came back out of the bodies of the two men in dark clothes. These two men were of the size of living men, but the others were small. He saw them for about half an hour and then the old man, he and the others were working, took a whip to them and said, 'Get on, get on, or we will have no work done.' I asked if the old man saw the fairies, too. Oh, yes, he saw them, but he did not want work he was paying wages for to be neglected.

Aristotle of the Books

The friend who can get the wood-cutter to talk more readily than he will to anybody else went lately to see his wife. She lives in a cottage not far from the edge of the woods, and is as full of old talk as her husband. This time the talk was about Goban, the legendary mason. She said: 'Aristotle of the Books was very wise too, and he had a great deal of experience, but did not the bees get the better of him in the end? He wanted to know how they packed the comb, and he wasted the better part of a fortnight watching them, and he could not see them doing it. Then he made a hive with a glass cover on it, and put it over them, and he thought to see. But when he went and put his eyes to the glass they had it all covered with wax, so that it was black as the pot; and he was as blind as before. He said he was never rightly kilt till then. They had him beat that time surely!'

58

'MORE CHAPTERS OF THE CELTIC TWILIGHT', V

from the *Speaker* (1902)

Miraculous Creatures

There are marten cats and badgers and foxes in the enchanted woods, but there are, of a certainty, mightier creatures, and the lake hides what neither net nor line can take. These creatures are of the race of the white stag, that flits in and out of the tales of Arthur, and of the evil pig that slew Diarmuid where Ben Bulben mixes with the sea wind. They are the wizard creatures of hope and fear, and they are of them that fly and of them that follow among the thickets that are about the Gates of Death. A man I know remembers 'that his father was one night in the wood of Inchy, where the lads of Gort used to be stealing rods.[1] He was sitting by the wall, and the dog beside him, and he heard something come running from Owbawn Weir, and he could see nothing, but the sound of its feet on the ground was like the sound of the feet of a deer. And when it passed him, the dog got between him and the wall and scratched at it there, as if it was afraid, but still he could see nothing but only hear the sound of hoofs. So when it was passed he turned and came away home.' 'Another time,' the man says, 'my father told me he was in a boat out on the lake with two or three men from Gort, and one of them had an eel-spear, and he thrust it into the water, and it hit something, and the man fainted, and they had to carry him out of the boat to land, and when he came to himself he said that what he struck was like a calf, but, whatever it was, it was not fish!' A friend of mine is convinced that these terrible creatures, so common in lakes, were set in there in old times by subtle enchanters to watch over the gates of wisdom. He thinks that if we sent our spirits down into the lakes we would make them of one substance, with strange moods of ecstasy and power, and go out it may be to the conquest of the world. We would, however, he believes, have first to outface and perhaps overthrow strange images full of a more powerful life than if they were really alive. It may be that we shall look at them without fear when we have endured the last adventure, that is death.

An Enduring Heart

One day a friend of mine was making a sketch of my Knight of the Sheep.[2] The old man's daughter was sitting by, and, when the conversation drifted to love and love-making, she said, 'Oh, father, tell him about your love affair.' The old man took his pipe out of his mouth, and said: 'Nobody ever marries the woman he loves,' and then, with a chuckle, 'there were fifteen of them I liked better than the woman I married,' and he repeated many women's names. He went on to tell how, when he was a lad, he had worked for his grandfather, his mother's father, and was called (my friend has forgotten why) by his grandfather's name, which, we will say, was Doran. He had a great friend, whom I shall call John Byrne; and one day he and his friend went to Queenstown to await an emigrant ship that was to take John Byrne to America. When they were walking along the quay, they saw a girl sitting on a seat, crying miserably, and two men standing up in front of her quarrelling with one another. Doran said: 'I think I know what is wrong. *That* man will be her brother, and *that* man will be her lover, and the brother is sending her to America to get her away from the lover. How she is crying! But I think I could console her myself.' Presently the lover and brother went away, and Doran began to walk up and down before her, saying, 'Mild weather, miss,' or the like. She answered him in a little while, and the three began to talk together. The emigrant ship did not arrive for some days, and the three drove about on outside cars very innocently and happily, seeing everything that was to be seen. When at last the ship came, and Doran had to break it to her that he was not going to America, she cried more after him than after the first lover. Doran whispered to Byrne as he went aboard ship, 'Now, Byrne, I don't grudge her to you, but don't marry young.'

When the story got to this, the farmer's daughter joined in mockingly with: 'I suppose you said that for Byrne's good, father.' But the old man insisted that he *had* said it for Byrne's good; and went on to tell how, when he got a letter telling of Byrne's engagement to the girl, he wrote him the same advice. Years passed by, and he heard nothing; and, though he was now married, he could not keep from wondering what she was doing. At last he went to America to find out, and though he asked many people for tidings, he could get none. More years went by, and his wife was dead, and he well on in years, and a rich farmer, with not a few great matters on his hands. He found an excuse in some vague business to go out to America again, and to begin his search again. One day he fell into talk with an Irishman in a railway carriage, and asked him, as his way was, about emigrants from this place and that, and at last, 'Did you ever hear of the miller's daughter from Innis Rath?' And he named the woman he was looking for. 'Oh, yes,' said the other, 'she is married to a friend of mine, John McEwin. She lives at such-and-such a street in Chicago.' Doran went to Chicago and knocked at her door. She opened the door herself, and was 'not a bit changed'. He gave her his real name, which he had taken again after his grandfather's death, and the name of the man he had met in the train. She did not recognise him, but asked him to stay to dinner, saying that her husband would be glad to meet anybody who knew that old friend of his. They talked of many things, but for all their talk, I do not know why, he never told her who he was. At dinner he asked her about Byrne, and she put her head down on the table and began to cry, and she cried so he was afraid her husband might be angry. He was afraid to ask what had happened to Byrne, and left soon after, never to see her again.

When the old man had finished the story, he said: 'Tell that to Mr Yeats, he will make a poem about it, perhaps.' But the daughter said: 'Oh no, father. Nobody could make a poem about a woman like that.' Alas! I have never made the poem, perhaps because my own heart, which has loved Helen and all the lovely and fickle women of the world, would be too sore. There are things it is well not to ponder over too much, things that bare words are the best suited for.

59

'AWAY'

from the *Fortnightly Review* (1902)

I

There is, I think, no countryside in Ireland where they will not tell you, if you can conquer their mistrust, of some man or woman or child who was lately or still is in the power of the gentry, or 'the others', or 'the fairies', or 'the sidhe', or the 'forgetful people', as they call the dead and the lesser gods of ancient times. These men and women and children are said to be 'away', and for the most part go about their work in a dream, or lie all day in bed, awakening after the fall of night to a strange and hurried life.

A woman at Gort, in County Galway, says: 'There was an old woman I remember was living at Martin Ruane's, and she had to go with them two or three hours every night for a while, and she'd make great complaints of the hardships she'd meet with, and how she'd have to spend the night going through little boreens, or in the churchyard at Kinvara, or they'd bring her down to the sea shore. They often meet with hardships like that those they bring with them, so it's no wonder they're glad to get back; this world's the best.' And an old pensioner from Kiltartan, a village some three miles from Gort, says: 'There is a man I knew that was my comrade after, used to be taken away at nights, and he'd speak of the journeys he had with them. And he got severe treatment and didn't want to go, but they'd bring him by force. He recovered after, and joined the army, and I was never so astonished as I was the day he walked in, when I was in Delhi.' There are a boy near Gort and a woman at Ardrahan close at hand, who are 'away', and this same man says of them: 'Mary Flaherty has been taken, and whenever she meets old Whelan the first thing she asks is for his son. She doesn't go to see him in the house, but travelling of nights they meet each other. Surely she's gone.

You have but to look in her face to see that. And whatever hour of the night she wants to go out, they must have the horse harnessed to bring her wherever she likes to go.'

The commonest beginning of the enchantment is to meet some one not of this earth, or in league with people not of this earth, and to talk too freely to them about yourself and about your life. If they understand you and your life too perfectly, or sometimes even if they know your name, they can throw their enchantment about you. A man living at Coole near Gort says: 'But those that are brought away would be glad to be back. It's a poor thing to go there after this life. Heaven is the best place, Heaven and this world we're in now. My own mother was away for twenty-one years, and at the end of every seven years she thought it would be off her, but she never could leave the bed. She could but sit up, and make a little shirt or the like for us. It was of the fever she died at last. The way she got the touch was one day after we left the place we used to be in, and we got our choice place on the estate, and my father chose Kilchreest. But a great many of the neighbours went to Moneen. And one day a woman that had been our neighbour came over from Moneen, and my mother showed her everything and told her of her way of living. And she walked a bit of the road with her, and when they were parting the woman said: "You'll soon be the same as such a one." And as she turned she felt a pain in the head. And from that day she lost her health. My father went to Biddy Early, but she said it was too late, she could do nothing, and she would take nothing from him.' Biddy Early[1] was a famous witch.

If you are taken you have always, it is said, a chance of return every seven years. Almost all that go 'away' among them are taken to help in their work, or in their play, or to nurse their children, or to bear them children, or to be their lovers, and all fairy children are born of such marriages. A man near Gort says: 'They are shadows, and how could a shadow have power to move that chair or that table? But they have power over mankind, and they can bring them away to do their work.' I have told elsewhere of a man who was 'away' with Maive Queen of the western sidhe as her lover, and made a mournful song in the Gaelic when she left him, and was mournful till he died.[2]

But sometimes one hears of people taken for no reason, as it seems, but that they may be a thing to laugh at. Indeed, one is often told that unlike 'the simple' who would do us an evil, 'the gentle' among 'the others' wish us no harm but 'to make a sport of us'.

And a man at Gort says: 'There was one Mahony had the land taken that is near Newtown racecourse. And he was out there one day building a wall and it came to the dinner hour, but he had none brought with him. And a man came by and said, "Is it home you'll be going for your dinner?" And he said, "It's not worth my while to go back to Gort, I'd have the day lost . . ." And the man said, "Well, come in and eat a bit with me." And he brought him into a forth and there was everything that was grand, and the dinner they gave him of the best, so that he eat near two plates of it. And then he went out again to build the wall. And whether it was with lifting the heavy stones I don't know, but with respects to you, when he was walking the road home he began to vomit, and what he vomited up was all green grass.'

You may eat their food, if they put it out to you, and indeed it is discourteous to refuse and will make them angry, but you must not go among them and eat their food, for this will give them power over you.

II

Sometimes one hears of people 'away' doing the work of the others and getting harm of it, or no good of it, but more often one hears of good crops or of physical strength or of cleverness or of supernatural knowledge being given and of no evil being given with it except the evil of being in a dream, or being laid up in bed or the like, which happens more or less to all who are 'away'. A woman near Craughwell says: 'There's a boy now of the Lydons, but I wouldn't for all the world let them think I spoke of him. But it's two years since he came from America and since that time he never went to mass, or to Church, or to market, or to fair, or to stand at the cross roads, or to the hurling. And if anyone comes into the house, it's into the room he'll slip not to see them. And as to work, he has the garden dug to bits and the whole place smeared with cow-dung, and such a crop as was never seen, and the alders all plaited that they look grand. One day he went as far as Peterswell Chapel, but as soon as he got to the door he turned straight round again as if he hadn't power to pass it. I wonder he wouldn't get the priest to read a mass for him or some such thing. But the crop he has is grand, and you may know well he has some that help him.'

Indeed, almost any exceptional cleverness, even the clever training of a dog may be thought a gift from 'the others'. I have been told of a boy in Gort 'who was lying in the bed a long time, and one day, the day of the races, he asked his father and mother were they going to the course, and they said they were not. Well, says he, "I'll show you as good sport as if you went." And he had a dog and he called to it and said something to it, and it began to take a run and to gallop and to jump backwards over the half door, for there was a very high half door to the house. "So now," says he, "didn't you see as good sport as if you were on Newtown racecourse?" And he didn't live long, but died soon after that.' And the same man whose mother had been away for twenty-one years says: 'There was one of the Burkes, John, was away for seven years, lying in his bed but brought away at nights. And he knew everything. And one Kearney up in the mountain, a cousin of his own, lost two hoggets and came and told him. And he knew the very spot where they were and told him, and he got them back again. But *they* were vexed at that, and took away the power, so that he never knew anything again, no more than another. There was another man up near Ballylee could tell these things too. When John Callan lost his wool he went to him, and next morning there were the fleeces at his door. Those that are away know these things. There was a brother of my own took to it for seven years, and he at school. And no one could beat him at the hurling and the games. But I wouldn't like to be mixed with that myself.' The wool and perhaps the hoggets had been taken by 'the others' who were forced to return them.

When you get a 'touch' you feel a sudden pain, and a swelling comes where you have felt the pain. I have been told that there is a fool and a queen 'in every household of them', and that nobody can cure the touch of the fool or the queen, but that the touch of anyone else among them can be cured.[3]

The people of the North are thought to know more about the supernatural than anybody else, and one remembers that the good gods of the Celts, the children of Danu, and the evil gods of the Celts the Fomor, came from the North in certain legends. The North does not mean Ulster, but any place to the north, for the people talk of the people of Cruachmaa, which is but a little north of Galway, as knowing much because they are from the North – one cannot tell whether the woman from the North in this tale was a mortal or an immortal. People 'away', like people taken by 'the others' from their death-beds, are confounded with the immortals, the true children of Danu, or the Dundonians, as I have heard them called in Clare. I have never heard the word 'Ingentry' for 'the others' at any other time.

Sometimes people who are 'away' are thought to have, like the dead who have been 'taken', that power of changing one thing into another, which is so constantly attributed to the Children of Danu in the Gaelic poems. The Children of Danu were the powers of life, the powers worshipped in the ecstatic dances among the woods and upon the mountains, and they had the flamelike changeability of life, and were the makers of all changes. 'The others', their descendants, change the colours of their clothes every moment, and build up a house 'in the corner of a field' and 'in ten minutes', 'finer than any gentleman's house'. An Irishwoman from Kildare that I met in London told me: 'There was a woman used to go away at night, and she said to her sister, "I'll be out on a white horse, and I'll stop and knock at your door as I pass," and so she used to do sometimes. And one day there was a man asked her for a debt she owed, and she said, "I have no money now." But then she put her hand behind her, and brought it back filled with gold, and then she rubbed it in her hand, and when she opened her hand again, there was nothing in it but dry cow-dung, and she said, "I could give you that, but it would be of no use to you."'

Those who are 'away' have sometimes, too, it seems, the power of changing their size and of going through walls as 'the others' themselves do. A man on Inisheer[4] says: 'There was a first cousin of mine used sometimes to go out of the house through the wall, but none could see him going. And one night his brother followed him, and he went down a path to the sea, and then he went into a hole in the rocks that the smallest dog wouldn't go into. And the brother took hold of his feet and drew him out again. He went to America after that, and is living there now, and sometimes in his room they'll see him beckoning and laughing and laughing, as if some were with him. One night there, when some of the neighbours from these islands were with him, he told them he'd been back to Inishmaan,[5] and told all that was going on, and some would not believe him. And he said, "You'll believe me next time." So the next night he told them again he had been there, and he brought out of his pocket a couple of boiled potatoes and a bit of fish, and showed them; so then they all believed it.' And an old man on Inisheer, who has come back from the State of Maine, says of this man: 'I knew him in America, and he used often to visit this island, and would know what all of them were doing, and would bring us word of them all, and all he'd tell us would turn out right. He's living yet in America.'

It often seems as if these enchanted people had some great secret. They may have taken an oath to be silent, but I have not heard of any oath, I am only certain that they are afraid or unable to speak. I have already told of Whelan and his nightly rides. I got a friend, with whom I was staying, to ask Whelan's father, who is a carpenter, to make a box and send it by his son. He promised to 'try and infatuate him to come', but did not think it would be of any use. It was no use, for the boy said, 'No, I won't go, I know why I am wanted.' His father says that he did not tell him, but that 'the others' told him, when he was out with them.

A man said to a friend of mine in the Abbey of Corcomroe among the Burren Hills in County Clare: 'There was one O'Loughlin that lies under that slab there, and for seven years he was brought away every night, and into this Abbey. And he was beat and pinched, and when he came home he'd faint. He told his brother-in-law, that told me, that in that hill beyond, behind this Abbey, there is the most splendid town that ever was seen, and grander than any city. Often he was in it and ought not to have been talking about it, but he said he wouldn't give them the satisfaction of it, he didn't care what they'd do to him. One night he was with a lot of others at a wake, and when he heard them coming for him he fainted on the floor. But after he got up he heard them come again and he rose to go, and the boys all took hold of him, Peter Fahey was one of them, and you know what a strong man he was, and *he* couldn't hold him. Drawn out of the door he was, and the arms of those that were holding him were near pulled out of their sockets.'

And a woman near Loughrea says: 'My mother often told me about her sister's child, my cousin, that used to spend the nights in the big forth at Moneen. Every night she went there, and she got thin and tired like. She used to say she saw grand things there, and the horses galloping and the riding. But then she'd say, "I must tell no more than that or I'll get a great beating." She wasted away, and one night they were so sure she was dead they had the pot full of water boiling on the fire to wash her. But she recovered again and lived five years after that.'

And an old man on the north isle of Aran says: 'I know a good many on the island have seen *those*, but they wouldn't say what they're like to look at, for when they speak of them their tongue gets like a stone.'

The most of what the country people have to tell of those who have been 'taken' altogether, and about the ways and looks of the 'others', has come from the frightened and rare confidences of people upon whom 'the others' cast this sleepy enchantment.

A man in the Burren Hills says: 'That girl of the Connors that was away for seven years, she was bid tell nothing of what she saw, but she told her mother some things, and told of some she met there. There was a woman, a cousin of my own, asked was her son ever there, and she had to press her a long time, but at last she said he was. And he was taken too, with little privication, fifty years ago.'

And a woman near Ardrahan says: 'There was a girl near Westport was away, and the way it came on her was she was on the road one day, and two men passed her, and one of them said, "That's a fine girl," and the other said, "She belongs to my town." And there and then she got a pain in her knee, and she couldn't walk home but had to be brought home in a cart, and she used to be away at night, and thorns in her feet in the morning, but she never said where she went. But one time the sister brought her to Kilfenora, and when they were crossing a bog near to there she pointed to a house in the bog and she said, "It's there I was last night." And the sister asked did she know anyone she met there, and she said, "There was one I knew that is my mother's cousin," and told her name. And she said, "But for her they'd have me ill-treated, but she fought for me and saved me!" She was thought to be dying one time, and my mother sent me to see her, and how she was. And she was lying on the bed, and her eyes turned back, and she was speechless, and I told my mother when I came home she hadn't an hour to live. And the next day she was up and about and not a thing on her. It might be the mother's cousin that fought for her again then. She went to America after.'

This girl fell under the power of 'the others' because the two men looked at her with admiration, 'overlooked her', as it is called, and did not say 'God bless her'. 'The others' can draw anything they admire to themselves by using our admiration as a bond between them and it.

III

In some barbarous countries no one is permitted to look at the king while he is eating, for one is thought to be less able to drive away malicious influence when one is eating, and most mortal influence must be malignant when one is representative and instrument of the gods. I have sometimes been told that nobody is ever allowed to see those who are 'away' eating. A woman near Gort says of Whelan the carpenter's son, 'He's lying in bed these four years, and food is brought into the room but he never touches it, but when it's left there it's taken away.' And a man at Coole says: 'I remember a boy was about my own age over at Cranagh on the other side of the water, and they said he was away for two years. Anyhow, for all that time he was sick in bed, and no one ever saw bit or sup pass his lips in all that time, though the food that was left in the room would disappear, whatever happened it. He recovered after and went to America.'

They are sometimes believed to hardly eat our food at all, but to live upon supernatural food. An old man from near Loughrea says: 'There was Kitty Flannery at Kilchreest, you might remember her. For seven years she had everything she could want, and music and dancing could be heard round her house every night, and all she did prospered. But she ate no food all that time, only she'd take a drink of the milk after the butter being churned. But at the end of the seven years all left her, and she was glad at the last to get Indian meal.'

But often one hears of their fearing to eat the food of 'the others' for fear they might never escape out of their hands. An old man on the Gortaveha mountain says: 'I knew one was away for seven years, and it was in the next townland to this she lived. Bridget Kinealy her name was. There was a large family of them, and she was the youngest, a very nice-looking fair-haired girl she was. I knew her well, she was the one age with myself. It was in the night she used to go to them, and if the door was shut she'd come in by the keyhole. The first time they came for her she was in bed between her two sisters, and she didn't want to go, but they beat her and pinched her till her brother called out to know what was the matter. She often spoke about them, and how she was badly treated because she wouldn't eat their food, and how there was a red-haired girl among them that would throw her into the river she'd get so mad with her. But if she had their food ate, she'd never have got away from them at all. She got no more than about three cold potatoes she could eat the whole time she was with them. All the old people about her put out food every night, the first of the food before they have any of it tasted themselves. She married a serving man after, and they went to Sydney, and if nothing happened in the last two years they're doing well there now.'

IV

The ancient peoples from whom the country people inherit their belief had to explain how, when you were 'away', as it seemed to you, you seemed, it might be, to your neighbours or your family, to be lying in a faint upon the ground, or in your bed, or even going about your daily work. It was probably one who was himself 'away' who explained, that somebody or something was put in your place, and this explanation was the only possible one to ancient peoples, who did not make our distinction between body and soul. The Irish country people always insist that something, a heap of shavings or a broomstick or a wooden image, or some dead person, 'maybe some old warrior', or some dead relative or neighbour of your own, is put in your place, though sometimes they will forget their belief until you remind them, and talk of 'the others' having put such and such a person 'into a faint', or of such and such a person being 'away' and being ill in bed. This substitution of the dead for the living is indeed a pagan mystery, and not more hard to understand than the substitution of the body and blood of Christ for the wafer and the wine in the mass; and I have not yet lost the belief that some day, in some village lost among the hills or in some island among the western seas, in some place that remembers old ways and has not learned new ways, I will come to understand how this pagan mystery hides and reveals some half-forgotten memory of an ancient knowledge or of an ancient wisdom. Time that has but left the lesser gods to haunt the hills and raths, has doubtless taken much that might have made us understand.

A man at Kiltartan, who thinks evil of 'the others', says: 'They have the hope of heaven or they wouldn't leave one on the face of the earth, and they are afraid of God. They'll not do you much harm if you leave them alone, it's best not to speak to them at all if you should meet them. If they bring anyone away they'll leave some good-for-nothing thing in its place, and the same way with a cow or a calf or such things. But a sheep or a lamb it's beyond their power to touch, because of our Lord.' And a woman near Ardrahan says: 'There was a cousin of my own was said to be "away", and when she died I was but a child, and my mother brought me with her to the house where she was laid out. And when I saw her I began to scream and to say, "That's not Mary that's in it, that's some old hag." And so it was, I know well it was not Mary that was lying there in the bed.' And a woman from near Loughrea says: 'Sure there was a fairy in a house at Eserkelly fourteen years. Bridget Collins she was called, you might remember Miss Fanny used to be bringing her gooseberries. She never kept the bed, but she'd sit in the corner of the kitchen on a mat, and from a good stout lump of a girl that she was, she wasted to nothing, and her teeth grew as long as your finger, and then they dropped out. And she'd eat nothing at all, only crabs and sour things. And she'd never leave the house in the daytime, but in the night she'd go out and pick things out of the fields she could eat. And the hurt she got, or whatever it was touched her, it was one day she was swinging on the Moneen gate, just there by the forth. She died as quiet as another, but you wouldn't like to be looking at her after the teeth fell out.'

And a man from Cahirglissane says: 'There was one Tierney on the road to Kinvara, I knew him well, was away with them seven years. It was at night he used to be brought away, and when they called him he should go. They'd leave some sort of a likeness of him in his place. He had a wart on his back, and his wife would rub her hand down to feel was the wart there before she'd know was it himself was in it or not. Himself and his pony used to be brought up into the sky, and he told many how he used to go riding about with them, and that often and often he was in that castle you see below. And Mrs Hevenor asked him did he ever see her son Jimmy that died, among them, and he told her he did, and that mostly all the people that he knew that had died out of the village were amongst them now. And if his wife had a clutch of geese they'd be ten times better than any other one's, and the wheat and the stock and all they had was better and more plentiful than what anyone else had. Help he got from them of course. But at last the wife got in the priest to read a mass and take it off him. And after that all that they had went to flitters.'

And a girl at Coole says of a place called 'The Three Lisses', where there are three of those old clay remnants of ancient houses or encampments so much haunted by 'the others': 'There must in old times have been a great deal of fighting there. There are some bushes growing on them, and no one, man or woman, will ever put a hand to cut them, no more than they would touch the little bush by the well beyond, that used to have lights shining out of it. And if anyone was to fall asleep within in the liss, himself would be taken away, and the spirit of some old warrior would be put in his place, and it's he would know everything in the whole world. There's no doubt at all but that there's the same sort of things in other countries, sure *these* can go through and appear in Australia in one minute, but you hear more about them in these parts because the Irish do be more familiar in talking of them.'

The chief way of bringing a person out of this state of dream is to threaten the dead person believed to have been put in his place. A man from County Clare says: 'I heard of a woman brought back again. It was told me by a boy going to school there at the time it happened, so I know there's no lie in it. It was one of the Lydons, a rich family in Scariff, whose wife was sick and pining away for seven years. And at the end of that time one day he came in, he had a drop of drink taken, and he began to be a bit rough with her. And she said, "Don't be rough with me now, after bearing so well with me all these seven years. But because you were so good and so kind to me all the time," says she, "I'll go away from you now, and I'll let your own wife come back to you." And so she did, for it was an old hag she was. And the wife came back again and reared a family. And before she went away she had a son that was reared a priest, and after she came back she had another that was reared a priest, so that shows a blessing came on them.'

The country people seldom do more than threaten the dead person put in the living person's place, and it is, I am convinced, a sin against the traditional wisdom to really ill-treat the dead person. A woman from Mayo who has told me a good many tales and has herself both seen and heard 'the royal gentry', as she calls them, was very angry with the Tipperary countryman who burned his wife, some time ago, her father and neighbours standing by. She had no doubt that they only burned some dead person, but she was quite certain that you should not burn even a dead person. She said: 'In my place we say you should only threaten. They are so superstitious in Tipperary. I have stood in the door and I have heard lovely music, and seen the fort all lighted up, but I never gave in to them.' 'Superstitious' means to her 'giving in' to 'the others', and 'giving in' means, I think, letting them get power over you, or being afraid of them, and getting excited about them, and doing foolish things. One does hear now and then of 'the dead person' being really ill-treated, but rarely. When I was last in Western Galway a man had just been arrested for trying to kill his sister-in-law, because he thought she was one of 'the others', and was tempting him to murder his cousin. He had sent his cousin away that she might be out of his reach in case he could not resist the temptation. This man was merely out of his mind, and had more than common reasons for his anger besides. A woman from Burren tells a tale more like the Tipperary tale. 'There was a girl near Ballyvaughan was away, and the mother used to hear horses coming about the door every night. And one day the mother was picking flax in the house and of a sudden there came in her hand an herb with the best smell and the sweetest that ever anyone smelled. And she closed it into her hand and called to the son that was making up a stack of hay outside, "Come in, Denis, for I have the best smelling herb that ever you saw." And when he came in she opened her hand and the herb was gone, clear and clean. She got annoyed at last with the horses coming about the door, and some one told her to gather all the fire into the middle of the floor and to lay the little girl upon it, and to see would she come back again. So she did as she was told, and brought the little girl out of the bed and laid her on the coals, and she began to scream and to call out, and the neighbours came running in, and the police heard of it, and they came and arrested the mother and brought her to Ballyvaughan, before the magistrate, Mr Macnamara, and my own husband was one of the police that arrested her. And when the magistrate heard all, he said she was an ignorant woman, and that she did what she thought right, and he would give her no punishment. And the girl got well and was married, and it was after she married I knew her.'

I was always convinced that tradition, which avoids needless inhumanity, had some stronger way of protecting the bodies of those, to whom the other world was perhaps unveiling its mysteries, than any mere command not to ill-treat some old dead person, who had maybe been put in the room of one's living wife or daughter or son. I heard of this stronger way last winter from an old Kildare woman, that I met in London. She said that in her own village, 'there was a girl used to be away with them, you'd never know when it was she herself that was in it or not till she'd come back, and then she'd tell she had been away. She didn't like to go, but she had to go when they called to her. And she told her mother always to treat kindly whoever was put in her place, sometimes one would be put and sometimes another, for, she'd say "If you are unkind to whoever is there, they'll be unkind to me."'

Sometimes the person is thought to be brought back by some one who meets him on his wanderings and leads him home. A woman near Kinvara says: 'There was a child was dying in some house in Burren by the sea, and the mother and all around it, thinking to see it die. And a boy came in, and he said when he was coming through a field beyond the house he heard a great crying, and he saw a troop of *them* and the child ran out from among them, and ran up to him and he took hold of its hand, and led it back, and then he brought it safe and well into the house. And the thing that was in the bed he took up and threw it out, and it vanished away into the air.'

An army pensioner says: 'My family were of the Finns of Athenry. I had an aunt that married a man of the name of Kane, and they had a child was taken. So they brought it to the Lady Well near Athenry, where there's patterns every 15th of August, to duck it. And such a ducking they gave it, that it walked away on crutches, and it swearing. And their own child they got back again, but he didn't live long after.' I have one tale in which a visit to Knock, the Irish Lourdes, worked the cure. 'There was a girl was overlooked got cured at Knock, and when she was cured she let three screams out of her, it was a neighbour of mine saw her and told me. And there are a great many cures done at Knock, and the walls thick with crutches and sticks and crooked shoes. And there was a gentleman from America was cured there, and his crutch was a very grand one, with silver on it, and he came back to bring it away, and when he did, he got as bad as ever he was before.' It was no doubt the old person who gave the three screams.

And sometimes a priest works the cure. A piper who wanders about County Galway says:– 'There was a girl at Kilkerran of the same name as my own, was lying on a mat for eight years. When she first got the touch the mother was sick, and there was no room in the bed; so they laid a mat on the floor for her, and she never left it for the eight years, but the mother died soon after. She never got off the mat for anyone to see, but one night there was a working man came to the house and they gave him lodging for the night. And he watched her from the other room, and in the night he saw the outer door open, and three or four boys and girls come in, and with them a piper or a fiddler, I'm not sure which, and he played to them, and they danced, and the girl got up off the mat and joined them. And in the morning, when he was sitting at breakfast, he looked over to her where she was lying, and said, "You were the best dancer among them last night."'

Many stories of the old Gaelic poems and romances become more fully intelligible when we read them by the light of these stories. There is a story about Cuchulain in *The Book of the Dun Cow*,[6] interpreted too exclusively as a solar myth by Professor Rhys,[7] which certainly is a story of Cuchulain 'away'. The people of Uladh, or Ulster, were celebrating the festival of the beginning of winter that was held the first day of November, on the days before and after.[8] A flock of wild birds lighted upon a lake near where Cuchulain and the heroes and fair women of Uladh were holding festival, and because of the bidding of the women Cuchulain caught the birds and divided them among them. When he came to his own wife Emer, he had no birds left, and promised her the finest two out of any new flock. Presently he saw two birds, bound one to the other with a chain of gold, and they were singing so sweetly that the host of Uladh fell in a little while into a magic sleep. Cuchulain cast a stone out of a sling, but missed them, and then another stone, but missed them, and wondered greatly, because he had not missed a cast from the day when he took arms. He threw his spear, and it passed through the wing of one of the birds, and the birds dived out of his sight. He lay down in great sorrow, because of his bad casting, and fell asleep and dreamed that two women, one dressed in green and one dressed in red, came to him, and first one and then the other smiled and struck him with a whip, and that they went on beating him until he was nearly dead. His friends came while he was still dreaming, but only saw that he slept and must not be awakened, and when at last he awoke, he was so weak that he made them carry him to his bed. He lay in his bed all through the winter, the time of the power of the gods of death and cold, and until the next November Eve, when those who watched beside him suddenly saw a stranger sitting upon the side of his bed. This stranger was Ængus, perhaps that Ængus, the master of love, who had made four birds out of his kisses, and he sang that Fand, the wife of Mannannan, the master of the sea, and of the island of the dead, loved Cuchulain, and that, if he would come into the country of the gods, where there was wine and gold and silver, she would send Leban, her sister, to heal him. Having ended his song, the stranger vanished as suddenly as he had come. Cuchulain, having consulted with his friends, went to the place where he had seen the swans and dreamed his dream, and there the woman dressed in green came and spoke with him. He reproached her, and she answered that she wished him no harm, but only to bring him to her sister Fand, who had been deserted by Mannannan, and who loved him passionately, and to bring him to help her own husband Labraid of the Swift Hand on the Sword in a one-day's battle against his enemies. After hearing what another mortal who had been to the country of Labraid had to tell, Cuchulain mounted into his chariot, and went to the country of Labraid, and fought a one-day's battle, and had Fand to wife for a month. At the month's end he made a promise to meet her at a place called 'The Yew at the Strand's End', and came back to the earth. When Emer, his mortal wife, heard of the tryst, she went with other women to the Yew at the Strand's End, and there she won again the love of Cuchulain. When Fand saw that she had lost his love she lamented her happy days with Mannannan when their love was new. Mannannan heard and came swiftly and carried her away to his own country.

When Cuchulain saw her leaving him his love for her returned, and he became mad and went into the mountains, and wandered there a long time without food or drink. At last the King of Uladh sent his poets and his druids to cure him, and though he tried to kill them in his madness, they chanted druid spells, so that he became weak. He cried out for a drink in his weakness, and they gave him a drink of forgetfulness; and they gave Emer a drink of forgetfulness, so that she forgot the divine woman.

Mr Frazer dicusses in, I think, the second volume of *The Golden Bough* – I am writing in Ireland and have not the book at hand and cannot give the exact reference – the beating of the divine man in ancient religious ceremonies, and decides that it was never for a punishment but always for a purification, for the driving out of something.[9] I am inclined, therefore, to consider the beating of Cuchulain by the smiling women, as a driving out or deadening, for a time, of his merely human faculties and instincts; and I am certain it should be compared with the stories told by the country people, of people over whom 'the others' get power by striking them (see my article in the *Nineteenth Century* for January, 1898, p. 69, for one such story[10]); and with countless stories of their getting power over people by giving them what is called 'the touch' – I shall tell and weigh a number of these stories some day – and perhaps with the common habit of calling a paralytic attack a 'stroke'. Cuchulain wins the love of Fand just as young, handsome countrymen are believed to win the love of fair women of 'the others', and he goes to help Labraid as young, strong countrymen are believed to help 'the others' who can do little, being but 'shadows' without a mortal among them, at the hurling and in the battle; and November Eve is still a season of great power among the spirits. Emer goes to the yew at the Strand End just as the wife goes to meet her husband who is 'away' or has been 'taken', or the husband to meet his wife, at midnight, at 'the custom gap' in the field where the fair is held, or at some other well known place; while the after madness of Cuchulain reminds me of the mystery the country people, like all premature people, see in madness, and of the way they sometimes associate it with 'the others', and of the saying of a woman in the Burren Hills, 'Those that are away among them never come back, or if they do they are not the same as they were before.' His great sorrow for the love of Fand reminds me of the woman told of in Aran, who was often heard weeping on the hill-side for the children she had left among 'the others'. One finds nothing in this tale about any person or thing being put in Cuchulain's place; but Professor Rhys has shown that in the original form of the story of Cuchulain and the Beetle of Forgetfulness,[11] Cuchulain made the prince who had come to summon him to the other world, take his place at the court of Uladh. There are many stories everywhere of people who have their places taken by Angels, or spirits, or gods, that they may live another life in some other place, and I believe all such stories were once stories of people 'away'.

Pwyll and Arawn in the *Mabinogion* change places for a year, Pwyll going to the court of the dead in the shape of Arawn to overcome his enemies, and Arawn going to the court of Dyved. Arawn said, 'I will put my form and semblance upon thee, so that not a page of the chamber, not an officer nor any other man that has always followed me, shall know that it is not I . . . And I will cause that no one in all thy dominions, neither man nor woman, shall know that I am not you, and I will go there in thy stead.' Pwyll overcomes Arawn's enemy with one blow, and Arawn's rule in Dyved was a marvel because of his wisdom, for in all these stories strength comes from among men, and wisdom from among gods who are but 'shadows'.

Professor Rhys has interpreted both the stories of Cuchulain and the story of Pwyll and Arawn as solar myths, and one doubts not that the old priests and poets saw analogies in day and night, in summer and winter; or perhaps held that the passing away for a time of the brightness of day or of the abundance of summer, was one story with the passing of a man out of our world for a time. There have been myth-makers who put the mountain of the gods at the North Pole, and there are still visionaries who think that cold and barrenness with us are warmth and abundance in some inner world; while what the Aran people call 'the battle of the friends' believed to be fought between the friends and enemies of the living among the 'others', to decide whether a sick person is to live or die, and the battle believed to be fought by the 'others' at harvest time, to decide, as I think, whether the harvest is to stay among men, or wither from among men and belong to 'the others' and the dead, show, I think, that the gain of the one country is the other country's loss. The Norse legend[12] of the false Odin that took the true Odin's place, when the summer sun became the winter sun, brings the story of a man who is 'away' and the story of the year perfectly together. It may be that the druids and poets meant more at the beginning than a love story, by such stories as that of Cuchulain and Fand, for in many ancient countries, as even among some African tribes to-day, a simulated and ceremonious death was the symbol, or the condition, of the soul's coming to the place of wisdom and of the spirits of wisdom; and, if this is true, it is right for such stories to remind us of day and night, winter and summer, that men may find in all nature the return and history of the soul's deliverance.

60

PREFACE TO LADY GREGORY'S *CUCHULAIN OF MUIRTHEMNE*

(1902)

I

I think this book is the best that has come out of Ireland in my time. Perhaps I should say that it is the best book that has ever come out of Ireland; for the stories which it tells are a chief part of Ireland's gift to the imagination of the world – and it tells them perfectly for the first time.[1] Translators from the Irish have hitherto retold one story or the other from some one version, and not often with any fine understanding of English, of those changes of rhythm for instance that are changes of the sense. They have translated the best and fullest manuscripts they knew, as accurately as they could, and that is all we have the right to expect from the first translators of a difficult and old literature. But few of the stories really begin to exist as great works of imagination until somebody has taken the best bits out of many manuscripts. Sometimes, as in Lady Gregory's version of Deirdre, a dozen manuscripts have to give their best before the beads are ready for the necklace. It has been as necessary also to leave out as to add, for generations of copyists, who had often but little sympathy with the stories they copied, have mixed versions together in a clumsy fashion, often repeating one incident several times, and every century has ornamented what was once a simple story with its own often extravagant ornament. One does not perhaps exaggerate when one says that no story has come down to us in the form it had when the story-teller told it in the winter evenings. Lady Gregory has done her work of compression and selection at once so firmly and so reverently that I cannot believe that anybody, except now and then for a scientific purpose, will need another text than this, or than the version of it the Gaelic League has begun to publish in Modern Irish.[2] When she has added her translations from other cycles, she will have given Ireland its *Mabinogion*,[3] its *Morte D'Arthur*,[4] its *Nibelungenlied*.[5] She has already put a great mass of stories, in which the ancient heart of Ireland still lives, into a shape at once harmonious and characteristic; and without writing more than a very few sentences of her own to link together incidents or thoughts taken from different manuscripts, without adding more indeed than the story-teller must often have added to amend the hesitation of a moment. Perhaps more than all she has discovered a fitting dialect to tell them in. Some years ago I wrote some stories of mediæval Irish life,[6] and as I wrote I was sometimes made wretched by the thought that I knew of no kind of English that fitted them as the language of Morris' prose stories[7] – the most beautiful language I had ever read – fitted his journeys to woods and wells beyond the world. I knew of no language to write about Ireland in but raw modern English; but now Lady Gregory has discovered a speech as beautiful as that of Morris, and a living speech into the bargain. As she moved about among her people she learned to love the beautiful speech of those who think in Irish, and to understand that it is as true a dialect of English as the dialect that Burns wrote in. It is some hundreds of years old, and age gives a language authority. One finds in it the vocabulary of the translators of the Bible, joined to an idiom which makes it tender, compassionate, and complaisant, like the Irish language itself. It is certainly well suited to clothe a literature which never ceased to be folk-lore even when it was recited in the Courts of Kings.

II

Lady Gregory could with less trouble have made a book that would have better pleased the hasty reader. She could have plucked away details, smoothed out characteristics till she had left nothing but the bare stories; but a book of that kind would never have called up the past, or stirred the imagination of a painter or a poet, and would be as little thought of in a few years as if it had been a popular novel.

The abundance of what may seem at first irrelevant invention in a story like the death of Conaire,[8] is essential if we are to recall a time when people were in love with a story, and gave themselves up to imagination as if to a lover. One may think there are too many lyrical outbursts, or too many enigmatical symbols here and there in some other story, but delight will always overtake one in the end. One comes to accept without reserve an art that is half epical, half lyrical, like that of the historical parts of the Bible, the art of a time when perhaps men passed more readily than they do now from one mood to another, and found it harder than we do to keep to the mood in which one tots up figures or banters a friend.

III

The Church when it was most powerful created an imaginative unity, for it taught learned and unlearned to climb, as it were, to the great moral realities through hierarchies of Cherubim and Seraphim, through clouds of Saints and Angels who had all their precise duties and privileges. The story-tellers of Ireland, perhaps of every primitive country, created a like unity, only it was to the great aesthetic realities that they taught people to climb. They created for learned and unlearned alike, a communion of heroes, a cloud of stalwart witnesses; but because they were as much excited as a monk over his prayers, they did not think sufficiently about the shape of the poem and the story. One has to get a little weary or a little distrustful of one's subject, perhaps, before one can lie awake thinking how one will make the most of it. They were more anxious to describe energetic characters, and to invent beautiful stories, than to express themselves with perfect dramatic logic or in perfectly-ordered words. They shared their characters and their stories, their very images, with one another, and handed them down from generation to generation; for nobody, even when he had added some new trait, or some new incident, thought of claiming for himself what so obviously lived its own merry or mournful life. The wood-carver who first put a sword into St Michael's hand would have as soon claimed as his own a thought which was perhaps put into his mind by St Michael himself. The Irish poets had also, it may be, what seemed a supernatural sanction, for a chief poet had to understand not only innumerable kinds of poetry, but how to keep himself for nine days in a trance. They certainly believed in the historical reality of even their wildest imaginations. And so soon as Christianity made their hearers desire a chronology that would run side by side with that of the Bible, they delighted in arranging their Kings and Queens, the shadows of forgotten mythologies, in long lines that ascended to Adam and his Garden. Those who listened to them must have felt as if the living were like rabbits digging their burrows under walls that had been built by Gods and Giants, or like swallows building their nests in the stone mouths of immense images, carved by nobody knows who. It is no wonder that one sometimes hears about men who saw in a vision ivy-leaves that were greater than shields, and blackbirds whose thighs were like the thighs of oxen. The fruit of all those stories, unless indeed the finest activities of the mind are but a pastime, is the quick intelligence, the abundant imagination, the courtly manners of the Irish country people.

IV

William Morris came to Dublin when I was a boy, and I had some talk with him about these old stories. He had intended to lecture upon them, but 'the ladies and gentlemen' – he put a communistic fervour of hatred into the phrase – knew nothing about them. He spoke of the Irish account of the battle of Clontarf, and of the Norse account, and said, that one saw the Norse and Irish tempers in the two accounts. The Norseman was interested in the way things are done, but the Irishman turned aside, evidently well pleased to be out of so dull a business, to describe beautiful supernatural events. He was thinking, I suppose, of the young man who came from Aebhen of the Grey Rock, giving up immortal love and youth, that he might fight and die by Murrugh's side.[9] He said that the Norseman had the dramatic temper, and the Irishman had the lyrical. I think I should have said epical and romantic rather than dramatic and lyrical, but his words, which have so much greater authority than mine, mark the distinction very well, and not only between Irish and Norse, but between Irish and other un-Celtic literatures. The Irish story-teller could not interest himself with an unbroken interest in the way men like himself burned a house, or won wives no more wonderful than themselves. His mind constantly escaped out of daily circumstance, as a bough that has been held down by a weak hand suddenly straightens itself out. His imagination was always running off to Tír na nÓg, to the Land of Promise, which is as near to the country-people of to-day, as it was to Cuchulain and his companions. His belief in its nearness, cherished in its turn the lyrical temper, which is always athirst for an emotion, a beauty which cannot be found in its perfection upon earth, or only for a moment. His imagination, which had not been able to believe in Cuchulain's greatness, until it had brought the Great Queen,[10] the red eyebrowed goddess to woo him upon the battlefield, could not be satisfied with a friendship less romantic and lyrical than that of Cuchulain and Ferdiad,[11] who kissed one another after the day's fighting, or with a love less romantic and lyrical than that of Baile and Aillinn,[12] who died at the report of one another's deaths, and married in Tír na nÓg. His art, too, is often at its greatest when it is most extravagant, for he only feels himself among solid things, among things with fixed laws and satisfying purposes, when he has reshaped the world according to his heart's desire. He understands as well as Blake that the ruins of time build mansions in eternity,[13] and he never allows anything, that we can see and handle, to remain long unchanged. The characters must remain the same, but the strength of Fergus may change so greatly, that he, who a moment before was merely a strong man among many, becomes the master of Three Blows that would destroy an army, did they not cut off the heads of three little hills instead, and his sword, which a fool had been able to steal out of its sheath, has of a sudden the likeness of a rainbow. A wandering lyric moon must knead and kindle perpetually that moving world of cloaks made out of the fleeces of Manannan; of armed men who change themselves into sea-birds; of goddesses who become crows; of trees that bear fruit and flower at the same time. The great emotions of love, terror, and friendship must alone remain untroubled by the moon in that world, which is still the world of the Irish country-people, who do not open their eyes very wide at the most miraculous change, at the most sudden enchantment. Its events, and things, and people are wild, and are like unbroken horses, that are so much more beautiful than horses that have learned to run between shafts. One thinks of actual life, when one reads those Norse stories, which were already in decadence, so necessary were the proportions of actual life to their efforts, when a dying man remembered his heroism enough to look down at his wound and say, 'Those broad spears are coming into fashion';[14] but the Irish stories make one understand why the Greeks called myths the activities of the dæmons. The great virtues, the great joys, the great privations come in the myths, and, as it were, take mankind between their naked arms, and without putting off their divinity. Poets have taken their themes more often from stories that are all, or half, mythological, than from history or stories that give one the sensation of history, understanding, as I think, that the imagination which remembers the proportions of life is but a long wooing, and that it has to forget them before it becomes the torch and the marriage-bed.

V

One finds, as one expects, in the work of men who were not troubled about any probabilities or necessities but those of emotion itself, an immense variety of incident and character and of ways of expressing emotion. Cuchulain fights man after man during the quest of the Brown Bull, and not one of those fights is like another, and not one is lacking in emotion or strangeness; and when one thinks imagination can do no more, the story of the Two Bulls, emblematic of all contests, suddenly lifts romance into prophecy. The characters too have a distinctness one does not find among the people of the *Mabinogion*, perhaps not even among the people of the *Morte D'Arthur*. One knows one will be long forgetting Cuchulain, whose life is vehement and full of pleasure, as though he always remembered that it was to be soon over; or the dreamy Fergus who betrays the sons of Usnach for a feast, without ceasing to be noble; or Conall[15] who is fierce and friendly and trustworthy, but has not the sap of divinity that makes Cuchulain mysterious to men, and beloved of women.

Women indeed, with their lamentations for lovers and husbands and sons, and for fallen rooftrees and lost wealth, give the stories their most beautiful sentences; and, after Cuchulain, one thinks most of certain great queens – of angry, amorous Maeve, with her long pale face; of Findabair, her daughter, who dies of shame and of pity; of Deirdre who might be some mild modern housewife but for her prophetic wisdom. If one does not set Deirdre's lamentations[16] among the greatest lyric poems of the world, I think one may be certain that the wine-press of the poets has been trodden for one in vain; and yet I think it may be proud Emer, Cuchulain's fitting wife, who will linger longest in the memory. What a pure flame burns in her always, whether she is the newly-married wife fighting for precedence, fierce as some beautiful bird, or the confident housewife, who would awaken her husband from his magic sleep with mocking words; or the great queen who would get him out of the tightening net of his doom, by sending him into the Valley of the Deaf, with Niamh, his mistress, because he will be more obedient to her; or the woman whom sorrow has set with Helen and Iseult and Brunnhilda, and Deirdre, to share their immortality in the rosary of the poets.

'"And oh! my love!" she said, "we were often in one another's company, and it was happy for us; for if the world had been searched from the rising of the sun to sunset, the like would never have been found in one place, of the Black Sainglain and the Grey of Macha, and Laeg the chariot-driver, and myself and Cuchulain."

'And after that Emer bade Conall to make a wide, very deep grave for Cuchulain; and she laid herself down beside her gentle comrade, and she put her mouth to his mouth, and she said: "Love of my life, my friend, my sweetheart, my one choice of the men of the earth, many is the women, wed or unwed, envied me until to-day; and now I will not stay living after you."'

VI

To us Irish these personages should be more important than all others, for they lived in the places where we ride and go marketing, and sometimes they have met one another on the hills that cast their shadows upon our doors at evening. If we will but tell these stories to our children the Land will begin again to be a Holy Land, as it was before men gave their hearts to Greece and Rome and Judea. When I was a child I had only to climb the hill behind the house to see long, blue, ragged hills flowing along the southern horizon. What beauty was lost to me, what depth of emotion is still perhaps lacking in me, because nobody told me, not even the merchant captains who knew everything, that Cruachan[17] of the Enchantments lay behind those long, blue, ragged hills!

61

'DREAMS THAT HAVE NO MORAL'

from *The Celtic Twilight* (1902)

The friend who heard about Maive and the hazel-stick[1] went to the workhouse another day. She found the old people cold and wretched, 'like flies in winter', she said; but they forgot the cold when they began to talk. A man had just left them who had played cards in a rath with the people of faery, who had played 'very fair'; and one old man had seen an enchanted black pig one night, and there were two old people my friend had heard quarrelling as to whether Raftery or Callanan was the better poet.[2] One had said of Raftery, 'He was a big man, and his songs have gone through the whole world. I remember him well. He had a voice like the wind'; but the other was certain 'that you would stand in the snow to listen to Callanan'. Presently an old man began to tell my friend a story, and all listened delightedly, bursting into laughter now and then. The story, which I am going to tell just as it was told, was one of those old rambling moralless tales, which are the delight of the poor and the hard driven, wherever life is left in its natural simplicity. They tell of a time when nothing had consequences, when even if you were killed, if only you had a good heart, somebody would bring you to life again with a touch of a rod, and when if you were a prince and happened to look exactly like your brother, you might go to bed with his queen, and have only a little quarrel afterwards. We too, if we were so weak and poor that everything threatened us with misfortune, would remember, if foolish people left us alone, every old dream that has been strong enough to fling the weight of the world from its shoulders.

There was a king one time who was very much put out because he had no son, and he went at last to consult his chief adviser. And the chief adviser said, 'It's easy enough managed if you do as

I tell you. Let you send some one,' says he, 'to such a place to catch a fish. And when the fish is brought in, give it to the queen, your wife, to eat.'

So the king sent as he was told, and the fish was caught and brought in, and he gave it to the cook, and bade her put it before the fire, but to be careful with it, and not to let any blob or blister rise on it. But it is impossible to cook a fish before the fire without the skin of it rising in some place or other, and so there came a blob on the skin, and the cook put her finger on it to smooth it down, and then she put her finger into her mouth to cool it, and so she got a taste of the fish. And then it was sent up to the queen, and she ate it, and what was left of it was thrown out into the yard, and there was a mare in the yard and a greyhound, and they ate the bits that were thrown out.

And before a year was out, the queen had a young son, and the cook had a young son, and the mare had two foals, and the greyhound had two pups.

And the two young sons were sent out for a while to some place to be cared, and when they came back they were so much like one another no person could know which was the queen's son and which was the cook's. And the queen was vexed at that, and she went to the chief adviser and said, 'Tell me some way that I can know which is my own son, for I don't like to be giving the same eating and drinking to the cook's son as to my own.' 'It is easy to know that,' said the chief adviser, 'if you will do as I tell you. Go you outside, and stand at the door they will be coming in by, and when they see you, your own son will bow his head, but the cook's son will only laugh.'

So she did that, and when her own son bowed his head, her servants put a mark on him that she would know him again. And when they were all sitting at their dinner after that, she said to Jack, that was the cook's son, 'It is time for you to go away out of this, for you are not my son.' And her own son, that we will call Bill, said, 'Do not send him away, are we not brothers?' But Jack said, 'I would have been long ago out of this house if I knew it was not my own father and mother owned it.' And for all Bill could say to him, he would not stop. But before he went, they were by the well that was in the garden, and he said to Bill, 'If harm ever happens to me, that water on the top of the well will be blood, and the water below will be honey.'

Then he took one of the pups, and one of the two horses, that was foaled after the mare eating the fish, and the wind that was after him could not catch him, and he caught the wind that was before him. And he went on till he came to a weaver's house, and he asked him for a lodging, and he gave it to him. And then he went on till he came to a king's house, and he went in at the door to ask, 'Did he want a servant?' 'All I want,' said the king, 'is a boy that will drive out the cows to the field every morning, and bring them in at night to be milked.' 'I will do that for you,' said Jack; so the king engaged him.

In the morning Jack was sent out with the four-and-twenty cows, and the place he was told to drive them to had not a blade of grass in it for them, but was full of stones. So Jack looked about for some place where there would be better grass, and after a while he saw a field with good green grass in it, and it belonging to a giant. So he knocked down a bit of the wall and drove them in, and he went up himself into an apple-tree and began to eat the apples. Then the giant came into the field. 'Fee-faw-fum,' says he, 'I smell the blood of an Irishman. I see you where you are, up in the tree,' he said; 'you are too big for one mouthful, and too small for two mouthfuls, and I don't know what I'll do with you if I don't grind you up and make snuff for my nose.' 'As you are strong, be merciful,' says Jack up in the tree. 'Come down out of that, you little dwarf,' said the giant, 'or I'll tear you and the tree asunder.' So Jack came down. 'Would you sooner be driving red-hot knives into one another's hearts,' said the giant, 'or would you sooner be fighting one another on red-hot flags?' 'Fighting on red-hot flags is what I'm used to at home,' said Jack, 'and your dirty feet will be sinking in them and my feet will be rising.' So then they began the fight. The ground that was hard they made soft, and the ground that was soft they made hard, and they made spring wells come up through the green flags. They were like that all through the day, no one getting the upper hand of the other, and at last a little bird came and sat on the bush and said to Jack, 'If you don't make an end of him by sunset, he'll make an end of you.' Then Jack put out his strength, and he brought the giant down on his knees. 'Give me my life,' says the giant, 'and I'll give you the three best gifts.' 'What are those?' said Jack. 'A sword that nothing can stand against, and a suit that when you put it on, you will see everybody, and nobody will see you, and a pair of shoes that will make you run faster than the wind blows.' 'Where are they to be found?' said Jack. 'In that red door you see there in the hill.' So Jack went and got them out. 'Where will I try the sword?' says he. 'Try it on that ugly black stump of a tree,' says the giant. 'I see nothing blacker or uglier than your own head,' says Jack. And with that he made one stroke, and cut off the giant's head that it went into the air, and he caught it on the sword as it was coming down, and made two halves of it. 'It is well for you I did not join the body again,' said the head, 'or you would have never been able to strike it off again.' 'I did not give you the chance of that,' said Jack. And he brought away the great suit with him.

So he brought the cows home at evening, and every one wondered at all the milk they gave that night. And when the king was sitting at dinner with the princess, his daughter, and the rest, he said, 'I think I only hear two roars from beyond to-night in place of three.'

The next morning Jack went out again with the cows, and he saw another field full of grass, and he knocked down the wall and let the cows in. All happened the same as the day before, but the giant that came this time had two heads, and they fought together, and the little bird came and spoke to Jack as before. And when Jack had brought the giant down, he said, 'Give me my life, and I'll give you the best thing I have.' 'What is that?' says Jack. 'It's a suit that you can put on, and you will see every one but no one can see you.' 'Where is it?' said Jack. 'It's inside that little red door at the side of the hill.' So Jack went and brought out the suit. And then he cut off the giant's two heads, and caught them coming down and made four halves of them. And they said it was well for him he had not given them time to join the body.

That night when the cows came home they gave so much milk that all the vessels that could be found were filled up.

The next morning Jack went out again, and all happened as before, and the giant this time had four heads, and Jack made eight halves of them. And the giant had told him to go to a little blue door in the side of the hill, and there he got a pair of shoes that when you put them on would go faster than the wind.

That night the cows gave so much milk that there were not vessels enough to hold it, and it was given to tenants and to poor people passing the road, and the rest was thrown out at the windows. I was passing that way myself, and I got a drink of it.

That night the king said to Jack, 'Why is it the cows are giving so much milk these days? Are you bringing them to any other grass?' 'I am not,' said Jack, 'but I have a good stick, and whenever they would stop still or lie down, I give them blows of it, that they jump and leap over walls and stones and ditches; that's the way to make cows give plenty of milk.'

And that night at the dinner, the king said, 'I hear no roars at all.'

The next morning, the king and the princess were watching at the window to see what would Jack do when he got to the field. And Jack knew they were there, and he got a stick, and began to batter the cows, that they went leaping and jumping over stones, and walls, and ditches. 'There is no lie in what Jack said,' said the king then.

Now there was a great serpent at that time used to come every seven years, and he had to get a king's daughter to eat, unless she would have some good man to fight for her. And it was the princess at the place Jack was had to be given to it that time, and the king had been feeding a bully underground for seven years, and you may believe he got the best of everything, to be ready to fight it.

And when the time came, the princess went out, and the bully with her down to the shore, and when they got there what did he do, but to tie the princess to a tree, the way the serpent would be able to swallow her easy with no delay, and he himself went and hid up in an ivy-tree. And Jack knew what was going on, for the princess had told him about it, and had asked would he help her, but he said he would not. But he came out now, and he put on the suit he had taken from the first giant, and he came by the place the princess was, but she didn't know him. 'Is that right for a princess to be tied to a tree?' said Jack. 'It is not, indeed,' said she, and she told him what had happened, and how the serpent was coming to take her. 'If you will let me sleep for awhile with my head in your lap,' said Jack, 'you could wake me when it is coming.' So he did that, and she awakened him when she saw the serpent coming, and Jack got up and fought with it, and drove it back into the sea. And then he cut the rope that fastened her, and he went away. The bully came down then out of the tree, and he brought the princess to where the king was, and he said, 'I got a friend of mine to come and fight the serpent to-day, where I was a little timorous after being so long shut up underground, but I'll do the fighting myself to-morrow.'

The next day they went out again, and the same thing happened, the bully tied up the princess where the serpent could come at her fair and easy, and went up himself to hide in the ivy-tree. Then Jack put on the suit he had taken from the second giant, and he walked out, and the princess did not know him, but she told him all that had happened yesterday, and how some young gentleman she did not know had come and saved her. So Jack asked might he lie down and take a sleep with his head in her lap, the way she could awake him. And all happened the same way as the day before. And the bully gave her up to the king, and said he had brought another of his friends to fight for her that day.

The next day she was brought down to the shore as before, and a great many people gathered to see the serpent that was coming to bring the king's daughter away. And Jack brought out the suit of clothes he had brought away from the third giant, and she did not know him, and they talked as before. But when he was asleep this time, she thought she would make sure of being able to find him again, and she took out her scissors and cut off a piece of his hair, and made a little packet of it and put it away. And she did another thing, she took off one of the shoes that was on his feet.

And when she saw the serpent coming she woke him, and he said, 'This time I will put the serpent in a way that he will eat no more king's daughters.' So he took out the sword he had got from the giant, and he put it in at the back of the serpent's neck, the way blood and water came spouting out that went for fifty miles inland, and made an end of him. And then he made off, and no one saw what way he went, and the bully brought the princess to the king, and claimed to have saved her, and it is he who was made much of, and was the right-hand man after that.

But when the feast was made ready for the wedding, the princess took out the bit of hair she had, and she said she would marry no one but the man whose hair would match that, and she showed the shoe and said that she would marry no one whose foot would not fit that shoe as well. And the bully tried to put on the shoe, but so much as his toe would not go into it, and as to his hair, it didn't match at all to the bit of hair she had cut from the man that saved her.

So then the king gave a great ball, to bring all the chief men of the country together to try would the shoe fit any of them. And they were all going to carpenters and joiners getting bits of their feet cut off to try could they wear the shoe, but it was no use, not one of them could get it on.

Then the king went to his chief adviser and asked what could he do. And the chief adviser bade him to give another ball, and this time he said, 'Give it to poor as well as rich.'

So the ball was given, and many came flocking to it, but the shoe would not fit any one of them. And the chief adviser said, 'Is every one here that belongs to the house?' 'They are all here,' said the king, 'except the boy that minds the cows, and I would not like him to be coming up here.'

Jack was below in the yard at the time, and he heard what the king said, and he was very angry, and he went and got his sword and came running up the stairs to strike off the king's head, but the man that kept the gate met him on the stairs before he could get to the king, and quieted him down, and when he got to the top of the stairs and the princess saw him, she gave a cry and ran into his arms. And they tried the shoe and it fitted him, and his hair matched to the piece that had been cut off. So then they were married, and a great feast was given for three days and three nights.

And at the end of that time, one morning there came a deer outside the window, with bells on it, and they ringing. And it called out, 'Here is the hunt, where is the huntsman and the hound?' So when Jack heard that he got up and took his horse and his hound and went hunting the deer. When it was in the hollow he was on the hill, and when it was on the hill he was in the hollow, and that went on all through the day, and when night fell it went into a wood. And Jack went into the wood after it, and all he could see was a mud-wall cabin, and he went in, and there he saw an old woman, about two hundred years old, and she sitting over the fire. 'Did you see a deer pass this way?' says

Jack. 'I did not,' says she, 'but it's too late now for you to be following a deer, let you stop the night here.' 'What will I do with my horse and my hound?' said Jack. 'Here are two ribs of hair,' says she, 'and let you tie them up with them.' So Jack went out and tied up the horse and the hound, and when he came in again the old woman said, 'You killed my three sons, and I'm going to kill you now,' and she put on a pair of boxing-gloves, each one of them nine stone weight, and the nails in them fifteen inches long. Then they began to fight, and Jack was getting the worst of it. 'Help, hound!' he cried out, then 'Squeeze, hair,' cried out the old woman, and the rib of hair that was about the hound's neck squeezed him to death. 'Help, horse!' Jack called out, then 'Squeeze, hair,' called out the old woman, and the rib of hair that was about the horse's neck began to tighten and squeeze him to death. Then the old woman made an end of Jack and threw him outside the door.

To go back now to Bill. He was out in the garden one day, and he took a look at the well, and what did he see but the water at the top was blood, and what was underneath was honey. So he went into the house again, and he said to his mother, 'I will never eat a second meal at the same table, or sleep a second night in the same bed, till I know what is happening to Jack.'

So he took the other horse and hound then, and set off, over hills where cock never crows and horn never sounds, and the devil never blows his bugle. And at last he came to the weaver's house, and when he went in, the weaver says, 'You are welcome, and I can give you better treatment than I did the last time you came in to me,' for she thought it was Jack who was there, they were so much like one another. 'That is good,' said Bill to himself, 'my brother has been here.' And he gave the weaver the full of a basin of gold in the morning before he left.

Then he went on till he came to the king's house, and when he was at the door the princess came running down the stairs, and said, 'Welcome to you back again.' And all the people said, 'It is a wonder you have gone hunting three days after your marriage, and to stop so long away.' So he stopped that night with the princess, and she thought it was her own husband all the time.

And in the morning the deer came, and bells ringing on her, under the windows, and called out, 'The hunt is here, where are the huntsmen and the hounds?' Then Bill got up and got his horse and his hound, and followed her over hills and hollows till they came to the wood, and there he saw nothing but the mud-wall cabin and the old woman sitting by the fire, and she bade him stop the night there, and gave him two ribs of hair to tie his horse and his hound with. But Bill was wittier than Jack was, and before he went out, he threw the ribs of hair into the fire secretly. When he came in the old woman said, 'Your brother killed my three sons, and I killed him, and I'll kill you along with him.' And she put her gloves on, and they began to fight, and then Bill called out, 'Help, horse.' 'Squeeze, hair,' called the old woman; 'I can't squeeze, I'm in the fire,' said the hair. And the horse came in and gave her a blow of his hoof. 'Help, hound,' said Bill then. 'Squeeze, hair,' said the old woman; 'I can't, I'm in the fire,' said the second hair. Then the hound put his teeth in her, and Bill brought her down, and she cried for mercy. 'Give me my life,' she said, 'and I'll tell you where you'll get your brother again, and his hound and horse.' 'Where's that?' said Bill. 'Do you see that rod over the fire?' said she; 'take it down and go outside the door where you'll see three green stones, and strike them with the rod, for they are your brother, and his horse and hounds, and they'll come to life again.' 'I will, but I'll make a green stone of you first,' said Bill, and he cut off her head with his sword.

Then he went out and struck the stones, and sure enough there were Jack, and his horse and hounds, alive and well. And they began striking other stones around, and men came from them, that had been turned to stones, hundreds and thousands of them.

Then they set out for home, but on the way they had some dispute or some argument together, for Jack was not well pleased to hear he had spent the night with his wife, and Bill got angry, and he struck Jack with the rod, and turned him to a green stone. And he went home, but the princess saw he had something on his mind, and he said then, 'I have killed my brother.' And he went back then and brought him to life, and they lived happy ever after, and they had children by the basketful, and threw them out by the shovelful. I was passing one time myself, and they called me in and gave me a cup of tea.

62

'POETS AND DREAMERS'

from the *New Liberal Review* (1903)

This new book of Lady Gregory's has brought to my mind a day two or three years ago when I stood on the side of Slieve Echtge looking out over Galway. The Burren Hills were to my left, and though I forget whether I could see the cairn over Bald Conan[1] of the Fianna, I could certainly see many places there of which I had been told stories and legends. In front of me, over many miles of level Galway plains, there was a low blue hill flooded with evening light. I asked a countryman who was with me what hill that was, and he told me it was Cruachmaa of the sidhe. I had often heard of that hill even as far north as Sligo, for I had heard from the country people a great many stories of the host of the Sidhe who live there, still fighting and holding festivals. I asked the old countryman more about it, and he told me many stories: of strange women who had come from it, and who would come into a house, having the appearance of countrywomen, but would know all that had happened in that house, and who would always pay back with increase, though not by their own hands, whatever was given to them. And he told me of people who had been carried away into the hill, and how one man went to look for his wife there, and how he dug into the hill and all but got his wife again; but at the very moment she was coming out to him, the pick he was digging with struck her upon the head and killed her. I asked him if he had himself seen any of its enchantments, and he said, 'Sometimes, when I look over to the hill, I see a mist lying on the top of it, that goes away after a while.'

A great part of the poems and stories in Lady Gregory's beautiful book were made or gathered between Burren and Cruachmaa and Echtge, for barren Echtge has its stories, too.

It was here that Raftery,[2] the wandering country poet of ninety years ago, praised and blamed, chanting fine verses or playing badly on his fiddle. It is here the ballads of meeting and parting have been sung; and some whose lamentations for defeat are still remembered may have passed through this plain flying from the battle of Aughrim.

'I will go up on the mountain alone, and I will come hither from it again. It is there I saw the camp of the Gael, the poor troop thinned, not keeping with one another. Och, Ochone!'[3]

And here, if one can believe many devout people, whose words are in this book, Christ has walked upon the roads, sending the needy to some warm fireside, and sending one of His saints to anoint the dying.

I do not think imagination has changed here for centuries, for it is still busy with these two themes of the ancient Irish poets, the sternness of battle and the sadness of parting and death. The emotion that in other countries has made many love-songs has here been given in a long wooing to danger, that ghostly bride. It is not a difference in the substance of things, that the lamentations that were sung after battles are now sung for men who have died upon the gallows in the fight with the stranger –

It was bound fast here you saw him, and you wondered to see him,
Our fair-haired Donough, and he after being condemned;
There was a little white cap on him in place of a hat,
And a hempen rope in the place of a neckcloth.

I am after walking here all through the night,
Like a young lamb in a great flock of sheep;
My breast open, my hair loosened out,
And how did I find my brother but stretched before me!

The first place I cried my fill was at the top of the lake;
The second place was at the foot of the gallows;
The third place was at the head of your dead body
Among the Gall, and my own head as if cut in two.

If you were with me in the place you had a right to be,
Down in Sligo or down in Ballinrobe,
It is the gallows would be broken, it is the rope would be cut,
And fair-haired Donough going home by the path.

O fair-haired Donough, it is not the gallows was fit for you;
But to be going to the barn, to be threshing out the straw;
To be turning the plough to the right hand and to the left,
To be putting the red side of the soil uppermost.

O fair-haired Donough, O dear brother,
It is well I know who it was took you away from me;
Drinking from the cup, putting a light to the pipe,
And walking in the dew in the cover of the night.

O Michael Malley, O scourge of misfortune!
My brother was no calf of a vagabond cow;
But a well-shaped boy on a height or a hillside,
To knock a low pleasant sound out of a hurling-stick.

And fair-haired Donough, is not that the pity,
You that would carry well a spur or a boot;
I would put clothes in the fashion on you from cloth that would be lasting;
I would send you out like a gentleman's son.

O Michael Malley, may your sons never be in one another's company;
May your daughters never ask a marriage portion of you;
The two ends of the table are empty, the house is filled,
And fair-haired Donough, my brother, is stretched out.

There is a marriage portion coming home for Donough,
But it is not cattle nor sheep nor horses;
But tobacco and pipes and white candles,
And it will not be begrudged to them that will use it.[4]

The emotion of battle has become not less but more noble than it was; for the man who goes to his death now, saying as in one of these ballads,

It is with the people I was,
It is not with the law I was,

has behind it generations of poetry.

The poets of to-day speak with the same voice as that unknown priest who wrote the *Sorrowful Lament for Ireland*[5] some two hundred years ago, which Lady Gregory has translated into her passionate and rhythmical English:

> I do not know of anything under the sky
> That is friendly or favourable to the Gael,
> But only the sea that our need brings us to,
> Or the wind that blows to the harbour
> The ship that is bearing us away from Ireland;
> And there is reason that these are reconciled with us,
> For we increase the sea with our tears,
> And the wandering wind with our sighs.

There is still in truth upon these great level plains a people, a community, bound together by imaginative possessions, by stories and poems which have grown out of their own life, and by a past of great passions which can still stir them to imaginative action. One could still if one had the genius, and had been born to Irish, write for these people plays and poems like those of Greece. Does not the greatest poetry always require a people to listen to it? England or any other country which takes its tune from the great cities, and gets its taste from schools and not from old custom, may have a mob, but it cannot have a people. In England there are a few groups of men and women who have good taste, whether in cookery or in books; and the multitude copy them badly or but copy their copiers. The poet must always prefer the community where the perfected minds express a people to a community which is vainly seeking to copy the perfected minds. To have, however perfectly, the thoughts that can be weighed, the knowledge that can be got from books, the precision that can be learned at school, to belong to any aristocracy, is to be a little pool that will soon dry up. A people alone is a great river; and that is why I am persuaded that where a people has died a nation is about to die.

63

'A CANONICAL BOOK'

from the *Bookman* (1903)

Sometimes I have made a list of books for some friend who wanted to understand our new Irish movement, but the list has seldom been much to my mind. One book would show the old poetry through the dark glass of a pompous translator, and another's virtue was in a few pages or even in a few lines. There was, however, one book that was altogether to my mind, *The Love Songs of Connacht*,[1] for it was all about beautiful things, and it was simply written; and now I know of two other books, which will be always a part of our canon, Lady Gregory's *Cuchulain of Muirthemne*,[2] which it is no longer necessary to praise, and this new book of hers, *Poets and Dreamers* (Dublin: Hodges and Figgis; London: John Murray). It is not as important as *Cuchulain of Muirthemne*, but it should be read with it, for it shows the same spirit coming down to our own time in the verses of Gaelic poets and in the stories of the country people. Her chapters on Raftery,[3] the wandering poet of some ninety years ago, on Irish Jacobite ballads, and old country love songs, and on the spells that are in herbs and the like, are necessary to anybody who would understand Ireland. She translates the ballads and love songs into prose, but it is that musical prose full of country phrases, which is her discovery and Dr Hyde's; and her own comments, for all their simplicity and charm, cannot hide from discerning eyes an erudition in simple things and a fineness of taste in great things, that are only possible to those who have known how to labour.

The towns, for our civilisation has been perfected in towns, have for a long time now called the tune for the poets, even as, I think, for the Lake poets. And because one is not always a citizen there are moods in which one cannot read modern poetry at all; it is so full of eccentric and temporal things, so gnarled and twisted by the presence of a complicated life, so burdened by that painful riddle of the world, which never seems inexplicable till men gather in crowds to talk it out. I could not imagine myself, though I know there are some who feel differently, reading modern poetry when in love or angry or stirred by any deep passion. It is full of thoughts, and when one is stirred by any deep passion one does not want to know what anybody has thought of that passion, but to hear it beautifully spoken, and that is all. Some seventeenth-century lyric, where the subtleties are of speech alone, or some old folk tale that had maybe no conscious maker, but grew by the almost accidental stringing together of verses out of other songs, commingle one's being with another age, or with the moods of fishers and turf-cutters. Sometimes, indeed, being full of the scorn that is in passion, one is convinced that all good poems are fruit of the Tree of Life, and all bad ones apples of the Tree of Knowledge. I find in this book many fruits of the Tree of Life, and am content that they offer me no consolation but their beauty.

A friend of mine once asked some Irish-speaking countrymen, who were learning to write and read in Irish, what poem they liked the best out of a bundle that had been given them. They said, 'The Grief of a Girl's Heart', an Aran poem, which is among those Lady Gregory has translated, and they added that the last verse of it was the best. This is the last verse: 'You have taken the east from me; you have taken the west from me; you have taken what is before me and what is behind me; you have taken the moon, you have taken the sun from me; and my fear is great that you have taken God from me.'[4] A few years ago, before the modern feeling for folk-thought on the one hand, and for certain schools of esoteric poetry on the other hand, had brought a greater trust in imagination, a verse like that would have seemed nonsense to even good critics, and even now a critic of the school represented by most of the writing in, let us say, the *Spectator*, would probably call it vague and absurd. The poet who made it lived when poetry, not yet entangled in our modern logic, a child of parliaments and law courts, was contented with itself, and happy in speaking of passions almost too great to be spoken in words at all. The poet had bitten deeply into that sweet, intoxicating fruit of the tree that was in the midst of the garden, and he saw the world about him with dim, unsteady eyes. Another verse of the Aran song, and all the song is lovely, would seem, I think, more wicked than foolish. The girl would give everything to her lover, and at last cries out: 'O, aya! my mother give myself to him; and give him all that you have in the world; get out yourself to ask for alms, and do not come back and forward looking for me.' A critic to whom the hidden life of the soul is of less importance than those relations of one person to another that grow in importance as life becomes crowded would find it hard to sympathise with so undutiful a daughter. He might, indeed, if he had learnt his trade in that singular criticism of Shakespeare[5] which has decided that *Hamlet* was written for a warning to the irresolute, and *Coriolanus* as a lesson to the proud, persuade himself that the poem was written to show how great passion leads to undutifulness and selfishness. He could hardly come to understand that the poet was too full of life to concern himself with that wisdom, which Nietzsche has called an infirmary for bad poets,[6] that if he had known of it he would have scorned it as deeply as any true lover, no matter how unhappy his love, would scorn the wizard drug, that promised him easy days and nights untroubled by his sweetheart's eyes. I would send any man who wants to be cured of wisdom to this book, and to *Cuchulain of Muirthemne*, and to books like them. The end of wisdom is sometimes the beginning of heroism, and Lady Gregory's country poets have kept alive the way of thinking of the old heroic poets that did not constrain nature into any plan of civic virtue, but saw man as he is in himself, as an amorous woman has seen her lover from the beginning of the world. Raftery, the peasant poet, praises one man 'because he had pleasantness on the tops of his fingers', 'because in every quarter that he ever knew he would scatter his fill and not gather . . . He would spend the estate of the Dalys, their beer and their wine'; and he praises another because 'He did not lower himself or humble himself to the Gall, but he died a good Irishman, and he never bowed the head to any man.'[7] In the presence of thoughts like these two aristocracies have passed away. The one, hearing them sung in its castles, perished fighting vainly against the stranger, and the other, hearing them in the praise and dispraise of the Celtic poor, felt without understanding what it felt, the presence of a tribunal more ancient and august than itself, and became spendthrift and fought duels across handkerchiefs, and at last, after a brief time of such eloquence that the world had hardly seen its like, passed away ignobly.

Lady Gregory finishes her book with translations of Dr Hyde's little plays. These plays, which are being constantly acted throughout Ireland, are typical of the new movement, so far as it is a movement, in Irish. Acted for peasants, and sometimes by them, and full of the peasant mind, they show how it keeps to-day the thoughts of Raftery and his predecessors back to the beginning of history. One play is about Raftery himself, one is about an imaginary poet, Hanrahan, one is about an old saint, one is a very beautiful Nativity.[8] They have an impartial delight in the sinless wandering saint, and in the drunken wandering poet with his mouth full of curses. Are not both of them fine creatures, and what does it matter if one has hard claws and the other carries no burdens? Is it not an illusion that man exists for man? was he not made for some unknown purpose, as the stones, and the stars and the clouds, or made, it may be, for his Maker's pleasure? I think the old poets thought that way, and the Irish countryman, who is prosaic enough in himself, is the clay where one finds their footsteps even yet.

64

PREFACE TO LADY GREGORY'S *GODS AND FIGHTING MEN*

(1904)

I

A few months ago I was on the bare Hill of Allen, 'wide Almhuin of Leinster', where Fionn and the Fianna lived, according to the stories, although there are no earthen mounds there like those that mark the sites of old buildings on so many hills. A hot sun beat down upon flowering gorse and flowerless heather; and on every side except the east, where there were green trees and distant hills, one saw a level horizon and brown boglands with a few green places and here and there the glitter of water. One could imagine that had it been twilight and not early afternoon, and had there been vapours drifting and frothing where there were now but shadows of clouds, it would have set stirring in one, as few places even in Ireland can, a thought that is peculiar to Celtic romance, as I think, a thought of a mystery coming not as with Gothic nations out of the pressure of darkness, but out of great spaces and windy light. The hill of Teamhair,[1] or Tara, as it is now called, with its green mounds and its partly wooded sides, and its more gradual slope set among fat grazing lands, with great trees in the hedgerows, had brought before one imaginations, not of heroes who were in their youth for hundreds of years, or of women who came to them in the likeness of hunted fawns, but of kings that lived brief and politic lives, and of the five white roads that carried their armies to the lesser kingdoms of Ireland, or brought to the great fair that had given Teamhair its sovereignty, all that sought justice or pleasure or had goods to barter.

II

It is certain that we must not confuse these kings, as did the mediæval chroniclers, with those half-divine kings of Almhuin. The chroniclers, perhaps because they loved tradition too well to cast out utterly much that they dreaded as Christians, and perhaps because popular imagination had begun the mixture, have mixed one with another ingeniously, making Fionn the head of a kind of Militia under Cormac MacArt, who is supposed to have reigned at Teamhair in the second century, and making Grania, who travels to enchanted houses under the cloak of Angus, god of Love, and keeps her troubling beauty longer than did Helen hers, Cormac's daughter, and giving the stories of the Fianna, although the impossible has thrust its proud finger into them all, a curious air of precise history. It is only when one separates the stories from that mediæval pedantry, as in this book, that one recognises one of the oldest worlds that man has imagined, an older world certainly than one finds in the stories of Cuchulain, who lived, according to the chroniclers, about the time of the birth of Christ. They are far better known, and one may be certain of the antiquity of incidents that are known in one form or another to every Gaelic-speaking countryman in Ireland or in the Highlands of Scotland. Sometimes a labourer digging near to a cromlech, or Bed of Diarmuid and Grania as it is called, will tell one a tradition that seems older and more barbaric than any description of their adventures or of themselves in written text or story that has taken form in the mouths of professed story-tellers. Fionn and the Fianna found welcome among the court poets later than did Cuchulain; and one finds memories of Danish invasions and standing armies mixed with the imaginations of hunters and solitary fighters among great woods. One never hears of Cuchulain delighting in the hunt or in woodland things; and one imagines that the story-teller would have thought it unworthy in so great a man, who lived a well-ordered, elaborate life, and had his chariot and his chariot-driver and his barley-fed horses to delight in. If he is in the woods before dawn one is not told that he cannot know the leaves of the hazel from the leaves of the oak; and when Emer laments him no wild creature comes into her thoughts but the cuckoo that cries over cultivated fields. His story must have come out of a time when the wild wood was giving way to pasture and tillage, and men had no longer a reason to consider every cry of the birds or change of the night. Fionn, who was always in the woods, whose battles were but hours amid years of hunting, delighted in the 'cackling of ducks from the Lake of the Three Narrows; the scolding talk of the blackbird of Doire an Cairn; the bellowing of the ox from the Valley of the Berries; the whistle of the eagle from the Valley of Victories or from the rough branches of the Ridge of the Stream; the grouse of the heather of Cruachan; the call of the otter of Druim re Coir'.[2] When sorrow comes upon the queens of the stories, they have sympathy for the wild birds and beasts that are like themselves: 'Credhe wife of Cael came with the others and went looking through the bodies for her comely comrade, and crying as she went. And as she was searching she saw a crane of the meadows and her two nestlings, and the cunning beast the fox watching the nestlings; and when the crane covered one of the birds to save it, he would make a rush at the other bird, the way she had to stretch herself out over the birds; and she would sooner have got her own death by the fox than the nestlings to be killed by him. And Credhe was looking at that, and she said: "It is no wonder I too have such love for my comely sweetheart, and the bird in that distress about her nestlings."'[3]

III

One often hears of a horse that shivers with terror, or of a dog that howls at something a man's eyes cannot see, and men who live primitive lives where instinct does the work of reason are fully conscious of many things that we cannot perceive at all. As life becomes more orderly, more deliberate, the supernatural world sinks farther away. Although the gods come to Cuchulain, and although he is the son of one of the greatest of them, their country and his are far apart, and they come to him as god to mortal; but Fionn is their equal. He is continually in their houses; he meets with Bodb Dearg,[4] and Angus, and Manannan, now as friend with friend, now as with an enemy he overcomes in battle; and when he has need of their help his messenger can say: 'There is not a king's son or a prince, or a leader of the Fianna of Ireland, without having a wife or a mother or a foster-mother or a sweetheart of the Tuatha Dé Danaan.' When the Fianna are broken up at last, after hundreds of years of hunting, it is doubtful that he dies at all, and certain that he comes again in some other shape, and Oisin, his son, is made king over a divine country. The birds and beasts that cross his path in the woods have been fighting men or great enchanters or fair women, and in a moment can take some beautiful or terrible shape. One thinks of him and of his people as great-bodied men with large movements, that seem, as it were, flowing out of some deep below the narrow stream of personal impulse, men that have broad brows and quiet eyes full of confidence in a good luck that proves every day afresh that they are a portion of the strength of things. They are hardly so much individual men as portions of universal nature, like the clouds that shape themselves and re-shape themselves momentarily, or like a bird between two boughs, or like the gods that have given the apples and the nuts; and yet this but brings them the nearer to us, for we can remake them in our image when we will, and the woods are the more beautiful for the thought. Do we not always fancy hunters to be something like this, and is not that why we think them poetical when we meet them of a sudden, as in these lines in 'Pauline':[5]

> An old hunter
> Talking with gods; or a high-crested chief
> Sailing with troops of friends to Tenedos?

IV

One must not expect in these stories the epic lineaments, the many incidents, woven into one great event of, let us say, the story of the War for the Brown Bull of Cuailgne, or that of the last gathering at Muirthemne. Even Diarmuid and Grania, which is a long story, has nothing of the clear outlines of Deirdre, and is indeed but a succession of detached episodes. The men who imagined the Fianna had the imagination of children, and as soon as they had invented one wonder, heaped another on top of it. Children – or, at any rate, it is so I remember my own childhood – do not understand large design, and they delight in little shut-in places where they can play at houses more than in great expanses where a country-side takes, as it were, the impression of a thought. The wild creatures and the green things are more to them than to us, for they creep towards our light by little holes and crevices. When they imagine a country for themselves, it is always a country where one can wander without aim, and where one can never know from one place what another will be like, or know from the one day's adventure what may meet one with to-morrow's sun. I have wished to become a child again that I might find this book, that not only tells one of such a country, but is fuller than any other book that tells of heroic life, of the childhood that is in all folk-lore, dearer to me than all the books of the western world.

V

Children play at being great and wonderful people, at the ambitions they will put away for one reason or another before they grow into ordinary men and women. Mankind as a whole had a like dream once; everybody and nobody built up the dream bit by bit, and the ancient story-tellers are there to make us remember what mankind would have been like, had not fear and the failing will and the laws of nature tripped up its heels. The Fianna and their like are themselves so full of power, and they are set in a world so fluctuating and dream-like, that nothing can hold them from being all that the heart desires.

I have read in a fabulous book that Adam had but to imagine a bird, and it was born into life, and that he created all things out of himself by nothing more important than an unflagging fancy; and heroes who can make a ship out of a shaving have but little less of the divine prerogatives. They had no speculative thoughts to wander through eternity and waste heroic blood; but how could that be otherwise, for it is at all times the proud angels who sit thinking upon the hill-side and not the people of Eden. One morning we meet them hunting a stag that is 'as joyful as the leaves of a tree in summer-time'; and whatever they do, whether they listen to the harp or follow an enchanter over-sea, they do for the sake of joy, their joy in one another, or their joy in pride and movement; and even their battles are fought more because of their delight in a good fighter than because of any gain that is in victory. They live always as if they were playing a game; and so far as they have any deliberate purpose at all, it is that they may become great gentlemen and be worthy of the songs of poets. It has been said, and I think the Japanese were the first to say it, that the four essential virtues are to be generous among the weak, and truthful among one's friends, and brave among one's enemies, and courteous at all times; and if we understand by courtesy not merely the gentleness the story-tellers have celebrated, but a delight in courtly things, in beautiful clothing and in beautiful verse, one understands that it was no formal succession of trials that bound the Fianna to one another. Only the Table Round, that is indeed, as it seems, a rivulet from the same river, is bound in a like fellowship, and there the four heroic virtues are troubled by the abstract virtues of the cloister. Every now and then some noble knight builds himself a cell upon the hill-side, or leaves kind women and joyful knights to seek the vision of the Grail in lonely adventures. But when Oisin or some kingly forerunner – Bran, son of Febal, or the like – rides or sails in an enchanted ship to some divine country, he but looks for a more delighted companionship, or to be in love with faces that will never fade. No thought of any life greater than that of love, and the companionship of those that have drawn their swords upon the darkness of the world, ever troubles their delight in one another as it troubles Iseult amid her love, or Arthur amid his battles. It is one of the ailments of our speculation that thought, when it is not the planning of something, or the doing of something or some memory of a plain circumstance separates us from one another because it makes us always more unlike, and because no thought passes through another's ear unchanged. Companionship can only be perfect when it is founded on things, for things are always the same under the hand, and at last one comes to hear with envy the voices of boys lighting a lantern to ensnare moths, or of the maids chattering in the kitchen about the fox that carried off a turkey before breakfast. This book is full of fellowship untroubled like theirs, and made noble by a courtesy that has gone perhaps out of the world. I do not know in literature better friends and lovers. When one of the Fianna finds Osgar dying the proud death of a young man, and asks is it well with him, he is answered, 'I am as you would have me be.'[6] The very heroism of the Fianna is indeed but their pride and joy in one another, their good fellowship. Goll, old and savage, and letting himself die of hunger in a cave because he is angry and sorry, can speak lovely words to the wife whose help he refuses. '"It is best as it is," he said, "and I never took the advice of a woman east or west, and I never will take it. And oh, sweet-voiced queen," he said, "what ails you to be fretting after me? and remember now your silver and your gold, and your silks . . . and do not be crying tears after me, queen with the white hands," he said, "but remember your constant lover Aodh, son of the best woman of the world, that came from Spain asking for you, and that I fought on Corcar-an-Dearg; and go to him now," he said, "for it is bad when a woman is without a good man."'[7]

VI

They have no asceticism, but they are more visionary than any ascetic, and their invisible life is but the life about them made more perfect and more lasting, and the invisible people are their own images in the water. Their gods may have been much besides this, for we know them from fragments of mythology picked out with trouble from a fantastic history running backward to Adam and Eve, and many things that may have seemed wicked to the monks who imagined that history, may have been altered or left out; but this they must have been essentially, for the old stories are confirmed by apparitions among the country-people to-day. The Men of Dea[8] fought against the misshapen Fomor, as Fionn fights against the Cat-Heads and the Dog-Heads;[9] and when they are overcome at last by men, they make themselves houses in the hearts of hills that are like the houses of men. When they call men to their houses and to their country Under-Wave[10] they promise them all that they have upon earth, only in greater abundance. The god Midir sings to Queen Etain in one of the most beautiful of the stories: 'The young never grow old; the fields and the flowers are as pleasant to be looking at as the blackbird's eggs; warm streams of mead and wine flow through that country; there is no care or no sorrow on any person; we see others, but we ourselves are not seen.'[11] These gods are indeed more wise and beautiful than men; but men, when they are great men, are stronger than they are, for men are, as it were, the foaming tide-line of their sea. One remembers the Druid who answered, when some one asked him who made the world, 'The Druids made it.' All was indeed but one life flowing everywhere, and taking one quality here, another there. It sometimes seems to one as if there is a kind of day and night of religion, and that a period when the influences are those that shape the world is followed by a period when the greater power is in influences that would lure the soul out of the world, out of the body. When Oisin is speaking with St Patrick of the friends and the life he has outlived, he can but cry out constantly against a religion that has no meaning for him. He laments, and the country-people have remembered his words for centuries: 'I will cry my fill, but not for God, but because Fionn and the Fianna are not living.'[12]

VII

Old writers had an admirable symbolism that attributed certain energies to the influence of the sun, and certain others to the lunar influence. To lunar influence belong all thoughts and emotions that were created by the community, by the common people, by nobody knows who, and to the sun all that came from the high disciplined or individual kingly mind. I myself imagine a marriage of the sun and moon in the arts I take most pleasure in; and now bride and bridegroom but exchange, as it were, full cups of gold and silver, and now they are one in a mystical embrace. From the moon come the folk-songs imagined by reapers and spinners of the common impulse of their labour, and made not by putting words together, but by mixing verses and phrases, and the folk-tales made by the capricious mixing of incidents known to everybody in new ways, as one deals out cards, never getting the same hand twice over. When one hears some fine story, one never knows whether it has not been hazard that put the last touch of adventure. Such poetry, as it seems to me, desires an infinity of wonder or emotion, for where there is no individual mind there is no measurer-out, no marker-in of limits. The poor fisher has no possession of the world and no responsibility for it; and if he dreams of a love-gift better than the brown shawl that seems too common for poetry, why should he not dream of a glove made from the skin of a bird, or shoes made from the skin of a fish, or a coat made from the glittering garment of the salmon?[13] Was it not Æschylus who said he but served up fragments from the banquet of Homer?[14] – but Homer himself found the great banquet on an earthen floor and under a broken roof. We do not know who at the foundation of the world made the banquet for the first time, or who put the pack of cards into rough hands; but we do know that, unless those that have made many inventions are about to change the nature of poetry, we may have to go where Homer went if we are to sing a new song. Is it because all that is under the moon thirsts to escape out of bounds, to lose itself in some unbounded tidal stream, that the songs of the folk are mournful, and that the story of the Fianna, whenever the queens lament for their lovers, reminds us of songs that are still sung in country-places? Their grief, even when it is to be brief like Grania's, goes up into the waste places of the sky. But in supreme art or in supreme life there is the influence of the sun too, and the sun brings with it, as old writers tell us, not merely discipline but joy; for its discipline is not of the kind the multitudes impose upon us by their weight and pressure, but the expression of the individual soul turning itself into a pure fire and imposing its own pattern, its own music, upon the heaviness and the dumbness that is in others and in itself. When we have drunk the cold cup of the moon's intoxication, we thirst for something beyond ourselves, and the mind flows outward to a natural immensity; but if we have drunk from the hot cup of the sun, our own fullness awakens, we desire little, for wherever one goes one's heart goes too; and if any ask what music is the sweetest, we can but answer, as Fionn answered, 'what happens'.[15] And yet the songs and stories that have come from either influence are a part, neither less than the other, of the pleasure that is the bride-bed of poetry.

VIII

Gaelic-speaking Ireland, because its art has been made, not by the artist choosing his material from wherever he has a mind to, but by adding a little to something which it has taken generations to invent, has always had a popular literature. One cannot say how much that literature has done for the vigour of the race, for one cannot count the hands its praise of kings and high-hearted queens made hot upon the sword-hilt, or the amorous eyes it made lustful for strength and beauty. One remembers indeed that when the farming people and the labourers of the town made their last attempt to cast out England by force of arms they named themselves after the companions of Fionn.[16] Even when Gaelic has gone, and the poetry with it, something of the habit of mind remains in ways of speech and thought and 'come-all-ye's' and poetical saying; nor is it only among the poor that the old thought has been for strength or weakness. Surely these old stories, whether of Fionn or Cuchulain, helped to sing the old Irish and the old Norman-Irish aristocracy to their end. They heard their hereditary poets and story-tellers, and they took to horse and died fighting against Elizabeth or against Cromwell; and when an English-speaking aristocracy had their place, it listened to no poetry indeed, but it felt about it in the popular mind an exacting and ancient tribunal, and began a play that had for spectators men and women that loved the high wasteful virtues. I do not think that their own mixed blood or the habit of their time need take all, or nearly all, credit or discredit for the impulse that made our modern gentlemen fight duels over pocket-handkerchiefs, and set out to play ball against the gates of Jerusalem[17] for a wager, and scatter money before the public eye; and at last, after an epoch of such eloquence the world has hardly seen its like, lose their public spirit and their high heart and grow querulous and selfish as men do who have played life out not heartily but with noise and tumult. Had they understood the people and the game a little better, they might have created an aristocracy in an age that has lost the meaning of the word. When one reads of the Fianna, or of Cuchulain, or of some great hero, one remembers that the fine life is always a part played finely before fine spectators. There also one notices the hot cup and the cold cup of intoxication; and when the fine spectators have ended, surely the fine players grow weary, and aristocratic life is ended. When O'Connell covered with a dark glove the hand that had killed a man in the duelling field, he played his part; and when Alexander stayed his army marching to the conquest of the world that he might contemplate the beauty of a plane-tree, he played his part. When Osgar complained as he lay dying, of the keening of the women and the old fighting men, he too played his part; 'No man ever knew any heart in me,' he said, 'but a heart of twisted horn, and it covered with iron; but the howling of the dogs beside me,' he said, 'and the keening of the old fighting men and the crying of the women one after another, those are the things that are vexing me.'[18] If we would create a great community – and what other game is so worth the labour? – we must recreate the old foundations of life, not as they existed in that splendid misunderstanding of the eighteenth century, but as they must always exist when the finest minds and Ned the beggar and Seaghan the fool think about the same thing, although they may not think the same thought about it.

IX

When I asked the little boy who had shown me the pathway up the Hill of Allen if he knew stories of Fionn and Oisin, he said he did not, but that he had often heard his grandfather telling them to his mother in Irish. He did not know Irish, but he was learning it at school, and all the little boys he knew were learning it. In a little while he will know enough stories of Fionn and Oisin to tell them to his children some day. It is the owners of the land whose children might never have known what would give them so much happiness. But now they can read this book to their children, and it will make Slieve-na-man, Allen, and Ben Bulben, the great mountain that showed itself before me every day through all my childhood and was yet unpeopled, and half the country-sides of south and west, as populous with memories as are Dundealgan and Emain Macha and Muirthemne; and after a while somebody may even take them to some famous place and say, 'This land where your fathers lived proudly and finely should be dear and dear and again dear'; and perhaps when many names have grown musical to their ears, a more imaginative love will have taught them a better service.

X

I need say nothing about the translation and arrangement of this book except that it is worthy to be put beside *Cuchulain of Muirthemne*. Such books should not be commended by written words but by spoken words, were that possible, for the written words commending a book, wherein something is done supremely well, remain, to sound in the ears of a later generation, like the foolish sound of church bells from the tower of a church when every pew is full.

65

'WITCHES AND WIZARDS AND IRISH FOLK-LORE'

from Lady Gregory's *Visions and Beliefs in the West of Ireland* (1920)

I

Ireland was not separated from general European speculation when much of that was concerned with the supernatural. Dr Adam Clarke[1] tells in his unfinished autobiography how, when he was at school in Antrim towards the end of the eighteenth century, a schoolfellow told him of Cornelius Agrippa's[2] book on Magic and that it had to be chained or it would fly away of itself. Presently he heard of a farmer who had a copy and after that made friends with a wandering tinker who had another. Lady Gregory and I spoke of a friend's visions to an old countryman. He said 'he must belong to a society'; and the people often attribute magical powers to Orangemen and to Freemasons, and I have heard a shepherd at Doneraile speak of a magic wand with Tetragramaton Agla[3] written upon it. The visions and speculations of Ireland differ much from those of England and France, for in Ireland, as in Highland Scotland, we are never far from the old Celtic mythology; but there is more likeness than difference. Lady Gregory's story of the witch who in semblance of a hare, leads the hounds such a dance, is the best remembered of all witch stories. It is told, I should imagine, in every countryside where there is even a fading memory of witchcraft. One finds it in a sworn testimony given at the trial of Julian Cox, an old woman indicted for witchcraft at Taunton in Somersetshire in 1663 and quoted by Joseph Glanvill.[4] 'The first witness was a huntsman, who swore that he went out with a pack of hounds to hunt a hare, and not far from Julian Cox her house he at last started a hare: the dogs hunted her very close, and the third ring hunted her in view, till at last the huntsman perceiving the hare almost spent and making towards a great bush, he ran on the other side of the bush to take her up and preserve her from the dogs; but as soon as he laid hands on her, it proved to be Julian Cox, who had her head grovelling on the ground, and her globes (as he expressed it) upward. He knowing her, was so affrighted that his hair on his head stood on end; and yet spake to her, and ask'd her what brought her there; but she was so far out of breath that she could not make him any answer; his dogs also came up full cry to recover the game, and smelled at her and so left off hunting any further. And the huntsman with his dogs went home presently sadly affrighted.' Dr Henry More,[5] the Platonist, who considers the story in a letter to Glanvill, explains that Julian Cox was not turned into a hare, but that 'Ludicrous Dæmons exhibited to the sight of this huntsman and his dogs, the shape of a hare, one of them turning himself into such a form, another hurrying on the body of Julian near the same place,' making her invisible till the right moment had come. 'As I have heard of some painters that have drawn the sky in a huge landscape, so lively, that the birds have flown against it, thinking it free air, and so have fallen down. And if painters and jugglers, by the tricks of legerdemain can do such strange feats to the deceiving of the sight, it is no wonder that these aerie invisible spirits have far surpassed them in all such prestigious doings, as the air surpasses the earth for subtlety.' Glanvill has given his own explanation of such cases elsewhere. He thinks that the sidereal or airy body is the foundation of the marvel, and Albert de Rochas[6] has found a like foundation for the marvels of spiritism. 'The transformation of witches,' writes Glanvill, 'into the shapes of other animals ... is very conceivable; since then, 'tis easy enough to imagine, that the power of imagination may form those passive and pliable vehicles into those shapes,' and then goes on to account for the stories where an injury, say to the witch hare, is found afterwards upon the witch's body precisely as a French hypnotist would account for the stigmata of a saint. 'When they feel the hurts in their gross bodies, that they receive in their airy vehicles, they must be supposed to have been really present, at least in these latter; and 'tis no more difficult to apprehend how the hurts of those should be translated upon their other bodies, than how diseases should be inflicted by the imagination, or how the fancy of the mother should wound the fœtus, as several credible relations do attest.'

All magical or Platonic writers of the times speak much of the transformation or projection of the sidereal body of witch or wizard. Once the soul escapes from the natural body, though but for a moment, it passes into the body of air and can transform itself as it please or even dream itself into some shape it has not willed.

> Chameleon-like thus they their colour change,
> And size contract and then dilate again.[7]

One of their favourite stories is of some famous man, John Haydon[8] says Socrates, falling asleep among his friends, who presently see a mouse running from his mouth and towards a little stream. Somebody lays a sword across the stream that it may pass, and after a little while it returns across the sword and to the sleeper's mouth again. When he awakes he tells them that he has dreamed of himself crossing a wide river by a great iron bridge.

But the witch's wandering and disguised double was not the worst shape one might meet in the fields or roads about a witch's house.

She was not a true witch unless there was a compact (or so it seems) between her and an evil spirit who called himself the devil, though Bodin[9] believes that he was often, and Glanvill always, 'some human soul forsaken of God', for 'the devil is a body politic'. The ghost or devil promised revenge on her enemies and that she would never want, and she upon her side let the devil suck her blood nightly or at need.

When Elizabeth Style[10] made a confession of witchcraft before the Justice of Somerset in 1664, the Justice appointed three men, William Thick and William Read and Nicholas Lambert, to watch her, and Glanvill publishes an affidavit of the evidence of Nicholas Lambert. 'About three of the clock in the morning there came from her head a glistering bright fly, about an inch in length which pitched at first in the chimney and then vanished.' Then two smaller flies came and vanished. 'He, looking steadfastly then on Style, perceived her countenance to change, and to become very black and ghastly and the fire also at the same time changing its colour; whereupon the Examinant, Thick and Read, conceiving that her familiar was then about her, looked to her poll, and seeing her hair shake very strangely, took it up and then a fly like a great miller[11] flew out from the place and pitched on the table board and then vanished away. Upon this the Examinant and the other two persons, looking again in Style's poll, found it very red and like raw beef. The Examinant ask'd her what it was that went out of her poll, she said it was a butterfly, and asked them why they had not caught it. Lambert said, they could not. I think so too, answered she. A little while after, the informant and the others, looking again into her poll, found the place to be of its former colour. The Examinant asked again what the fly was, she confessed it was her familiar and that she felt it tickle in her poll, and that was the usual time for her familiar to come to her.' These sucking devils alike when at their meal, or when they went here and there to do her will or about their own business, had the shapes of pole-cat or cat or greyhound or of some moth or bird. At the trials of certain witches in Essex in 1645 reported in the English state trials a principal witness was one 'Matthew Hopkins, gent'. Bishop Hutchinson, writing in 1730,[12] describes him as he appeared to those who laughed at witchcraft and had brought the witch trials to an end. 'Hopkins went on searching and swimming poor creatures, till some gentlemen, out of indignation of the barbarity, took him, and tied his own thumbs and toes as he used to tie others, and when he was put into the water he himself swam as they did. That cleared the country of him and it was a great pity that they did not think of the experiment sooner.' Floating when thrown into the water was taken for a sign of witchcraft. Matthew Hopkins's testimony, however, is uncommonly like that of the countryman who told Lady Gregory that he had seen his dog and some shadow fighting. A certain Mrs Edwards of Manintree in Essex had her hogs killed by witchcraft, and 'going from the house of the said Mrs Edwards to his own house, about nine or ten of the clock that night, with his greyhound with him, he saw the greyhound suddenly give a jump, and run as she had been in full course after a hare; and that when this informant made haste to see what his greyhound so eagerly pursued, he espied a white thing, about the bigness of a kitlyn,[13] and the greyhound standing aloof from it; and that by and by the said white imp or kitlyn danced about the greyhound, and by all likelihood bit off a piece of the flesh of the shoulder of the said greyhound; for the greyhound came shrieking and crying to the informant, with a piece of flesh torn from her shoulder. And the informant further saith, that coming into his own yard that night, he espied a black thing proportioned like a cat, only it was thrice as big, sitting on a strawberry bed, and fixing the eyes on this informant, and when he went towards it, it leaped over the pale towards this informant, as he thought, but ran through the yard, with his greyhound after it, to a great gate, which was underset with a pair of tumble strings, and did throw the said gate wide open, and then vanished; and the said greyhound returned again to this informant, shaking and trembling exceedingly.' At the same trial Sir Thomas Bowes, Knight, affirmed 'that a very honest man of Manintree, whom he knew would not speak an untruth, affirmed unto him, that very early one morning, as he passed by the said Anne West's door' (this is the witch on trial) 'about four o'clock, it being a moonlight night, and perceiving her door to be open so early in the morning, looked into the house and presently there came three or four little things, in the shape of black rabbits, leaping and skipping about him, who, having a good stick in his hand, struck at them, thinking to kill them, but could not; but at last caught one of them in his hand, and holding it by the body of it, he beat the head of it against his stick, intending to beat out the brains of it; but when he could not kill it that way, he took the body of it in one hand and the head of it in another, and endeavoured to wring off the head; and as he wrung and stretched the neck of it, it came out between his hands like a lock of wool; yet he would not give over his intended purpose, but knowing of a spring not far off, he went to drown it; but still as he went he fell down and could not go, but down he fell again, so that he at last crept upon his hands and knees till he came at the water, and holding it fast in his hand, he put his hand down into the water up to the elbow, and held it under water a good space till he conceived it was drowned, and then letting go his hand, it sprung out of the water up into the air, and so vanished away.' However, the sucking imps were not always invulnerable for Glanvill tells how one John Monpesson, whose house was haunted by such a familiar, 'seeing some wood move that was in the chimney of a room, where he was, as if of itself, discharged a pistol into it after which they found several drops of blood on the hearth and in divers places of the stairs'. I remember the old Aran man who heard fighting in the air and found blood in a fish-box and scattered through the room, and I remember the measure of blood Odysseus poured out for the shades.[14]

The English witch trials are like the popular poetry of England, matter-of-fact and unimaginative. The witch desires to kill some one and when she takes the devil for her husband he as likely as not will seem dull and domestic. Rebecca West told Matthew Hopkins that the devil appeared to her as she was going to bed and told her he would marry her. He kissed her but was as cold as clay, and he promised to be 'her loving husband till death', although she had, as it seems, but one leg. But the Scotch trials are as wild and passionate as is the Scottish poetry, and we find ourselves in the presence of a mythology that differs little, if at all, from that of Ireland. There are orgies of lust and of hatred and there is a wild shamelessness that would be fine material for poets and romance writers if the world should come once more to half-believe the tale. They are divided into troops of thirteen, with the youngest witch for leader in every troop, and though they complain that the embraces of the devil are as cold as ice, the young witches prefer him to their husbands. He gives them money, but they must spend it quickly, for it will be but dry cow dung in two circles of the clock. They go often to Elfhame or Faeryland and the mountains open before them and as they go out and in they are terrified by the 'rowtling and skoylling' of the great 'elf bulls'. They sometimes confess to trooping in the shape of cats and to finding upon their terrestrial bodies when they awake in the morning the scratches they had made upon one another in the night's wandering, or should they have wandered in the images of hares the bites of dogs. Isobell Godie who was tried at Lochlay in 1662 confessed that 'We put besoms in our beds with our husbands till we return again to them . . . and then we would fly away where we would be, even as straws would fly upon a highway. We will fly like straws when we please; wild straws and corn straws will be horses to us, and we put them betwixt our feet and say horse and hillock in the devil's name. And when any see these straws in a whirlwind and do not sanctify themselves, we may shoot them dead at our pleasure.'[15] When they kill people, she goes on to say, the souls escape them 'but their bodies remain with us and will fly as horses to us all as small as straws'. It is plain that it is the 'airy body' they take possession of; those 'animal spirits' perhaps which Henry More thought to be the link between soul and body and the seat of all vital function. The trials were more unjust than those of England, where there was a continual criticism from sceptics; torture was used again and again to distort confessions, and innocent people certainly suffered; some who had but believed too much in their own dreams and some who had but cured the sick at some vision's prompting. Alison Pearson who was burnt in 1588 might have been Biddy Early or any other knowledgeable woman in Ireland today.[16] She was convicted 'for haunting and repairing with the Good Neighbours and queen of Elfhame, these divers years and bypast, as she had confessed in her depositions, declaring that she could not say readily how long she was with them; and that she had friends in that court who were of her own blood and who had great acquaintance of the queen of Elfhame. That when she went to bed she never knew where she would be carried before dawn.' When they worked cures they had the same doctrine of the penalty that one finds in Lady Gregory's stories.[17] One who made her confession before James I was convicted for 'taking the sick party's pains and sicknesses upon herself for a time and then translating them to a third person'.

II

There are more women than men mediums to-day; and there have been or seem to have been more witches than wizards. The wizards of the sixteenth and seventeenth centuries relied more upon their conjuring book than the witches whose visions and experiences seem but half voluntary, and when voluntary called up by some childish rhyme:

> Hare, hare, God send thee care;
> I am in a hare's likeness now,
> But I shall be a woman even now;
> Hare, hare, God send thee care.

More often than not the wizards were learned men, alchemists or mystics, and if they dealt with the devil at times, or some spirit they called by that name, they had amongst them ascetics and heretical saints. Our chemistry, our metallurgy, and our medicine are often but accidents that befell in their pursuit of the philosopher's stone, the elixir of life. They were bound together in secret societies and had, it may be, some forgotten practice for liberating the soul from the body and sending it to fetch and carry them divine knowledge. Cornelius Agrippa in a letter quoted by Beaumont[18] has hints of such a practice. Yet, like the witches, they worked many wonders by the power of the imagination, perhaps one should say by their power of calling up vivid pictures in the mind's eye. The Arabian philosophers have taught, writes Beaumont, 'that the soul by the power of the imagination can perform what it pleases; as penetrate the heavens, force the elements, demolish mountains, raise valleys to mountains, and do with all material forms as it pleases'.

> He shewed hym, er he wente to sopeer,
> Forestes, parkes ful of wilde deer;
> Ther saugh he hertes with hir hornes hye,
> The gretteste that evere were seyn with yë.
>
> . . .
>
> Tho saugh he knyghtes justing in a playn;
> And after this, he dide hym swich plaisaunce,
> That he hym shewed his lady on a daunce
> On which hymself he daunced, as hym thoughte.
> And whan this maister, that this magyk wroughte,

Saugh it was tyme, he clapte his handes two,
And, farewel! al our revel was ago.[19]

One has not as careful a record as one has of the works of witches, for but few English wizards came before the court, the only society for psychical research in those days. The translation, however, of Cornelius Agrippa's *De Occulta Philosophia* in the seventeenth century, with the addition of a spurious fourth book full of conjurations, seems to have filled England and Ireland with whole or half wizards. In 1703, the Reverend Arthur Bedford of Bristol who is quoted by Sibley[20] in his big book on astrology wrote to the Bishop of Gloucester telling how a certain Thomas Perks had been to consult him. Thomas Perks lived with his father, a gunsmith, and devoted his leisure to mathematics, astronomy, and the discovery of perpetual motion. One day he asked the clergyman if it was wrong to commune with spirits, and said that he himself held that 'there was an innocent society with them which a man might use, if he made no compacts with them, did no harm by their means, and were not curious in prying into hidden things, and he himself had discoursed with them and heard them sing to his great satisfaction'. He then told how it was his custom to go to a crossway with lantern and candle consecrated for the purpose, according to the directions in a book he had, and having also consecrated chalk for making a circle. The spirits appeared to him 'in the likeness of little maidens about a foot and a half high . . . they spoke with a very shrill voice like an ancient woman' and when he begged them to sing, 'they went to some distance behind a bush from whence he could hear a perfect concert of such exquisite music as he never before heard; and in the upper part he heard something very harsh and shrill like a reed but as it was managed did give a particular grace to the rest'. The Reverend Arthur Bedford refused an introduction to the spirits for himself and a friend and warned him very solemnly. Having some doubt of his sanity, he set him a difficult mathematical problem, but finding that he worked it easily, concluded him sane. A quarter of a year later, the young man came again, but showed by his face and his eyes that he was very ill and lamented that he had not followed the clergyman's advice for his conjurations would bring him to his death. He had decided to get a familiar and had read in his magical book what he should do. He was to make a book of virgin parchment, consecrate it, and bring it to the cross-road, and having called up his spirits, ask the first of them for its name and write that name on the first page of the book and then question another and write that name on the second page and so on till he had enough familiars. He had got the first name easily enough and it was in Hebrew, but after that they came in fearful shapes, lions and bears and the like, or hurled at him balls of fire. He had to stay there among those terrifying visions till the dawn broke and would not be the better of it till he died. I have read in some eighteenth-century book whose name I cannot recall of two men who made a magic circle and who invoked the spirits of the moon and saw them trampling about the circle as great bulls, or rolling about it as flocks of wool. One of Lady Gregory's story-tellers considered a flock of wool one of the worst shapes that a spirit could take.

There must have been many like experimenters in Ireland. An Irish alchemist called Butler[21] was supposed to have made successful transmutations in London early in the eighteenth century, and in the *Life of Dr Adam Clarke*, published in 1833, are several letters from a Dublin maker of stained glass describing a transmutation and a conjuration into a tumbler of water of large lizards. The alchemist was an unknown man who had called to see him and claimed to do all by the help of the devil 'who was the friend of all ingenious gentlemen'.

66

'COMPULSORY GAELIC: A DIALOGUE'

from the *Irish Statesman* (1924)

PERSONS: PETER, a Senator.
PAUL, a Deputy.
TIMOTHY, an elderly student.[1]

PETER

We will catch nothing, so I may as well listen to you. They have dynamited the fish, and several seasons will pass before there are trout enough to make a day's fishing. Let us put our rods against a tree and eat our lunch. I see Timothy coming along the river path, and I do not suppose he has had any better luck. While I am making the fire, you can explain that incredible doctrine of yours.

PAUL

Which doctrine, for I have a number which you consider incredible.

PETER

I mean what you said in the train, when you told me that you were about to vote scholarships or something of that kind for Gaelic speakers.

PAUL

Our general culture cannot be better than that of the English-speaking world as a whole, and is more likely to be worse. We are on the banks of a river that flows through an industrial town and bathe in its waters. But visit certain small nations – one of the Scandinavian nations, let us say – and you will notice at once that not only education, but general well-being are better distributed there, and when you ask how they manage it, somebody says 'our people are so few that we can reach everybody'. Everybody you meet speaks several languages well enough for commercial purposes and travel, but only one well enough for intimacy. Kings, nobles, farmers, professional men, socialists and reactionaries, novelists and poets grow up with a common life, from which nothing can separate them. Their rich or able men seldom drift away permanently, for if they find themselves in London or New York or Paris, they feel but strangers there. They may perhaps be less rich than men of equal ability, who belong to some English-speaking nation, and so manipulate greater resources, material or living, but their ability or their riches create in their own country a habit of energy and a tradition of well-being. No bond constrains, because no man compels; they but accept a limitation like that imposed upon a sculptor by the stone in which he works. Would not Ireland have gained if Mr Bernard Shaw and Oscar Wilde, let us say, and the various Ryans and O'Briens who have enriched America, had grown up with such a limitation, and thought they were strangers everywhere but in Ireland. Then, too, I could discover with a little research the names of actors and singers who might at this moment be performing in some Dublin State Theatre or State Opera House, but for the damnable convenience of the English tongue.

PETER

If we have no State Theatre or State Opera House, we have the Abbey Theatre, and have all commended *Juno and the Paycock*.[2]

PAUL

We may keep the author of the play, but how long shall we keep the players that give it so great a part of its life? A great Empire buys every talent that it can use and for the most part spoils what it buys. If we keep a good comedian, it is generally because his art, being an art of dialect, interests few but ourselves. A play called *Peg o' my Heart* – a stage mechanism without literary value – because it contained one dialect part, robbed the Abbey Theatre of four actresses, and almost brought it to an end.[3] If they had been bound to Ireland by a separate language, they would not have gone, they would not have desired to go.

PETER

You mean that if enforced bonds make hatred those that are obeyed though not enforced, make love.

PAUL

Norway could never have created the greatest dramatic school of modern times if it had spoken a world-wide language.

PETER

But surely a nation like Ireland or Norway should be able to pay an actress enough to keep her at home in comfort.

PAUL

World-wide commercial interests exploit whatever form of expression appeals to the largest possible audience; that is to say, some inferior form; and will always purchase executive talent. The chief actress of Norway, some few years ago, had to threaten to stop acting altogether to get her salary raised from £200 a year. If she had spoken English she could have earned more than that in a week, at some English or American music-hall.

PETER

Your point seems to be that no nation can prosper unless it uses for itself the greater portion of its talent.

PAUL

I am not thinking only of talent. The greater part of its creative life – that of the woman of fashion, not less than that of the founder of a business or of a school of thought, should be the jet of a fountain that falls into the basin where it rose.

PETER

That may or may not be true, but what has it to do with practical affairs? I have heard a man discuss for an hour what would have happened if the library of Alexandria had never been burnt, and another bored me through a windy day on an outside car by describing what Europe might have been if Constantinople had never fallen. The Irish language can never again be the language of the whole people.

PAUL

Why not?

PETER

Because the Irish people will not consent that it should, having set their hearts on Glasgow and New York.

PAUL

We shall have to go slowly, making our converts man by man, and yet Ireland should become bilingual in three generations.

PETER

Those three generations may be the most important since the foundation of Christianity. Architecture, and all the arts associated with architecture are being re-born as though to express a new perception of the inter-dependence of man. Drama and poetry are once more casting out photography, becoming psychological and creative. The experimental verification of a mathematical research – research made possible by the Irishman Rowan Hamilton[4] – has changed the universe into a mathematical formula, and a formula so astounding that it can but alter every thought in our heads. Psychical research interpreted by that formula in thirty years will once more set man's soul above time and change, and make it necessary to reconsider every secular activity. Nations are made neither by language nor by frontier, but by a decision taken in some crisis of intellectual excitement like that which Italy took at the Renaissance, Germany at the Reformation, moments of fusion followed by centuries of cooling and hardening. The whole world draws to such a crisis, and you would cut Ireland off from Europe and plunge it into a controversy that will be incredibly bitter, because it can be fought without ideas and without education.

PAUL

I see no reason why the Gaelic movement should cut Ireland off from Europe, and I have never spoken a bitter word about an opponent.

PETER

I know a man who, after certain years of dependence in a great house, has set up as a picture-framer in a country town. He employs a young man, poverty-stricken like himself at the same age, and though this young man is as well educated as himself, compels him to take his meals in the kitchen with the servants. The great house had not driven him to the kitchen, but his offended dignity has demanded an offering. Spinoza thought that nations were like individuals, and that it was no use pulling down a tyrant, for a tyrant is what he is, because of something in the nation. 'Look at the people of England,' he said, or some such words. 'They have pulled down Charles, but have had to push up Cromwell in his place.'[5] Can you read an Irish propagandist newspaper, all those threatenings and compellings, and not see that a servitude, far longer than any England has known, has bred into Irish bones a stronger sub-conscious desire than England ever knew to enslave and to be enslaved? There is no public emotion in the country but resentment, and no man thinks that he serves his cause who does not employ that emotion. If we praise, the praise is unreal, and but given to some reflection of ourselves, but our vituperation is animated and even joyous. We think it effeminate to trust in eloquence and patience, and prefer to make men servile, rather than permit their opinions to differ from our own, and if there is a man notable for intellect and sincerity, we fit some base motive to his every act that he may not prevail against us. We had eloquence some hundred years ago, and had, it seems, when we spoke in Gaelic, popular poetry, but now we have neither – possessing indeed every quality of the negro but his music. We were a proud people once, but have grown so humble, that we have no method of speech or propaganda that the knave cannot use and the dunce understand.

PAUL

There are a great many people in this country who neither threaten nor impute base motives, and besides what you say, in so far as it is true, describes half the democracy of Europe.

PETER

Yes, all those who have pulled down a tyrant and would put another in his place.

PAUL

All this passion means, I suppose, that you object to our teaching Gaelic to those who do not want it.

PETER

I object to every action which reminds me of a mediaeval humorist compelling a Jew to eat bacon. Especially as in this case Jew compels Jew.

PAUL

Yet, if a Government can enforce Latin it has a right to enforce Gaelic.

PETER

I do not deny the right, but I deny that it should be employed in this country except within the narrowest limits.

PAUL

Ruskin once contended that reading and writing should be optional, because what a fool reads does himself harm, and what a fool writes does others harm.[6] That may be a convincing argument, but as our Government accepts the modern theory, I do not see why Gaelic should not be compulsory also. I have had nothing to do with that, however. My work, if I have a work, is to keep it from stupefying. I want the Government to accept the recommendation of the Senate and spend £5,000 a year on Gaelic scholarship; to train a small number of highly-efficient teachers of the living tongue, who should have general European culture; to found scholarships for the best pupils of those teachers; to endow a theatre with a Gaelic and English company, and to make Gaelic an instrument of European culture. There is already a Gaelic company performing Tchekov,[7] and there is much European literature, especially that of countries like Spain and Italy which have a long-settled peasantry that would go better into Gaelic than into English. After all, Sancho Panza is very nearly a Munster farmer. I want the Government to find money for translation by ceasing to print Acts in Gaelic that everybody reads in English.

PETER

As soon as a play or book is translated, which goes deep into human life, it will be denounced for immorality or irreligion. Certain of our powerful men advocate Gaelic that they may keep out the European mind. They know that if they do not build a wall, this country will plunge, as Europe is plunging, into philosophic speculation. They hope to put into every place of authority a Gaelic speaker, and, if possible, a native speaker, who has learned all he knows at his mother's knee.

PAUL

I have always opposed the making of Irish obligatory for any post not connected with the language. I want everywhere the best man with the knowledge appropriate to his post.

PETER

Once you make Gaelic a political question you are helpless. They have made it obligatory, and will continue to do so.

PAUL

That will last a few years. We are all new to public life, but the choice between wisdom and fanaticism will be good for our intelligence.

PETER

We are agreed that the future of Ireland depends upon the choice.

PAUL

If Gaelic cannot become as I would make it, a disturbing intellectual force, it means . . .

PETER

A little potato-digging Republic.

PAUL

No, but Ireland a dull school-book, consequent apathy and final absorption in the British Empire.

PETER

You are ready to chance all that?

PAUL

I believe in the intellectual force created by years of conflict as by a flint and steel.

[*They are joined by Timothy*]

TIMOTHY

I see that you have the kettle boiling.

PAUL

Had you any luck?

TIMOTHY

Not a rise, but I saw some good fish floating with their bellies up. I am glad to sit down, for I am old enough to grow tired standing with a useless rod in my hand. What were you disputing about? Peter, you looked a moment ago as if you would fling the kettle into Paul's face, and Paul's face is red.

PETER

At present we speak English and Gaelic is compulsory in the schools, but Paul wants us to speak Gaelic and make English compulsory in the schools, and I am not sufficiently attracted by the change to plunge the country into a permanent condition of bad manners.

TIMOTHY

Whatever imagination we have in Ireland to-day, we owe to Gaelic literature or to the effect of Gaelic speech upon the English language. Think of the dialect plays of Synge and of Lady Gregory – of Lady Gregory's translations of the stories of Fionn and of Cuchulain, which have given new classics to the English tongue. I can read a little Gaelic, but I often think I would give some years of life if I could read in the original one of those old poems translated by Kuno Meyer,[8] and the lamentations of Deirdre and read well enough to feel the quality of their style. We can only feel the full beauty of a poem in another language when we can understand without translating as we read, when we can become for the time being a Frenchman, a German, or a Gael, and I sometimes wonder if that is really possible. Those lamentations of Deirdre have a poignancy unlike anything in any other European tongue. Surely, there must be something in the vocabulary, in the cadence, corresponding to it, and when I think that these poems were written in this country and by and about its people, it seems to me unbearable that I should be shut out, or partly shut out, from it all.

PAUL

Then you want to make Gaelic the language of the country?

TIMOTHY

But, Paul, I am so uncertain about everything, and there is so much to be said upon every side. English literature is, perhaps, the greatest in the world, and I am not in politics. If I were in politics, I would have to be certain, whereas I am an elderly student. I cannot even call myself a scholar, for I know nothing properly. Politics are a roulette wheel with various colours, and if a man is to take a part in the game, he must choose. If he prefers some colour that is not there, or if he be quite undecided, he must put that away and bang down his money firmly. So Peter must oppose the Gaelic movement and you must defend it.

PAUL

If Ireland gives up Gaelic, it will soon be a suburb of New York.

PETER

Like somebody in Shakespeare, I think nobly of the soul and refuse to admit that the soul of man or nation is as dependent upon circumstance as all that.[9]

TIMOTHY

I have held both opinions in the same hour, perhaps in the same minute. It sometimes seems to me, too, that there must be a kind of politics where one need not be certain. After all, imitation is automatic, but creation moves in a continual uncertainty. If we were certain of the future, who would trouble to create it?

PAUL

I cannot see any means whereby a Parliament can pass uncertainty into law.

TIMOTHY

I have no practical experience, but perhaps it might be possible to choose a schoolmaster as we choose a painter or a sculptor. 'There is so-and-so,' we would say, 'who thinks that Ireland should be Gaelic-speaking, and because he is a very able, cultivated and learned man we will give him a school and let him teach. We ourselves think that he may be wrong, but, after all, what does anybody know about it?' I think the knowledge of the Greek language must have come to Renaissance Italy in much that way. No two men, perhaps, would have agreed about its future. To some it meant a better knowledge of the New Testament, and to others – some at the Platonic Academy of Florence, for instance – a re-established worship of the Homeric gods. I am not sure that I like the idea of a State with a definite purpose, and there are moments, unpractical moments, perhaps, when I think that the State should leave the mind free to create. I think Aristotle defined the soul as that which moves itself, and how can it move itself if everything is arranged beforehand?[10]

PETER

Do you mean to say that you would appoint a schoolmaster, not only to teach Irish, but that it must be the living language of Ireland, although you thought what he attempted neither desirable nor possible?

TIMOTHY

Perhaps neither desirable nor possible, but remember I would not appoint him if I did not like him, and because I have always liked Peter, if he wanted to teach that English was the only proper language for the Irish people, I would appoint him also. I generally dislike the people of Ulster, and want to keep them out – when I was in Belfast a few years ago they had only one bookshop – but I am told the Government wants to bring them in, so it might be well to give a school to some likeable Orangeman and let him teach Orangeism there. In fact, I am almost certain that the Education Office that would please me best, would choose schoolmasters much as a good hostess chooses her guests. It should never invite anybody to teach who is a bore or in any way disagreeable.

PETER

Timothy, you have not shed any light upon the subject.

PAUL

None whatever.

67
INTRODUCTION TO *THE MIDNIGHT COURT*
(1926)

Months ago Mr Ussher asked me to introduce his translation of *The Midnight Court*. I had seen a few pages in an Irish magazine; praised its vitality; my words had been repeated; and because I could discover no reason for refusal that did not make me a little ashamed, I consented. Yet I could wish that a Gaelic scholar had been found, or failing that some man of known sobriety of manner and of mind – Professor Trench[1] of Trinity College let us say – to introduce to the Irish reading public this vital, extravagant, immoral, preposterous poem.

Brian Mac Giolla Meidhre – or to put it in English, Brian Merriman – wrote in Gaelic, one final and three internal rhymes in every line, pouring all his mediaeval abundance into that narrow neck. He was born early in the eighteenth century, somewhere in Clare, even now the most turbulent of counties, and the countrymen of Clare and of many parts of Munster have repeated his poem down to our own day. Yet this poem which is so characteristically Gaelic and mediaeval is founded upon *Cadenus and Vanessa*,[2] read perhaps in some country gentleman's library. The shepherds and nymphs of Jonathan Swift plead by counsel before Venus:

> Accusing the false creature man.
> The brief with weighty crimes was charged
> On which the pleader much enlarged,
> That Cupid now has lost his art,
> Or blunt the point of every dart.

Men have made marriage mercenary and love an intrigue; but

the shepherds' counsel answers that the fault lies with women who have changed love for 'gross desire' and care but for 'fops and fools and rakes'. Venus finds the matter so weighty that she calls the Muses and the Graces to her assistance and consults her books of law – Ovid, Virgil, Tibullus, Cowley, Waller[3] – continuously adjourns the court for sixteen years, and then after the failure of an experiment gives the case in favour of the women. The experiment is the creation of Vanessa, who instead of becoming all men's idol and reformer, all women's example, repels both by her learning and falls in love with her tutor Swift.

The Gaelic poet changed a dead to a living mythology, and called men and women to plead before Eevell of Craglee, the chief of Munster Spirits, and gave her court reality by seeing it as a vision upon a midsummer day under a Munster tree. No countryman of that time doubted, nor in all probability did the poet doubt, the existence of Eevell, a famous figure to every storyteller.[4] The mediaeval convention of a dream or vision has served the turn of innumerable licentious rhymers in Gaelic and other languages, of Irish Jacobites who have substituted some personification of Ireland, some Dark Rosaleen,[5] for a mortal mistress, of learned poets who call before our eyes an elaborate allegory of courtly love. I think of Chaucer's *Romaunt of the Rose*, his *Book of the Duchess*, and of two later poems that used to be called his, *Chaucer's Dream* and *The Complaint of the Black Knight*. But in all these the vision comes in May.[6]

> That it was May, me thoughte tho,
> It is fyve yere or more ago;
> That it was May, thus dreamed me
> In tyme of love and jolitie
> That all things ginneth waxen gay.[7]

One wonders if there is some Gaelic precedent for changing the spring festival for that of summer, the May-day singing of the birds to the silence of summer fields. Had Mac Giolla Meidhre before his mind the fires of St John's Night, for all through Munster men and women leaped the fires that they might be fruitful, and after scattered the ashes that the fields might be fruitful also.[8] Certainly it is not possible to read his verses without being shocked and horrified as city onlookers were perhaps shocked and horrified at the free speech and buffoonery of some traditional country festival.

He wrote at a moment of national discouragement, the penal laws[9] were still in force though weakening, the old order was a vivid memory but with the failure of the last Jacobite rising hope of its return had vanished, and no new political dream had come. The state of Ireland is described: 'Her land purloined, her law decayed . . . pastures with weeds o'ergrown, her ground untilled . . . hirelings holding the upper hand,' and worst of all – and this the fairy court has been summoned to investigate – 'the lads and lasses have left off breeding'. Are the men or the women to blame? A woman speaks first, and it is Swift's argument but uttered with voluble country extravagance, and as she speaks one calls up a Munster hearth, farmers sitting round at the day's end, some old farmer famous through all the countryside for this long recitation, speaking or singing with dramatic gesture. If a man marries, the girl declares, he does not choose a young girl but some rich scold 'with a hairless crown and a snotty nose'. Then she describes her own beauty and asks if she is not more fit for marriage? She has gone everywhere 'bedizened from top to toe', but because she lacks money nobody will look at her and she is single still.

> After all I have spent upon readers of palms
> And tellers of tea-leaves and sellers of charms.

Then an old man replies, and heaps upon her and upon her poverty-stricken father and family all manner of abuse: he is the champion of the men, and he will show where the blame lies. He tells of his own marriage. He was a man of substance but has been ruined by his wife who gave herself up to every sort of dissipation – Swift's argument again. A child was born, but when he asked to see the child the women tried to cover it up, and when he did see it, it was too fine, too handsome and vigorous to be a child of his. And now Swift is forgotten and dramatic propriety, the poet speaks through the old man's mouth and asks Eevell of

Craglee to abolish marriage that such children may be born in plenty.

> For why call a Priest in to bind and to bless
> Since Mary the Mother of God did conceive
> Without calling the Clergy or begging their leave,
> The love-gotten children are famed as the flower
> Of man's procreation and nature's power,
> For love is a lustier sire than law,
> And has made them sound without fault or flaw
> And better and braver in heart and head
> Than the puny breed of the marriage bed.

The bastard's speech in *Lear* is floating through his mind mixed up doubtless with old stories of Diarmuid's and Cuchulain's loves, and old dialogues where Oisin railed at Patrick;[10] but there is something more, an air of personal conviction that is of his age, something that makes his words – spoken to that audience – more than the last song of Irish paganism. One remembers that Burns is about to write his beautiful defiant 'Welcome to his love-begotten daughter' and that Blake who is defiant in thought alone meditates perhaps his *Marriage of Heaven and Hell*.[11] The girl replies to the old man that if he were not so old and crazed she would break his bones, and that if his wife is unfaithful what better could he expect seeing that she was starved into marrying him. However, she has her own solution. Let all the handsome young priests be compelled to marry. Then Eevell of Craglee gives her judgment, the Priests are left to the Pope who will order them into marriage one of these days, but let all other young men marry or be stripped and beaten by her spirits, and let all old bachelors be tortured by the spinsters. The poem ends by the girl falling upon the poet and beating him because he is unmarried. He is ugly and humped, she says, but might look as well as another in the dark.

Standish Hayes O'Grady[12] has described the *Midnight Court* as the best poem written in Gaelic, and as I read Mr Ussher's translation I have felt, without sharing what seems to me an extravagant opinion, that Giolla Meidhre, had political circumstances been different, might have founded a modern Gaelic literature. Mac

Conmara, or Macnamara, though his poem is of historical importance, does not interest me so much. He knew Irish and Latin only, knew nothing of his own age, saw vividly but could not reflect upon what he saw, and so remained an amusing provincial figure.

68

'THE GREAT BLASKET'

from the *Spectator* (1933)

Aran was John Synge's first choice. There he thought himself happy for the first time, 'having escaped the squalor of the poor and the nullity of the rich'.[1] There he and Lady Gregory saw one another for the first time, looked at one another with unfriendly eyes without speaking, not knowing that they were in search of the same thing.[2] Then others came and he fled to the Great Blasket. He told me upon his return that he found an old crippled pensioner visiting there, that they had come away together, stayed in the same little hotel in Ventry or Dingle. One morning the pensioner was not to be found. Synge searched for him everywhere, trying to find out if he had gone back to the Island, jealous as if the Island had been a woman. A few years ago the Irish Government, lacking texts for students of modern Irish, asked Mr Robin Flower to persuade one of its oldest inhabitants to write his life.[3] After much toil he got the main facts on to a sheet of notepaper and thought his task at an end. Then Mr Flower read him some chapters of Gorki's *Reminiscences*.[4] Now all was well, for to write like that was to write as he talked, and he was one of the best talkers upon the Island where there is no written literature. Then came a long delay; scholars had to pronounce upon the language, moralists upon the events; but when the book was published the few Gaelic speakers of my acquaintance passionately denied or affirmed that it was a masterpiece. Then a Blasket Islander settled in Dublin began to read out and circulate in manuscript poems that pleased a Gaelic scholar whose judgement I value, but were too Rabelaisian to please the eye of Government. Then Mr Maurice O'Sullivan, a young Civic Guard, who had lived upon the Island until he reached manhood, wrote his life, called it *Twenty Years A-Growing*, and Chatto and Windus have published a translation.

All this writing comes from the sheep runs and diminishing fisheries of an Island seven or eight miles long and a mile broad, from its hundred and fifty inhabitants who preserve in their little white cottages, roofed with tarred felt, an ancient culture of the song and the spoken word, who consult neither newspaper nor book, but carry all their knowledge in their minds. A few more years and a tradition where Seventeenth Century poets, Mediaeval storytellers, Fathers of the Church, even Neoplatonic philosophers have left their traces in whole poems of fragmentary thoughts and isolated images will have vanished. 'The young people are no use,' said an old man to Synge. 'I am not as good a man as my father was and my son is growing up worse than I am.'

Mr Maurice O'Sullivan, by a series of episodes, his first days at school, his first day puffin hunting, a regatta at Ventry, a wake, a shipwreck, a night upon a deserted neighbouring Island, calls up a vision of the sea, dark or bright, creates by the simplest means a sense of mystery, makes us for the moment part of a life that has not changed for thousands of years. And he himself seems unchanging like the life, the same when a little boy playing truant as when a grown man travelling by rail for the first time. It is not a defect that there is no subjectivity, no development; that like Helen during the ten years' siege he is untouched by time. Upon this limitation depend the clarity and the gaiety of his work. Fate has separated his people from all that could not sustain their happiness and their energy, from all that might confuse the soul, given them the protection that monks and nuns find in their traditional rule, aristocrats in their disdain.

Much modern Irish literature is violent, harsh, almost brutal, in its insistence upon the bare facts of life. Again and again I have defended plays or novels unlike anything I have myself attempted, or anything in the work of others that has given me great pleasure, because I have known that they were medicinal to a people struggling against secondhand thought and insincere emotion. Mr O'Sullivan's book is not a great book, the events are too unrelated, but it is perfect of its kind, it has elegance; Mr E. M. Forster compares it with a sea-bird's egg; and I am grateful.[5] He has found admirable translators – Mrs Llewellyn Davies and Professor George Thompson, who teaches Greek through the vehicle of Gaelic in Galway University. They have translated his Gaelic into a dialect that has taken much of its syntax from Gaelic. Dr Douglas Hyde used it in the prose of his *Love Songs of Connacht*; he was the first. Then Lady Gregory, in her translation of old Irish epics; then Synge and she in their plays. In late years it has superseded in the works of our dramatists and novelists the conventional speech nineteenth-century writers put into the mouth of Irish peasants. To Lady Gregory and to Synge it was more than speech, for it implied an attitude towards letters, sometimes even towards life, an attitude Lady Gregory was accustomed to define by a quotation from Aristotle: 'To think like a wise man but to express oneself like the common people.'[6]

NOTES

1 *Introduction to* Fairy and Folk Tales of the Irish Peasantry

In July 1887 Yeats wrote to his friend John O'Leary (1830–1907) to say that he had been asked to contribute an Irish volume to the Camelot Series of reprints edited by Ernest Rhys, who was to become a valuable friend. At first he thought he would edit Thomas Crofton Croker's *Fairy Legends and Traditions of the South of Ireland* (1825 and 1828); instead the volume became an anthology of fairy and folktales that included twelve items from Croker. He worked on the anthology from July 1887 to September 1888. He made use of material from authors and folklorists such as Croker, William Carleton, Samuel Lover, Patrick Kennedy, Nicholas O'Kearney, Letitia McClintock, Douglas Hyde, Mr and Mrs Samuel Carter Hall; he drew from anonymous contributors on fairy and folklore in the *Dublin University Magazine*; and used county histories, such as William Shaw Mason's *A Statistical Account of the Parochial Survey of Ireland, Drawn Up from the Communications of the Clergy* (1814–19). He included extracts from the *Topographia Hibernica* of Giraldus Cambrensis; and he anthologized poetry by William Allingham, Samuel Ferguson, J. J. Callanan, and James Clarence Mangan.

As an anthologist Yeats selected material from Irish fairy belief that, in his view, had its origins in ancient Druidic religion. He avoided tales that depicted the Irish peasant as ridiculous or gullible and instead included work that showed him, or her, to be imaginative, passionate and visionary.

1. Richard Corbet (or Corbett) (1582–1635), Bishop of Oxford, then Norwich; author of *Certain Elegant Poems* (1647), which includes 'A Proper New Ballad, Entitled "The Fairies' Farewell"', from which come the lines quoted by Yeats.
2. Title of an 1825 volume of essays by William Hazlitt (1778–1830).

3. Giraldus Cambrensis (1146?–1220?), Gerald of Wales, a scholar and chronicler from Pembrokeshire. In 1184 he accompanied Prince John to Ireland. His *Topographia Hibernica* is a description of Ireland, and the *Expugnatio Hibernica* an account of the Norman conquest.
4. Probably Inishturk, an island off the south coast of Co. Mayo.
5. A word of Breton origin that has been used to describe megalithic chamber tombs, or dolmens, prehistoric burial structures most often made from large stones. It is no longer favoured because in Brittany the word designates not a tomb but a stone circle. There are more than twelve hundred such tombs in Ireland, often known in folk tradition as the beds of Diarmuid and Gráinne, after the two lovers, who are said to have slept in them on their elopement. See glossary entry **Dermod**.
6. Hallowe'en, the night of 31 October, before All Saints' Day. In Irish tradition Samhain, the beginning of the winter half of the year, fell on 1 November; and on the eve of Samhain the natural and supernatural worlds interacted.
7. See headnote above.
8. The Royal Dublin Society was founded in 1731 to encourage art, science, industry and agriculture. Yeats later wrote a play on the Deirdre theme (1907).
9. 'John-O-Daly' would appear to have been Carroll O'Daly. Lissadell is the home of the Gore-Booth sisters, and Yeats included an elegy on them, 'In Memory of Eva Gore-Booth and Con Markiewicz', in *The Winding Stair* (1933). 'Eibhlín a Rúin' is a famous traditional song, said to have been composed by Cearbhall Ó Dálaigh (*fl.* 1597–1630) of Co. Wexford (not Sligo) for Elinor, daughter of Sir Murrough Cavanagh. See Pádraig de Brún, Breandán Ó Buachalla and Tomás Ó Concheanainn (eds.), *Nua Dhuanaire I* (1975), p. 126. G. F. Handel (1685–1759) visited Dublin, where his *Messiah* was first performed (1741). 'O'Donahue of Kerry', probably a version of 'Do Chuala Scéal do Chéas Gach Ló Mé' ('I Heard a Tale that Distracted Me Daily') by Seafraidh Ó Donnchadha (Geoffrey O'Donoghue), composed some time in the seventeenth century; its theme is Ireland's subjection to Britain.
10. Source untraced.
11. B— is Ballisodare, Co. Sligo.
12. The Irish for a fairy hill or fort is *sí*; but the word can also be used as an adjective to mean 'gentle', 'bewitched', 'peaceful' or 'enchanting'.

13. The fairies; often referred to thus or as 'the good people', in order to fend off their ill will.
14. Yeats now tells a story of Columcille and his mother and gives a brisk sketch of his informant, Paddy Flynn, both of which he used in *CT, 1893* in a piece called 'A Teller of Tales'. It is omitted here and given in the later version (see item 23), preferred in this edition because it becomes a satisfying piece in itself in *CT, 1893*.
15. See 'Belief and Unbelief' from *CT, 1893*, included in this volume (item 24), for another reference to this man and a different account of him.
16. Thomas Crofton Croker (1798–1854), Irish folklorist. Born in Cork, he had little formal education. Having worked in his native city as an apprentice accountant, he found employment in the Admiralty in London. From around the age of fourteen he collected folk material and traditions of various kinds in the south of Ireland; and when he moved to London he returned frequently to continue his fieldwork. Yeats drew upon the following collections by Croker when compiling his anthologies of Irish folk material: *Researches in the South of Ireland, Illustrative of the Scenery, Architectural Remains, and the Manners and Superstitions of the Peasantry* (1824); and *Fairy Legends and Traditions of the South of Ireland* (1825), the first collection of oral legends published in either Britain or Ireland.
17. Samuel Lover (1797–1868), writer and painter. Born in Dublin, he began as a painter of marine themes. Yeats drew upon his anthology *Legends and Stories of Ireland* (1831).
18. Writers such as the cultural politician Thomas Davis (1814–45), novelist William Carleton (1794–1869), the polemicist John Mitchel (1815–75) and the poet James Clarence Mangan (1803–49). All were informed by the spirit of the Young Ireland movement, which sought to combine idealistic nationalism, an awareness of Ireland's distinctive cultural traditions, and a plan of political and economic reform. Young Ireland's aim was the repeal of the Act of Union; in 1848 there was an ineffective insurrection. For Carleton, see note 19 below; for Mangan, see item 18, note 3.
19. William Carleton, writer of fiction. Born in Prillisk, Co. Tyrone, he attended a local hedge school. He intended to become a Catholic priest, but instead became a schoolmaster for a time before walking to Dublin in search of success as a writer. He converted to Protestantism and wrote many novels and sketches based on his experiences of country life in Ireland. Among them are: *Traits and Stories of the*

Irish Peasantry (1830), *Fardorougha the Miser* (1839) and *The Black Prophet* (1847). Yeats anthologized his tales and sketches in *FFTIP* and *Representative Irish Tales* (1891); he also produced an edition of his stories for the Camelot Series (1889).

20. Patrick Kennedy (1801–73). Born in Co. Wexford, he worked as a teacher and later as a bookseller. Author of *Legendary Fictions of the Irish Celts* (1866).
21. Lady Jane Francesca Wilde (1826–96), a Young Irelander who wrote as 'Speranza' in the *Nation*, the paper of the Young Ireland movement. Born in Dublin, she became a nationalist when she saw the funeral of Thomas Davis. She married Sir William Wilde in 1851, who was a surgeon and an antiquarian. She published *Ancient Legends of Ireland* (1887) and *Ancient Cures* (1890). See item 10.
22. Folklorist and author from Co. Donegal. She contributed pieces on her native county to the *Dublin University Magazine* and published an anti-Land League novel, *The Boycotted Household* (1880).
23. Douglas Hyde (1860–1949), folklorist, Gaelic scholar and first President of Ireland (1937–45). Grew up in Frenchpark, Co. Roscommon, where his father was the Church of Ireland rector. From his early teens he developed his knowledge of Irish. He helped found the Gaelic League in 1893 and was its first president. He won the battle to make Irish a compulsory matriculation subject in the new National University of Ireland; and he was appointed Professor of Modern Irish at UCD in 1909. Among his publications are: *Beside the Fire* (1891); *Love Songs of Connacht* (1893); *A Literary History of Ireland* (1899); *Songs Ascribed to Raftery* (1903); *Religious Songs of Connacht* (1905–6).
24. Edward Walsh (1805–50), poet and nationalist, born in Derry, he became a hedge-school master. He wrote for the *Nation* and published *Reliques of Irish Jacobite Poetry* (1844) and *Irish Popular Songs* (1847). J. J. Callanan (1795–1829), poet and collector of folklore. Born in Cork, he studied for the priesthood at Maynooth. He left and after a period at Trinity College, Dublin, he returned to Cork, from where he made trips into west Cork collecting poetry and legend. *The Poems of J. J. Callanan* (1861) was edited by M. F. McCarthy.
25. The name given to the popular literature that was handed around at fairs and other meeting places by itinerant ballad-men or chapmen. Often illustrated by woodblock engravings, chapbooks contained tales, satiric verse, moralistic sketches, and other such material.
26. London.

27. The translation of the introductory conversation in Plato's *Phaedrus* is by Benjamin Jowett, who published a translation of the dialogues of Plato in 1871.

2 *'The Irish Fairies'*

From July 1887 to September 1888, in preparation for *FFTIP*, Yeats worked hard to familiarize himself with all the writings, whether imaginative, scholarly or scientific, on fairy tradition and folklore in Ireland. The results of this painstaking research can be seen both in the general introduction (item 1 in the present collection) and also in the prefaces he wrote for the different sections of his book, here gathered together. These brief prefaces show that he is capable of integrating the various conjectures on the origins of the fairies, which he had distilled from his sources, and of classifying them under different headings within two broad categories: trooping or sociable fairies, and solitary fairies. This analytical approach indicates that Yeats was attempting to clarify, both for himself and for his readers, the bewildering variety of often contradictory material he had carefully worked through. It was the approach he was to continue to adopt to all supernatural, mythological or occult learning. Mary Helen Thuente observes: 'Yeats's categories and his carefully prepared introductions indicate a much more serious, intellectual approach than in any previous Irish folklorist' (*WBYIF*, p. 84).

1. Written in the ninth century, *The Book of Armagh* contains Latin lives of St Patrick, his confessions and some material in Irish. In one of these lives St Patrick's biographer speaks of the fairies as: 'side aut deorum terrenorum' ('*sí*, or gods who dwell in the earth').
2. See glossary.
3. May Eve: the eve of Bealtaine, 1 May. Midsummer Eve: 23 June, also St John's Eve. November Eve: the eve of Samhain, 1 November. For Plain-a-Bawn, see glossary.
4. A fetch is a ghost or spirit. For pooka, see glossary.
5. 'The Pretty Girl Milking the Cow' ('Cailín Deas Crúite na mBó'), well-known Irish folksong. For rath, see glossary.
6. Toirdhealach Ó Cearbhalláin (Turlogh O'Carolan) (1670–1738), harper and composer. Born in Co. Meath, he was blind from youth. He found patrons among the surviving Gaelic nobility. Edward Bunting collected many of his airs at the end of the eighteenth century and in the first decades of the nineteenth.
7. Blake, in conversation, claimed to have had a vision in which he 'saw

a procession of creatures of the size . . . of grasshoppers, bearing a body laid out on a rose leaf'. J. W. Foster Damon, *William Blake: His Philosophy and Writings* (1924), p. 200.

8. See 'The Stolen Child', *The Wanderings of Oisin and Other Poems* (1889), *CP*, p. 20.
9. For Lady Wilde, see item 1, note 21. See Thomas Wright (ed.), *The Historical Works of Giraldus Cambrensis* (1863), p. 74 (see also item 1, note 3).
10. Nicholas O'Kearney (1802–74), Irish poet and scribe, born outside Dundalk. He spent most of his life in Co. Louth. A contributor to the *Nation* and a member of the Ossianic Society, he edited Irish texts and corresponded with the Dublin bookseller and publisher John O'Daly.
11. Nicholas O'Kearney (ed.), *Feis Tighe Conáin* (1855), p. 17, defines *leith-phrogan* as 'artisan of the shoe or brogue'. Many of Yeats's following definitions come from O'Kearney.
12. See 'All Souls' Night', *Seven Poems and a Fragment* (1922), *CP*, p. 256.
13. See glossary.
14. 'fairy blast': *sí-ghaoth*.
15. See Thomas Wright (ed.), *The Historical Works of Giraldus Cambrensis*, pp. 79–84.
16. M. De La Boullage Le Cong unidentified.
17. See *The Wanderings of Oisin* (1889), *CP*, p. 409.
18. Mangan's (item 1, note 18; item 18, note 3) translation of a poem attributed to Alfred in James Hardiman's *Irish Minstrelsy* (1831) and published in H. R. Montgomery's *Specimens of the Early Native Poetry of Ireland* (1846). 'Inisfail' means the 'Island of Destiny'.

3 'Irish Fairies, Ghosts, Witches'

Lucifer was the journal of Madame Blavatsky's London Theosophical Society. For the issue of 15 January 1889 Yeats reworked material he had used in the prefaces to the different sections of *FFTIP*, which had appeared the previous October. This article represents another attempt by Yeats to classify the fairies; it includes additional information and reflects continued research. On 9 November 1888 Yeats wrote to Douglas Hyde, requesting information on the *fear sí* (the male equivalent of the banshee); but on 21 December, in a letter to Katharine Tynan, he said: 'I must be careful in no way to suggest that fairies or something like them do veritably exist.' (See *CL, I*, pp. 105, 117.) The fresh material from *Lucifer*, not duplicating that in item 2, is reprinted here. The article is written with a theosophical readership in mind, and it shows how Yeats's study of folklore and his occult interests overlapped.

1. Theophrastus Bombastus von Hohenheim Paracelsus (1493–1541), mystic and alchemist, famous in his day and since, and author of studies of occult power, including *De Nymphis* . . . (1658). Adolphe d'Assier, author of *Essai sur l'humanité posthume et le spiritisme, par un positive* (1883), translated by H. S. Olcott as *Posthumous Humanity: A Study of Phantoms* (1887).
2. The 'loyal minority' are the Northern Presbyterians. See item 4. Yeats's source was Samuel McSkimin, *The History and Antiquities of the Co. and Town of Carrickfergus, from the Earliest Records to the Present Time* (Belfast, 1832), where this incident is described as having occurred in 1711.
3. For Croker, see item 1, note 16. Thomas Keightly (1789–1872), author of *Fairy Mythology* (1828).
4. See item 2, note 6.
5. For Lady Wilde, see item 1, note 21. For Kennedy, see item 1, note 20.
6. David Rice McAnally Jr, author of *Irish Wonders* (1888). See item 5.
7. See glossary; 'Ganconagh' was the pseudonym Yeats adopted for his short stories *John Sherman and Dhoya* (1891).
8. See glossary.
9. For Cleena, see glossary. John O'Donovan (1809–61) was a scholar and antiquarian. Born in Co. Kilkenny; he worked in the Ordnance Survey under George Petrie. Edited the *Annals of the Four Masters* (1848–51) and prepared a *Grammar of the Irish Language* (1845). See item 8, note 8.
10. The Eoghanacht, or the race of Eoghan Mór, was a dynasty that established its supremacy in Munster in the second half of the fifth century. A traditional name for Munster people. See item 8, note 9.
11. piglets, from the Irish *banbh*.
12. Yeats derived his antithesis between the gods of light and those of darkness from John Rhys's *Lectures on the Origin and Growth of Religion as Illustrated by Celtic Heathendom* (1888) and Henri d'Arbois de Jubainville's *Le Cycle mythologique irlandais et la mythologie celtique* (1884, translated 1903). For Rhys, see also item 41, note 2.
13. From the Fir Domhnann, a tribe of early settlers in Ireland, equated by Yeats, and by many of his predecessors in Irish tradition, with the forces of darkness against which the Tuatha Dé Danann fight at the battle of Moytirra.

4 'Scots and Irish Fairies'

Published in the *Scots Observer*, 2 March 1889. The magazine was edited by William Ernest Henley (1849–1903) from January 1889. In November 1890 the journal changed its name to the *National Observer*. This essay Yeats collected in *CT, 1893* under the more humorously argumentative title 'A Remonstrance with Scotsmen for Having Soured the Disposition of Their Ghosts and Faeries'. *CT, 1893* is without the opening paragraph.

1. Thomas of Ercildoune (*fl.* 1220–97), a visionary and poet, supposed prophet and author of a poem on the Tristram legend.
2. Charmed or enchanted, from Lowland Scots.
3. John Francis Campbell (1825–85), editor of *Popular Tales of the West Highlands Orally Collected* (1860–62).
4. Lowland Scots word for a water-spirit, usually appearing as a horse.
5. Untraced.
6. See item 3, note 2.
7. See item 2, note 6.

5 'Irish Wonders'

This piece is a review of David Rice McAnally Jr's book *Irish Wonders: The Ghosts, Giants, Pookas, Demons, Leprechawns, Banshees, Fairies, Witches, Widows, Old Maids and Other Marvels of the Emerald Isle* (1888), published in the *Scots Observer*, 30 March 1889. Yeats is impatient of McAnally's stage-Irishry, because, having collected folklore himself and read a great deal of the relevant material, he has a confidence in folk tradition based on experience and knowledge.

1. See item 1, note 19.
2. An epic poem in Sanskrit, dealing with the conflict between two great families; from *maha* (great) and *bharata* (storm). One of the most famous episodes of the *Mahabbharata* is the *Bhagavad-Gita*.
3. Father of Lies, Beelzebub.

6 'Village Ghosts'

This essay appeared in William Ernest Henley's *Scots Observer* for 11 May 1889. Yeats used part of it in an article for the *Leisure Hour* (item 11) and reprinted it in *CT, 1893* under the same title. It reflects an interest in folk and fairy lore in his later teens, the period during which he lived in Howth, the village of the title. It also shows that in his early manhood Yeats was collecting and organizing material relating to the supernatural from oral tradition. See item 11.

1. Howth, near Dublin. The Yeats family lived at Howth from 1881 to 1884, during which time Yeats got to know the local people and some of their stories.
2. First wife of Adam, according to Jewish tradition. She was said to be created at the same time as him but refused to accept him as her master. She slept with him after the Fall, and their progeny were demons.
3. In 1902 Yeats wrote the following footnote: 'I wonder why she had a white border to her cap. The old Mayo woman, who has told me so many tales, has told me that her brother-in-law saw "a woman with white borders to her cap going round the stacks in a field, and soon after he got a hurt, and he died in six months".' Yeats's old Mayo woman is 'Biddy Hart'. See item 7, note 3, item 8, note 4, and item 15, note 1.

7 *'Kidnappers'*

This piece appeared in William Ernest Henley's *Scots Observer* for 15 June 1889. Part of it was used in the essay on 'Irish Fairies' for the *Leisure Hour*, October 1890 (item 11), which had been occupying him since July 1887. The piece was included, under this title, in *CT, 1893*.

1. William Lilly (1602–81), famous English astrologer, who wrote a *Christian Astrology* (1647).
2. In *Lamia* (1819) by Keats, the goddess Lamia has a secret palace in Corinth where she takes her beloved, Lycius.
3. Yeats based a poem 'The Host of the Air' in *The Wind Among the Reeds* (1899) on this story. The friend is 'Biddy Hart'.
4. In a note to *CT, 1902*, which included this essay, Yeats tells us that he has heard that it was not the Kirwans but the Hacketts, their predecessors at Castle Hackett, who were descended from a mortal and a spirit.
5. See Yeats's account of Paddy Flynn in items 1 and 23.
6. A hobble.

8 *'Columkille and Rosses'*

Published in William Ernest Henley's *Scots Observer* for 5 October 1889, and republished in *CT, 1893* as 'Drumcliff and Rosses'.

NOTES

1. From 'The Fairies' by William Allingham (1824–89), poet, born in Ballyshannon, Co. Donegal. He worked as a customs officer, then settled in London to a literary career. His first book, *Poems* (1850), contained the poem from which these verses come. Author of a verse novel on Irish affairs, *Laurence Bloomfield in Ireland* (1864). Yeats admired his simplicity and his popularity amongst Ballyshannon and Donegal people.
2. In item 7.
3. Columcille (521–97), one of the patron saints of Ireland. Born in Gartan, Co. Donegal. He was given the name 'Columcille', meaning 'dove of the Church', by angels. He founded monasteries at Derry, Kells and other places; and in 563 went into exile on Iona, whence he converted the Picts. In 575 he attended the convention of Druim Ceat, where he prevented the abolition of the poetic caste, which had grown arrogant and very numerous. He is said to have written three hundred books. Also known sometimes as Columba. 'Bigging' is Hiberno-English for 'building'.
4. See the introduction to *Irish Fairy Tales* (1892), item 15 in this volume, which is a sketch of 'Biddy Hart'. Yeats calls her husband 'Michael Hart'. These may or may not be the actual names of Yeats's informants.
5. See glossary.
6. A rich and fertile island of fable off the west coast of Ireland described in James Hardiman's *Irish Minstrelsy* (1831).
7. See glossary.
8. *The Annals of the Four Masters*, a chronicle of Irish history from the earliest times to 1616. Compiled by Mícheál Ó Cléirigh, Cúigcoigríche Ó Duibhgeannáin, Fearfeasa Ó Maoilchonaire and Cúigcoigríche Ó Cléirigh (the four masters). The work was undertaken between 1632 and 1636 by the River Drowse on the border between present-day counties Donegal and Leitrim. It was edited and translated by John O'Donovan from 1848 to 1851. See item 3, note 9.
9. According to tradition, Conn of the Hundred Battles (Conn Cétchathach) and Mugh Nuadhat (also known as Eoghan Mór) divided Ireland between them, Conn taking the upper half, Mugh the lower. A person from the Northern half of Ireland could describe himself as 'of the race of Conn'; someone from the Southern half could designate himself as being 'of the race of Eoghan'. See item 3, note 10.
10. The 'sweet Harp-String' is Douglas Hyde (see item 1, note 23). His pen-name was 'An Craoibhínn Aoibhinn', the 'Sweet Little Branch',

which Yeats mistranslates. A 'gauger' was a customs officer specializing in inspecting liquor for excise purposes, who in Ireland had a special responsibility for tracking down the illegal distillers, the makers of poteen (Irish *poitín*).

9 *'Bardic Ireland'*

A review of Sophie Bryant's *Celtic Ireland* (1889), published in the *Scots Observer*, 4 January 1890, which shows that Yeats has familiarized himself with a wide range of Irish legendary material. However, he laments what he regards as the incompleteness of ancient Irish tradition, its 'wild anarchy of legends', and regrets the apparent lack of some original ordering intelligence that could have shaped the material into a coherent narrative.

1. Literally the *Great Learning*, the name given to a body of Irish legal knowledge, written down by the eighth century, but which originated in pre-Christian Druidic tradition. The *Senchus Mór*, which John O'Donovan began to edit (see item 3, note 8), is one of the most important collections of ancient Irish law, but it is not the only one, as is sometimes stated. See Brian Ó Cuív (ed.), *Seven Centuries of Irish Learning* (1971), p. 54.
2. Known in Irish as *Leabhar na h-Uidhre*, a manuscript compilation written at Clonmacnoise by a scribe called Maolmuire, who died in 1106. Legend has it that the vellum was made from the hide of a cow that followed St Ciarán to the monastery of Clomacnoise, hence its name: *uidhre* means brown or dun cow. It contains versions of *The Voyage of Bran* and of the *Táin Bó Cuailnge*. See glossary entries **Bran** and **Tain Bo**.
3. Standish James O'Grady (1846–1928), novelist and historian, author of *The History of Ireland: Heroic Period* (1878–80), as well as novels such as *Red Hugh's Captivity* (1889) and *The Flight of the Eagle* (1897).
4. Mary Catherine Ferguson (1823–1905), née Guinness; married Samuel Ferguson in 1848 and wrote *Sir Samuel Ferguson in the Ireland of His Day* (1896); also *Ireland before the Conquest* (1868), the correct title.
5. Sir Samuel Ferguson (1810–86), Irish poet and scholar, born in Belfast and educated at the Royal Belfast Academical Institution and Trinity College, Dublin. He wrote fiction, cultural analysis, propaganda and translations from the Irish for the conservative *Dublin University Magazine*. He published *Lays of the Western Gael* (1865), an epic, *Congal* (1872), and a work of scholarship on the *Ogham Inscriptions*

in Ireland, Wales and Scotland (1887). Yeats's first published piece of criticism was an article, in effect an obituary, on Ferguson for the *Irish Fireside* in 1886.

6. Aubrey de Vere (1814–1902), poet, born at Curragh Chase, Co. Limerick. In 1851 he converted to Catholicism under the influence of the Oxford movement. He wrote an analysis of Anglo-Irish relations, *English Misrule and Irish Misdeeds* (1848); *Inisfail* (1864), a lyrical chronicle of Ireland; *The Foray of Queen Maeve* (1882); and his *Recollections* (1897).
7. Richard de Clare, second Earl of Pembroke (d. 1176), known as Strongbow, who assisted Diarmuid MacMurrough, under the authority of Henry II, to regain the kingship of Leinster, thereby initiating the Norman invasion.
8. St Patrick (d. *c.* 490), patron saint of the Irish. Born probably in Britain, he was captured by Irish raiders and sold into slavery in Ireland, where he tended sheep on Slemish mountain in present day Co. Antrim. He escaped to Britain; but, according to tradition, heard the voices of the Irish calling him back. He returned as a missionary and converted Ireland to Christianity with remarkable rapidity in the second half of the fifth century. He is said to have died on 17 March at Downpatrick.
9. The high king (*ardrí*) who crossed the Alps was King Dathi.
10. Men of learning in Gaelic tradition. The word *bard* designated a somewhat lesser person in the Irish hierarchy of learning than the *file*, or poet-seer. 'Bardic' is now widely used as a term to refer to traditional poetic learning.
11. This forms the subject of the king tale *Fledh Dún na nGédh* (*The Feast of Dún na nGédh*) and was the inspiration for Samuel Ferguson's *Congal* and Yeats's play *The Herne's Egg* (1938).
12. The word 'Fenian' derives from *fiann*, meaning a troop of warriors. According to Irish learned tradition Fionn mac Cumhail had command of the warriors, the Fianna, of Cormac mac Airt, said to have lived in the third century. The Fianna inspired a branch of storytelling known as the Fenian cycle. See glossary entry under **Fionn mac Cumhail.**
13. The Ulster cycle of tales, which recounts the doings of Cuchulain and other warriors based at Emhain Macha, known also as the Tales of the Red Branch. It derives this alternative title from the name given to the lodging house near Emhain Macha where the warriors were quartered: An Craobh Rua, the 'Red Branch'.

14. The Fianna became, in time, rebellious, and conflict broke out between them and Cairbre, son of Cormac mac Airt. Cairbre defeated them at the battle of Gavra in Co. Meath, after which Oisín went to Tír na nÓg with Niamh.
15. *The Book of Invasions* is a legendary history of Ireland, compiled in the twelfth century. Known in Irish as *Leabhar Gabhála Éireann*, it gives a pseudo-historical account of the successive waves of settlers in Ireland. For the Fomorians and the Milesians, see glossary entry **Tuatha Dé Danann**.
16. See item 3, note 12.
17. The system of law administered in Gaelic Ireland, one of the significant collections of which is the *Senchus Mór* (see note 1 above).
18. *Nibelungenlied*: a thirteenth-century heroic German poem, related to the *Edda*. *Edda*: the name given to a collection of old Norse material. The poetic *Edda* date from Viking times (800–1000); the prose *Edda* were written by Snorri Sturlson in the early fourteenth century and, like the poetic *Edda*, contain tales about heroes and Norse gods.
19. Edgar Quinet (1803–75), author of *Génie des religions* (1844), where he argues as Yeats indicates. For Conchobar, see glossary.
20. The Parsees practised a religion of Zoroastrian origin, dedicated to the worship of the god of light and fire. They were expelled from Persia in the eighth century and settled in India.

10 'Tales from the Twilight'

A review of Lady Wilde's *Ancient Cures, Charms, and Usages of Ireland* (1890), which appeared in the *Scots Observer*, 1 March 1890. He made use of her earlier book *Ancient Legends, Mystic Charms and Superstitions of Ireland* (1887) for *FFTIP* (1889) and met her in 1888. From this time on he often was a visitor at her house in Chelsea. In 1895, in a letter to the Dublin *Daily Express* for 27 February, he described Lady Wilde's *Ancient Legends* as the most imaginative collection of Irish folklore, but suggested that it should be read in conjunction with Douglas Hyde's *Beside the Fire* (1891). (See *CL, I*, p. 433.) Yeats admired her circumstantiality and her attention to detail.

1. See item 1, note 21.
2. An island off the Co. Sligo coast, inhabited until 1947.
3. Sir William Wilde (1815–76), antiquarian and surgeon, husband of Lady Wilde and father of Oscar. Born in Castlerea, Co. Roscommon, he qualified as a surgeon in 1837. He specialized in operations on the ear and eye, and wrote books on Irish topography, among them

Lough Corrib and Lough Mask (1867), as well as studies and surveys of medical topics.

4. See item 3, note 2.
5. A remote island west of Inishbofin off the Connemara coast.
6. Holland-tide is Hallowe'en, the eve of 1 November, Samhain. The story of the dead riding the waves is reflected in the poem 'Byzantium' (1932); and the following paragraph appears in *CT, 1893* under the title 'Concerning the Nearness Together of Heaven, Earth, and Purgatory'.
7. More correctly Brocken, the highest peak of the Harz Mountains in Germany, significant in German folklore. The night before 1 May the Devil and his witches hold their festival there, called the Walpurgisnacht.
8. See 'All Souls' Night', *Seven Poems and a Fragment* (1922), *CP*, p. 256.

11 'Irish Fairies'

This essay appeared in the *Leisure Hour* for October 1890. Part of it had been used in previous essays for the *Scots Observer*; but he had been working on an article on Irish fairies for the *Leisure Hour* from as early as July 1887, when he wrote to Katharine Tynan saying as much (*CL, I*, p. 25). Parts of this article, including the pieces he had used in 'Village Ghosts', 'Kidnappers' and 'Columkille and Rosses' (items 6, 7 and 8), appeared in *CT, 1893*. They are deleted from this item and allowed to stand as they occur in their separate forms. These deletions are indicated in the following annotations and the reader is referred to the items that include them in this edition.

1. See item 6, note 1.
2. Some material following deleted. Yeats used it in *CT, 1893* in 'Belief and Unbelief'. See item 24.
3. Edward Walsh: see item 1, note 24. This poem is to be found in Denis Florence McCarthy (ed.), *The Book of Irish Ballads* (1869) under the title 'The Fairy Nurse'. For *koel shee*, see glossary.
4. Some material following deleted. Yeats used it in *CT, 1893* under the title 'The Three O'Byrnes and the Evil Faeries'. See item 30.
5. The song is 'Bean na Cleithe Caoile' by Seán Ó Tuama an Ghrinn and may be found in John O'Daly (ed.), *Poets and Poetry of Munster* (1850) with a translation by James Clarence Mangan.
6. Some material following deleted. Yeats used it in the section called 'Drumcliffe and the Rosses' in *CT, 1893*. It had appeared in 'Columkille and Rosses' in the *Scots Observer*, 5 October 1889. See item 8.

7. Daithí Ó hÓgáin points out that a common saying in Irish is: 'Ní troimide an loch an loch, is ní troimide an lacha an snámh.' Translated, 'The lake is no heavier for the lake, and the duck is no heavier for being able to swim.' This became one of Yeats's favourite proverbs at this time: see item 13, note 20, and item 15, note 5.

12 *'Invoking the Irish Fairies'*

This article appeared in the first issue of the *Irish Theosophist* (October 1890), signed D.E.D.I., 'Demon est Deus Inversus' ('a Demon is an Inverted God'), Yeats's name in the Order of the Golden Dawn, which he joined in March 1890. The Order was dedicated to the study of magic.

1. D.D.: probably Florence Farr, whose acronym in the Golden Dawn was S.S.D.D, 'Sapientia Sapienti Dono Data' ('Wisdom is Given to the Wise as a Gift'). Florence Farr Emery (1860–1917) was an actress and friend of Yeats's in the nineties and during the first decade of the twentieth century. She played Dectora in a production of *The Shadowy Waters* for the Theosophical Society in 1905. In 1912 she went to Ceylon, where she ran a school.
2. Cardinal Pietro Bembo (1460–1547), an Italian humanist and scholar who revised Baldassare Castiglione's (1478–1529) *The Book of the Courtier* (1528).
3. Hebrew word for demons, from the Kabbalistic tradition.

13 *'Irish Folk Tales'*

Yeats had taken great trouble, from August 1889, to persuade Hyde (see item 1, note 23), who had reservations about publishing folktales in translation, to edit and translate a selection of the folktales he had gathered in Connacht. Yeats arranged that they be published by Alfred Nutt, publisher of the *Folk Lore Journal*, organ of the Folk Lore Society (*CL, I*, pp. 182, 185). Through the remainder of 1889 he badgered Hyde about this book, which finally appeared in January 1891 as *Beside the Fire*. This piece, a review of Hyde's volume, appeared in the *National Observer* for 28 February 1891. Yeats included it in *CT, 1893* as 'The Four Winds of Desire'. Nutt (1856–1910) contributed notes and a commentary to *Beside the Fire*. A publisher (he ran the family firm) and a folklorist, Nutt provided an extensive commentary for Kuno Meyer's translation of *The Voyage of Bran* in 1895 and 1897, which Yeats reviewed in the *Bookman* in 1898. See item 41.

1. Hyde had written 'throughout'.
2. Matthew Arnold's (1822–88) famous phrase from his essay on Joseph Joubert of 1864, which appeared in *Essays in Criticism* (1865).
3. See item 1, note 16.
4. See item 1, note 20.
5. Gerald Griffin (1803–40), novelist and poet, author of *Holland Tide* (1826) and *The Collegians* (1829). He entered the Christian Brothers in 1838 and ceased to write.
6. See item 1, notes 19 and 17.
7. See item 1, note 21.
8. David Fitzgerald (1843–1916), folklorist and author of a number of articles on folklore in *Revue celtique*.
9. See item 5, headnote.
10. Jeremiah Curtin (1838–1906), folklorist and writer. An Irish-American, he wrote *Myths and Folklore of Ireland* (1890–1911) and *Hero Tales of Ireland* (1894). He was on the staff of the Ethnology Department in the Smithsonian Institution and also wrote a history, *The Mongols* (1908).
11. See item 4, note 3.
12. See glossary.
13. 'Teig O'Kane' had been included in *FFTIP*.
14. Hyde published his first book, *Leabhar Sgéulaigheachta* (*A Book of Stories*), a volume of folklore, in Irish in 1889.
15. See glossary.
16. Hyde translated: 'and there he saw the loveliest woman that was, he thought, upon the ridge of the world. The rose and the lily were fighting together in her face and one could not tell which of them got the victory'.
17. Hyde translated: 'the sharp whistle of the fadogues and fibeens [golden and green plover], rising and lying, lying and rising, as they do on a calm night'.
18. Emanuel Swedenborg (1688–1772), Swedish mystic and student of the supernatural. He studied in Uppsala and became a scientist. Later in his life he had visions. He died in London and has been an influence on Blake, Yeats and many writers who assert the primacy of imagination. The material and spiritual worlds interpenetrate in Swedenborg's system. His *Spiritual Diary* was published in English in 1846.
19. Source untraced.
20. This proverb was a favourite of Yeats's at this time. See item 11, note 7, and item 15, note 5.

14 *'An Irish Visionary'*

This article appeared in William Ernest Henley's *National Observer* on 3 October 1891. Yeats reprinted it as 'A Visionary' in *CT, 1893* with some changes. A different poem, for example, is given in *CT, 1893*. It is a description of George William Russell (AE). Russell (1867–1935) was born in Lurgan, Co. Armagh. His family moved to Dublin, and he attended the Metropolitan School of Art, where he met Yeats. A theosophist, he shared with Yeats an interest in the supernatural, and in mythology and folklore. Yeats initially admired Russell's spiritual receptivity, but later became critical of his tendency towards abstraction. Russell, when Yeats first knew him, was a clerk; he later acted as a rural organizer for the Irish Agricultural Organization; in 1905 he was appointed editor of the *Irish Homestead*, the weekly journal of the cooperative movement, which published James Joyce's early *Dubliners* stories. His *Collected Poems* first appeared in 1913, the year in which he spoke out against the lock-out of Dublin strikers by employers.

1. See AE, *Collected Poems* (1919), p. 45, in which the poem has the title 'Childhood' and begins: 'How I could see through and through you'.
2. See item 4, note 1.
3. Yeats based his poem 'The Lamentation of the Old Pensioner' (originally titled 'The Old Pensioner' when it first appeared in 1890) on this encounter, which George Russell described in an extract from his unpublished autobiography, 'The Sunset of Fantasy', which was published in the *Dublin Magazine* for January 1938. The old man was a veteran of the Crimean War (*CL, I*, p. 232).
4. See glossary.

15 *'An Irish Storyteller'*

Irish Fairy Tales appeared in T. Fisher Unwin's Children's Library in May 1892. Yeats described it as a 'supplementary volume' to *FFTIP*. It contained two illustrations by his brother, the artist Jack B. Yeats. Different in approach to the introduction to the earlier volume of folklore, which ranges widely, this piece is a vignette of 'Biddy Hart', one of the Sligo country people Yeats drew upon for local stories and legends. As such it reflects an increased interest in the personalities of the people who believed in the fairies and the otherworld, as distinct from those beliefs themselves, which continued to preoccupy him. At the back of this volume Yeats included a classification of the Irish fairies, largely repeating material he had used in the appendix to *FFTIP*; he also gave a list of sources for Irish folklore, which reflects his wide reading in the available material. An anecdote included in the appendix on the classification of fairies, not available elsewhere, relates to an anthropologist who assured Yeats that he heard the banshee on 1 December 1867 in Pital, near Libertad, Central America, as he rode through the tropical forest. She was dressed in pale yellow, had a cry like the cry of a bat, and came to announce his father's death. Yeats gives her transcribed cry, which is G♯/B, then high D, skipping an octave, prolonged. The same anthropologist saw her on 5 February 1871 at 16 Devonshire Street in London, when she announced the death of his eldest child; and in 1884 at 20 East Street, at the death of his mother.

1. 'Biddy Hart' and her husband, 'Michael', were among Yeats's informants on folk and fairy lore in Co. Sligo. It is uncertain if Hart was their real name. In *CT, 1893* they are referred to as Mrs H— and Michael H—. See also item 8, note 4.
2. John Yeats, who had the living of Drumcliffe in Co. Sligo.
3. *OED*: tow-row, an uproar, hubbub. See *A*, p. 35.
4. A suburb of Dublin.
5. See item 11, note 7, and item 13, note 20.

16 'The Last Gleeman'

First published in the *National Observer* for 6 May 1893. A study of Michael Moran (1794–1846), the Dublin street rhymer and balladeer, it was based on a *Memoir of the Great Original Zozimus (Michael Moran)* (1871), by 'Gulielmus Dubliniensis Humoriensis'. A gleeman is a minstrel.

1. Yeats's source gives the following additional information: Richard Madden, author of a poem called 'Farnham Hall'; John Kearney; John Martin; John McBride, a hedge poet.
2. The *Aislinge Meic Conglinne* (*The Vision of Mac Conglinne*) is a twelfth-century parody of the vision genre, in which Mac Conglinne, a wandering scholar, satirizes the monks of Cork for their meanness.
3. The author of Yeats's source.
4. Hiberno-English for a witty saying, often saucy or facetious.
5. A policeman, named after Sir Robert Peel, who set up the police force during his period of office as Home Secretary (1828–30).
6. Yeats follows his source's spelling.
7. See glossary.

8. Bad luck in Hiberno-English, from 'cess', meaning taxation or valuation. *Garra* comes from the Irish exclamatory particle *Dhera*, which is generally depreciative.

17 'A Literary Causerie'

The *Speaker* was a London weekly of Liberal views. At the time Yeats contributed this piece to it, it regularly carried a literary 'causerie' (a chatty piece of writing); he had been waiting since July 1892 to do such a piece for this journal (see *CL, I*, p. 302); this contribution appeared on 19 August 1893. On the editorial staff was Richard Barry O'Brien, a Parnellite. Yeats's 'causerie' was a review of T. F. Thistelton Dyer's *The Ghost World* (1893). The review was edited extensively in proof, but not all of Yeats's corrections were incorporated. This printing follows *UP, I* in including all of Yeats's revisions. *UP, I* prints it as 'The Message of the Folklorist'. Yeats had been working with the poet Edwin Ellis (1848–1916) on an edition of Blake, and this review reveals an emphasis on the imagination. The contemporary interest in folklore Yeats interprets as a revival of Blakean imagination, the folklorist's 'message', as against the spirit of realism and science.

1. Edward Young (1683–1765), satirist and author of *The Complaint, or Night Thoughts on Life, Death and Immortality* (1742–5), said to be a commemorative elegy on his dead wife.
2. William Blake (1757–1827), poet and prophet, and one of Yeats's major influences. Yeats edited his works with Edwin Ellis; their edition was published by Quaritch in 1893. Blake engraved and illustrated Young's *Night Thoughts* (1796–7). Yeats's 'William Blake and His Illustrations to Dante' (1897) discusses Blake's work as an artist. See *Essays and Introductions* (1961).
3. *The Tempest*, I, ii, 50.
4. John Keats's 'The Eve of St Agnes' contains the line (stanza VI) 'Upon the honey'd middle of the night'.
5. A scald or skald (Old Norse) means poet or minstrel.
6. Jacob Boehme (1575–1624), a German mystic who earned his living as a cobbler. *UP, I* can find no such assertion in any of Boehme's works, but suggests that Yeats may be drawing upon a commentary by Boehme's English disciple William Law (1688–1721).
7. *The Voyage of Maeldune*: in Irish *Imram Curaigh Maíle Dúin*, preserved in the *Book of Leinster* and in other manuscripts and dating from the tenth century. In Old Irish tradition there was a genre of

'voyage' tales known as *imramma*. Tennyson wrote a poem on this subject.

8. In Yeats's late poem 'Cuchulain Comforted' this is what happens to the hero.
9. In P. B. Shelley's *Prometheus Unbound* (1820) the spirit of the hour is the offspring of Prometheus and his beloved Asia; the evil voices are those of the Furies, messengers of the tyrant Jupiter, who tempt Prometheus to submit.
10. See Yeats's essay 'The Philosophy of Shelley's Poetry' (1900) in *Essays and Introductions* (1961).

18 'Old Gaelic Love Songs'

Yeats reviewed Douglas Hyde's *Love Songs of Connacht* (1893) for the *Bookman* (October 1893). He had been an enthusiastic champion of Hyde's work in folklore since the mid 1880s and he included Hyde's translation of 'Teig O'Kane', a Gaelic folktale, in *FFTIP*. In 1891 Yeats had thought that *Beside the Fire*, a collection of Gaelic tales with facing translations, broke new ground in Irish folklore (see item 13), and his praise for the *Love Songs of Connacht* is very high indeed. The *Love Songs* is a remarkable book: a collection of outstanding Gaelic love songs with facing verse translations and accompanied also by literal prose versions, it conveys the immediacy, originality and force of Irish folksong. Yeats had taken pains to familiarize himself with Irish folktales, and, in particular, those tales to do with fairy lore; here, in Hyde's literal and colloquial prose, and in strong verse translations, was the imaginative scope of Gaelic verse. It was one of the most influential books of the Irish literary revival, and Yeats registers it as such. The perfection he finds in Connacht folksong may be contrasted with his view of the fragmented anarchy of the legendary material he describes in item 9.

1. The preceding 'chapters' of the collection the *Songs of Connacht* were: 'Carolan and His Contemporaries'; 'Songs in Praise of Women'; and 'Drinking Songs', and they appeared in the *Nation* and the *Weekly Freeman*. These four were followed by three further chapters, the 'Songs Ascribed to Raftery' and the two chapters on the 'Religious Songs of Connacht'.
2. Untraced.
3. James Clarence Mangan, poet and translator, and someone in whom Yeats was interested for a time. Mangan wrote powerful nationalistic poems, such as 'Dark Rosaleen'; poems of dismal self-disgust and

self-parody; and translations from German, French and languages he purported to know, such as Persian. An exotic figure, he was a mid-century Dublin *poète maudit*, whose intensity and force of character is expressed through a variety of disguises and personages. He translated a good deal of Irish poetry, with the help of scholars such as John O'Donovan and John O'Daly. See also item 1, note 18. For Walsh, see item 1, note 24.

4. *The Poets and Poetry of Munster*, First Series (1850).

19 *'An Impression'*

Published in the *Speaker* for 21 October 1893. Yeats took his title from a tale by Gerald Griffin, 'The Knight of the Sheep', in *Tales of My Neighbourhood* (1835), which Yeats included in *Representative Irish Tales* (1891). This tale opens with an account by Griffin of how strong sheep farmers, when they had acquired substance and standing, were given the title 'Knight of the Sheep' (*ridire caorach* in Irish). Yeats's farmer is a strong personality as well as being wealthy, and is forceful and passionate in words and action. Yeats used this piece in *CT, 1893*, and for *CT, 1902* he added a further story about him, 'An Enduring Heart'. See item 58 in the present collection.

20 *'Our Lady of the Hills'*

This sketch was published in the *Speaker* for 11 November 1893. Here Yeats is not being a folklorist; rather he is trying to understand the minds of country children, while at the same time acknowledging the fact that he, like the young Protestant girl of this narrative, is, to some extent, outside the cultural framework he is attempting to describe. Yeats used this article in *CT, 1893* and *CT, 1902*.

21 *'Michael Clancy, the Great Dhoul, and Death'*

This appeared in the Christmas annual the *Old Country* in 1893. It was reprinted, with a prefatory letter, in the *Kilkenny Moderator*, edited by Standish James O'Grady, in its 1898 Christmas number; and Yeats included it in his *Collected Works* of 1908. Based on a story Yeats heard in Co. Sligo when he was 'about eighteen' (*UP, I*, p. 310), it is, strictly speaking, a work of fiction, but one that is an attempt, on Yeats's part, to compose in the folklore mode; and to give an impression, in the use of dialect, of the extravagant rhetoric storytellers use.

1. Pouch.
2. See glossary.
3. See glossary.
4. See glossary.
5. Diarmuid was gored to death on top of Ben Bulben by the boar, his dead foster-brother, who had been restored to life through Fionn's intervention. See glossary entry **Dermod**.
6. 'Creepy' is Scots for a low stool.

22 *Preface to* The Celtic Twilight

The Celtic Twilight represents a flowering of Yeats's research into written and oral folk tradition. *FFTIP* anthologized material from written sources, while, in the main, *The Celtic Twilight* comes out of his own collection of folklore. It was planned as a volume for T. Fisher Unwin that would collect Yeats's writing on folklore in the *Scots Observer* and the *National Observer* (*CL, I*, p. 255), with twenty illustrations by Jack B. Yeats. However, Lawrence & Bullen published the book and it had a frontispiece by John B. Yeats, the poet's father. A great many of the pieces had appeared previously, but the book also contained new material. Those items previously published are given, in this edition, in the chronological sequence in which they appeared; the freshly written pieces are given together here, although even the present item was published immediately in advance, in *United Ireland* for 11 November 1893. Exceptions are items 23 and 24. See item 1, note 14, and headnotes to items 23 and 24. *The Celtic Twilight* was reissued in 1902, with new material that had been written in the intervening years. *The Celtic Twilight*, in its two editions, in the variety of material they incorporate, and in the research and collecting that led to them, shows us Yeats at pains to master and verify a difficult body of information and knowledge.

1. In 1902 Yeats added the following additional paragraph:

> I have added a few more chapters in the manner of the old ones, and would have added others, but one loses, as one grows older, something of the lightness of one's dreams; one begins to take life up in both hands, and to care more for the fruit than the flower, and that is no great loss perhaps. In these new chapters, as in the old ones, I have invented nothing but my comments and one or two deceitful sentences that may keep some poor story-teller's commerce with the devil and his angels,

> or the like, from being known among his neighbours. I shall publish in a little while a big book about the commonwealth of faery, and shall try to make it systematical and learned enough to buy pardon for this handful of dreams.

This systematical book was eventually the two-volume *Visions and Beliefs in the West of Ireland* (1920) by Lady Gregory, which Yeats collaborated in.

23 *'A Teller of Tales'*

Yeats had earlier described this teller of tales, Paddy Flynn, in *FFTIP* (item 1); Yeats's account of him, and the story of Columcille and his mother, was deleted from the text at that point and is given here in the *CT, 1893* version. In the introduction to *FFTIP* this material is given incidentally; in *CT, 1893* Yeats gives it a small essay to itself.

1. See the essay 'The Moods', *Essays and Introductions* (1961); and 'The Moods', *The Wind Among the Reeds* (1899), *CP*, p. 62.

24 *'Belief and Unbelief'*

This piece is made up of a very different version of the account of the 'Sceptic' in item 1; and of a part of item 11, 'Irish Fairies'. Both accounts were deleted at these points and are given here. *CT, 1902* deletes the last paragraph. See item 1, note 15, and item 11, note 2.

1. See glossary.

25 *'The Sorcerers'*

An account of an experience with some practitioners of black magic. Yeats records how he successfully resisted the power emanating from one of the sorcerers; the atmosphere is one of evil.

1. In 1902 Yeats wrote: 'I know better now. We have the dark powers much more than I thought, but not as much as the Scottish, and yet I think the imagination of the people does dwell chiefly upon the fantastic and capricious.'

26 *'Regina, Regina Pigmeorum, Veni'*

In a letter of *c.* 15 October 1892 to the poet Richard Le Gallienne Yeats described the incident that inspired this essay (*CL, I*, p. 321):

> Last night I had a rather interesting magical adventure. I went to a great fairy locality – a cave by the Rosses sands – with an Uncle & a cousin who is believed by the neighbours & herself to have narrowly escaped capture by that dim kingdom once. I made a magical circle & invoked the fairys. My uncle – a hard headed man of about 47 – heard presently voices like those of boys shouting and distant music but saw nothing. My cousin however saw a bright light & multitudes of little forms clad in crimson as well as hearing the music & the[n] the far voices. Once their was a great sound as of little people cheering & stamping with their feet away in the heart of the rock. The queen of the troop came then – I could see her – & held a long conversation with us & finally wrote in the sand 'be careful & do not seek to know too much about us'. She told us before she wrote this however a great deal about the economy of the dim kingdom. One troop of the creatures carried quicken berries in their hands. My cousin saw them very plainly.

The account in *CT, 1893* is different. Yeats says here that he had an 'impression' rather than a vision. The title of the piece is based upon the invocation the astrologer William Lilly claimed was used by Ellen Evans, daughter of Lilly's tutor in magic, when she gazed into her crystal. It means: 'Queen, Queen of the Fairies, come!' See William Lilly, *History of His Life and Times* (1715), p. 102. Yeats's uncle, George Pollexfen (1839–1910), was a keen student of the occult, and he and Yeats conducted magical experiments together (see *A*). The cousin Lucy Middleton was known locally as a witch. This essay also appeared in the *Irish Home Reading Magazine* for May 1894.

1. Yeats made the following comment in 1902: 'The people and fairies in Ireland are sometimes as big as we are, sometimes bigger, and sometimes, as I have been told, about three feet high. The old Mayo woman I so often quote thinks that it is something in our eyes that makes them seem big or little.' The 'old Mayo woman' is Mary Battle, servant of George Pollexfen. In *A*, Yeats wrote: 'Much of my *Celtic Twilight* is but her daily speech' (p. 71).
2. In a note of 1924 Yeats wrote: 'The word "trance" gives a wrong impression. I had learned from MacGregor Mathers and his pupils to so suspend the will that the imagination moved of itself. The girl was, however, fully entranced, and the man so affected by her that he heard the children's voices as if with his physical ears. On two

occasions, later on, her trance so affected me that I also heard or saw some part of what she did as if with physical eyes and ears.' MacGregor Mathers (1854–1918), originally Samuel Liddell Mathers (he changed his name for magical reasons) and also self-styled 'Comte de Glenstrae', was one of the three chiefs of the Order of the Golden Dawn in England. He wrote *The Kabbalah Unveiled* (1887) and experimented with magic. For a time he had a profound influence on Yeats.

3. This last paragraph was deleted from subsequent editions. The Gate of Horn is the gate through which true dreams pass (*Odyssey*, XIX).

27 *'The Untiring Ones'*

This is a most interesting piece in that it shows how Yeats gained authentic contact with folk tradition through both his reading and oral sources. He cannot remember exactly who told him the story, but that there almost certainly was an oral source is attested to by the convincing distortion of Cailleach Bérri into Clooth-na-Bare, which is a worthy but inaccurate phonetic transcription.

1. See Yeats's poem 'He tells of the Perfect Beauty' in *The Wind Among the Reeds* (1899), *CP*, p. 74, in which he swears that his 'heart will bow, / . . . until God burn time, / Before the unlabouring stars and you.'
2. See 'The Rose of Battle' in *The Countess Kathleen and Various Legends and Lyrics* (1892), *CP*, p. 42, where Yeats, invoking the Rose of the World, its hidden principle of energy, declares that 'Beauty grown sad with its eternity / Made you [the Rose] of us, and of the dim grey sea', implying an interaction between abstract form (Rose) and actuality.
3. In a note in the 1902 edition Yeats wrote: 'Doubtless Clooth-na-Bare should be Cailleac Beare, which would mean the Old Woman Beare. Beare or Bere or Verah or Dera or Dhera was a very famous person, perhaps the Mother of the gods herself. Standish O'Grady found her, as he thinks, frequenting Lough Leath, or the Grey Lake on a mountain of the Fews. Perhaps Lough Ia is my mishearing, or the storyteller's mispronunciation of Lough Leath, for there are many Lough Leaths.' In 'Red Hanrahan's Song about Ireland' Yeats used Clooth-na-Bare as a place-name.

   In his notes to *Collected Poems* (1933, retained in *CP* and reprinted in Richard J. Finneran's *W. B. Yeats: The Poems – A New Edition*) Yeats says that he has forgotten where he heard the story, but that it may have been from a priest in Colooney.

   G. Wood Martin's *History of Sligo, County and Town* (Dublin,

1882–92, Vol. III, p. 354) tells how a goddess called Veragh is drowned. (See *The Poems – A New Edition*, p. 602; but also *WBYIF*, pp. 144–7).

Yeats's Clooth-na-Bare is distantly connected to the Cailleach Bérri, the Hag of Beare, associated with the Beara peninsula in Co. Cork. Yeats's story connects Clooth-na-Bare with the landscape that the ancient legends also do; and we are also told that she had seven periods of youth; whereas Yeats's girl, from a 'village in the South of Ireland', had seven husbands. In the eighth or ninth century in a famous poem she is imagined as an old nun, converted from paganism, and looking back with regret on the days of her vigorous love. *Cailleach* can mean nun as well as old woman. See *CM*, pp. 94–5.

29 'A Coward'

1. The strong sheep farmer of item 19.

30 'The Three O'Byrnes and the Evil Faeries'

This tale had appeared as part of an essay for the *Leisure Hour*, October 1890. Item 11 of this collection, which reprints much of that article, omits the material of this story, as it is given in *CT, 1893* in a more organized and arresting fashion. The opening paragraph has an air of oral narration about it, in its emphatic repetition, which modulates into speculation.

'The Collar-bone of a Hare' in *The Wild Swans at Coole* (1917) reverses the perspective at the end of this story: in the poem the mortal looks at the 'bitter world' of actuality from the land of faery, to which he has departed (*CP*, p. 153).

31 'The Thick Skull of the Fortunate'

1. Hero of the Icelandic saga *Egil*, which deals with the exploits of Egil, son of Skallagrim, enemy of Eric Bloodaxe.
2. In 1902 Yeats added the following note: 'I wrote all this years ago, out of what were even then old memories. I was in Roughley the other day, and found it much like other desolate places. I may have been thinking of Moughorow, a much wilder place, for the memories of one's childhood are brittle things to lean upon.'

34 'The Eaters of Precious Stones'

Yeats thought that there was one universal mind, and that the individual mind overlapped with a collective memory. His folklore studies were part of his attempt to understand the contents of his own mind; and his experiments in occult psychology, a number of which are briefly referred to here, were means whereby the world of folklore and its knowledge were tested and personalized.

35 *'The Golden Age'*

The fairies and the good spirits are a reminder to human consciousness of the Golden Age. We hear, Yeats says, their lamentation for its passing in the wind among the reeds: hence the title of his collection of poems in 1899. The Order of the Golden Dawn, which Yeats joined on 7 March 1890, was dedicated to the resuscitation of the Golden Age through study and practical magic.

36 *'The Evangel of Folk-lore'*

This review of William Larminie's *West Irish Folk Tales and Romances* (1893) appeared in the *Bookman* for June 1894. Larminie (1849–1900) was born in Castlebar, Co. Mayo, of a Huguenot family. He worked with the India Office and wrote poetry as well as collecting folktales. *Fand and Other Poems* (1892) made use of assonantal rhyming in imitation of Gaelic verse. Here Yeats is speaking confidently about a revival in Irish literature, and linking that to the awakening of interest in folk wisdom and knowledge.

1. Yeats is thinking of the writers of Young Ireland. See item 1, note 18.
2. Jane Barlow (1857–1917), born Clontarf, Co. Dublin. She published stories of Irish life, beginning with *Bogland Studies* (1892), which was in verse and used dialect. Her best-known volume of stories was *Irish Idylls* (also 1892).
3. Emily Lawless (1845–1913), poet and novelist. Born in Lyons Castle, Co. Kildare, she published a great many novels, among them *Hurrish* (1886) and *With Essex in Ireland* (1890). *With the Wild Geese* (1902) is a collection of verse.
4. Katharine Tynan-Hinkson (née Tynan) (1861–1931), poet and novelist, and close friend of Yeats's in his young manhood. Born in Dublin, her first collection was *Louise de la Vallière* (1885), followed by, among others, *Ballads and Lyrics* (1891) and *The Wind in the Trees* (1898). Extremely prolific, she wrote scores of novels and four volumes of memoirs. For Standish O'Grady, see item 9, note 3.
5. See, respectively: item 13, note 10; item 1, note 21; item 1, note 23; item 3, note 6, and headnote to item 5; and item 13, note 8.

6. See 'The Secret Rose', *The Wind Among the Reeds* (1899), *CP*, p. 78, which uses this image of shining hair from Larminie.
7. See 'The Woman Who Went to Hell' in *West Irish Folk Tales and Romances.*
8. From 'The Story of Bioultach' in *West Irish Folk Tales and Romances.*
9. See 'The Story of Bioultach' in *West Irish Folk Tales and Romances.*
10. Willie Steenson in Sir Walter Scott's *Redgauntlet* (1824).

37 *'The Tribes of Danu'*

This essay appeared in the *New Review* for November 1897. It is the first creative outcome of his friendship with Lady Augusta Gregory (1852–1932). They met in 1894, but their friendship developed after a second meeting at Tulira Castle, the home of the playwright Edward Martyn, in August 1897 (see item 48, note 1). That September Yeats went to stay at Coole, Lady Gregory's fine house near Gort in Co. Galway, and he was to spend part of each summer there for the next twenty years. She began seriously to learn Irish in 1897 and to develop further the interest in Irish folklore that she had before she met Yeats. He was grateful for the friendship, and Coole became a refuge where his nervous temperament could steady itself in the calm routine and in the invigorating fieldwork on folklore upon which he and Lady Gregory collaborated. He always dressed in black, so that the country people around Gort thought he was a Protestant minister. See John Kelly, 'Friendship is the Only House I Have' in Ann Saddlemyer and Colin Smythe (eds.), *Lady Gregory, Fifty Years After* (1987) for an account of their collaboration. They planned a large comprehensive work on folklore: she to be responsible for the information presented; he to shape and interpret it. This essay and five others came out of this collaboration (items 38, 39, 46, 50, 59) and show Yeats's continuing preoccupation with folk belief and wisdom. The six essays were to be taken by the *New Review*, but the journal changed its policy and they were published elsewhere (see *Lady Gregory, Fifty Years After*, p. 325). These pieces are based upon his summer fieldwork with Lady Gregory; their collaboration also bore fruit in the two volumes of *Visions and Beliefs in the West of Ireland, Collected and Arranged by Lady Gregory; with Two Essays and Notes by W. B. Yeats* (1920; see item 65). She helped Yeats make the language of his Red Hanrahan stories more immediate by using dialect speech. Encouraged by Yeats, she wrote *Cuchulain of Muirthemne*, with a preface by Yeats; and *Gods and Fighting Men*, also prefaced by Yeats (see items 60 and 64). She collaborated with him on a number of plays and began writing drama herself.

She helped Yeats set up the Irish Literary Theatre in 1899, which later became the Abbey; and saw her own plays produced and become part of its repertoire. Among them are: *Spreading the News* (1904), *Kincora* (1905), *Hyacinth Halvey* (1906) and *Dervorgilla* (1908).

Yeats's writing here, and in the five other essays that followed this one in the series, is marked with a new-found reassurance that came out of his fieldwork and his growing confidence in the reality of the otherworld.

1. See glossary entry **Tuatha Dé Danann.**
2. For Gráinne, see glossary entry **Dermod**. For Fómhoire, see glossary entry **Tuatha Dé Danann.**
3. The hazel (*coll* in Irish) was sacred to the Druids; and the salmon was associated with wisdom.
4. Edward Calvert (1799–1883), a visionary artist who was a disciple of Blake.
5. Fiachna is an otherworld being who comes to Connacht to ask Laoghaire, the king's son, to help him in his conflict in the otherworld. He recites this poem to describe the world from which he has come. The tale describing Laoghaire's adventures in the otherworld is called *Echtrae Laoghaire* (*Laoghaire's Adventure*) and is preserved in the *Book of Leinster* and the *Book of Fermoy*.
6. Dubhaltach mac Firbisigh (*c.* 1585–1670), scribe and scholar, born in Laccan Castle, Co. Sligo. The 'old book' is *The Book of Genealogies*.
7. See glossary for these peoples.
8. The links and contrasts between Celtic and Greek conceptions of the otherworld are considered in the chapter on 'The Belief in the Immortality of the Soul in Ireland and in Gael' in H. d'Arbois de Jubainville, *The Irish Mythological Cycle and Celtic Mythology*, translated by R. I. Best (1903). See item 3, note 12.
9. Cormac mac Airt, high king of Ireland in the time of Fionn mac Cumhail, exchanged his wife and children for a magic branch with golden apples, the sound of which removes all memory of sorrow and brings on a Druidic swoon (*UP, II*, p. 59). See also glossary entry **Cormac.**
10. Biddy Early (1798–1874). Born Bridget Ellen Connors in Faha, near Feakle, Co. Clare, she married a number of times, but was always known by her mother's name, Early. She was widely known as a healer, and was said to be able to foretell the future from a blue bottle she kept in the kitchen dresser. See item 46 for a full account of her healing powers. She is referred to in the introductory poem to the play *The Shadowy Waters* (1900).

11. See glossary.
12. From this point on begins a section which Yeats reprinted in *CT, 1902* as 'The Friends of the People of Faery'.
13. Hylae (or Hyle) is a town on the island of Crete sacred to Apollo, who was surnamed Hylatus.
14. See glossary.
15. Probably not Lady Gregory in this case, according to Colin Smythe, but her friend Miss Charlotte Elizabeth MacManus, a novelist, from Killeaden, Co. Mayo. See Colin Smythe, 'Lady Gregory's Contribution to Periodicals: A Checklist', in Ann Saddlemyer and Colin Smythe (eds.), *Lady Gregory, Fifty Years After*, p. 325.
16. Hiberno-English word meaning 'in front of'.
17. As in note 16 above.
18. Hiberno-English word meaning a 'blow'.
19. At this point the story of the 'wee woman' of Co. Tyrone finishes in *CT, 1902*, whereas here further material is given.
20. The period of darkness, beginning each year with Samhain. See item 1, note 6.
21. See 'Nineteen Hundred and Nineteen', *The Tower* (1928), where 'Herodias' daughters' are said to have come again (*CP*, p. 237 and note, p. 534).

38 'The Prisoners of the Gods'

This essay, the second of the six essays that arose out of his fieldwork and collaboration with Lady Gregory (see headnote to 'The Tribes of Danu', item 37), appeared in the *Nineteenth Century* for January 1898. It shows an increasing interest, due, probably, to his renewed contact with country people while staying at Coole in 1897, in Hiberno-English speech, in particular its rhythm and syntax.

1. Another of Yeats's variant spellings of the Irish for fairy host. See glossary entry **slooa-shee**, which is phonetically quite accurate.
2. The nymphs of the sea.
3. In a note Yeats wrote: 'These names are not, of course, the real names. It seems better to use a name of some kind for everyone who has told more than one story, that the reader may recognise the great number of strange things many a countryman and woman sees and hears. I keep the real names carefully, but I cannot print them.'
4. In 1879 Michael Davitt (1846–1906) and Charles Stewart Parnell (1846–91) founded the Land League, which aimed to reform the

abuses of landlordism. Its membership comprised mainly tenant farmers. The Land War, which it waged successfully, finally gained tenant ownership through a series of Land Acts, employing methods such as withholding rent and the 'boycott', the latter term from an evicting landlord, Captain Charles Cunningham Boycott, in Co. Mayo. For Cruach-na-Sheogue, see glossary.

5. St Patrick's Purgatory is on Station Island in Lough Derg, Co. Donegal. A famous place of pilgrimage from early times, St Patrick had a vision of the next world there.
6. Pounding cloth.
7. Hiberno-English word, from Irish *scraith*, meaning sod or layer of lea surface.
8. Hiberno-English word, possibly from Scots, meaning ear.
9. Meaning uncertain, but possibly derived from *lóiche*, meaning light, bright, and by association, intelligent, wise.
10. See glossary and item 45.

39 *'The Broken Gates of Death'*

This essay is the third of the six essays that arose out of his collaboration with Lady Gregory (see headnote to 'The Tribes of Danu', item 37). It appeared in the *Fortnightly Review* for April 1898. Yeats's fascination with folklore concerning the interrelations between the living and the dead is much in evidence. The essay would appear to consist largely of material contributed by Lady Gregory that was taken down from oral narration.

1. 'Was over': from the Irish *fiach do bhí air*, a debt that was on him.
2. See glossary.
3. Hiberno-English for an illegitimate child.
4. See item 37, note 10.
5. For Midir and Etaín, see glossary entry **Midir**; for Oisín and Niamh, see glossary entry **Oisin**; for Conla, Bran, Cormac, Miluchra, Manannán, see glossary entries for those names; for Cuchulain's 'divine woman', see **Fand** in glossary and item 40, note 34.

40 *'The Celtic Element in Literature'*

This essay, which first appeared in *Cosmopolis*, a journal of arts and letters, for June 1898, shows Yeats uniting his interest in folklore with his study of mythology, and integrating both with his sense of mission as an

Irish writer above all else. Starting with Matthew Arnold and Ernest Renan, both of whom he has studied carefully, he argues that the 'Celtic' element is significant for modern literature because Irish folklore retains connections with the primary impulses of human nature that are evident in Irish and Celtic mythology. The argument evolves from Arnold but becomes quite different: Arnold holds that Celtic sensibility was crucial in order to make the Saxon or Germanic temperament more sensitive; whereas Yeats's contention is that the Celtic (therefore Irish) genius, as expressed in its folklore and mythology, is universal, therefore absolutely valid.

1. Ernest Renan (1823–92), philologist, Celticist and historian of religion. Born in Brittany, he studied for the priesthood, but left the seminary and applied himself to a scientific investigation of Christianity. Author of *Vie de Jésus* (1863) and, in the field of Celtic studies, the influential essay of 1854, 'De la poésie des races Celtiques', translated by William G. Hutchinson in *Ernest Renan: The Poetry of the Celtic Races and Other Essays* (1896).
2. Matthew Arnold published *On the Study of Celtic Literature* in 1867; Yeats takes his phrases from various parts of the work, but he does not distort Arnold's essential point.
3. Johann Wolfgang von Goethe (1749–1832) wrote *Faust* (Part I, 1808; Part II, 1832) and *The Sorrows of Young Werther* (1774).
4. The *Kalevala* is an epic poem of Finland, based on the oral poetry of Karelia on the Finnish–Russian border, compiled by Elias Lönnrot (1802–84) and published in 1835. It was translated into English by John Martin Crawford in 1888. For the *Eddas*, see item 9, note 18.
5. A collection of Welsh tales translated by Lady Charlotte Guest (1838–49). *On the Study of Celtic Literature* quotes passages describing the making of 'Flower Aspect', *Blodeuwedd*, from the fourth branch of the *Mabinogion*. The passage about the tree half in leaf recurs in the poem 'Vacillation', *Words for Music Perhaps and Other Poems* (1932), *CP*, p. 282.
6. The two Keats quotations are from 'Ode to a Nightingale' and 'Bright star! Would I were steadfast as thou art'. 'Oblations' should read 'ablutions' and 'shore' should read 'shores'.
7. This and preceding quotations from *The Merchant of Venice*, V, i.
8. From *A Midsummer Night's Dream*, II, i.
9. Arnold distinguishes four ways of 'handling nature' – the conventional, the faithful, the Greek and the Celtic: 'in the faithful way . . . the eye is on the object, and that is all you can say; in the Greek,

the eye is on the object, but lightness and brightness are added; in the magical, the eye is on the object, but charm and magic are added.'

10. From Keats's 'Ode on a Grecian Urn'. Yeats misquotes: 'mountain built' should be hyphenated, 'quiet' should be 'peaceful' and 'its' in line 3 should read 'this'.
11. From *A Midsummer Night's Dream*, II, i.
12. The first quotation from Virgil is from *Eclogue VII*, l. 45, '[You] mossy springs and grass softer than sleep . . .'; the second from *Eclogue II*, ll. 47–8: '[the beautiful Naiad] gathering pale violets and the heads of poppies / mingles the narcissus and the flower of the sweet-smelling fennel . . .'
13. A medieval French romance that celebrates a victory of Charlemagne over the armies of Islam. The Mahomedan king is Marsile.
14. Yeats is recalling a 'Love Song' from the Gaelic, based on Edward Walsh's translation of 'Éamonn an Chnoic' in *Irish Popular Songs* (1847), which he published in *Poems and Ballads of Young Ireland* (1888) but never reprinted. See Timothy Webb (ed.), *W. B. Yeats: Selected Poetry* (1991), p. 230.
15. The lay in which Oisín describes to St Patrick the origin of the blackbird of Derrycairn is amongst the best-known of the Ossianic lays or songs. They were edited in the *Transactions of the Ossianic Society* (1859 and 1861).
16. From Douglas Hyde's *Love Songs of Connacht* (1893), pp. 134–5.
17. A literal version of 'Róisín Dubh', best known in James Clarence Mangan's translation 'Dark Rosaleen'. Yeats's source possibly was Ferguson's literal translation in the *Dublin University Magazine* for August 1834.
18. From 'The Dirge of O'Sullivan Bear' by J. J. Callanan, a poem based on Gaelic originals collected by Callanan in west Cork. The lines cursing the killers of O'Sullivan Bear read:

    May the hearth stone of hell
    Be their best bed for ever!

    Yeats's source was T. Crofton Croker's *Researches in the South of Ireland* (1824).
19. The poem is the Irish poem beginning 'Triúr atá ag brath ar mo bhás' and may be found in Tomás Ó Rathile (ed.), *Measgra Dánta II* (1927, reprinted 1977), p. 186. Ó Rathile argues that the author was probably a Franciscan called Francis O'Molloy, who wrote a *Grammatica Latino-Hibernica* in 1676.

20. From 'Illusion', to be found in AE, *Collected Poems* (1919), p. 175. For AE, see headnote to item 14.
21. In a note of 1924 Yeats reveals that the friend was William Sharp ('Fiona Macleod') (1855–1915), a Scottish writer who came under the influence of the Celtic revival of the late nineteenth century and who achieved some fame under his feminine pseudonym. Yeats also expresses the view that, though this proverb was probably invented, it remains true for all that.
22. The phrases are from Hutchinson's translation of Renan. See note 1.
23. A translation of this poem can be found in Lady Gregory's *Gods and Fighting Men* (1904), p. 460. The original she found in *The Book of the Dean of Lismore* (1862); Yeats follows Lady Gregory's mistranslation of the first line, which correctly should be: 'Tonight is long in Elphin'. Yeats provides a defiant version of this lament in *The Wanderings of Oisin* (1889), where Oisín turns aside from St Patrick's Christianity at the close (*CP*, p. 447).
24. Quoted in Arnold's *On the Study of Celtic Literature* (see headnote and note 2 above) from *Canu Llywarch Hen* (*The Song of Llywarch the Old*), a cycle of Welsh poems about Llywarch and his sons, dating from the ninth or tenth century.
25. From the opening paragraphs of Douglas Hyde's *Love Songs of Connacht*. For Douglas Hyde, see item 1, note 23.
26. From a sketchbook of Samuel Palmer's, written 1823/4, quoted in A. H. Palmer (ed.), *The Life and Letters of Samuel Palmer* (London, 1892), p. 16. Palmer (1805–81), artist and engraver, was a disciple of William Blake.
27. In 1924 Yeats added a note: 'I should have added as an alternative that the supernatural may at any moment create new myths, but I was too timid.'
28. The vat the Daghda has beneath Newgrange, from which no one departs unsatisfied.
29. In novels such as *Waverley* (1814), *The Antiquary* (1816), *Old Mortality* (1816) and *Rob Roy* (1817).
30. Richard Wagner (1813–83), the German composer, based many of his operas on Nordic mythology; William Morris retold Norse material in *Sigurd the Volsung* (1876). For Morris, see item 42, note 2.
31. Heroine of *Longes meic nUisnigh* (*The Exile of the Sons of Uisnech*) preserved in the *Book of Leinster* and elsewhere in a version of the eighth or ninth century. An early form of the story of Tristan and Isolde, it tells a tale of tragic doomed love, wandering and human malice. Deirdre's story is the basis of Yeats's play of 1907.

32. *Oidheadh Chlainne Tuireann* (*The Death of the Children of Tuireann*) tells of the adventures of the children of Tuireann, as they discharge tasks imposed upon them by the son of a man they have killed. They eventually die in carrying out the duties laid upon them.
33. *Oidheadh Chlainne Lir* (*The Death of the Children of Lir*) tells how the four children of Lir, one of the Tuatha Dé Danann (see glossary), are transformed through the sorcery of a jealous stepmother into four swans, and in this shape they live on the seas off Ireland until the coming of St Patrick.
34. In *Serglighe Con Chulainn* (*The Wasting Sickness of Cuchulain*), preserved in the twelfth-century *Book of the Dun Cow*, Cuchulain is cast into a trance by two otherworld women who beat him; after a year in this state he is taken to the otherworld, where he fights for Fand's love against a host of the *sídh* on behalf of Labhraidh, himself one of the *sídh*. Having spent a month with Fand, he is won back by Emer, his earthly wife. Yeats based his play *The Only Jealousy of Emer* (1919) on this tale. The friend is Ferdia; see glossary entry **Tain Bo**.
35. See glossary entry **Dermod**.
36. The Pre-Raphaelite Brotherhood was a group of artists and poets (D. G. Rossetti, Holman Hunt, William Morris among them) who developed a cult of simplicity, naïvety and medievalism in art. They flourished in the 1850s, but they continued to influence literature and painting for a considerable time after.
37. Philippe-Auguste Villiers de L'Isle-Adam (1838–89), French writer and aesthete whose *Axël* (1890) was a formative symbolist visionary drama.
38. Stéphane Mallarmé (1842–98), an influential French symbolist poet, who experimented with the musical and suggestive possibilities of verse.
39. Maurice Maeterlinck (1862–1949), Belgian playwright and symbolist.
40. Gabriele D'Annunzio (1863–1938), Italian writer who experimented in a wide range of forms.
41. In 1902 Yeats wrote 'Verhaeren'. Émile Verhaeren (1855–1916), Belgian poet and Rosicrucian, who united symbolism and social awareness. He knew Maeterlinck (see note 39 above).
42. In 1902 he added: 'I could have written this essay with much more precision and have much better illustrated my meaning if I had waited until Lady Gregory had finished her book of legends, *Cuchulain of Muirthemne*, a book to set beside the *Morte d'Arthur* and the *Mabinogion*.'

41 *'Celtic Beliefs about the Soul'*

This article, which is a review of Kuno Meyer's and Alfred Nutt's commentary and edition of *The Voyage of Bran* (1895 and 1897), appeared in the *Bookman* for September 1898. For an account of this tale, see glossary entry **Bran**. Kuno Meyer (1838–1919) was born in Hamburg and became Professor of Teutonic Languages in Liverpool University. He helped to establish the school of Irish Learning in 1903. He published *Ancient Irish Poetry* (1911), a deeply influential book, which compared early Irish nature poetry to Japanese verse, and which accompanied the texts with limpid translations. For Alfred Nutt, see headnote to item 13.

1. For D'Arbois de Jubainville, see item 3, note 12.
2. John Rhys (1840–1915) published *Lectures on the Origin and Growth of Religion as Illustrated by Celtic Heathendom* (Hibbert Lectures, 1888). He was first Professor of Celtic at Oxford, a chair established largely as a result of Matthew Arnold's pleading (see item 40). Principal of Jesus College in 1895. He wrote on Celtic philology, mythology and folklore. See also item 3, note 12.
3. See item 38.
4. Sir James George Frazer (1854–1941), Professor of Social Anthropology in Liverpool, he published the first volume of *The Golden Bough*, a comparative study of belief and ritual, in 1890; the twelfth and final in 1915.
5. Andrew Lang (1844–1912), poet, novelist and anthropologist, whose *Myth, Ritual and Religion* appeared in 1887.

42 *'The Academic Class and the Agrarian Revolution'*

A letter to the *Daily Express*, published 11 March 1899. The Viceregal Commission on Intermediate Education began its work on 13 January 1899, and part of its brief was to consider Irish language and literature as an element in the curriculum. J. P. Mahaffy, Provost of Trinity College, Dublin, attacked the Irish language in the *Daily Express* on 16 February; followed by Robert Atkinson, Professor of Romance Languages, Sanskrit and Comparative Philology, on 22 February. On 25 February Douglas Hyde, President of the Gaelic League, entered the controversy and debunked Atkinson as a 'prig'. Atkinson had said that Irish literature tended towards the 'silly' or 'indecent'; he had deprecated Hyde's own work; and called all folklore 'abominable'. This letter is a statement of Yeats's pride in being Irish; and an assertion that such a pride is possible without bitterness.

1. Sir Edward Burne-Jones (1833–98), the Pre-Raphaelite artist, was much impressed by Celtic romance, in particular by James Macpherson's *Ossian*, an eighteenth-century Scottish forgery loosely based on stories about Fionn mac Cumhail. See glossary entry **Fionn mac Cumhail**.
2. William Morris (1834–96), poet and social and cultural reformer; an early friend of Yeats's. A Pre-Raphaelite who combined socialism with aestheticism.
3. Edward Dowden (1843–1913), Professor of English at Trinity College, Dublin, and author of studies of Shakespeare, Shelley and Browning. Yeats came to dislike Dowden, once a friend of the family, for his lack of commitment to Irish literature.

43 *'A Note on "The Hosting of the Sidhe"'*

This piece and the two items following appeared as lengthy notes in *The Wind Among the Reeds* (April 1899). This one is on the poem 'The Hosting of the Sidhe'. In a letter, quoted by Alan Wade in *A Bibliography of the Writings of W. B. Yeats* (1968), p. 48, Yeats described these notes as 'elaborate essays in the manner of *The Celtic Twilight*'.

1. See item 37, note 21, for cross-reference to poems.
2. *CT, 1893* and *CT, 1902*; and the six essays he wrote with Lady Gregory's help. See item 37, headnote.
3. See item 59.
4. Standish James O'Grady, *History of Ireland: Critical and Philosophical* (1881), p. 354, was the source. See *NCJ*, p. 43.
5. See item 27, headnote. For Maeve, see glossary.
6. See *NCJ*, p. 44, citing W. G. Wood-Martin, *History of Sligo, County and Town* (1882–92), Vol. III, p. 384; and his *Pagan Ireland* (1895), p. 126; and item 27.
7. Standish James O'Grady, *The Flight of the Eagle* (1897), pp. 255–7, 296–7. See *NCJ*, p. 44.
8. See glossary entry **Miluchra**.
9. See item 40, note 33.
10. P. W. Joyce (1827–1914), author of *Old Celtic Romances* (1879), *A Social History of Ancient Ireland* (1903) and *English as We Speak It in Ireland* (1910). Aebhen, more properly Aoibheall of Carraig Liath,

is a tutelary goddess of north Munster, with her rath near Killaloe in Co. Clare. She features in Brian Merriman's *The Midnight Court* (see item 67) and in Yeats's poem 'The Grey Rock', *Responsibilities* (1914), *CP*, p. 115. See glossary entry and item 60, note 9.

44 *'A Note on "The Host of the Air"'*

This piece appeared as a lengthy note on the poem 'The Host of the Air' in *The Wind Among the Reeds* (1899).

1. See item 43, note 10. Yeats is citing the story 'Fergus O'Mara and the Demons' from P. W. Joyce's *Good and Pleasant Reading* (1892), which he included in *Irish Fairy Tales* (1892).
2. Satan is the prince of the air; and for the *sídhe* as wind, see item 43.
3. A headland north-west of Kinvarra, Co. Clare.
4. See item 46 for another account of the 'touch'.
5. Hypnosis.
6. Lady Gregory.
7. See glossary entry **Midir**. Echuid (Uchee) is Etaín's mortal husband, Midir her immortal lover. Their story is the subject of Yeats's poem 'The Two Kings', *Responsibilities* (1914), *CP*, p. 503.
8. Yeats's source was Kuno Meyer and Alfred Nutt (eds.), *The Voyage of Bran* (1895–7). See item 41.

45 *'A Note on "The Valley of the Black Pig"'*

This piece appeared as a lengthy note on Yeats's poem 'The Valley of the Black Pig' in *The Wind Among the Reeds* (1899).

1. An undefined valley where an apocalyptic battle will be fought. A Black Pig's Dyke extends through counties Cavan, Longford and Leitrim. See item 56, 'War'.
2. See item 56, note 3.
3. See item 38, note 4.
4. Yeats is referring to *Scéle Mucce Meic Dathó* (*The Story of Mac Datho's Pig*), in which the Ulster and Connacht champions argue over who has the right to carve the pig at a feast. After much boasting the warriors fall into dissension that develops into brutal carnage.
5. See item 3, note 12.
6. Adonis (see glossary entry **Dermod**) is the beloved of Venus, and is gored by the boar he hunts. Attis, beloved of the goddess Cybele, is

driven mad by her when he falls in love with a mortal. He castrates himself at the foot of a pine tree and dies. See Yeats's poem 'Vacillation', *Words for Music Perhaps and Other Poems* (1932), *CP*, p. 282. Typhon could take many animal forms, amongst them the pig.

7. See item 41, note 4.
8. See item 3, note 12.
9. *Cath Maige Tuired*, a ninth-century tale, recounts the struggle between the Tuatha Dé Danann and the Fómhoire. See glossary entry **Tuatha Dé Danann**. Moytirra overlooks Lough Arrow in Co. Sligo.
10. See item 38.

46 *'Ireland Bewitched'*

The fourth of the six essays that arose out of Yeats's collaboration with Lady Gregory. This essay appeared in the *Contemporary Review* for September 1899. It is devoted almost exclusively to folklore concerning the Clare healer Biddy Early (see item 37, note 10). Much of this material was republished in Lady Gregory's *Visions and Beliefs in the West of Ireland* (1920).

1. From the Irish *a rogha rud*, his choice thing, i.e., anything he likes.
2. See section II, 'The Tower' in *The Tower* (1928), *CP*, p. 220.
3. From the Irish *cúig ráithe*, five seasons or quarters.
4. The friend here is probably Lady Gregory, whose *Visions and Beliefs in the West of Ireland*, Vol. I, pp. 25–37, gives an account of this visit to Biddy Early.
5. 'Phillibine' comes probably from Irish *pilibín*, meaning a lapwing or plover, extended to refer to something small; therefore a small bush, such as blackthorn; hence, possibly, 'magpie bush' because of its dark branches and white flowers.
6. Boundaries are places of power and danger; twilight is the boundary between night and day.
7. Possibly some kind of wide-brimmed cap, from (?) Irish *lán* (full) and *beirrdeis* (border/edge).

47 *'Dust Hath Closed Helen's Eye'*

First published in October 1899 in the *Dome* and included in *CT, 1902*.

1. From 'In Time of Pestilence' by Thomas Nashe (1567–1601), one of Yeats's favourite poems.
2. The castle at Baile Laoi (anglicized as Ballylee), or Thoor Ballylee,

became Yeats's property in March 1917, and he lived there during the summer months for many years to follow.

3. See item 37, note 10, and item 46.
4. Hiberno-English meaning gnarled, from Irish *creanncaí*.
5. Anthony Raftery (Antoine Ó Reachtabhra) (1784–1835), a Mayo poet, famous in his own time, and a major figure in the folklore of Mayo and Galway. Blinded by smallpox in youth, he became a symbol of Gaelic Ireland for Yeats and Lady Gregory.
6. Known in Irish as 'An Pósaidh Glégeal' ('The Bright Posy') or 'Máire ní Eidhin' ('Mary Hynes').
7. This poem was 'Seanchas na Sceiche' ('The Story-telling of the Bush').
8. Lady Gregory: see item 37, headnote.
9. This whole passage lies behind the second section of 'The Tower' in *The Tower* (1928). See Lady Gregory's *Gods and Fighting Men* (1904), p. 434, for a translation of the poem Yeats has in mind. Lady Gregory took it from Standish Hayes O'Grady's *Silva Gadelica* (1892), p. 172. Standish Hayes O'Grady (1846–1928), was an historian and novelist, and a cousin of Standish James O'Grady; see item 43, note 4.
10. 'An Pósaidh Glégeal': see note 6 above.
11. Hiberno-English for a festival in honour of a saint.
12. (Pool) of the fairy women.
13. See item 1, note 23.
14. In *CT, 1902* Yeats added the following passage:

> When I was in a northern town a while ago I had a long talk with a man who had lived in a neighbouring country district when he was a boy. He told me that when a very beautiful girl was born in a family that had not been noted for good looks, her beauty was thought to have come from the sidhe, and to bring misfortune with it. He went over the names of several beautiful girls that he had known, and said that beauty had never brought happiness to anybody. It was a thing, he said, to be proud of and afraid of. I wish I had written out his words at the time, for they were more picturesque than my memory of them.

48 'Maeve *and Certain Irish Beliefs*'

Beltaine, a journal devoted to explaining the plans and methods of the Irish Literary Theatre, was first published in May 1899. It took its name from the pagan Irish festival associated with 1 May. There followed two further issues, in February and April 1900; from 1901 the journal was called *Samhain*, named after the other pagan Irish festival of 1 November. This article was printed in the issue for February 1900.

1. Edward Martyn (1859–1923), playwright and landowner. He lived at Tulira Castle on the family estate in Co. Galway. With Yeats and Lady Gregory he founded the Irish Literary Theatre in 1899. *The Heather Field* was produced by this theatre in that year. *Maeve* (which Yeats often spelled 'Maive') was performed in 1900. Maeve is the Queen of Connacht, in the Ulster cycle of tales; but she is also the goddess of Irish sovereignty, a female symbol of Ireland itself. Her name means intoxication (Medb is linked to mead). Peg Inerny is her incarnation in the play.
2. See item 37, note 10, and item 46.
3. Possibly he was thinking of Aogán Ó Rathille (1670–1726), whose poem 'Gile na Gile' (translated 'Brightness of Brightness') is one of the most famous of all Irish *aislingí*, or vision poems, in which the poet has a vision of the otherworld goddess of Irish sovereignty, called the *spéirbhean*, or sky-woman.
4. See glossary entry **Midir** for the characters mentioned. The following passage is from the *Tochmharc Etaíne* (*The Wooing of Etaín*).
5. Yeats reused the material from this point onwards in a section of *CT, 1902* called 'And Fair, Fierce Women', which he published in the *Speaker* for 1902 before *CT, 1902*. It is given in the *Speaker* version in item 57, where this material is expanded and developed.

49 *'Irish Fairy Beliefs'*

This review of Daniel Deeney's *Peasant Lore from Gaelic Ireland* (1900) appeared in the *Speaker* for 14 July 1900. Yeats asserts that the world from which Deeney's tales come is that of human reality; and he is aware that Hiberno-English, as a literary convention, is often flawed.

1. *FFTIP*.
2. For William Larminie, see headnote to item 36; for Jeremiah Curtin, see item 13, note 10; for Douglas Hyde, see item 1, note 23.
3. This book was *Tales of the Fairies and of the Ghost World Collected from Oral Tradition in South-west Munster* (1895). See *UP, II*, p. 217.
4. For Thomas Crofton Croker, see item 1, note 16; for Samuel Lover, see item 1, note 17.
5. For Yeats's review of *Beside the Fire*, see item 13.

50 'Irish Witch Doctors'

This essay, the fifth that grew out of his collaboration with Lady Gregory (see headnote to item 37), appeared in the *Fortnightly Review* for September 1900. Although heavily dependent on the material that Lady Gregory took down from oral narration, Yeats's recounting of the various episodes that comprise the essay is vivid and dramatic. The story of the herdsman who saw a woman before a fire in a room in the ruins of Lydican Castle anticipates the scenes evoked in the play *Purgatory* (1939).

1. *Táin Bó Cuailnge*: see glossary entry **Tain Bo.**
2. See item 37, note 10, and item 46.
3. A woman's short coat or jacket, named after Earl Spencer (1758–1834).
4. The Irish poet is AE. See the sketch of him entitled 'An Irish Visionary', item 14. For Swedenborg, see item 13, note 18.
5. In John Rhys's *Lectures on the Origin and Growth of Religion as Illustrated by Celtic Heathendom* (1888) there is much discussion linking Jupiter, Thor (whence Thursday), Celtic Taranis and Irish Tórna. See pp. 54–73.
6. In John Rhys's *Lectures on the Origin and Growth of Religion as Illustrated by Celtic Heathendom*, the nine hazels that surround the pool of the salmon of knowledge are linked to the 'nine-night week of the ancients' (p. 558).
7. See item 3, note 12.
8. See item 3, note 12, and item 41, note 2.
9. John Millington Synge (1871–1909), playwright, born in Rathfarnham, Co. Dublin. Having travelled in Europe as a young man, he met Yeats in Paris in 1896. Encouraged by Yeats, he went to Aran and studied the Irish language and the life of the people there and in West Kerry; these experiences inspired his plays *Riders to the Sea* (1904) and the *Playboy of the Western World* (1907). *The Aran Islands* (1907) is Synge's account of island life.
10. In the preface to *Jerusalem* Blake wrote: 'We who dwell on earth can do nothing of ourselves; every thing is conducted by spirits, no less than digestion or sleep.'
11. For *file* and *imbas forosnai*, see glossary.
12. Coole House was Lady Gregory's house at Coole Park near Gort, Co. Galway.
13. See glossary entry **coach-a-bower.**
14. The scene of Yeats's play *Purgatory.*

15. A river rises in Coole demesne, spreads to a lake, then drops into a cavern. See Yeats's poem 'Coole Park and Ballylee, 1931', *The Winding Stair and Other Poems* (1933), *CP*, p. 275.

51 *'To D. P. Moran's* Leader'

A letter written for the first number of the *Leader*, 1 September 1900, at the request of David Patrick Moran, its editor. Moran (1871–1936), a strong advocate of an Irish Ireland philosophy, had attacked Yeats's Anglo-Irishness in articles in the *New Ireland Review*. Yeats's letter avoids wrangling and asserts the vitality of the imagination as a means of expression for Irish writers, free of specific political commitment. He also makes clear his unease with the formulation 'Anglo-Irish literature'. From his comments it is clear that his views on Arnold in 'The Celtic Element in Literature' (item 40) were misinterpreted; his attitude to the 'Celt' was diametrically opposed to that of Arnold.

1. *An Claidheamh Soluis* (*The Sword of Light*) was the journal of the Gaelic League. The League was founded in 1893 to encourage knowledge of, and respect for, the Irish language and had as its aim the revival of Irish as the everyday spoken medium of the majority of Irish people. *An Claidheamh Soluis* absorbed the earlier *Fáinne an Lae* (*The Dawning of the Day*), founded in 1898.
2. See headnote to item 42, for the Viceregal Commission on Intermediate Education and the Irish language controversy of 1899. The Commission reported in August 1899, and its findings were debated in the House of Commons in 1900, where the Irish MPs spoke against the Irish language.
3. Charles Gavan Duffy (1816–1903), one of the founders of the *Nation* (1842), was active in the Young Ireland movement with Thomas Davis. In 1848 Duffy was arrested on suspicion of treason. In 1855 he went to Australia, where he became Prime Minister of Victoria (1871). He returned to Europe in 1880 and in the early nineties tried to get the Irish literary revival, which was spearheaded by Yeats, to recreate the spirit of Young Ireland.
4. See item 47, note 5.
5. See item 1, note 23, and item 13.
6. See item 8, note 1, for William Allingham, author of 'Farewell to Ballyshannon'; 'The Absent-Minded Beggar' is by Rudyard Kipling (1865–1936), a poem that appeared in the *Daily Mail* in 1899, inviting subscriptions to a fund for the wives and children of soldiers fighting in the Boer War. It was put to music by Sir Arthur Sullivan.
7. St Columbanus (*c.* 543–615), Leinster saint who travelled in Europe

preaching the Gospel. Founded monasteries at Luxeuil, Fontaines and Bobbio.

8. For AE, see headnote to item 14.
9. Lady Gregory, in her diary for 24 December 1900, noted Hyde's account of a conversation with D. P. Moran. Hyde had said Moran should not attack his friends, 'whereat M. said: "Your enemies don't mind what you say, but if you attack your friend, he is the boy that will feel it."' Moran had attacked Yeats in the *New Ireland Review*. See *UP, II*, p. 241.
10. See item 40.

52 *'The Fool of Faery'*

First published in the *Kensington* for June 1901.

1. The story of Lomna the fool is in Lady Gregory's *Gods and Fighting Men* (1904), pp. 270–71. See glossary entry **Lomna**.
2. The Welsh story of Bran is in the *Mabinogion*; and the severed head that replaces the Grail is to be found in the Welsh tale *Peredur*.
3. For Aengus, see glossary.
4. From P. B. Shelley, 'Rosalind and Helen' (1819), ll. 1121–9. The 'minstrelsy' is the song of the nightingale, which Lionel is listening to.

53 *'By the Roadside'*

First published in *An Claidheamh Soluis* (see item 51, note 1) for 13 July 1901, later in *CT, 1902*.

1. 'An Pósaidh Glégeal', Raftery's song, see item 47, note 6; for 'Eibhlín a Rúin', see item 1, note 9; for ''Sa Mhuirnín Dílis', see glossary.
2. Cormac mac Carthy, king of Munster, built a chapel in the Hiberno-Romanesque style on the Rock of Cashel in 1134. The setting for the poem 'The Double Vision of Michael Robartes', *The Wild Swans at Coole* (1919), *CP*, p. 192.
3. John 19:12.

54 *'New Chapters of the Celtic Twilight', I*

First published in the *Speaker* for 18 January 1902 under the title 'New Chapters of the Celtic Twilight', it formed part of a series of five 'chapters' in the *Speaker* that were gathered together for *CT, 1902*. The first 'chapter' contained the essay 'Enchanted Woods'. The vision the hedgecutter recounts is very similar to the vision of the girl in 'The Song of Wandering Aengus', written probably in 1893, a likeness Yeats himself commented upon in a note to that poem. See *NCJ*, p. 47.

1. 'In the Seven Woods', title-poem of a collection (1903).
2. See glossary.
3. See glossary.
4. 'Dim Inchy wood, that hides badger and fox / And martin-cat . . .' From the dedication (to Lady Gregory), *The Shadowy Waters* (1900).
5. A reference to the first section of the *Phaedrus*, quoted in the introduction to *FFTIP* (item 1).
6. A poem by William Morris (see item 42, note 2), published 1868–70.

55 *'New Chapters of the Celtic Twilight', II*

The second of five 'New Chapters of the Celtic Twilight' for the *Speaker* (see headnote to item 54). This 'chapter' contained the essay 'Happy and Unhappy Theologians' and was published in the *Speaker* for 15 February 1902. It was gathered in *CT, 1902*.

1. Mary Battle (see item 26, note 1), the 'happy' theologian, as distinct from the man from Galway in the second part of the essay.
2. Yeats noted: 'The religious society she had belonged to.'
3. Such as the *Fís Adamnán*, the *Vision of Adamnán*, said to have been written by St Adamnán, Abbot of Iona (625–704). It describes heaven and hell.
4. Rory O'Connor (1116–98), last of the Irish high kings.

56 *'New Chapters of the Celtic Twilight', III*

Third of the five 'New Chapters of the Celtic Twilight' published in the *Speaker* in 1902 and gathered that year in *CT, 1902*. This 'chapter', which contained 'The Old Town', 'War' and 'Earth, Fire, and Water', appeared on 15 March 1902.

1. The United Irishmen uprising of 1798, when French revolutionary forces landed in Ireland to assist the Irish insurgents.
2. A congested district was one in which 'the total rateable value divided by the number of inhabitants amounted to less than thirty shillings per person', F. S. L. Lyons, *Ireland since the Famine* (1973), p. 206. It was, in other words, a poor area.
3. The Fenians were a secret revolutionary group, also known as the Irish Republican Brotherhood (IRB). Founded in 1858 on St Patrick's Day by James Stephens, it was dedicated to the cause of Irish independence and did not rule out the use of force.

4. See item 45.
5. Possibly Ernest Renan, whose *Histoire du peuple d'Israel* (1887) argues something very like this.
6. The Parsees. See item 9, note 20.
7. Greek philosopher (233–304), Neo-Platonist and follower of Plotinus. In an interpretation of a passage of Homer, Porphyry maintains that water symbolizes the flow of energetic thought from life's spiritual source. See Yeats's essay 'The Philosophy of Shelley's Poetry', *Essays and Introductions* (1961), p. 83; and 'Coole Park and Ballylee, 1931', *The Winding Stair and Other Poems* (1933), *CP*, p. 275, which contains the line 'What's water but the generated soul?'

57 *'New Chapters of the Celtic Twilight', IV*

Fourth of the five 'New Chapters of the Celtic Twilight' published in the *Speaker* in 1902 and gathered that year in *CT, 1902*. This 'chapter', which contained 'A Voice', 'The Swine of the Gods', 'The Devil', 'And Fair, Fierce Women', 'Mortal Help', and 'Aristotle of the Books', appeared in the *Speaker* for 19 April 1902.

1. See item 54, note 4.
2. Aengus's beloved is Etaín; see glossary entry **Midir.**
3. Untraced.
4. Queen Victoria.
5. See glossary.

58 *'More Chapters of the Celtic Twilight', V*

Fifth in the five 'New Chapters of the Celtic Twilight', published in the *Speaker* in 1902 and gathered in that year in *CT, 1902*. This chapter, which appeared on 26 April, contained the essays 'Miraculous Creatures' and 'An Enduring Heart'.

1. See item 54, note 4.
2. For the 'knight of the sheep', see item 19. The friend was possibly George Russell (AE). See headnote to item 14.

59 *'Away'*

The sixth and last of the essays that grew out of his collaboration and fieldwork with Lady Gregory (see headnote to item 37). It appeared in the *Fortnightly Review* for April 1902, and it reveals Yeats's continuing and intensifying interest in the interaction between the living and the dead.

1. See item 37, note 10, and item 46.
2. In '*Maeve* and Certain Irish Beliefs', item 48.
3. A section, retelling the story of 'a woman from the North' from '*Maeve* and Certain Irish Beliefs', item 48, is omitted here.
4. The most easterly of the Aran Islands. Inishmaan is further west, with Inishmore being the most westerly.
5. See note 4 above.
6. See item 9, note 2.
7. See item 41, note 2.
8. There follows the story of *Serglighe Con Chulainn* (*The Wasting Sickness of Cuchulain*); see item 40, note 34. Yeats based his play *The Only Jealousy of Emer* (1919) on this tale.
9. In the ninth volume of *The Golden Bough* (pp. 259, *et seq.*) J. G. Frazer discusses the scapegoat. See *UP, II*, p. 281.
10. See item 38.
11. A mysterious task laid upon Cuchulain is the discovery as to where the sons of Doel Dermait are; Doel Dermait, according to Rhys, means 'beetle of forgetfulness'. See John Rhys, *Lectures on the Origins and Growth of Religion as Illustrated by Celtic Heathendom* (1888), p. 345.
12. In *Skiruismal*, one of the poems of the *Edda* (see item 9, note 18), the warrior Freyr goes into Hlidskjalf, Odin's tower, and while there sees Gerdr, daughter of the giant Gymir, with whom he falls in love.

60 *Preface to Lady Gregory's* Cuchulain of Muirthemne

Lady Gregory's *Cuchulain of Muirthemne* (1902), with Yeats's preface, appeared in April 1902. Yeats develops the idea that the stories of Cuchulain, which his friend has united into a coherent narrative, carry a life of their own, larger and more intense than mere actuality, which, though traditional, appeals to the modern imagination.

1. In the Scylla and Charybdis episode of *Ulysses*, Buck Mulligan, 'chanting with waving graceful arms', mocks Yeats's praise of 'that old hake Gregory' and, jesting, suggests to Stephen Dedalus that he do 'the Yeats touch': 'The most beautiful book that has come out of our country in my time.'

2. Douglas Hyde planned to translate portions of *Cuchulain of Muirthemne* into Irish in 1901, but the translation did not materialize.
3. See item 40, note 5.
4. Sir Thomas Malory (d. 1471) is said to be the author of *Le Morte D'Arthur*, an integration of various Arthurian tales into a coherent narrative, printed by William Caxton in 1485.
5. See item 9, note 18.
6. *The Secret Rose* (1897).
7. Yeats wrote an essay on William Morris, 'The Happiest of the Poets', in 1902. See item 42, note 2. Amongst the stories Yeats admired were *The Wood Beyond the World* (1894) and *The Well at the World's End* (1896).
8. The story is *Togail Bruidne Da Derga* (*The Destruction of Da Derga's Hostel*). Conaire, high king of Ireland, is killed at Da Derga's hostel by an invading band of British marauders, who are aided by three relatives of the king himself.
9. Theme of the poem 'The Grey Rock' in *Responsibilities* (1914), *CP*, p. 115. Aoibheall is the fairy goddess of Carraig Liath near Killaloe in Co. Clare, who offered her lover a long life if he did not fight alongside Murrchadh, Brian Boru's son, at the Battle of Clontarf. He did fight and was killed, along with his friend. See item 43, note 10.
10. See glossary entry **Maeve**.
11. Cuchulain's friend, induced by Maeve to fight him.
12. An apple tree grew out of Aillinn's grave, a yew out of Baile's. Their burial place was Baile's Strand near Dundalk, setting for Yeats's play of that name. The Irish original is *Scél Baile Binn Bérlaigh* (*The Story of Baile of the Clear Voice*), a tale preserved in an eleventh-century version.
13. William Blake, 'Proverbs of Hell' in *The Marriage of Heaven and Hell* (1790).
14. In chapter 45 of the Norse *Grettis* saga, which dates from the early fourteenth century, Atli, the brother of Grettir, says this just before he dies.
15. See glossary.
16. At the end of *The Exile of the Sons of Uisnech* (see item 40, note 31), a pre-tale to *The Cattle Raid of Cooley* (see glossary entry **Tain Bo**) and translated in *Cuchulain of Muirthemne*.
17. The palace of the kings and queens of Connacht, and therefore the fortress of Queen Maeve; near the village of Tulsk in Co. Roscommon.

61 *'Dreams That Have No Moral'*

First published in *CT*, *1902*.

1. See item 54. Yeats seems to have joined the figure of the hedgecutter with the imaginary scene of 'Song of Wandering Aengus'. The friend is Lady Gregory.
2. For Raftery, see item 47, note 5; Callanan was a rival of Raftery.

62 *'Poets and Dreamers'*

This piece is a review of Lady Gregory's *Poets and Dreamers: Studies and Translations from the Irish* (1903), which appeared in the *New Liberal Review* for March 1903. Reprinted as 'The Galway Plains' in *Ideas of Good and Evil* (1903), it appeals to the people's acceptance as the most authentic sanction of art.

1. Conán Maol mac Mórna, the fool and jester of the Fianna. See glossary entry **Fionn mac Cumhail.**
2. See item 47, note 5.
3. Lady Gregory's translation of 'Slán le Pádraig Sáirséal' ('Farewell to Patrick Sarsfield') from *Poets and Dreamers*.
4. Lady Gregory's translation of 'Donnchadh Bán' ('White-haired Donough') from *Poets and Dreamers*.
5. 'Deorchaoineadh na Hérionn' by Séamus Carthún, edited by Rudolf Thurneysen in *Revue celtique*, XIV, 1893, pp. 153–62.

63 *'A Canonical Book'*

Yeats's second review of *Poets and Dreamers: Studies and Translations from the Irish* (1903), which appeared in the *Bookman* for May 1903. The other review had appeared in March (see item 62). In this review Yeats equates the Gaelic and the Anglo-Irish aristocracies.

1. For Yeats's review of the *Love Songs of Connacht*, see item 18.
2. For his preface to *Cuchulain of Muirthemne*, see item 60.
3. See item 47, note 5.
4. Lady Gregory's translation of 'Dónal Og' from *Poets and Dreamers*.
5. Yeats's essay on Shakespeare, 'At Stratford-on-Avon', was written in May 1901.

6. In the section entitled 'Of the Famous Philosophers' in *Thus Spoke Zarathustra*, Nietzsche wrote, of those who behave in 'too familiar a way with the spirit', that they make of wisdom 'a poorhouse and hospital for bad poets'.
7. 'Antoine Ó Dálaigh' in Douglas Hyde (ed.), *Songs Ascribed to Raftery* (1903), p. 128.
8. The plays were: *The Marriage*, *The Twisting of the Rope*, *The Lost Saint* and *The Nativity*.

64 *Preface to Lady Gregory's* Gods and Fighting Men

Lady Gregory's *Gods and Fighting Men* (1904) appeared in January, with Yeats's preface. This volume, a companion piece to *Cuchulain of Muirthemne*, retold a selection of the legends and tales of the Irish mythological and Fionn (or Fenian) cycles. Yeats argues for a return to simplicity; in order to achieve imaginative vitality, the modern artist must get back to bedrock.

1. Residence of the Irish high kings in Co. Meath.
2. See 'Oisin and Patrick: The Arguments' in *Gods and Fighting Men*.
3. See 'Cael and Credhe' in *Gods and Fighting Men*. See also glossary entry **Credhe**.
4. See glossary.
5. Robert Browning's first published poem, 1833, describing his impressions of Greek literature; these lines are cited in 'Are You Content?', *New Poems* (1938), *CP*, p. 370.
6. See 'The Battle of Gabhra' in *Gods and Fighting Men*.
7. See the 'Death of Goll' in *Gods and Fighting Men*. Yeats's poem 'The Madness of King Goll' appeared in *The Wanderings of Oisin and Other Poems* (1889), *CP*, p. 17. See also glossary entry.
8. Tuatha Dé Danann.
9. See *Gods and Fighting Men*, pp. 266, *et seq*.
10. Tír Fó Thoinn: another name for Tír na nÓg.
11. See *Gods and Fighting Men*, p. 96.
12. See *Gods and Fighting Men*, p. 456.
13. Phrases echoed from the love song 'Dónal Og' in *Poets and Dreamers* (see item 63).
14. In Aristophanes' *The Frogs*, presented in 405 BC, Aeschylus pays tribute to Homer as the 'matrix' from which he has moulded the forms of his own characters.
15. See *Gods and Fighting Men*, p. 312.

16. See item 56, note 3.
17. Untraced.
18. See *Gods and Fighting Men*, p. 429.

65 'Witches and Wizards and Irish Folk-lore'

Published in *Visions and Beliefs in the West of Ireland* (1920), Vol. I, and dated there 1914. For Vol. II Yeats wrote 'Swedenborg, Mediums, and the Desolate Places', an essay that more properly belongs in a volume devoted to occult writings. This two-volume compendium of folk belief, with its analyses of that belief by Yeats, represents the culmination of over twenty years of shared study, fieldwork and thought with Lady Gregory.

1. Adam Clarke (1762–1832), Wesleyan preacher and theological writer, born in Co. Derry. *An Account of the Infancy, Religious and Literary Life of Adam Clarke* by a member of his family was published in 1833 in three volumes, the first of which was an autobiography.
2. Henricus Cornelius Agrippa von Nettesheim (1486–1535), famous necromancer and magus, and author of *De occulta philosophia libri tres* (1529).
3. 'Tetragrammaton' is the ineffable name of God in the Kabbalah, the Jewish mystic tradition, and comprises the first letters of the Hebrew words for the four elements. 'Agla' is a Kabbalistic invocation, meaning 'Thou art powerful and eternal, Lord.'
4. Joseph Glanvill (1636–80) was chaplain to Charles II and a rector of the Abbey Church in Bath. He wrote *Philosophical Considerations Touching Witches and Witchcraft* (1666), and his *Sadducismus Triumphatus* (1681) contained some material by Henry More, who is said to have edited the volume from Glanvill's papers.
5. Henry More (1614–87), fellow of Christ's College, Cambridge. A Neo-Platonist, he wrote much philosophy and poetry, including *Psychozoia Platonica; or, a Platonicall Song of the Soul* (1642).
6. Eugène Auguste Albert de Rochas, a nineteenth-century spiritualist thinker.
7. From 'The Præexistency of the Soul' in A. B. Grosart (ed.), *The Complete Works of Henry More* (privately printed, 1878), p. 123. More has been describing the properties of the spirits of the air.
8. An astrologer who published much in the seventeenth century. See *The British Library Catalogue*.
9. Untraced.

10. Yeats is drawing upon Glanvill's accounts; see note 4 above.
11. A white or white-powdered insect.
12. Francis Hutchinson (1660–1739), bishop of Down and Connor in 1721. His first preferment was in Hoxne, Suffolk, where he interested himself in the history of witchcraft in the area, whence his *An Historical Essay Concerning Witchcraft* (1718). Afterwards in Ireland he was a tolerant and ecumenical churchman who learned Irish. He published *A Defence of the Antient Historians* (1734), the volume to which Yeats refers.
13. Kitten or the young of any animal.
14. See item 38 for the account of the Aran man. In Book XI of *The Odyssey*, Odysseus makes a blood sacrifice to the shades so that Tiresias may come from Hades and advise him about his journey home to Ithaca.
15. In a note Yeats says that he has anglicized the Lowland Scots from Pitcairn's 'Criminal Trials'. Robert Pitcairn (1793–1855) published in 1833 *Trials and Other Proceedings in Matters Criminal before the High Court of Justice in Scotland*.
16. See item 37, note 10, and item 46.
17. A cure often had to be paid for by someone else's suffering.
18. Possibly J. Beaumont (1616–99), Master of Peterhouse College and Chaplain in Ordinary to the king, who rebuked Henry More (see note 5 above) with *Some Observations upon the Apologie of Dr Henry More* (1665).
19. The magical scenes conjured by the wizard of Orleans in Chaucer's *The Franklin's Tale*.
20. Ebenezer Sibley (or Sibly) (d. 1800) published *A New and Complete Illustration of the Celestial Science of Astrology* (1787). He is said to have cast the horoscope of Richard Brinsley Sheridan.
21. John Butler, probably the astrologer attacked by Henry More (see note 5 above and *The British Library Catalogue*).

66 'Compulsory Gaelic: A Dialogue'

This dialogue appeared in the *Irish Statesman*, edited by George Russell (AE), for 2 August 1924. Yeats, a Senator of the Irish Free State since 1922, had acted as chairman of a Senate committee which had recommended increased expenditure on the Irish language earlier in the summer of 1924. The dialogue is uncertain about the desirability of compulsory Gaelic, though it acknowledges the part Gaelic tradition has played in the development of modern Irish imaginative life. It concludes with a welter of hesitancies, mischievously asserted.

1. Paul argues for compulsory Gaelic; Peter against.
2. *Juno and the Paycock* was first performed in the Abbey in 1924 and met with great success. Barry Fitzgerald and F. J. McCormick took the roles of Joxer and Captain Boyle.
3. J. Hartley Manners (1870–1928), the American dramatist, wrote *Peg o' My Heart*. First produced in 1912, it became very popular. Sara Allgood (1883–1950) left the Abbey in 1915 and toured in the title part of Manners's play in Australia and elsewhere. However, she returned to the Abbey to play Juno in *Juno and the Paycock* (see note 2 above) in 1924.
4. William Rowan Hamilton (1805–65), a mathematical prodigy who, while still an undergraduate at Trinity College, Dublin, was appointed Professor of Astronomy. His mathematical researches brought him European eminence.
5. In Chapter XVIII of *Tractatus Theologic-Politicus* (1670) Spinoza argues that the English tried to find legal grounds for removing the king but then failed to 'change the form of the state'.
6. In 'Education and Art' (1858) John Ruskin wrote: 'We have all of us probably known persons who, without being able to read or write, discharged the important duties of life wisely and faithfully; as we have also known others able to read and write whose reading did little good to themselves and whose writing little good to anyone else.' See E. T. Cook and Alexander Wedderburn (eds.), *The Works of John Ruskin* (1905), Vol. XVI, pp. 143–4.
7. An Comhar Drámaíochta, founded in 1922 to foster the performance of plays in Irish.
8. For Kuno Meyer, see headnote to item 41.
9. Yeats is possibly thinking of Hamlet's speech to Horatio (III, ii, 73–6):

   Since my dear soul was mistress of her choice
   And could of men distinguish her election,
   S'hath sealed thee for herself, for thou hast been
   As one, in suff'ring all, that suffers nothing.

10. Aristotle (384–322 BC) argues in *On the Soul* that it is the soul that animates life.

67 *Introduction to* The Midnight Court

An introduction to Percy Arland Ussher's translation *The Midnight Court and the Adventures of a Luckless Fellow* (1926). Ussher (1899–1980) was an English-born man of letters, who learned Irish and wrote studies of Shaw, Yeats and Joyce, and a critique of Existentialism. Brian Merriman (*c.* 1740–1805) was a hedge-school master in Feakle, Co. Clare, and a farmer. *The Midnight Court* (*Cúirt an Mheáin-Oíche*), written around 1780, is one of the great poems of Irish literature. Racy, turbulent, ribald, the poem's language is eloquent and charged with intellectual force and energy; it is also very funny. Donnchadh Rua Mac Con Mara (1715–1810) was a hedge-school master in Co. Waterford. He is said to have emigrated to Newfoundland, and the preparation for his journey and the events thereon form the subject of *The Adventures of a Luckless Fellow* (*Eachtra Ghiolla an Amarráin*).

1. Wibraham Fitzjohn Trench (1873–1939), appointed Professor of English literature at Trinity College, Dublin, in 1913. Before that Professor of English at Galway.
2. A poem by Jonathan Swift based on his relationship with Esther Vanhomrigh (Vanessa), published in 1713. Yeats gives the following note:

   > Mr Robin Flower pointed this out to me [that *The Midnight Court* was founded on Swift's poem]. *Cadenus and Vanessa*, which has the precision of fine prose, is the chief authority for the first meeting of Swift and Esther Vanhomrigh. I think it was Sir Walter Scott who first suggested a 'constitutional infirmity' to account for Swift's emotional entanglement, but this suggestion is not supported by Irish tradition. Some years ago a one-act play was submitted to the Abbey Theatre reading committee which showed Swift saved from English soldiers at the time of the *Drapier Letters* by a young harlot he was accustomed to visit. The author claimed that though the actual incident was his invention, his view of Swift was traditional, and enquiry proved him right. I had always known that stories of Swift and his serving-man were folk-lore all over Ireland and now I learned from country friends why the man was once dismissed. Swift sent him out to fetch a woman, and when Swift woke in the morning he found that she was a negress.

The *Drapier's Letters* were a series of pamphlets published by Swift in in 1724, campaigning against the patent acquired by William Wood, which enabled him to supply copper coins to Ireland, on the grounds that 'Wood's halfpence' would debase Irish currency. Robin Flower was an Irish scholar who translated *An tOileánach* (*The Islandman*). See item 68.

3. Ovid (43 BC–AD 18) wrote the *Ars Amatoria*; Virgil's (70–19 BC) *Aeneid* tells of the love of Dido and Aeneas; Tibullus (48–19 BC) wrote elegiac love poetry; Abraham Cowley (1618–67) was a seventeenth-century amatory poet; and Edmund Waller (1606–87) wrote love poems to his mistress 'Sacharissa'.
4. See glossary entry **Aebhen** and item 60, note 9.
5. Title of James Clarence Mangan's poem, which is based on a Gaelic song 'Róisín Dubh'.
6. *Chaucer's Dream*, a long poem once thought to be Chaucer's, also known as *The Isle of Ladies*; 'The Complaint of the Black Knight' is now known to be by John Lydgate (1370?–1449). See Albert E. Hartnung (gen. ed.), *A Manual of the Writings in Middle English*, Vol. IV (1973), pp. 1096–7.
7. From the Middle English translation of *Le Roman de la Rose* by Guillaume de Lorris and Jean de Meun, ll. 49–53. Chaucer may have translated parts of the English work.
8. The traditional bonfires, lit on St John's Eve (23 June) were a survival of pagan custom. Bones of animals were kept and burnt that night and the resulting bonemeal used as fertilizer. Jumping through the fire was a fertility rite, still practised by Irish tinkers.
9. A series of enactments beginning in 1695, designed to protect the interests of the Protestant minority. Catholics were not allowed to buy land from a Protestant, lease it for longer than thirty-one years, or leave it to one offspring. They were excluded from Parliament, the army and the other professions; nor could they send their children abroad to be educated. They could not own a horse worth more than five pounds. Although all of these laws were not strictly enforced all the time, many remained on the statute book until Catholic Emancipation in 1829.
10. In medieval and early modern Gaelic tradition many poems and ballads of Fionn and Oisín are narrated to St Patrick by Oisín or Caoilte after Ireland has been converted to Christianity. They look back longingly on a free, pagan life. The bastard's speech in *King Lear* is Edmund's at the beginning of I, ii, where he declares that

bastards have 'more composition and fierce quality' than those conventionally sired.

11. Burns's illegitimate daughter, Bess, was born in 1785; her mother was Lizzie Paton, a servant girl. Blake's *Marriage of Heaven and Hell* was etched from 1790 to 1793.
12. For Standish Hayes O'Grady, see item 47, note 9.

68 *'The Great Blasket'*

An appreciation of Muiris Ó Súilleabháin's *Fiche Bliain ag Fás* (1933), an autobiographical account of life on the Great Blasket Island off the coast of Kerry. Ó Súilleabháin (1904–50) lived there from the age of seven until he joined the Irish Civic Guards in 1927. Yeats's piece appeared in the *Spectator* for 2 June 1933.

1. J. M. Synge, *The Aran Islands* in *Collected Works* (1966), Vol. II, p. 103.
2. Lady Gregory, 'Synge', the *English Review*, March 1913, p. 556. See Lady Gregory, *Our Irish Theatre*, Vol. IV (1972), pp. 73–83.
3. This was Tomás Ó Criomhthain's *An tOileánach* (1929), which Robin Flower translated as *The Islandman* (1934).
4. It would appear that the person who read Gorky to Ó Criomhthain was the island schoolteacher Brian Ó Ceallaigh. See Tomás Ó Criomhthain, *Allagar na hInise* (*Island Talk*) (1977), p. ix.
5. In an introductory note to *Twenty Years A-Growing*.
6. In the *Nicomachean Ethics* Aristotle envisages the good man as someone inspired by virtue and conscious of social obligation. The precise source is untraced.

GLOSSARY

Although he did not know Irish, Yeats sought the advice of such as Douglas Hyde, Lady Gregory, Frank O'Connor and F. R. Higgins on the Irish language and Gaelic tradition at different points in his career. In his writings on folklore, legend and myth he went to considerable pains to find out what Gaelic words meant and to provide his readers with an anglicization that would not entirely misrepresent the sound of the word or words in Irish. Also, almost invariably, he provided an explanation, sometimes based on expert advice; these explanations are, however, sometimes inaccurate. The present glossary lists all Yeats's anglicizations of Irish words in the present text, gives Yeats's explanation (where available), corrects Yeats's explanation wherever necessary, and gives a corrected form in modern standard Irish. It also provides phonetic transcriptions to help pronunciation wherever it seemed helpful.

Aebhen: Fairy queen of Carraig Liath. Standard spelling: Aoibheall. Also spelled Eevell by Yeats.

Aengus: Irish god of love, who lives at Brugh na Bóinne (Newgrange).

Amadán-na-Breena: A fool of the forth, Yeats (correctly) explains. Standard Irish: *amadán na bruíona*, *bruíon* being a word for rath or fort or forth.

ard-reigh: (awrd-ree) High king. Standard spelling: *ard rí*.

Augh-iska: (Ach-ishke) The water-horse, which in standard spelling would be Each Uisce.

banshee: Fairy woman. Standard spelling: *bean sí*.

banyan: Piglet, from the Irish *banbh*.

Bodb Dearg: (Bov Darug) One of the Tuatha Dé Danann (see glossary entry), son of the Daghda.

bracket: From the Irish *breacadh*, meaning speckled or variegated or striped.

Bran: The hero of *Eachtre Brain meic Febhail* (*The Adventure of Bran, Son of Febhal*), preserved in an early version from the seventh century. Bran, having had a vision of the otherworld, sets out to sea to find it with twenty-seven companions. He meets the sea god Manannán mac Lir; he visits the island of women and stays there many years, but one of his companions longs for Ireland. They go back and leave him there, but depart again.

bucalauns: Yeats defines as ragweed. Standard spelling: *buachalán*.

Caetchen: (Caught-hen) Cat-head; Fionn mac Cumhail and the Fianna fight an army of cat-headed men in one of the Ossianic tales. See Lady Gregory, *Gods and Fighting Men* (1904), p. 266.

Caolte: (Kweelte) A warrior in Fianna Éireann. See glossary entry **Fionn mac Cumhail**. Standard spelling: Caoilte.

Cleena: An ancient Irish goddess, now a Munster *sheogue*, according to Yeats. One of the four waves of Ireland, the wave of Clíodhna (as the name is usually spelled) sounds off Glandore in Co. Cork.

Cluricaun: A sprite of some kind. Yeats cites an etymology from Nicholas O'Kearney that he does not explain (see notes for item 2) but describes him as perhaps 'the lepracaun on a spree'. Standard spelling would be *clúracán*, meaning an elf or sprite.

coach-a-bower: No explanation given by Yeats: literally a deaf coach, a dead coach, the coach of death. Standard spelling: *cóiste bodhar* (Coishta bower).

cohullen druith: Yeats describes this as a red cap worn by the merrow on land. Standard spelling would be *cochaillín draoi*, meaning a magical hood or cowl.

Conall: (Cunal) Conall Cearnach, hero of the Ulster cycle, linked to the Celtic deity Cernunnos, the horned god.

Conchobar: (Crohoore) King of the Ulstermen and chief of the warriors of the Red Branch.

Conla: (Cun-la) Son of Conn of the Hundred Battles, high king of Ireland in the second century AD. His story *Eachtre Connli* (*The Adventure of Conli*) is preserved in an eighth-century version in the *Yellow Book of Lecan* and elsewhere. A *leannán sí* comes to Conli the Red to entice him into the otherworld. Her power is resisted by Conli, who then languishes; she comes to him again and this time he departs with her in a glass boat.

Cormac: (Curmuck) High king of Ireland during the time of Fionn mac Cumhail. His full name is Cormac mac Airt, Cormac son of Art. Art was a son of Conn of the Hundred Battles. See glossary entry **Conla**. The story of Cormac's adventures in the otherworld is preserved in the *Yellow Book of Lecan* under the title *Eachtre Cormaic*. When Cormac's wife is taken into the otherworld, he follows her, a mist descends, and he has a number of baffling experiences, all later explained. He encounters Manannán (see glossary), wins back his wife, and returns with a gold cup, symbolic of truth and sovereignty.

Credhe: (Krayd-e) Fairy bride of Cael, a warrior of the Fianna. He is killed at the Battle of Ventry, defending Ireland against invaders, and she mourns him in a famous poem.

Cruach-na-Sheogue: Yeats's anglicization of a place-name, meaning the Hill of the Fairies. Standard spelling: Cruach na Sióg.

Cuchulain: (Coohullin) Hero of the Ulster cycle; his name derives from Cú Chulainn: the hound of Culann the Smith. Standard spelling: Cúchulainn. Emer was his wife. Yeats's spellings have been standardized.

Dallahan: A headless spirit.

daoine maithe: Means the good people, the fairies. He also uses *dinny math*.

Dermod: (Dear-mid) Diarmuid Ó Duibhne, hero of *Toraíocht Dhiarmada agus Gráinne* (*The Elopement of Diarmuid and Gráinne*). Gráinne's lover and antagonist of Fionn mac Cumhail, to whom she was promised. Mortally wounded by a boar, Diarmuid was killed on Ben Bulben. Fionn could have saved him with a drink of water from a pool, but twice he allowed the water to drain through his fingers; the third time it was too late.

Dhoul: Not explained by Yeats, but means devil, *diabhal*.

dinny math: See glossary entry **daoine maithe.**

Domnu: The Fir Domhnann; see glossary entry **Laighin**.

Fand: (Fon) Otherworld lover (*leannán sí*] of Cuchulain in the tale *Serglighe Con Chulainn* (*The Wasting Sickness of Cuchulain*), in which she is reached by sailing across a lake in a ship of bronze.

Fear-Gorta: An emaciated fairy that roams the land in times of famine.

Fergus, son of Roy: An Ulsterman who fought on the Connacht side in *Táin Bó Cuailnge*; in Irish, Fergus mac Roich. In the *Táin Bó* there is some phallic joking about Fergus and his sexual prowess (or lack of it).

File: A poet or seer. The *file* in Christianized Old Irish society was the inheritor of the function of the pagan Druid. He was a poet but also a seer, a teacher, an adviser in all matters involving knowledge and wisdom.

Fionn mac Cumhail: (Fionn mock Cooill) The leader of Fianna Éireann, the 'Fenian militia' (Yeats's term) under the high king Cormac mac Airt in the third country. Yeats's spellings have been standardized.

Firbolg: One of the legendary peoples of Ireland, preceding, according to tradition, the Tuatha Dé Danann. Defeated at the first Battle of Moytirra they retired to the islands around Ireland, among them Aran, Islay, Man and Rathlin. *Bolg* is the Irish for bag or belly, and they are said to have been slaves in Greece, and to have carried earth in bags about their waists.

Fir Darrigs: Red Men, Yeats translates, and also, correctly, points out that the colour red is always a sign of the underworld. Standard spelling would be Fir Dhearga (Fir Yarga).

Fir Morca: A semi-legendary Munster tribe.

Fomorians: See glossary entry **Tuatha Dé Danann.**

Gailioin: (Galyeoin) See glossary entry **Laighin.**

geabheadh tu an sonas aer pighin: Yeats explains, fairly correctly, 'you can buy joy for a penny'. Standard spelling: *gheobhaidh tú an sonas ar phingin*, 'you will get happiness for a penny'.

glugger-a-bunthaun: Not explained by Yeats, but most likely an anglicization of a Gaelic term for 'yellow rattle' (*bodach* *gliogair*), *Rhinanthus minor*, a scrophulariaceous plant having a capsule in which the seeds rattle.

Goibnui: (Guivknew) The god of the Smiths, as Yeats correctly defines him. A more standard form of orthography for his name would be Goibhniu. He is the equivalent of Vulcan and Hephaestos. As An Gobán Saor, he has entered folklore as a master mason who is able effortlessly to outwit others.

Goll: (Gull) Goll mac Mórna, enemy of Fionn mac Cumhail.

Gonconer: Yeats's explanation, which he got from Nicholas O'Kearney (see item 2, note 10) is unlikely. *Geancánach* is a fairy cobbler (Niall Ó Dónaill, *Foclóir Gaeilge-Béarla*, Oifig an tSoláthair, Baile Átha Cliath, 1977).

Goborchin: (Gower-hin) Goat-headed otherworld creatures. Standard spelling: *gabhar-cheann*.

grainne oge: (grawinoge) Correctly defined as hedgehog by Yeats. More correctly: *gráinneog*.

Guleesh na Guss Dhu: Guleesh of the Black Feet, title of a story in Douglas Hyde's *Beside the Fire* (1891). Standard spelling: Goilís na gCos nDubh.

imbas forosna: (imbass forusknee) or *imbas forosnai* as it is more often written. Defined by Yeats as 'science which enlightens', it is an ancient term for a technique of divination practised by the poet/seer (*file*), in which he chewed on a piece of meat, chanted over it, slept, and dreamed the knowledge sought.

koel shee: (keoghl shee) Fairy music (Yeats). Standard spelling: *ceol sí*.

Laighin: (La Yin) A group of tribes, including the Fir Domhnann and the Gaileoin (or Gailioin), who, according to tradition, settled in Leinster from Armorica. Gave their name to the province of Leinster (in Irish, Cúige Laighean).

Leanhaun Shee: (Lanawn Shee) Fairy mistress (Yeats), often equated with the muse. Standard spelling would be *leannán sí*, a phantom lover, either female or male.

lepracaun: The fairy shoemaker, according to Yeats. Douglas Hyde told Yeats that it came 'from the Irish *leith brog* – *i.e.*, the One-shoemaker, since he is generally seen working at a single shoe'. In Irish *leipreachán*, meaning a sprite or (as in P. S.

Dineen, *An Irish–English Dictionary*, Irish Texts Society, Dublin, 1927) 'a kind of sub-aqueous sprite'. Yeats's spellings have been standardized.

liss: Yeats's version of the Irish *lios*, a fairy fort or rath.

Lomna: A fool, or jester, amongst the Fianna, who reveals to Fionn that a wife has been unfaithful to him. The adulterer, Coirpre, kills the fool and keeps his head on a spike, but when the Fianna come, the head rebukes Coirpre, who is then slain. See Lady Gregory's *Gods and Fighting Men* (1904).

Maeldun: (Maledoon) Warrior hero of a tenth-century voyage tale entitled *Immran Curaigh Máile Dúin* (*The Voyage of Maeldun's Boat*) preserved in the *Book of the Dun Cow* and in other manuscript collections. Maeldun visits thirty-one islands on a voyage undertaken as penance for breaking a Druidic taboo.

Maeve: (Mayv) Tutelary goddess of Connacht, Queen of Connacht in the Ulster cycle of sagas, and antagonist of the Ulstermen. She is warlike and associated with fertility. Her fort is at Cruachan. Her name (in Irish, Medhbh) links her with sweetness (mead, honey) and also means intoxication. Origin of Shakespeare's Queen Mab. Yeats often spells her name Maive.

Mannanan: (Mananawn) The Irish sea god, whose name is usually written Manannán mac Lir.

Marcra shee: The fairy cavalcade (Yeats). Standard spelling: *marcra sí*.

Merrow: Yeats's anglicization of what he writes as *Moruadh* or *Murrughach*, deriving the Irish from *muir* (sea) and *oigh* (maid). Standard spelling would be *murrúch*, and a merman is *murrúch fir*.

Midir: (Mithir, *th* as in 'there') Fairy king of Bri Leith, a fairy rath, and otherworld lover of Etaín in *Tochmharc Etaíne* (*The Wooing of Etaín*), a ninth-century mythological tale preserved in the *Yellow Book of Lecan* and the *Book of the Dun Cow*. Standard spelling would be Midhir. He is a figure in Yeats's poem 'The Two Kings'.

Milesians: See glossary entry **Tuatha Dé Danann**.

Mill: According to tradition the sons of Míl, or the Milesians, defeated the Tuatha Dé Danann (see glossary entry).

Miluchra: A fairy woman who lures Fionn mac Cumhail away to Slieve Collin in Co. Antrim, where, through trickery, she gets him to swim in the bewitched Grey Lake, thus turning him into a weak old man. The Fianna, Fionn's soldiers, bring him to Miluchra's father in Slieve Fuaid in Co. Armagh, where, after a show of force, the curse is lifted.

Oinseachs: (Oweinshuck) Apes, Yeats says. An anglicized plural of *óinseach*, which is defined more correctly as a fool, especially a female one.

Oisin: (Usheen) The son of Fionn mac Cumhail, poet and seer, correctly written Oisín. After the Fianna are defeated at the Battle of Gavra, he goes with Niamh to Tír na nÓg, where he spends many years before returning again to a Christian Ireland. His adventures in Tír na nÓg are the subject of Yeats's *The Wanderings of Oisin* (1889).

Payshtha: (Payshte) A lake-dragon (Yeats). Standard spelling: *péiste*.

Plain-a-Bawn: Not glossed by Yeats in his text, but probably from *plé an bháin*, a contending or conflict of the pasture, indicating that the fairies fought in the air above a smooth expanse of grass or lea.

pooka: The nightmare, according to Yeats, who troubles drunkards in particular. In Irish *púca*, related to Puck, in English tradition.

rann: (rown) Irish for verse or stanza.

rath: A fairy fort or mound.

''Sa Mhuirnín Dílis': A love song, possibly a version of the love song 'Mo Mhúirnín Bán'.

sennachie: (shannachee) Storyteller. Standard spelling: *seanchaí*.

sheehogue: Yeats's anglicization of the Irish for fairy, which he gives as *sidheóg*; standard spelling would be *síóg*. Yeats says it is the diminutive of *sí* (shee), as in banshee, which is correct.

slooa-shee: The fairy host (Yeats). Standard spelling: *slua sí*.

sowlth: A ghost, from standard Irish *samhailt*.

Tain Bo: (Tawin Bow) The greatest of all the epics (Yeats). Correctly known as *Táin Bó Cuailnge* (*The Cattle Raid of Cooley*), it is the central tale of the Ulster cycle of sagas and tells of the conflict between the Connacht men under Queen Medhbh, and Cuchulain, who defends Ulster heroically and single-handedly because the Ulstermen are laid low by a curse.

Tash: (Tosh) Ghosts (Yeats). Yeats gives the Gaelic *tais*, which is the singular form. *Taisí* would be ghosts.

Tír na nÓg: The Country of the Young (Yeats). Other names: Tír Fó Thoinn (The Land Under Wave); Magh Mell (The Honey Plain).

Thevshi: (Taivshe) Ghosts (Yeats). Yeats also gives a Gaelic spelling, *taidhbhse*, which would now be simplified to *taibhsí*.

Tuatha Dé Danann: (Tooaha Day Donon) A branch of the gods of pagan Ireland. The peoples of Dé Danann are said to have occupied Ireland before the Celts. Their name connects them to the Hindu mother goddess Danu. They defeated their undersea opponents, the Fómhoire, at the battle of Moytirra, near Lough Arrow in Co. Sligo. The Tuatha Dé Danann were themselves defeated by the Celts (the sons of Míl, Milesians) at Tailtiu: the Milesians took the upper, visible world; the Tuatha Dé Danann were given jurisdiction over the lower world, the underworld, access to which may be gained through the fairy raths or mounds. Among their heroes were Lugh, the Daghda, Nuadha. Yeats's spellings have been standardized.

vanathee: Not explained by Yeats, but means woman of the house, *bean an tí*.

APPENDIX:

Contents of the 1893 and 1902 Editions of *The Celtic Twilight*

1893

APPENDIX

1902

TIME DROPS IN DECAY
THE HOST
THIS BOOK
A TELLER OF TALES
BELIEF AND UNBELIEF
MORTAL HELP
A VISIONARY
VILLAGE GHOSTS
'DUST HATH CLOSED HELEN'S EYE'
A KNIGHT OF THE SHEEP
AN ENDURING HEART
THE SORCERERS
THE DEVIL
HAPPY AND UNHAPPY THEOLOGIANS
THE LAST GLEEMAN
REGINA, REGINA PIGMEORUM, VENI
'AND FAIR, FIERCE WOMEN'
ENCHANTED WOODS
MIRACULOUS CREATURES
ARISTOTLE OF THE BOOKS
THE SWINE OF THE GODS
A VOICE
KIDNAPPERS
THE UNTIRING ONES
EARTH, FIRE, AND WATER
THE OLD TOWN
THE MAN AND HIS BOOTS
A COWARD
THE THREE O'BYRNES AND THE EVIL FAERIES
DRUMCLIFF AND ROSSES
THE THICK SKULL OF THE FORTUNATE
THE RELIGION OF A SAILOR
CONCERNING THE NEARNESS TOGETHER OF
HEAVEN, EARTH, AND PURGATORY
THE EATERS OF PRECIOUS STONES
OUR LADY OF THE HILLS

IRISH FOLKLORE, LEGEND AND MYTH

THE GOLDEN AGE

A REMONSTRANCE WITH SCOTSMEN FOR HAVING SOURED THE DISPOSITION OF THEIR GHOSTS AND FAERIES

WAR

THE QUEEN AND THE FOOL

THE FRIENDS OF THE PEOPLE OF FAERY

DREAMS THAT HAVE NO MORAL

BY THE ROADSIDE

FOUR WINDS OF DESIRE

INTO THE TWILIGHT

READ MORE IN PENGUIN

Penguin Twentieth-Century Classics offer a selection of the finest works of literature published this century. Spanning the globe from Argentina to America, from France to India, the masters of prose and poetry are represented by the Penguin.

If you would like a catalogue of the Twentieth-Century Classics library, please write to:

Penguin Marketing, 27 Wrights Lane, London W8 5TZ

(Available while stocks last)